THE
O'BRIENS

SEAN

M.L. TERRY

LifeRich
PUBLISHING®

LifeRich Publishing is a registered trademark of
The Reader's Digest Association, Inc.

LifeRich Publishing books may be ordered
through booksellers or by contacting:

LifeRich Publishing
1663 Liberty Drive
Bloomington, IN 47403
www.liferichpublishing.com
844-686-9607

ISBN: 978-1-4897-3055-8 (sc)
ISBN: 978-1-4897-3056-5 (hc)
ISBN: 978-1-4897-3069-5 (e)

Library of Congress Control Number: 2020917047

Print information available on the last page.

LifeRich Publishing rev. date: 09/22/2020

CHAPTER ONE

*H*e stood in the doorway waiting.

In his line of work patience was not a virtue; it was a necessity.

He had been waiting for her, carefully choosing the best spot to observe . . . but not be seen. Twice he had subtly changed his appearance. Removing his bowtie, slipping it into his pocket and placing the glasses he was wearing in his suit jacket.

The entryway he chose was seldom used since the building had recently been purchased and the new owners were set to demolish it. It was an older office building, the entrance narrow and shaded so he could step back into the shadows if she happened to glance his way.

Not that she had, he smiled to himself, she had passed right in front of him on the way to her destination. Every Friday, like clockwork, she was here waiting in front of the building where her cousin Luke Noonan and his partner Jay O'Brien shared a law office. At precisely five o'clock her cousin Luke would appear, pick up her sample case and the two of them would walk two blocks to a little neighborhood restaurant for dinner.

Careful and quiet inquiries had netted the information that although they were only cousins, she and Luke were as close as brother and sister.

Her mother's untimely death had brought Alison to the States to live with her mother's twin sister when she was five years old, and she had been with them until six months ago when she moved into her own apartment.

He had done his homework; he knew everything there was to know about her. The only thing he didn't know was why somebody wanted her dead. Nor did he care.

He allowed himself a glance in her direction. She was a pretty little thing with her blond curly hair and trim figure, and no one could ever say that he didn't appreciate a pretty face, but he had never allowed sentiment to get in the way of a job, and he wasn't about to start now.

He had planned everything carefully. The street was bustling, and as in most big cities, at five o'clock people were on the move.

He shifted restlessly, sliding deeper into the shadow of the doorway. He couldn't afford to draw attention to himself. No one would remember him. He had perfected the art of blending in, and that was what made him so successful. Be seen, but not remembered. Just blend in like the tiny chameleon that had become his calling card.

Days from now when questions were asked no one would be able to pick him out from a crowd. His clothing never drew attention. Everything he wore was indistinguishable, picked right off the rack of a local store. Silently he chuckled to himself. If the people surrounding him only knew. He could afford the very best, but when he was working, he prided himself on being invisible.

He allowed himself to step out of the shadows for a moment, pausing to look up and down the street as if watching for a late arrival, and then glanced down at his watch.

Everything was going as planned. She looked perfectly relaxed leaning against the brick building, but he knew that was her persona. She was a master of hiding her feelings and he admired her for it. But he also knew that she had to be worried.

In two days, she was leaving on a plane for London.

And he was being paid to be sure she never made it.

She glanced his way and he shifted further back into the shadows.

It wouldn't be long now. Just a few more minutes and the surrounding office buildings would start emptying and he would find the cover he was looking for.

He'd slipped up in the past, but he promised himself it wouldn't happen again.

Eyes darting back and forth, he waited, and watched.

Finally, he spotted a group heading his way, chatting with each other and laughing. Reaching up he unbuttoned the top button of his shirt and laid his jacket over his arm. This group suited him perfectly.

There were only two women and they were lagging behind, one of them on a cell phone. The rest were men, with several wearing jackets, while others carried them over their arms.

He smiled as he watched them approach. No one would ever notice that the smile never reached his eyes. Silently he congratulated himself. If they only knew the jacket he had draped so casually over his arm was so very different from theirs.

This one had been specially made for him by a master craftsman, and tailored to fit his precise instructions.

Cut much fuller than the ones he normally wore, it had a pocket hidden deep in the lining which completely concealed his gun with its silencer.

He smoothed his hand over the jacket as if it were a woman, caressing the spot where the gun lay hidden. He had other guns, but this one was his favorite...small, lethal, and easy to hide. One shot, one precise shot, and it slipped back into its pocket. Sadly, no one would ever know the genius of his design because the master craftsman who had created it for him was dead- and dead men don't talk.

He stepped out of the doorway, blending seamlessly into the rear of the group. He matched his steps to theirs and smiled at passers-by as he strolled along. No one would notice or remember him. Just another guy going for a beer with his buddies or on his way home to his wife and kids.

CHAPTER TWO

Whisper tilted the oversized briefcase against the wall of the tall brick building that housed her cousin Luke's law office and rubbed her arm.

Her sample case toppled over and she bent and straightened it silently berating herself for being such a fool. Agreeing to take home these sheets of blue marble samples was just another indication of how stressed she was.

Leaning back against the building she slipped off one of her shoes and bent down to rub her foot. She knew she looked silly standing on a main street in Boston with one shoe on and the other one in her hand, but damn she'd forgotten how uncomfortable these shoes were.

Her stomach knotted as she already regretted taking time out of her busy schedule to have dinner with Luke. Missing one week of sharing family gossip and griping about the challenges of their respective careers wouldn't kill them – but she knew if she skipped tonight Luke would come looking for her and it would be easier to have dinner with him, and then leave.

She loved Luke, but there were times when his take charge attitude drove her crazy, and she was sure that tonight was going to be one of those nights. She just hoped that the two of them would be able to get through dinner without either of them coming to bodily harm.

Reaching up she ran her fingers through her curls, ruing the fact that no matter how hard she tried to tame them, they seemed to have developed a mind of their own. She had tried pushing, pulling, and tying them down with scarves, but they always managed to escape. And instead of the poised professional look she was constantly striving for, there were times when she still looked like a teenager playing grown up.

She had seen pictures of her mother Alise in her modeling days and her blond hair had always looked sleek and sophisticated. But she and her Aunt Annette, her mother's twin, had both inherited the curly hair of her grandmother.

Glancing down to make sure that the sample case was still upright she allowed her thoughts to wander back to the last customers of the day.

If it wasn't for those two, -- in retrospect she should have been warned when she had heard the raised voices of the cantankerous older man, and his young bride, as they arrived at her office door five minutes before closing She tried not to listen as they stood outside, but it was impossible not to hear their words since neither of them seemed inclined to keep their voices down.

Slipping from behind her desk, she plastered a smile on her face before she stepped out into the hall and invited them in. She refused to let their attitudes discourage her, since she still viewed every assignment as a challenge, and the cash that every sale brought to the business helped keep the wolf from the door, and from the sound of things this assignment was going to be her greatest challenge yet, and she was going to earn every penny.

She sighed, and rubbed her forehead remembering the encounter.

Two minutes into their meeting the new wife had made it perfectly clear that she had no intention of living in her husband's house without removing all reminders of the first wife's tastes.

Thank heavens I agreed to talk to them, Whisper thought, if I had sent them to Sylvia, ten minutes into the conversation she would have been threatening to kill them both. Sylvia, who had the face of an angel and the business acumen of a shark.

The first day on the job, Sylvia had taken one look at her books and screamed. Literally screamed. Staff had come running from all over the office to see if anybody was being killed, and after five minutes of Sylvia's tirade about their lack of organization, and their lackadaisical bookkeeping- they were contemplating murdering her themselves.

From that day on Sylvia had become the financial wizard of the company. Lately she had been giving a lot of thought to making Sylvia a partner but she would have to wait until she returned from London before she approached her.

She winced, trying to get the couple out of her office had been a feat in itself, they had argued about everything, and when the new bride insisted that the bathroom tile match the blue of her eyes, she thought the husband was going to strangle her.

Finally in desperation, she had promised to take home some sample tiles, and squeeze in a few minutes to look them over to see if she could find just the right shade.

After some pouting by the bride, because Whisper couldn't assure her that the tiles would exactly match her eyes, she had promised that she would do her very best, and finally they left.

Closing her eyes, she tried rubbing away the headache that was starting behind her eyes, and she decided that should she read in the paper that the husband had murdered his new wife, she might consider it justifiable homicide.

But she reminded herself, this wasn't the time for her to be worrying about blue tile, not when she needed to prepare herself for the looming battle with Luke. Luke was used to doing battle in a courtroom. He was not only a skilled interrogator but he was coolly logical and her reasons for refusing to let him accompany her to London would no doubt result in a heated argument. Unfortunately for Luke this was one battle she didn't intend to lose.

She realized that her lack of sleep was contributing to her overall anxiety and apprehension, and tossing and turning most of the night before had left her not only tired, but irritable.

And for the last few nights, ever since she had gotten the phone call-- the dream had returned.

The dream had begun when she was just a child, right after her mother died, and although for the last few years it had appeared less frequently, when it happened, she always woke with her heart pounding, her hands clenched, struggling to breathe. She would crawl out of bed and spend the rest of the night prowling around her apartment praying that morning would come quickly.

Sometimes she swore that the air around her became musty, and no matter the type of weather she would flee out into the night and walk until she was so exhausted that she would return to her apartment and fall into a restless sleep.

She never told anyone about these walks because her Aunt Annette and Uncle Craig, would surely insist that she move back in with them- and that wasn't going to happen. She loved them all dearly but she needed to be on her own.

Refusing to allow her thoughts to dwell on her night terrors, she fumbled in her suit jacket for the small piece of paper where she'd jotted down her notes.

How she was ever going to get everything accomplished before she boarded the plane, she had no clue, and by agreeing to look over these samples of tiles she'd managed to add another layer to her stress.

The case shifted, and she bent and pushed it back against the building glaring at it as if by sheer will she could keep it in its place. She glanced at her watch and realized it was a little after five and Luke should be arriving any minute. She had visited Luke and Jay's office frequently, but from the street level she never could determine which of the windows on the tenth floor belonged to the law offices of Noonan and O'Brien.

She chuckled softly, how her cousin Luke and Jay O'Brien had ever become best friends was beyond her.

The friendship had evolved from a friendly competition in grammar school to a knockdown drag out fight over a girl in eighth grade. They had both ended up bruised and bloody, and in deep trouble with two sets of parents. After that day they had made a sacred vow to never let a girl come between them again. And they never had.

They had grown up tough and wise to the ways of the Boston streets, and that same toughness had carried over into their fledgling law practice.

She loved her aunt and uncle and her other cousins, but Luke was special to her. After the death of her mother the Noonan family had taken her into their arms and hearts, and she had become as much a part of the family as if she had been born into it.

But Luke had a special place in her heart. He had been there for her from the first day. He had taken her under his wing, and had let her tag along even though his circle of friends was older. He had always been her champion, and though there were times when the two of them fought, nothing ever changed the special bond between them.

But tonight was going to strain that bond. She had grown up aware that her father had brought her to the states hoping that a change of scenery and the knowledgeable physicians that were available in the states would help her to deal with the trauma of witnessing her mother's death.

Her Aunt Annette had explained to her, as soon as she felt that Whisper could understand, how helpless her father had felt as he watched his only child trying to deal with her grief over her mother's death, and the nightmares she suffered had shaken him. But it was only when physician after physician had been unable to unlock the reason for her refusal to speak that he had turned to his wife's twin sister Annette and her Uncle Craig for help.

It was supposed to be a temporary move, but each time her

father came to bring her home she became hysterical, so they agreed to wait until she was a little older to return her to London.

Only that day never came until now.

She bent and picked up her purse from where she had tucked it behind her briefcase and fumbling in the bottom looked for an aspirin. Surely one of those blessed little tablets must have dropped into the bottom of this black hole she called a pocketbook.

Finding one, she grimaced as she popped it into her mouth and looked at her watch. Luke was usually on time, but her aunt had warned her that he and Jay were preparing a big case, and they had been working late every night.

But Friday night was their night, and she jealously guarded these few hours with Luke. The two of them shared secrets they had never told anyone else. He knew about her nightmares and how they would happen when she least expected them; and he had confessed that he was in love with Jay's sister Colleen. As if that was a surprise.

Taking a couple of deep breaths, she concentrated on trying to quell the butterflies in her stomach.

Had it really only been three days since she received the call from her father asking her to return to London? The call had shaken her, chilling her to the core and as she listened to the anxiety in his voice she had felt as if the blood had drained from her body.

Her strong and invincible father, how could this be happening to him? A virus, a stupid virus, and now he was facing life threatening surgery to repair the damage the virus had done to the valves of his heart.

And he wanted her to come home.

She shuddered, she was going to have to go back home, home to London, only London wasn't home anymore, Boston was.

She had no choice; she would never forgive herself if something happened to her father and she had to live with the knowledge that she had been too much of a coward to return.

Tears formed in her eyes, and she quickly reached up and wiped them away. No matter what, she couldn't let Luke see how frightened she was, yet she couldn't shake the feeling that there was something evil in that ancient mansion where her father lived, where she'd been born-- and where her mother had died.

After her father's call she had ordered her airline tickets, and then and only then, had she called her aunt, knowing she would try to dissuade her from returning home until someone could go with her.

Within an hour after her call to her aunt, Luke had come storming through her office door.

Their quarrel had gotten quite heated when she rejected the idea of his going with her, and she had stubbornly refused to discuss the matter any further with him. She was going back to face her fears . . . alone.

Shivering even though the late afternoon was warm, she silently assured herself that she could handle Luke. She would deal with her own demons later, knowing if she gave him just the tiniest hint of how frightened she was, he would press her to let him accompany her and that just wasn't going to happen.

As the briefcase threatened to topple again, she pushed it back against the building with her foot. The first thing she was going to do when Luke arrived was hand him this damn thing to carry.

Through the large plate glass window of the building Whisper spotted him. It was easy to pick him out because he moved with a quickness that left others in his wake, and he towered over most of them.

Whisper bent to retrieve her briefcase, her arms still aching from carrying it from her office so she shifted it up against her chest.

Just as the bullet struck.

The sample case exploded and she staggered back from the impact. Pieces of blue tile littered the ground in front of her and beside her. Fragments were caught in the fabric of her coat.

Blood seemed to be spattered everywhere. Her cheeks stung and she could feel a warm liquid running down her face. She tried to reach up to wipe it away but a sharp pain in her arm halted her movement. She looked down but couldn't seem to focus. Was that blood seeping through her jacket? Where had that come from?

Her vision began to blur as her stomach roiled and she gasped for breath. Where was Luke? He'd fix this; he'd fix whatever had happened. He always did.

The light began to fade and she thought this is crazy I'm going to faint... I never faint, even as her knees buckled and she slumped back, sliding down the uneven wall behind her.

CHAPTER THREE

No, he couldn't believe it.

It was a perfect shot; he had gauged it precisely. She should be dead, but now she was sitting on the sidewalk staring up at him.

He had thought when she fell that it was over, but something had made him pause, and when her hand moved, he realized that she had fainted.

Now the group he'd used for cover had doubled back and were standing next to him staring down at her.

As more people crowded around them, he knew that he couldn't just walk away, that would raise a red flag to anyone watching. So, with a barely perceptible movement, he checked to be sure that the gun had dropped down into the hidden lining of his jacket.

Finding it secure he tossed the jacket down, then kicking shards of sharp tile aside he dropped to one knee, "Lady, are you all right?"

The voice seemed concerned, and Whisper looked up into dark eyes.

"I'm not sure." Her voice was weak and she struggled to stay conscious.

He looked around and spotting a woman talking into a cell phone yelled, "Call 9-1-1 this lady is hurt."

With a startled look, the woman punched in the numbers,

while another stepped forward and tearing the scarf from around her neck offered it to him to press against the wound.

Luke walking out of the office building glanced curiously at the crowd gathering on the sidewalk. Where the hell was Whisper? He might have to cut their dinner short because he and Jay were behind on the brief they were preparing for their Monday morning court case.

Not seeing her, he walked toward the crowd, if someone had fallen, he might be of some assistance since he and Jay had a first aid kit in their office, and it would only take a few minutes to run back up and get it.

Pushing his way through the crowd he spotted her.

She was sitting in a pool of blood while some guy tried to stem the flow of the precious liquid that was running down her arm and onto the sidewalk. Red streaks ran down the side of her face and he could see a jagged cut on the side of her head and smaller ones on her cheeks.

"What the hell?" Luke shoved the man kneeling over her aside, and grabbing the scarf from his hand, pressed it tightly against her arm.

"What the hell happened?"

"I don't know." Whisper's voice was strained and he could barely hear the words. Her face was pale, her eyes glazed, and he knew she was going into shock.

"Hang in there honey." He sought to reassure her past the lump in his own throat. The scarf under his hand was turning dark, and he could feel the warm stickiness of her blood running onto his hands, and he was afraid to let the pressure up for even a second.

"Where the hell is the ambulance?"

He had no sooner uttered the words than the scream of approaching sirens deafened him. An ambulance shot to the curb, barely stopping before a tiny blond jumped out and ran over dropping down beside Luke.

Grabbing rubber gloves out of her pocket she leaned toward Whisper her soft voice reassuring as she quickly noted the blood covering Luke's hands and still seeping down Whisper's arm.

"I need to see the wound," she murmured to Luke gently pulling the scarf away.

"Gunshot." she looked up at her partner. "Call it in and get the PD moving this way."

Glancing over at Luke her voice became crisp. "Here, don't let up on that scarf till I tell you."

With deft movements she reached into the black bag she had flung on the ground beside them and retrieved a large bandage and tourniquet.

Quickly and efficiently she cut away the ragged sleeve from Whisper's jacket then with a sharp glance at Luke instructed him. "When I tell you, move the scarf and let me get this bandage on. But don't move it till I tell you to."

Luke nodded, his eyes glued to Whisper's pale face.

Since issuing the orders to Luke, the paramedic had not acknowledged Luke or anyone else in the crowd, only glancing up at her partner as she mumbled, "I don't like the look of this it's too near the artery, we need to get her to trauma now!"

Jumping to her feet she bent as if to help her partner lift Whisper onto the stretcher but Luke was there before her.

"I'll do it." His tone brooked no argument and the paramedic took a step back before turning and running ahead of him to climb into the back of the ambulance.

Cradling Whisper in his arms he held her for a second before laying her on the stretcher. She seemed so fragile that he was afraid to put her down, afraid if he did, he would lose her. God, she was dearer to him than his own brothers. He held his breath as she was bundled into the interior of the ambulance and the doors slammed shut behind her.

He stood stunned as the ambulance took off, sirens wailing

and lights flashing. Luke glanced around him suddenly aware that the street was alive with cops and cruisers.

As the screech of the ambulance faded, Luke stood staring down at his hands and the blood soaking into the sidewalk and onto the shattered sample case. Cops moved through the crowd searching for witnesses while others stretched out the yellow tape that marked off a crime scene.

"Luke, what the hell happened?"

Lieutenant Eric O'Brien of the Boston Crime Squad strode up to Luke.

"I heard the call on the radio about a shooting and I knew it was your building." He looked at the blood staining Luke's hands and jacket. "Who got shot?"

"Shot?" Luke tried to focus on Eric's question but he kept seeing Whisper's ashen face before his eyes. "Whisper."

"Your cousin? How the . . .?"

He never got to finish his question as Luke pushed past him, "Later- I have to find a cab."

"Don't be an ass!" Eric grabbed his arm and guided him toward the patrol car. "Get in, did anybody see anything?"

"How the hell do I know...all I could see was Whisper."

He felt sick to his stomach as he thought about all the blood and how pale she had been—damn if anything happened to her ...he couldn't even think about it.

"Yeah, well the guys will know if anyone saw anything." He nodded to the cops who were standing with clusters of people.

"Maybe they should ask the guy who was helping her when I got there."

But the Good Samaritan who had come to Whisper's aid had disappeared.

Three blocks away, the Good Samaritan smiled to himself. That whole scenario had been a stroke of genius, his genius.

First he shot her, then he saved her. How ironic.

It had always been the thrill of the hunt that made each job a challenge and he had survived by practicing three cardinal rules; follow your prey, learn everything there is to know, and then move in quickly for the kill.

After his first couple of hits, he'd laughed when he'd heard that his ability to blend in or to disappear had earned him the nickname of Chameleon by the punks who lived on the streets. He'd even adopted the name and left his calling card after he completed a job. Word spread fast and now the gangs were all afraid of him, and he encouraged and nurtured that fear, knowing none of them would be tempted to turn on him.

He never thought of his targets as people, they were nothing, just things to be eliminated, and the fact that each job paid very well helped him to live the kind of life he'd dreamed about as a kid.

Growing up on the streets had taught him how to survive.

His eyes narrowed, and his breathing became slow and deep. He was only sixteen when his slut of a mother had died of an overdose, and although he was only a kid himself, he'd had his eight-year-old brother Teddy to worry about. It didn't take him long to realize that if he wanted to keep Teddy with him, he had to earn some money and fast. He'd begun by selling crack but he soon discovered that was penny ante stuff and so when he was approached about eliminating the head of a rival street gang, he discovered he had another and a much more lucrative skill set. Murder.

But right now, he couldn't think about Teddy. He was gone, killed in prison; and the man who had sent him there, and cost Teddy his life, would pay, and pay dearly.

He looked down at the stains that marred his jacket, and of course his pants were ruined, kneeling in the blood had been messy, but sometimes those kinds of sacrifices had to be made.

People would remember that he had been the one to stop and help. The newspapers might even be looking for the hero who had saved her; after all she was a member of a very prominent Boston family.

He frowned, of course this job didn't pay as well as most since he was doing it as a favor to Max. Well not exactly a favor he mused, he was still getting a fifty-thousand-dollar retainer out of the deal, and another twenty-five when she was dead.

Max was the only other person beside Teddy he trusted.

They'd met when a local gang didn't like him selling in their neighborhood and had come after him. He'd been taking quite a beating when Max had appeared. Not liking the odds, Max had come to his aid.

That night he had learned a valuable lesson, always be prepared and if you're going to be in a fight, be in it to win. The next day he went to a friend and bought a gun.

For years he and Max had drifted in and out of each other's lives till finally down on his luck Max had approached him about a job. He'd hired him immediately. Within months Max became his Arranger and setup the jobs and collected the payoffs. No one messed with Max. But if they wanted a job done it was Max they approached---only Max, he never allowed anyone to see him.

But Max had a couple of weaknesses that still made him nervous, he talked too much, and he was a sucker for a sob story. Over and over he had warned Max, but Max just laughed and assured him he was careful. He had better be, or friend or not, those flaws just might prove fatal.

He slipped on the rubber gloves he always carried and unlocked the door to the used car he kept hidden in the city. It was because of Max he was working this hit. The stupid bastard had met some guy in a hotel bar and after listening to him for a couple of hours, had offered to help the guy out by having the little problem he was dealing with eliminated.

But eliminating that little problem was proving more difficult then he'd anticipated. She seemed to have a guardian angel.

He started the car and sat for a moment staring out at the

street in front of him. He'd have to stop and slip into the condo he rented on the edge of the city, shower and change his clothes.

It wouldn't do if he went home with blood on him, he couldn't take a chance on Nola asking any questions.

Nola, his wife, wouldn't she be surprised if she knew what was financing her next diamond bracelet. Beautiful and dumb, she was the perfect mate. When he met her, she had been a stripper in a cheap club out west. No family, no one to ask questions. It had taken him awhile to get rid of the trashy things she loved, but now she looked, talked, and acted like a businessman's wife. He laughed to himself, because he came and went at all hours of the day and night she probably thought he was also a drug dealer. He wondered how she would react, and if she would even care if she knew that her husband was a paid assassin.

His thoughts returned to the woman he had just shot, let them patch her up. He had seen her up close and she had seen him, but the fact that she never knew that he had her life in his hands made it that much more exciting. When he moved in for the final kill, he might just let her see him one more time.

Right before she died.

CHAPTER FOUR

Lieutenant Eric O'Brien stood in the emergency room with only a thin curtain between him, his brother Mike, and Whisper. It had been a harrowing two hours since he and Luke had rushed through the doors following Whisper's stretcher. The emergency room staff had been waiting on the platform, alerted by Eric, and as soon as the ambulance rolled to a stop, they had torn open the doors and began scrambling inside.

Helplessly Luke and Eric had watched, and it was only when Whisper had been whisked away to surgery that Eric had caught a glimpse of his brother Mike. Dressed in his scrubs he was striding along with the stretcher. Eric and Luke glanced at each other reassured that whatever Whisper needed she had the best physician in the hospital caring for her.

He should have remembered that his brother Mike would be on duty tonight. Mike thrived on the chaos and challenge of the busy Boston hospital on a Friday night, and although his position as Emergency Room Director afforded him evenings and weekends off, he never seemed to take them. For a man still in his thirties, being the head of the ER was quite an achievement and he had fought hard to earn his reputation as an outstanding physician.

Recognized throughout the state, and if true, from the murmurings that had reached Eric's ears, Mike wasn't only recognized as an exceptionally skilled and experienced surgeon here, but was sought after to lecture and assist with delicate surgeries throughout the country. He was also the first person the hospital called when there was trouble.

But it came as no surprise to the O'Brien family that along with that well deserved reputation he was also known to be hardheaded, opinionated and cantankerous.

Always the maverick of the family, never backing down from a fight, wherever trouble was, there was Mike.

His best friend Ollie had been just the opposite, soft spoken, jolly and a peacemaker. Totally different in personality, they had somehow established a bond that dated back to their days in kindergarten. They argued, and laughed, and watched each other's backs, and anyone thinking that because Ollie was easy going and passive, he was an easy target soon found out to their chagrin that a challenge to Ollie was a challenge to Mike. Where one was, you always knew the other one wasn't far away.

But their senior year in high school that all changed, walking home after a particularly grueling soccer practice, Ollie had called out to Mike as he began to cross the intersection toward home.

It was the last gesture and words that Ollie ever spoke.

As he began to cross the street a drunk careened around the corner. Ollie never had a chance.

Mike never saw the drunk driver; he only heard the screech of brakes, and a thump, and turned to see Ollie flying through the air. He had thrown his equipment to the ground and raced into the street.

Throwing himself down, he had gathered Ollie into his arms. Ollie had opened his eyes once and tried to smile, but Mike knew from the amount of blood coming from Ollie's nose and mouth that he was dying.

Oblivious to the cars that had stopped, forming a barrier around the two boys, he had held onto Ollie, clutching his hand to his chest as if by shear will he could keep Ollie alive. His frustration at not being able to help his friend tore at him. He never saw the crowd gathered around them, or heard the sad wail of the ambulance as it arrived, it was only when his father lifted him from beside his buddy, that Mike realized Ollie was gone.

He stood shaking and staring after the ambulance until his father placed him gently in his patrol car and drove him home.

On the day of Ollie's funeral Mike stood by his grave and made his friend a promise. He would never feel that helpless again. From that day on the old Mike was gone, he finished his senior year at the top of his class, with one goal in mind, becoming a doctor. With steely determination he put himself through medical school, graduating at the top of his class, and then immediately took an internship studying abroad with some of the best-known physicians in the United Kingdom.

Yet despite his thorny reputation Eric knew Mike's staff adored him; and heaven help the hapless soul who made a derogatory comment about him within earshot of any of them.

Eric rubbed his head, he and Luke hadn't been surprised when Whisper had been returned to the emergency room instead of being admitted to a floor after her surgery, since they were pretty sure that Mike wouldn't let her out of his sight. The Noonan's and the O'Brien's were exceptionally close and Whisper had long ago been accepted as one of the O'Brien's. Luke and Eric had sat beside her bed in the emergency room until she had started to open her eyes and then they had slipped out so that Mike and the nurses could attend to her.

But from the argument going on between his brother and Whisper, she was obviously now fully awake and was demanding that she be allowed to go home.

He glanced down the corridor to where Luke stood cell phone to his ear and beckoned to him, hoping that he would get the message and conclude his conversation and get back before all hell broke loose.

Luke was probably the only one that Whisper would listen

to because it sure didn't sound like Mike was getting anywhere with her.

Although still groggy, Whisper's voice had a hint of stubbornness in it; while Mike's tone was brusque. That, Eric knew from experience was a huge mistake.

Whisper might have the deceptive look of a fragile doll, with her soft blond hair, emerald green eyes and a model's face, but he also knew from past experience that she could hold her own in any argument and she had a very formidable stubborn streak.

As the voices in the room continued to rise, Eric gestured to Luke so he would get the hell off the phone. If Luke didn't persuade Whisper to do as Mike asked this could turn into a very long night. His brother might be a skilled physician, but as far was Eric was concerned, he had the bedside manners of a goat.

If this whole damn thing wasn't so serious, he'd be tempted to laugh. Luke had started to make his calls from outside Whisper's room, but because of the racket coming from the adjoining cubicle he'd been forced to move up the hall. A frantic mother, a furious father and five-year-old twins who had super glued their hands together definitely had not been conducive to a quiet conversation.

As he watched Luke pace, Eric knew to anyone seeing him Luke looked in complete control, but there was no doubt in Eric's mind that he was raging inside. Too many times he had sat in a courtroom and watched Luke and Jay at work. While Jay was more flamboyant Luke was a deadly adversary who had perfected an almost relaxed manner that often-encouraged opposing attorneys to believe he would be easy to beat. Only after he had slashed and burned their arguments did they realize that it had been a tactical mistake to underestimate him.

Shoving his phone into his pocket Luke strode down the corridor toward Eric. Spotting the uniformed cop who had quietly come into the ER and moved into place besides Whisper room, his roar of outrage had people stopping to stare at him.

"What the hell is going on?"

Surging to his feet, Eric reached out and shoved Luke into a nearby empty room.

"What the hell do you think is going on? I called the precinct and ordered an officer stationed outside her room for the night."

"We don't need an officer, if she has to stay the night, I'll stay with her."

Eric's eyes narrowed. "Really? And what would you do if it was a guy with a gun? Throw a bedpan at him?"

Pushing Luke down into a nearby chair, Eric hesitated for a moment knowing what he was about to tell Luke was going to scare the hell out of him.

"Look I know how you feel but while you were on the phone, I got a call from the station. One of the detectives just filed a report and from what he's written he's pretty sure that bullet was meant for her."

Eric reached out and grasped Luke's shoulder. "He's still got some checking to do, but according to him and his partner, this was no drive by, this was up close and personal and if she hadn't been lifting those tiles and that gun had been more powerful. . .

"Jesus." Luke's face was white.

"They traced the trajectory of the bullet and the damage to the building behind her and there was no mistaking the intent of the shooter. Three witnesses swore she had been standing alone with no one in any close proximity when the bullet struck. And there was no indication that any other shots had been fired."

"Who the hell would want her dead?" Luke voice was low and raspy.

"I don't know, but you can be sure that every available officer is working on it."

Straightening up, Eric tried not to grin, "But right now you have a more immediate problem."

"And what could be more important than someone trying to kill her?"

"You. . .You need to go into that room with Mike and persuade her that she needs to stay overnight."

Luke groaned. "My folks will be here in a few minutes I'm sure my mother. . ."

"Come on, suck it up, she's your cousin she'll listen to you. Mike can't stay in there all night arguing with her he's got an emergency room to run."

"Whisper listen to me? Since when? When has she ever listened to anyone once she makes up her mind?"

Eric looked at Luke his eyes narrowed. "Tonight, you make her listen. I want her where she is surrounded by people while we figure out the hell is going on."

He turned and started out the door and Luke stood and fell in beside him stopping once to square his shoulders before stepping behind the curtain into Whisper's room.

Hearing Luke's soothing voice and the soft murmur of Whisper's responses, Eric breathed a sigh of relief.

Moving with a panther like grace that seemed out of character for such a big man, Eric quietly drifted toward a group of chairs lined up against the wall and dropped into one. Slouching down he made himself as inconspicuous as possible. Friday nights in a Boston emergency room were always hectic, and sitting here in full uniform was bound to make a few of the patients and visitors nervous.

Patting his pocket, Eric reassured himself that the small plastic bag Whisper's nurse had handed him a few moments ago was still there.

Her terse, "Here you'll want this," was all the acknowledgement Eric got as she disappeared back into Whisper's room.

Eric reached up and rubbing the back of his neck tried to recall what he'd overheard at the station. He'd been booking a suspect but he could swear he'd overheard Whisper's name but he hadn't put two and two together till tonight. His shift was over but as soon as he was sure Whisper was going to stay put, he was heading back to the station.

He looked up as Mike stepped out and headed toward him. The scowl on his face told Eric that the battle with Whisper had probably been won, but not without some cost.

As Mike strode toward him the lines of an old childhood rhyme played in Eric's head. Rich man, poor man, beggar man, thief, doctor, lawyer, Indian Chief, the same one the kids in the neighborhood had taunted his adopted brother R. W. with until the day Sean heard it . . . and then...

He shook his head, that was then and this was now, ironic how that silly rhyme had come true. His brother Mike a doctor, Jay a lawyer, and he imagined his adopted brother R.W. would be a tribal Chief if he ever decided to leave Boston and return to the home of his birth. As far as that rich man stuff, his brother Sean was well on his way to fulfilling that prophesy, while Connor in his undercover work with the CIA had probably been a beggar and a thief. And poor man- well not exactly poor, but as a kid Patrick never could keep a nickel in his pocket.

Where that left him, he had no idea.

Wearily Mike dropped into a chair beside Eric. "I left her with Luke, but as soon as he's out of there I need him to stop and see me I've just given her a shot for pain, so she should be out of it for a while."

His face was somber as he looked at Eric. "That bullet missed the main artery in her arm by a fraction of an inch; and she's lost a lot of blood, so I'm glad he persuaded her to stay so we could watch her.'

"I know, but you're going to have a hell of a job getting Luke to leave her tonight, especially if he thinks she's in danger."

"Tough, she's my patient," his voice softened, "I know he's shook up, anyone would be, but he needs to go home and just let her rest. You talk to him; I'm worn out from arguing with her."

He shook his head, "Did you hear the argument I had with that woman? I never met such a stubborn female in my life."

"Oh, really? Surprised, are you?" Eric leaned back in his chair and folded his arms across his chest as he gazed up at the ceiling with a grin on his face.

"I seem to remember a time when you pestered her to get you a date with one of the most popular cheerleaders in her class and she point blank refused -insisted that she wouldn't fix you up because she wasn't the right girl for you and as I recall no matter how much you hassled her–"

"Shut up" Mike growled, "How was I to know Clarise was sleeping with half the football team?"

Eric laughed, "Saved your ass, didn't she? When your cute little cheerleader turned up pregnant and her Daddy was looking for the culprit--your name never came up..."

The two men looked at each other and grinned. But Mike's grin quickly disappeared.

"Listen I meant what I said, I'm not going to discharge her, she's staying here where I can keep an eye on her. Everything looks o.k. but infection is always a possibility and I want to watch her all night."

"Then Joe stays too." Eric nodded toward the uniformed cop that was leaning against a wall outside of Whisper's room. Eric's gaze was somber. "I'll make sure he's relieved at midnight."

"You really think a cop outside her room is necessary?"

Eric didn't hesitate, "Yes, I do."

Identical brown eyes met in the silent communication of siblings, and as Mike pushed himself up out of the chair he reached over and gave his older brother a light punch on the arm. "Be careful I've had to deal with a series of gunshot wounds lately from what you boys so quaintly refer to as random shootings."

"Only this one wasn't random was it?"

"From a physician's perspective, I don't know, from a friend's perspective, no, it wasn't."

Before Eric could ask him what he meant, a nurse stepped out into the hall and frantically waved to Mike and without another word he turned and sprinted down the corridor.

Eric watched his brother for a moment before he disappeared into a room and then he shifted his weight and moved his gun belt a little further on his hip so his back could rest more comfortably against the chair. A young nurse walked by and smiled at him, and he winked at her.

He tilted his head back giving the impression of being relaxed, but under his half-closed eyelids, he missed nothing.

The nurses' station a few feet away was alive with activity yet more than a few nurses threw admiring glances in Eric's direction. One young student was rewarded with a sharp poke in the ribs by a colleague, when she stared openly at him.

Eric wasn't conventionally handsome, but none of the O'Brien brothers were, yet they all possessed a potent masculinity that had women immediately responding. Eric was the only one who had inherited the quick smile and offbeat sense of humor of his grandfather Archie.

His body was lean though his upper torso was muscular, and his body tapered down to slender hips and long legs. He considered his body a weapon and worked out regularly to keep it honed. Yet when threatened it was not so much his body that gave perpetrators pause, but his eyes, they would narrow and darken to a midnight hue that gave a silent warning. His colleagues on the job recognized the look and when it happened, they wisely moved out of the way.

Ignoring the nurses' scrutiny, Eric crossed his arms over his chest and the muscles on his arms tightened against the sleeves of his shirt.

With a gasp, a young nurse dropped the chart she was carrying and the sound of the clipboard hitting the floor had his head swiveling just as his brother Mike reappeared barking orders.

A movement caught his attention and he watched as Luke

stepped out and headed back toward him. He was sure that one of Luke's earlier calls had been to his mother and probably the second one to Jay. He had specifically ordered Luke to keep the rest of the Noonan and O'Brien families in the dark because he had something in mind that he wanted to put into motion before the two families descended to offer aid and comfort. The element of surprise was essential when he talked to his brother Sean and he desperately needed Sean's help in discovering who and why someone had attempted to kill Whisper.

Luckily his sister Colleen was out of town at an FBI school or she would have been working the second shift at the PD and he was sure that no matter what her assignment was she would have been here when Whisper arrived. They were extremely close and nothing would have kept her away.

Luke's quick steps and crisp demeanor warred with Eric's recollections of the two scruffy kids that many nights graced the O'Brien dinner table; Jay with his dark hair and brown eyes; and Luke Noonan, his best friend, who was blessed with the fair coloring of some distant ancestor. Together they had gotten into more trouble than all the rest of the boys combined, except for Mike, and they always seemed to be just one step ahead of disaster.

Now they were successful trial lawyers and sometimes he still couldn't believe it, he'd always thought the two of them would end up breaking rocks and doing hard time somewhere.

"Well, did you see Mike? Did he say anything else?" Luke's face was ashen and although he was doing his best to remain calm, Eric noted his hands were trembling.

"God." he rubbed his forehead, "She's so damn pale, and before the shot took affect every time she moved, she winced." Rage radiated from him and although his voice was low there was determination in his words. "When I find whoever did this, I'll kill the bast..."

Uncoiling himself from the chair, Eric pushed Luke into the seat next to him.

"Any idea who would want her dead?"

Luke stared at him. "What the hell kind of a question is that? She hasn't got a single enemy that I know of. Christ people fall all over themselves to spend time with her."

"Then you have no idea who would want her dead bad enough to shoot her, at close range on a busy sidewalk . . . and with a .22?"

Reaching into his pocket Eric pulled out the small plastic bag with the bullet tucked neatly inside that the OR nurse had handed him.

"This little baby had her name on it that guy knew who he was after."

Luke dropped his head into his hands, "I don't know, I can't even think of anyone who would want to hurt her."

Eyes narrowed Eric gazed at Luke, "So from what you're telling me she's a saint without an enemy in the world."

Luke's head shot up and he glared at Eric. "What are you talking about? You know yourself she's no saint. She's stubborn, opinionated and extremely independent, and I was preparing to do battle with her tonight myself!" His voice broke, "But damn I love her as if she was my sister. Does that make me a prime suspect?"

"Only if you can be in two places at once, since everyone at the scene saw you arrive." Eric leaned forward and stared at Luke, "So we've established she's no saint and you were about to argue with her. Mind telling me about what?"

"Sure, she got a phone call from her father and he's scheduled for some major heart surgery and he wants her to come home to London. So, she's going back and I want to go with her."

At Eric's lifted brow Luke growled, "I know I'm over protective, but damn it the nightmares have started up again and there is something over there that frightens her."

Eric frowned, "Well that sure as hell complicates things, I had hoped we could keep an eye on her here but. . .London."

Eric vaguely remembered hearing something about Whisper being brought to the states by her father, but she'd been part of the Noonan family for so long that the reason she had been brought up by her aunt and uncle eluded him.

"Yeah London, it's her home but it really isn't . . . but it's a long story. Her father needs her now and has asked her to come back . . . and she swears she's going." He looked over at Eric, "But I really think she's afraid to go back and that's why I want to go with her."

"Afraid? What's she afraid of? Wasn't she just a kid when she got here?"

"Yeah, but she's tight lipped about the whole thing but she finally admitted to me about her nightmares returning, I don't know if it has to do with the accident that killed her mother but tonight I was going to press the issue."

"Well it's obvious she's in no condition to answer questions so you'll just have to wait to get those answers. . ."

Hearing a commotion in the corridor, Luke rose, "That will be my folks, what am I going to tell them?"

"Just tell them that we think it was a random shooting, don't tell them we suspect anything else."

Eric stood, and leaning down put his hand on Luke's shoulder. "Meet me tomorrow at Sean's office at one o'clock, and we'll try to make some sense out of this," he paused, "and tell Jay to keep his mouth shut, the less people know the easier it's going to protect her--- the last thing we needs is a lot of idle speculation."

Eric started down the hall then turned back. "Keep your folks busy, so they won't have time to ask too many questions. There are some papers that have to be signed at the nurses' station, but remember don't say anything to anybody, the less people know what happened the better."

"Wait, suppose Sean can't see us tomorrow. Jay said he's getting ready to go on vacation."

"Oh, he'll see us, don't worry about that; you know my brother he'll move heaven and hell to find out who did this."

Luke nodded, knowing that Sean O'Brien had the reputation of being a pit bull when it came to finding his man. He had worked hard to obtain the reputation of being the best private investigator in Boston and he never backed down from a challenge.

Spotting his parents, Luke headed toward them, while Eric slipped down a side corridor. Although he was very fond of Luke's parents, he didn't need to be there when Luke told them what happened. This way he was free to do some checking without having to answer any questions.

He grinned knowing Luke's mom, the interrogation that Luke was about to face would make any questioning at the station look like child's play.

Exiting the hospital, Eric climbed into the squad car and picked up his cell phone. Punching in a few numbers he waited till a pleasant voice on the other end answered. Eric chatted for a moment with Sean's secretary, then asked to speak to his brother.

"Do you know what the hell time it is? The office is closed." Sean's voice growled at him.

"Ah" Eric said, "I can see you're your usual charming self."

Sean O'Brien's snarled a few choice words that made Eric grin.

"I'm coming to see you tomorrow at one o'clock and I'm bringing some friends."

Holding the phone away from his ear, he didn't bother to listen to his brother's words instead he concentrated on trying not to laugh.

He waited for a momentary lull, and then in a patient voice answered "Yes I know its Saturday, and I know you're scheduled to go out on an assignment tonight," he paused, "And I am also aware that you're getting ready to go on vacation, but you won't want to miss this."

With those cryptic words, Eric hung up.

He leaned back against the seat and laughed; he could just picture his brother's face. His notorious Irish temper would be at the boiling point and he could almost hear him bellowing at his secretary to get him back on the line, but it was already too late, the minute he hung up, he'd shut off his phone.

As he started the patrol car and pulled out into traffic, the grin was still there, he loved his older brother, but every once in a while it felt good to remind Sean that he wasn't afraid of him, or his bark. Yes, tomorrow promised to be a very interesting day.

CHAPTER FIVE

Hearing the soft click, Erik opened the door to his brother Sean's office and slipped inside. He quickly moved to the wall behind the desk and reaching into his back pocket retrieved a small handmade tool and proceeded to dismantle the alarm.

He chuckled to himself. He wondered how much Sean had paid for this latest security purchase.

For a half hour he had quietly waited in his car outside the building until he spotted Sean's secretary, who was also their Aunt Emma, leaving for lunch.

No sense in giving his aunt a heart attack by slipping thru the locked door to Sean's office while she was still in there.

It was Saturday and if everything ran true to form, the office was closed, the door locked and Emma certainly would not be expecting a visitor.

But getting in without being seen or heard was the challenge.

Dismantling the lock that let him into Sean's inner office Eric entered.

Looking around he realized that nothing had changed.

No matter how successful Sean became, there were some things in his life that would always remain the same.

Wandering over to the massive bookcase that lined one wall, he picked up the framed family photo that Sean proudly displayed there.

Very few people made it into this office, and those that did had earned his trust, so Sean was not afraid to display his family pictures.

Two doors down, off the hall, was a large conference room where Sean met with guests, and it didn't matter if it was CIA, FBI, or various government, state or city officials. They met there. No one got into his office - no matter how powerful they might think they were.

Reaching up, he picked up the carving of a snarling black bear that someone had given Sean, and if you looked closely you could see the small animal cowering behind its left leg.

The first time he had looked at it he had missed the small animal, until something had made him go back and pick it up again.

It was obvious the bear was protecting something smaller, and weaker, from whatever predator was threatening it.

After that, he had always thought whoever gave Sean the carving had chosen the perfect gift, since the bear and the small animal he was protecting portrayed the essence of his brother.

Hearing a sound in the outer office, Eric silently went over and pushed some of the files that were strewn around on Sean's desk to one-side.

He glanced at the top one with CIA scrawled across it but had no desire to even peak at it. That wasn't his style.

He grabbed a new magazine that was on the corner of the desk, sat down--and waited.

Sean O'Brien pushed open the door to his office and stepped inside.

Eyes narrowed, he glared at his brother who was languishing in his chair, feet on his desk, reading a magazine.

Tossing his keys onto a small marble top table, he leaned against the wall, his arms folded across his chest.

"How long did it take this time?"

Eric glanced up from the magazine and peered at his watch. "Seven minutes."

"Jesus, don't you ever get tired of breaking into my office?"
"Nope."

Sean winced, as he pushed himself away from the wall, his shoulder still aching from the wrestling match he'd had with one of the drug dealers. He was tired, and lately he'd begun questioning whether at thirty-five he was getting too old for these middle of the night raids.

The only positive thing as far as he could see, was that if he was aching, the bastard he had been wrestling with was nursing a lot more bruises than he was, and would be out of commission for quite a long time.

"You know I just had another new security system installed."

"Yeah, I heard..." Eric couldn't contain his grin, "Wasted your money."

Since a child, Eric had considered every locked door a personal challenge, and he had developed an uncanny knack of being able to pick any lock, or open any door.

Now he had made it a personal challenge to test every new security system that Sean installed.

The first time Eric had slipped into his office, Sean had been furious, but Eric had just shrugged and his response had Sean choking back his words.

"Take your pick- either I test your security system —or someone else will."

Sean recognized the truth in his brother's words, knowing that the highly confidential files he stored in his office would cause a major international incident if his security was ever breached.

Disgustedly Sean shook his head. "All right, you made your point, now get the hell out of my chair."

Watching as Sean moved toward him, Eric felt a sense of pride.

Owner of one of the most prestigious detective agencies in Boston, Sean had let nothing stand in his way. Five years ago, Sean had decided to leave the Boston police department and strike out on his own. As soon as he opened the doors to his agency, word had spread, and the FBI, CIA, and other agencies the average joe didn't even know about, began knocking on his door.

Yet, despite his success, he never quite threw off the mantle of being a street cop and once in a while, he and the special OPS guys who worked for him, went back to assist his old department.

Eric had heard rumors for weeks that something big was going down, and that the department was calling in some very special help. The whole thing was supposed to be highly classified and secret, but in a city like Boston it was hard to keep the street cops from knowing what was going on.

A little after midnight, Eric had sat in an unmarked car, and watched Sean and his men enter the warehouse.

He'd almost lost his brother once, and he intended to be around in case something went wrong. There was no question in his mind that the special help the department called in was Sean's, since it was well known that Sean despised predators and especially those that targeted children, and this raid was on a crack house that specialized in selling drugs to kids.

Eric pushed himself up out of Sean's chair, and stepped aside grinning at the disgusted look on Sean's face.

Dressed in black, dungarees stained and the sleeve of his tee shirt partially torn off there was still an element of danger surrounding him. The small stream of dried blood on his arm and the bruise on his cheek was a mute testament to the fact that he had taken part in a dangerous and potentially deadly operation.

The brothers looked enough alike to be twins, but now the sprinkling of silver at Sean's temples added a bit of a roguish look to him. He wore his hair in a traditional cut since it annoyed him that it had a tendency to curl, while Eric's was longer and pulled away from his face and clubbed back with a black leather band.

Eric's defiance of the police dress code had caused his bosses a great deal of grief, but finally they had thrown up their hands and decided that keeping such a valuable cop on the streets was worth turning a blind eye to his idiosyncrasies.

Dropping into his chair Sean studied Eric. He wasn't fooled by the smile on his face there was a distinct air of tension surrounding him.

"O.K. spit it out – what is so damn important that you have to see me the day before I'm leaving on vacation."

"Wait for Jay and Luke, there is no sense giving you half a story when you're going to need all the pieces."

"Pieces?" Sean glared at him. "Listen, I was up all night and I am in no mood for all this mystery crap, so spit it out, why are Jay and Luke coming here? I thought they had some big case they were working on"

"They are, but this is more important."

Shifting in his chair Sean felt the familiar twinge of pain in his back. He glanced over at Eric to see if he noticed, but his brother seemed engrossed in the papers he had pulled from his pocket.

But Eric had noticed.

The fleeting glimpse of pain that crossed Sean's face was a cruel reminder of how close he had come to losing him, and for Eric it still brought back the panic and the painful memories.

It was as vivid as if it had happened yesterday when in actuality it had happened seven years ago.

The call had come at the change of shift and although Sean was technically off duty, that night the department was flat out with a domestic, a hit and run, and a burglary, all taking place within minutes of each other. With his buddies spread so thin, and most of the evening shift guys being held over, he had offered to take it.

The dispatcher had been trying to calm the hysterical caller down as Sean climbed into the patrol car and headed for the alley where the call had come from.

The info he had was sketchy. He'd caught just enough to

know that the victim had been beaten, and she was afraid her boyfriend was coming back to kill her.

What no one knew was the boyfriend was still there, high on drugs and carrying a knife. A very large knife.

It was the one and only time in his job that Sean allowed emotion to overrule his survival instinct. He never let it happen again.

It was a hot night, and he'd discarded his vest, throwing it on the back seat at the end of his shift. He arrived without lights or sirens, not wanting to draw attention to himself, or alert the perpetrator.

As soon as he exited his patrol car, he spotted her. She was unconscious; lying in the alley, her face bruised and badly swollen, her clothes torn from her body and he could see blood on one of her breasts. She looked like she was barely breathing, and without thinking he dropped to one knee to check her vitals. Too late he saw her eyes open in fear just as the knife was plunged deep into his back.

He had struggled to rise as his attacker yanked out the knife and lunged for his throat. Deflecting the thrust, he swung around and realized he was facing a kid about twenty years old.

Sean didn't hesitate, he could tell from the crazed look on the kids face that there were a lot of drugs pumping through his system, and they were arming him with a strength that belied his slight build. Weak from the loss of blood, Sean had thrown his arms around the kid hoping that he would be able to remain conscious long enough for help to arrive.

He'd been dimly aware of squealing tires, and the sound of pounding feet running toward them, and then the blood curdling shout of his brother Eric.

Eric had been a few streets away writing a speeding ticket when he'd had heard Sean sign out at the scene. Knowing Sean was going off duty, he decided to head that way to relieve him.

A sudden chill and then a feeling of apprehension began in his belly, and he had turned on his lights and siren and hit the gas.

The car had barely stopped when he hit the pavement, and his shout had temporarily distracted Sean's attacker. It took only an instant for him to yank Eddie Little away from Sean, and take him down and cuff him.

Weak from the loss of blood Sean began swaying, and Eric could tell it was taking all of his strength to remain standing. Sean put his hand out toward Eric, then slumped to the pavement.

It was months before Sean learned that as Eric reached out to grab him, his hands had become covered with blood. Lifting Sean off the pavement and into his arms Eric had desperately tried to stop the bleeding as he watched his brother's life flowing from him.

Cursing, he'd called for help holding onto Sean and praying that the emergency crew would get there in time. As soon as he heard the sound of sirens, and saw the flashing lights of two ambulances, Eric lifted Sean in his arms and ran to the curb.

As the back doors of the first ambulance opened, he stepped in, and laid Sean on the stretcher. "Get going I'll be there as soon as I take care of the little bastard that jumped him."

As the light from the ambulance illuminated Sean's face Eric saw the ugly gash over Sean's lip and the bleeding nicks on his throat.

With a cry of rage Eric jumped from the ambulance, and had started back down the alley after the assailant, and it had taken the combined strength of fellow officers, who had arrived at the scene, to keep Eric from getting to him.

Throwing him into the back of a patrol car, the driver had swiftly left the scene.

For three weeks Sean lay in the critical care unit. His parents and sister keeping vigil until all of his brothers began arriving. Twenty-four hours a day an O'Brien sat outside or in the unit.

There was never a question in their minds as to whether he would survive or not, he was an O'Brien.

Eric had been the one sitting by his bedside when Sean finally opened his eyes.

"You look like hell." Sean's voice was raspy and weak.

"Yeah, well you're no sleeping beauty." Eric's voice broke and he reached down and grasped Sean's hand. The hand he held was weak and trembling, but its warmth comforted Eric since it had been icy cold when they brought him in.

"Scared you, did I?"

"Nah... I kept telling everybody you were too damn ornery to die--" but his voice broke, and tears slid silently down his cheeks.

The unspoken bond that existed between the two brothers was reinforced as Sean tightened his grip on Eric's hand.

Shaking off the memories of the past, Eric realized that Sean was talking to him.

"This meeting had better be important, I'm going on vacation tomorrow," but his sentence was interrupted as the door to his office opened.

To the casual observer the two men that entered were a study in contrasts.

Jay O'Brien, although as tall as his brothers, had always been considered the handsome one in the family, his face lean but his cheekbones less pronounced thereby giving him a warmer countenance.

Luke Noonan, his partner and best friend, had an athlete's build, and the look and the coloring of some long forgotten Nordic ancestor. While Jay's eyes were brown, Luke's were a cool blue and he wore his blond hair cropped short.

As they entered Sean watched the two of them carefully, being out of their law office together spelled trouble; and he hoped to hell he wasn't going to be in the middle of it.

Tension radiated in the room and Sean watched warily as

Luke tossed his briefcase down, and walked over to stare out of the floor length windows at the Boston skyline.

Jay paused for a moment watching Luke, then dropped into a chair next to Eric.

"You two have a lover's quarrel?" Sean nodded his head toward Luke who stood silently at the window.

"Go to hell." Jay growled as Eric sat with an amused look on his face.

The three brothers that were gathered in Sean's office had no idea that their size alone seemed to diminish the substantial dimensions of the room. Each man stood over six feet and they had all been blessed with the rock-solid build of their father. They had inherited their parent's rich Irish coloring; with dark eyes that ranged from Sean's deepest brown to the lighter coffee color of Jay's. They were sturdy looking, and rumors that they were descended from men who were not averse to making their living as gamblers and pirates probably were true.

Fortunately for the city of Boston, the men in this room had all chosen to uphold the law, not break it.

Glancing from Jay to Eric, Sean saw a sudden tightness in Eric's jaw, which was out of character for the family's most stoic poker player, and the same concern was mirrored on Jay's face. Without a word Sean swung his chair around and addressed Luke knowing instinctively that the key to this unscheduled visit lay with him.

"Hey buddy you here to talk to me or because you enjoy the view?"

He waited not pushing, Luke had a reputation both in the courtroom and on the street for his rapier wit, and his silence was so out of character that it made Sean uneasy. Receiving no answer Sean's tone became abrupt.

"Look, if there's something bothering you, spit it out. I don't have time for games I'm leaving on vacation tomorrow."

Luke swung around, and Sean was startled to see that all the color had drained from his face. Moving deliberately, he stepped away from the window and dropped into a chair directly in front of Sean desk.

"Yesterday my cousin Whisper was shot."

The roar that followed his statement and the massive fist that slammed down on the desk, startled the men as the papers that had been piled neatly on its corner jumped, and tumbled to the floor.

Sean's furious voice rumbled out of his chest.

"What the hell are you talking about? She was shot yesterday? Yesterday? And you asses just got around to telling me? What the hell is the matter with all of you?"

He surged to his feet, and furiously rounded on Eric. "You didn't think to tell me that when you called? I could have had men on the street in five minutes – we could have found the son of a..."

Eric's voice was calm, and his gaze steady as he met Sean's eyes.

"No, there was nothing you could do, it was over, my guys had taken statements, the scene was being scrubbed . . ."

Cursing, Sean interrupted his words. "Nothing I could do? What the hell do you mean there was nothing I could do? Do you know how fast my men could have covered this city? We'd have caught him before he got" --

"No you wouldn't, and it was my idea to keep her shooting quiet." Eric replied softly. "I told them not to say anything."

Sean slumped back down into his chair, as he struggled to control his temper, but his eyes still blazed angrily. "Mind telling me why?"

"First of all, nobody saw anything. It happened in broad daylight in front of scores of people, but there wasn't a single person who could tell us a thing. It seemed as if the bullet came out of thin air. You would have been chasing a ghost. Besides it would have been useless to give you half a story and I still didn't have all the pieces."

"And now you do?"

"Not all, but let's just say a few more."

His eyes still glittering with suppressed anger Sean turned his attention to Luke. "Look I'm sorry my first question should have been, is she all right?"

Luke shrugged, anguish reflected in his voice, "Yeah as good as you can be when a doctor has just dug a bullet out of your arm and you have a bunch of stitches in your head."

Sean eyes narrowed as he waited for Luke to go on.

The man standing in front of him was nothing like the kid who spent more time at the O'Brien supper table than he did in his own home. The round face of youth was gone. This man had the long sleek look of a predator. He was wiry and tough in addition to being a brilliant lawyer, and as far as Sean could tell, he had only one weakness, and that was Colleen. He had fallen in love with Sean's sister when they were just kids; but so far he hadn't made a move.

Luke's voice interrupted his thoughts, "I better start at the beginning, do you remember my cousin Whisper?" He paused. "Maybe not, you were already a rookie on the force while she was still in college school."

"Sure, I remember she had that silly nickname but as I recall her real name," he mused" is Anna or Annette or something..."

"Alison"

"Cute kid, she was always following you around," he grinned "Seems I remember a couple of times she interrupted you when you were making a move."

"Yeah, well those days are over, and when I make my moves now – you can bet she's nowhere in sight."

Sean smiled. He picked up a pen and pulled a pad toward him. "All right, now that we've established that I still remember her, let's get on with it."

Luke paused, "Whisper came to live with us when she was about five --right after her mother died."

As Luke spoke Sean recalled hearing something about a tragedy in the Noonan family, but it had happened years ago and the details eluded him.

Luke continued, "Even though she's closer in age to my brother Rusty, there has always been a special bond between us. It began the night she moved in. I was the only one who heard her crying so I went into her room and picked her up and climbed into a chair with her. I was only a kid myself but somehow, I knew she needed someone to hold her. She cuddled up in my arms and went to sleep. I spent the whole night sitting holding her, and I did the same thing every night for a week."

"That was all it took, I never thought of her as my cousin again, she's become my sister in all but name, and since that time I've watched out for her."

He stopped, and looked down at his clenched fist. "Only yesterday I wasn't there when some bastard tried to kill her."

"Not your fault." Sean leaned forward his voice reassuring. "You can't look into the future any more than I can. Besides it might have been random, or the hit might have been intended for someone else, anyway there was no way you could have stopped it."

"No," Eric interrupted abruptly, pushing himself to his feet. "That bullet was meant for her. First of all, that shot was too personal."

As one the men turned and stared at him, "After I left the hospital yesterday I went back to the station, at first it was just a hunch, some gut feeling I couldn't shake, so I ran her name, funny the things that have happened to her lately."

Reaching into his pocket he pulled out a small notebook. "About a week ago a runaway cab nearly hit her, then a few days later the elevator she was on plunged five floors before a safety stopped it, and yesterday she was shot." He lifted his head and looked around at the men staring at him in stunned silence.

"Shit, either she's the unluckiest person in the world, or you're right she was the target."

Shaking his head Sean leaned forward and concentrated on Eric's words. "Start with the cab and then the elevator."

"I found the officer's report on the cab incident in the computer, so following a hunch I paid a little visit this morning to the security guard in her office building. She's one of his favorites, so he keeps an eye on her. Usually when she leaves the building, she's carrying something, so he watches to make sure she gets across the street to the parking garage safely. Three days ago, she left the building and was halfway across the street when it happened."

A muscle in his cheek twitched as he continued, "Said it was the spookiest thing he ever saw, the cab had nobody in it when it left the curb. She was in the middle of the street, her arms full of rug samples, and if it hadn't been for some woman who screamed and shoved her out of the way, they both might have been killed. She was scraped and bruised from the fall, as was the other woman. Both refused medical treatment. Needless to say, the cab was stolen. It was towed from the scene and the guys from my station had it impounded."

His eyes swept over the men in the room, "But listen to this, the cab was started and steered by remote control, the guys in the crime lab went nuts, they had never seen such an elaborate setup. Whoever wired it was a genius."

Then on Wednesday she has an appointment with a client on the tenth floor of one of the downtown office buildings. She takes the elevator up to where she's supposed to meet the client only no client, no office...just a storage area. She climbs back onto the elevator, and it begins a free fall. This time she's alone. The super tells me it's an old building and the safety on the elevator was scheduled to be repaired. However, on this day it decides to work. On the fifth floor it engages. Again, cuts and bruises, from the fall, only she doesn't report it to the police, the super does. Seems he's been trying to get the landlord to correct the problem for months and her falling scared the devil out of him. The reason that he called the station was the sign on the elevator door that said it was unsafe was stolen. When she got on it she didn't know it had been taken out of service. Luckily, he took her name for insurance purposes, and when the report was typed up all the info was in it."

As he listened Luke's eyes glittered with anger. "She never told me anything, the shooting was the only thing I knew about. If what Eric said is true then she definitely is the target, and yesterday if she hadn't been carrying those tiles." He shuddered.

Sean swiveled his chair around and stared out into the bright afternoon sunshine, a glorious day, and yet he knew somewhere on the streets of Boston someone was being mugged, shot or stabbed—only he was sure of one thing, the next victim would not be Whisper.

"All right," he swung around and faced the men, "It's obvious you guys have a plan or you wouldn't be here. It's a little late to try and find this guy. . ."

"We don't want you to find him, we're hiring you to protect her." Jay interrupted.

"You're hiring me to protect her?" Sean's eyes snapped with anger- "why the hell do you think you have to hire me?"

"Because," Jay glanced over at the two men flanking him – "you'll be protecting her in London."

"What?" London? Are you crazy? I'll have a couple of my best guys follow her."

"No, it has to be you." Luke's interrupted, his voice adamant. Reaching into his briefcase he removed a folder and handed it to Sean. "Look at these photos, two are of Whisper, and one is her mother."

Sean reached for the folder as he looked at Luke quizzically. "Mind telling me why you call her Whisper?"

Luke looked pained, "It's my fault, well not all my fault, but when she came to live with us, my brothers and I thought she was just shy that was the reason her voice was so muted. So of course we took to calling her Whisper to tease her --and it stuck. But my parents were suspicious that shyness wasn't the cause of her muted voice and so they took her to a bunch of doctors, and they all said the same thing, somehow she had suffered some type of trauma to her vocal chords."

Opening the folder Sean grinned.

Here was the teenager Sean remembered. She stood in the center of a group of high school boys, with a football under one arm and a devilish grin on her face. Sean could make out Luke, and two of his own brothers in the background, and although they looked pretty beat up, the girl seemed to have escaped any major mauling.

When Sean picked up the next picture, he caught his breath.

Luke watching Sean's reaction smiled. "She turned out to be a knockout, didn't she? That one was taken for a magazine layout last year. She's a very sought-after interior designer."

Glancing around the office, he grinned, "You probably could use her in here."

When Sean's head shot up, Luke quickly interjected, "Not that there's anything wrong with your office, and the last picture is of her mother."

Sean didn't answer just continued to stare at the photographs that he held in his hands.

The mother had the classic high cheekbones of a model, while the daughter's face was slightly more rounded. Yet it was the daughter he found himself staring at.

He couldn't believe his eyes, what the hell had happened to the skinny little teenager he remembered? This beauty's blond hair tumbled around her face and onto her shoulders and the photographer obviously knew what he was doing, since her head was tilted to so that anyone seeing the picture would feel the full effect of her smile. Dark lashes framed eyes that he was positive were looking directly at him.

He had seen those amazing emerald eyes before, only then they had been sparkling with tears. It was the day before he was to report for duty with the Marines. On an impulse he had swung by the high school to say goodbye to some of the guys on his old football team, but the team bus was just leaving, and he had only been able to give them a quick salute as they pulled out. As he rounded the corner of the building, he had practically stumbled over a young girl sitting on the sidewalk rubbing her ankle. He had dropped to one knee and the eyes that turned up toward him were sparkling with tears. She obviously was on the cheerleading squad since she was wearing a short red skirt and a white sweater with the school logo emblazoned on it.

Bending down he took her ankle in his hands to check it. She had winced as he gently touched it.

"Is it broken?" her soft voice asked pleadingly.

"I don't think so, but it looks like you've got yourself one heck of a bruise."

"Well" she sighed "I guess that's the end of cheerleading for a while."

"I think so."

Bending down he scooped her up into his arms, "Where do you live? You're going to need a ride home."

"Do you know Luke Noonan? I live with him and my aunt and uncle."

"Do I know Luke Noonan?" He grinned at her "He practically lives at our house."

"You're Sean, Sean O'Brien, I know all about you."

He laughed. "Whatever you heard, I'm guilty as charged."

"And you're going in the service tomorrow, your brothers are always bragging about you."

"Not the service cupcake, The Marines Corps, and don't believe half the stuff they tell you."

"Oh, I won't --- maybe." She said laughing at the look on his face.

He had taken her home that day and carried her up the steps to the front door. Her aunt had answered his knock, and he had set her down carefully on the couch. He had offered to take her to the doctor, but her aunt had insisted she could take it from there, and he had left her clucking over her niece.

He never mentioned it to anyone because he left at dawn the next day.

And now they had come full circle.

Sean's palms became damp and he struggled to keep his reaction to Whisper's picture to himself. Somehow he knew, this is the one damn it, she was the one he had been waiting for.

He was no stranger to attractive women, but there had always been something missing.

Carefully keeping his voice neutral he laid the photos down on his desk, "Yeah, they're both beautiful."

Not by a look, or any inflection of voice, would he let on what was going through his head. He knew his brothers; they had ingrained radar that would immediately pick up on any of his vibes. .. and he wasn't ready to share.

Scowling he turned to Luke. "All right let's go over everything again, it's obvious from what Eric says that all of these attempts on her started within the last week."

Luke shook his head, "I can't be sure but it might have started about the same time she got the phone call from her father. She's flying to London because her father has some major health issues and he wants her to come home."

"And," Sean said, "It's my guess that somebody doesn't want her to come home—so they obviously intend to keep her here---permanently."

Sitting back Sean looked at the three men, "Start at the beginning, I want to know everything. When she came to live with your family, what's her family like, who might have a grudge against her, then we'll go over all the incidents leading up to yesterday's shooting. Before you leave here, I want to know everything there is to know about," he paused, "Whisper."

Within minutes Luke had reviewed everything, while Eric filled in all the details that he had gathered.

When the two men finished there was dead silence in the room as each man digested what had been said, and how different the outcome might have been.

Reaching into his pocket Eric extracted a few more papers and threw them onto Sean's desk. "It's all here, the police report, pictures of the scene, statements, everything."

He frowned, "There's only one thing that puzzled me, Dave, who was the first officer to arrive on the scene, says that the guy who stopped to help Whisper disappeared before he could get his statement."

Eric frowned as he looked at his brother.

"Usually people who help out in an emergency will hang around to see what happens, or to give a statement, but this guy simply vanished into thin air."

Sean eyes narrowed; he didn't like the sound of that. "Does anybody know who the guy is? Or get a description of him."

"Nah, he was just some guy walking along with everybody else and nobody had seen him before."

Throwing down his pen, Sean turned to Luke, "O.K. – just so I am clear on this- you want me to protect Whisper by being her bodyguard."

"No." For the first time there was lightness in Luke's voice.

"No?" His tone became suspicious. "Then just what the hell do you want?"

Luke started to speak then glanced at Jay. "It's kind of a touchy situation, you remember Whisper as a kid – well things have changed. She is now a successful businesswoman. Independent, stubborn, sassy—so your job won't be easy. She's not going to want anybody to take care of her."

At the frown on Sean's face he hastily continued, "You're going to have to meet her accidentally, because if she suspects what we're up to – she'll skin each of us alive."

He took a few steps back before he continued, "We talked it over before we got here, and we've decided the only chance this has of working is if you just happen to run into her. Then you make sure she's interested in you," he grinned, "But we all agreed since we're hiring you for this job –we're not paying you to sleep with her."

"What?" Sean's voice was incredulous.

Luke tried not to laugh, and glanced over at Jay whose face was flushed from trying to contain his chuckle, while Eric was suddenly intently interested in a mark on his shoe.

"Look, you don't know her like we do; she's stubborn and she'd never stand for a bodyguard, and since you'd have to have a reason to be with her, so we talked it over, and decided you will have to pretend an interest in her. No one will know," Luke paused, "Since you'll be in London."

"First of all, you're not hiring me, and second are you guys out of your mind? If you think any woman would fall for a hare-brained scheme like that – especially one as smart as you say she is –."

Luke grinned, "Well, as lawyers, Jay and I toyed with the idea of asking you to 'court her' but then Jay thought that might be pushing it."

"You're both asses."

Eric stifled his laughter as he looked at his brother, "Look it's worth a shot – Luke's right she'd never go along with the bodyguard thing – so our only hope is that with your Irish charm and good looks."

He ducked as Sean threw a paperweight at him "She might not be able to resist you."

"Go to hell," Sean snapped glaring at Eric. "And if I did agree to this crazy scheme, how do you geniuses propose that I meet her, it's been years since I've seen her, and suddenly out of the blue I just appear in her life?"

"We already figured that out," Jay said, "You've got a satellite office in London. So, you've got the perfect excuse for traveling over there, and all we have to do is see that she sits next to you on the plane. By the time the flight is over with your charming personality we're sure you'll be able to arrange to see her again."

At the sound of Eric's chuckle, Sean swung around, and Eric quickly turned his laughter into a cough that didn't fool anyone.

"Alright," Sean sighed, "I still think it's an asinine idea but I'm willing to give it a try. What about your family Luke, do they have any idea what's going on?"

"My parents know that we want someone to look after her while she's in London, but my brother Chris's wife is due to have her baby any time, and Rusty is on assignment with the military, so they have a lot on their plate right now."

Sean rubbed his hands across his eyes, and swiveled his chair around and stared out of the window.

Damn it, he already had his plane and hotel reservations and he was planning on leaving tomorrow, he deserved this vacation, he had struggled to make this agency successful, giving up nights and weekends, carefully choosing cases that had some substance. Yet from the moment he had seen Whisper's picture he had known he was going to throw it all away and do whatever it took to keep her safe.

Turning back to the men, his gaze piercing, he shifted into professional mode.

"I said I'd do it, and I will, but you guys will have to take care of the details. Luke, you find out what time she's leaving, and what airline she'll be on, and as soon as you get that info, Jay you've got buddies over at the airline call them and see if they can help you set up this trip because at this late date it is going to be impossible for me to get reservations on the same plane."

Leaning over he hit the intercom, "Em, can you come in for a moment?"

Diminutive and with curly gray hair and a peaches and cream complexion, the woman who entered looked like a tiny doll, but none of the men in the room were deceived. Emma was no one to mess with.

She stalked through the door with a scowl on her face and her eyes narrowed as she surveyed them all.

"This," she said, "had better be good."

Hearing no response, she fastened a piercing gaze on Eric "You talked him out of taking his vacation, didn't you? Do you have any idea what this does to me? May I remind all of you" she paused, "Today is Saturday, and in case you haven't noticed I'm working—working, because he was leaving on vacation tomorrow and now..."

Sean interrupted her tirade by laughing. "You're still going to get that rest, it's just a change of plans.... I'm going to London."

"London? What happened to all that talk about sun, sand, sky and no phones?"

Trying not to grin Sean anticipated her reaction to his next words. "I guess that will just have to wait, but in the meantime, I need you to call Archie and tell him I am going to need some help while I'm there."

A look of horror crossed Em's face and her voice took on a screeching tone, "You want me to call your Grandfather and tell him you want his help you while you're in London? Are you out of your mind? That crazy old man will get you arrested or worse."

The disbelief in her tone had all the men in the room grinning.

Archie McGinty was well known in the family for his eccentric ways, but all the O'Brien kids loved him and after her mother died, their mom Nellie was constantly after her dad to move to the states to be near her. So far it hadn't worked.

"I think he'll be able to help – he knows the area well and he's dying for something to do –this will be the perfect job for him."

"You're crazy." Em sniffed, "But just remember this office will be closed while you're gone and when you need bail money, do not call me!"

Tossing her head, and glaring at the men in the room, she turned and stalked out leaving the four men trying to contain their laughter.

"Archie?" Eric raised an eyebrow, "She's right you know...he will get you into trouble, remember when you were sixteen and went to England for a visit, as I recall he took you to a pub and Grandma had to go get both of you out of. . ."

"Shut up." Sean growled "And get the hell out of here so I can get some of work done." He settled back in his chair and then looked over at Eric with a grin.

"I have a lot of loose ends I have to clean up so --- you're taking my place at dinner tonight."

"Why do I have a feeling I'm not going to like this?"

"You're going to love it, a home cooked meal and Nellie promised me pot roast, mashed potatoes, pie."

"Why aren't you going if this whole thing is so great?" Eric's eyes narrowed suspiciously.

"Well," Sean couldn't contain his chuckle. "She's invited a special guest named Maureen for me to meet. But since I'm going to be tied up – you're taking my place, and you get to meet this wonderful girl named Maureen."

Eric groaned and put his head in his hands. "Damn, I've seen a picture of this wonderful girl Nellie wants you to meet, and she has picket fence and kids written all over her."

Muttering he stood and headed for the door.

Jay rose, but as Luke reached for the folder on his desk, Sean's hand shot out and grasped Luke's wrist. "Leave it, I may need to study these pictures some more." At Luke's quizzical look, Sean let go of his wrist and sat back, offering no further explanations.

"O.K. I'll be in touch with you as soon as I know Whisper has finalized all her plans."

Sean stood and reaching out shook Luke's hand, "Good, and don't worry about her, I'll do everything in my power to keep her safe."

"I know you will," Luke's eyes met Sean's, and what he saw there reassured him. Turning he followed Eric and Jay out of the office feeling better than he had in days.

CHAPTER SIX

S ean had called in some favors.

Now he and the pilot stood silently and watched as a handler and his bomb sniffing dog walked slowly and carefully through the plane. He'd been concerned that the pilot might balk when he discovered Sean had the security clearance to carry his gun on board. But the guy had flown combat missions in Iraq and Afghanistan and wasn't the least bit intimidated by having a detective with a loaded gun as a passenger.

Earlier an FBI ace mechanic had checked out the engines, and once the dog was through, he would be satisfied that everything had been covered.

Sean had an uneasy feeling that frustration was building in the killer because of his three failed attempts on Whisper's life. And although the odds were slim that he knew exactly when she was leaving the country, he was taking no chances.

Especially after what he had witnessed this morning.

He'd stopped by the crime lab to see the cab that had almost hit Whisper and he'd come away shaking his head. The guy who wired it was a freaking genius. He could have been anywhere when that cab left the curb, all he had to do was hit a remote and it followed a preprogrammed path.

And the bullet that hit Whisper had been fired from close range and yet nobody had seen anything.

Who the hell was this guy? Where was he, and why the hell did he want Whisper dead?

The more he learned about this guy the more he realized that they were not only dealing with a freaking genius, but also a diabolical killer.

Dropping into his seat, Sean reached into his briefcase and pulled out the papers that had been faxed by his London staff.

When he had been approached, and encouraged, to open an overseas branch he had been reluctant, since the Boston office was booming and he had more cases than he could handle.

But after a late-night visit from a high-ranking government official he had seen the benefit of expanding his operation.

Luckily, he had hired a competent manager for his London office, and the only major disagreement had occurred when she insisted on adding what she referred to as two computer whizzes to the staff.

That battle had been an epic one. He threatened to fire her, and she in turn threatened to quit; but for all his bluster nothing had deterred her, and in the end, she had just smiled and sent him two payroll slips to sign.

Now grudgingly he had to admit that when he called his overseas office looking for answers within a half an hour his fax machine would start humming.

How the hell they did it he didn't know, nor did he care, all he knew was when he asked about the gaps in the life of Alison Alexander, they had filled them in.

He scanned the information again wanting to be sure he had missed nothing.

Alison Alexander, the only child of Sir Stephen Alexander and his wife Alise. They met at a cocktail party, an Englishman with titles that went back centuries, and a famous American model and actress. They fell in love, he pursued her across Europe, and then back to the states. She refused his proposal numerous times because of her concerns about their diverse backgrounds.

She and her twin sister had been raised dirt poor on a farm in South Carolina, and Stephen had been born into money. A lot of money.

After months of ardent pursuing he had finally persuaded her to marry him. He brought her back to London and they had been deliriously happy, and their joy at Alison's birth had been noted in the newspapers.

But their happiness had been short lived. Two days after Alison's fifth birthday Alise had tumbled down a staircase and died. Her loss had dealt Stephen a severe blow, and then to have his only child begin to experience nightmares and refuse to communicate, had devastated Stephen.

In desperation he had taken his child away from the scene of her mother's death, and brought her to his wife's twin sister Annette and her husband Steve in Boston.

He visited her as often as he could, trying to juggle the wellbeing of his daughter, and the responsibilities he faced at home.

There were several mentions of the damage to her vocal cords but no explanation as to the cause.

But any talk of her returning with him would result in the nightmares returning. Gradually he became resigned to the fact that she now considered Boston her home.

Sean flipped the rest of the pages of the report, scanning it for any telltale item he might have missed. His own digging into the Alexander family had unearthed the fact that Stephen Alexander was a still a very wealthy man, a titled landowner with diversified investments in the U.S. and the United Kingdom.

As the son and heir of a very old and very prominent family he had inherited several titles that had been handed down from some of England's most famous nobility. He never remarried after the loss of his wife although occasionally he was seen squiring some beauty around town, but it never amounted to anything.

His only sibling was his sister Charlotte, and she was an heiress in her own right. She never married, and had adopted her son Edward when he was just a baby. Edward had inherited a sizeable sum from his grandparents upon their deaths, and as her only child he would inherit a fortune from Charlotte.

Sean flipped the page and stared at the photographs of the two of them. Charlotte was still beautiful but seemed to have an air of sadness about her.

Sean stopped and shook his head, now where the hell had that come from?

There was nothing in the article to reinforce that thought --- but still he paused for a moment before he went back to scanning the article. He stared at the picture, she was standing in front of a stable, patting the neck of a thoroughbred while her son looked on. She had just won best in class and the article raved that in addition to her charity work she raised horses as a hobby, and also dabbled in painting.

Her son stood a little behind her and didn't look too happy to be having his picture taken. The article mentioned that Edward worked for the prestigious St. James architectural firm and there were rumors that he was being considered for a partnership.

He flipped a few more pages and silently whistled to himself — the mansion where the two of them lived was on the grounds of Stephen's estate, and was magnificent.

It was obvious that they wouldn't need to harm Whisper for money — and from all he read there was no hint of scandal attached to either of them. So there was no reason why either of them would want Whisper dead.

Sean winched as he moved his shoulder, although it didn't look like either of them had a motive, he had learned the hard way that not everything was as it seemed. And he wasn't ready quite yet to eliminate her relatives as potential murders.

Folding the papers up, he stuck them back in the briefcase.

If his watch was right passengers should be boarding in just a few minutes so he reached into the bag his sister Colleen had left for him in his car. The two of them shared the same love of mysteries, and whenever he was leaving on a trip, she would provide him with the latest magazines and novels.

He glanced down at the magazine in his hand not really seeing it, more intent on watching the passengers as they began boarding.

To the casual observer his interest might seem cursory, and few would recognize the intense alertness, or the dark eyes that constantly scanned the interior of the aircraft. His size and soft-spoken manner had led a few lawbreakers to think he was just a sleepy big bear of a man, only to discover they had made a disastrous mistake. They rarely made that mistake again.

Now those dark eyes were anchored on the passengers as they appeared in the hatchway.

Getting the airline to rearrange the seating so he could be seated next to Whisper had taken some arm twisting, but somehow Jay had pulled it off.

Sean shifted his weight trying to find a comfortable position. Fitting a six-foot five frame into an economy class seat was never easy, and flying to London would certainly put both his physical well-being as well as his patience to the test. Not that his patience was ever very good, but at least since he had opened his agency, he had learned to temper it a little.

Finally, he spotted her. She was a lot smaller than he expected. Even though she was five foot six according to her driver's license, somehow in person she looked fragile and petite, or maybe he mused, she might just seem that way because of his own size.

Not bad, he thought as he watched her move toward him. Mentally he reviewed everything he knew about her. Twenty-seven years old, a graduate of a prestigious school of design; raised by her mother's twin sister and her husband, three cousins, all men who doted on her, and from everything he'd learned she was a level headed and exceptionally caring person.

It didn't hurt that she was a knockout with hair the color of soft ash and emerald eyes surrounded by thick dark lashes that could flash with warmth or temper. From what he'd learned about her, she wasn't afraid to stand her ground and if pushed, she pushed back.

All in all he'd already decided she was the perfect woman for him.

Yet some of the things he'd learned about her still puzzled him. On her days off, she volunteered at a women's shelter and other days she worked long hours at a soup kitchen. Something didn't add up, if she was so damn perfect why the hell was some son of a bitch trying to kill her?

And why was there no man in her life? She dated, but before anything developed, or things looked like they were getting serious -- she backed off. Yet these splits always seemed amicable. That ruled out a jealous or disgruntled boyfriend. In one or two instances she had even fixed her dates up with friends, resulting in her being a bridesmaid at more than one wedding. The more he learned about her the more baffled he became.

The day after the meeting in his office he had gone to Luke's office and they had contacted Whisper's father. Sean had learned a lot from that conversation. It was obvious that Stephen was really frightened for his daughter's safety, and when he learned of her other 'so called accidents' Sean could hear the tremor in his voice. They spent an hour discussing various scenarios, but couldn't come up with a single reason that anyone would want her dead.

As soon as he got back to the office Sean had immediately set a few safeguards in place. He knew he couldn't just move in with Whisper while they were in England, so he had done the next best thing, and without Stephen knowing, he had quietly arranged to put two of his best operatives in the Alexander home.

The fact that Stephen's chauffeur had just retired was perfect, and the man he had in mind for the job fit right in. With a little persuasion from his brother Mike, who had interned in London under Stephen's surgeon, a nurse had been assigned to care for Stephen around the clock and Sean just happened to have a woman in mind that fit that bill also.

As each passenger reached their assigned seat Sean carefully scanned them. He had specifically requested seats toward the back of the plane so that he would see anyone coming toward them.

As Whisper moved closer to him, he was stunned, the picture Luke had shown him didn't do her justice. Her sun streaked blonde hair was pulled back away from her face, revealing high cheekbones and a flawless complexion. She wore the least little bit of color on her cheeks and lips, and his gut tightened as he realized the daughter was becoming a carbon copy of the beautiful woman whose picture he had seen.

He frowned as he saw that the only thing marring her perfection were a few small blue bruises marking the spots high on her forehead where she had been hit by the exploding tiles, and a row of tiny stitches at her hairline.

He watched as she stopped to let passengers stow their bags, and never looked the least bit impatient. The genuine warmth of her smile amazed him as she thanked other passengers who moved aside to let her pass. He winced when one of the passengers accidentally bumped her arm, and he saw the fleeting look of pain that crossed her face.

This lady was full of surprises, flying economy class, when he knew for sure daddy could have hired a pilot and plane to get her to England.

Pretending to be engrossed in his magazine he kept his head down until she was directly next to him.

"Excuse me, but I think I have the seat next to you."

He had forgotten what her voice sounded like and he was unprepared for the caress of it, and by his instant reaction. Sean looked up into amazing emerald eyes, and smiled.

"You have the window seat?" At her nod, he unwounded himself and moved into the aisle to let her pass.

Whisper's eyes widened and she stared up at Sean. "Sean... Sean O'Brien? What," she hissed, "are you doing here?"

"Pardon me?" Sean kept his voice low and suddenly wished he had spent some time taking acting lessons.

"You're Sean O'Brien!"

Putting his hands into the air, Sean grinned "Guilty as charged but---"

"Never mind but...what are you doing on this plane and did Luke put you up to this?"

"Lady," Sean started, he wanted to laugh but he knew that would be like throwing a match into a powder keg.

The way her expressive eyes were snapping she didn't look like she was in any mood to be toyed with.

Whisper struggled to control her temper. "If Luke put you up to this..."

"Luke didn't put me up to anything, I'm on my way to London to a business meeting, but if you'd like me to move..." keeping his voice low and hoping that his calm demeanor would defuse the situation he tried another tack, "Look I don't know what's going on in your head, but I wouldn't be sitting next to you if the airline hadn't messed up my plane ticket. I didn't know they had assigned two people to the same seat until I boarded."

He held his breath hoping she would buy it.

Although her eyes narrowed, when she didn't attack immediately, he continued. "If you'll feel more comfortable, I'll see if the stewardess can find me another seat."

She thought for a moment and then looked up at him and sighed. "Sorry," she mumbled "You must think I'm crazy... but Luke-"

Glancing at the passengers standing behind her who were watching with grins on their faces, he gently took her arm being careful not to jar it.

"What do you say that we start over after we're seated?"

He moved into the aisle and Whisper found herself up staring at him. She had forgotten how big he was.

She remembered the day she had fallen as she ran to catch the team bus, and he had found her crying. He had picked her up in his arms and carried her to his car, and then driven her home. She had been broken hearted about having to miss the game, but by the time they reached her home he had had her laughing. She could still feel the strength of the arms, and the musky fragrance of the aftershave he used as he leaned over to pick her up and carry her into the house.

She'd woven a few teenage daydreams about that day but before she could run into him again, he had left for Marine boot camp.

Of course, over the years she'd asked about him several times, and had heard snatches of conversation about him, and she had worried along with his family when she heard he had been stabbed.

Strangely enough she had a picture of him at home. Of course, he had been a lot younger, probably seventeen or eighteen. He was part of a state championship football team and it was his senior year in school. Luke, although only a freshman, was the quarterback, and he had pointed out all the O'Brien brothers in the picture to her. She remembered thinking if she had seen that line of O'Brien's running toward her, she would have turned and run the other way. In fact, some of the teams they played did.

She settled into her seat and turned to look at him but he had his back to her as he stepped across the aisle to help stow a bag for an elderly passenger.

His shoulders were encased in a jacket that was tailored to fit; tapering down to a torso that looked like it didn't have an ounce of fat on it.

He had towered over her as they stood in the aisle but even as angry as she was, she had noticed that he had dark brown eyes framed by the most incredible black eyelashes she had ever seen. His ebony hair had just a hint of silver at the temples, and he wasn't handsome in the conventional sense, his nose a little crooked, with a mean looking scar above his lip, and although she was sure he was trying to contain his grin as she argued with him, she knew by the set of his chin, he had a stubborn streak to match those features.

Dropping into the seat next to her, Sean caught a whiff of the delicate floral scent she was wearing and instinctively he leaned closer.

Good Lord, he silently warned himself, stop behaving like a horny teenager. He'd better keep his mind on what he was doing and get a hold of himself. Damn this whole thing was a stupid idea and he should never have listened to those idiots. He should have just told her he was going with her, and that was that.

"Sean?" When he turned to look at her he saw a tentative smile on her face. .'I'm sorry for jumping to conclusions but Luke has been driving me crazy about making this trip and it just seemed like too much of a coincidence that an O'Brien would be sitting next to me on the plane."

"Well I admit it probably does look funny," inwardly he cringed, good god he was babbling "but there was some mix-up at the airline so I had to take the first available seat and it was either take this flight or wait for one tomorrow."

Mentally he crossed his fingers and vowed that he would make his peace later with the good Lord for lying.

"Me too. They had to switch my seat at the last minute."

"Probably some computer glitch, hate the damn things myself."

"You do? In my business I have to use them constantly."

Before she could say anything more the stewardess appeared and began to go through the flight instructions.

Mentally Sean gave a sigh of relief. He wasn't sure how much longer he could have held out with those dazzling eyes questioning him.

As Whisper listened to the instructions her mind wandered and she wished that she could shake the feeling that somehow Luke's fine hand was involved in arranging for an O'Brien to sit next to her on the plane. He had been driving her crazy fretting over this trip ever since she had told him she was returning home. He'd been calling her at work and at home, and generally getting on her nerves, right up till the time she boarded the plane. She knew he'd been upset when she told him that he couldn't make this trip, but she had no idea how long her father's recuperation would take and she had no intention of leaving him until he was on his feet again.

And now this was just too much, Sean O'Brien sitting next to her on the same plane, and the same flight heading for the same destination.

If somehow Luke and Sean had pulled this off it was a pretty neat trick, but sooner to later one of them would slip, and if she found out . . . as though Sean knew what she was thinking his eyes swept around and met hers.

Her eyes challenged his, and he knew that this woman would be a worthy opponent. She wasn't intimidated by him, not by his size, his demeanor or anything else. As they stared at each other he swore he could feel his blood begin to bubble in his veins.

He needed to find out who was trying to kill her, and do it quickly, so he could throw himself into the most important battle of his life, winning her.

But this was no time to lose track of what he was here for. There were too many questions about the attempts on her life and he didn't like questions; he liked answers.

He needed to know more. No other woman had ever affected him so quickly, there was something about her he tried to shake off the images that kept sneaking into his mind. He didn't usually fantasize about women preferring to just let things happen and sometimes he had been pleasantly surprised and sometimes he'd been disappointed. Yet pictures of her kept slipping unbidden into his head, that glorious hair spread out on a pillow; soft candlelight, smooth skin under his hand . . . His palms began to sweat, one more minute and his telltale body was going to embarrass him.

Mentally he shook himself, he'd better get it together, her life was at stake and he couldn't afford to be distracted. He'd better put his fantasies on hold, someone wanted her dead and he damn well better concentrate on keeping her alive.

CHAPTER SEVEN

It was cold, with a bone chilling dampness that silently seeps into a person. . . and dark.

She felt something scurry past her, and she tucked her small feet closer to her body. She had to be quiet, very quiet, so no one would know she was there.

Whisper raised her hand to brush away the cobwebs that surrounded her, frantically clawing at them – unaware that her whimpers and frenzied movements were alarming Sean.

He had watched as her eyes fluttered closed, and he knew she needed to rest. Luke had told him that she had finally confessed to him that her nightmares had returned, and that she was unable to sleep at night. So it was not unexpected that the warmth and the drone of the plane's engines might soothe her, and she might be able to rest.

Now he watched as her hands moved toward her face and she began brushing at her cheeks... the pulse in her throat beating erratically with her head thrashing from side to side.

Her eyes suddenly flew open, terror mirrored in them, and he knew whatever she was seeing was real to her. Her breath became shallow and as she opened her mouth to scream, he leaned over and kissed her.

Her lips were soft and warm, and it was all he could do not to scoop her up out of her seat and hold her close to him. But instead his kiss was soft, a gentle kiss, one to comfort and to calm, a kiss to soothe.

"Whisper, wake up," he murmured the words against her warm lips, his voice soft and reassuring. "You're having a nightmare."

Slowly she opened her eyes and stared into dark eyes filled with concern.

"Take a deep breath."

For a moment she didn't know where she was and her eyes darted frantically around the interior of the plane.

Fighting to stifle a sob, she leaned her head against the cool window beside her and tried to ease her breathing. A large hand reached out and unclasped her fingers from the armrest, and gently began to massage them until some of their color and warmth returned. Gently laying that hand in her lap he reached across her body for the other one. His large arm lay across her breasts and the heat from his body chased away the chill.

"I'm so sorry," she whispered, tears glistening in her eyes.

"For what? For giving me an opportunity to kiss a beautiful woman in a plane high above an ocean? Baby," he grinned at her "That's what dreams are made of."

"Not my dreams I'm afraid."

"Want to talk about it?"

"No. I can handle it. I'm just a little tired and stressed right now." She glanced over at him. "I didn't mean to alarm you." she said, "It's just a silly dream."

"Not very silly if it frightens you."

"Yes, well" She hesitated and then looked up into his eyes, "But you kissed me, why did you kiss me?"

Sean leaned his head close to hers, "Well I had a choice, I could either let you scream, and scare half the people on this plane to death, or I could kiss you, and baby believe me, I made the right choice. But if you had screamed, I still could have handled it.

He grinned, "I've handled screaming women before, once I was kissing this girl and these two kids. . ."

"You mean the night Luke and Jay caught you kissing Mary Margaret O'Toole out in your backyard and dropped the snake out of a tree on her?"

Whisper wiped the tears from her eyes and a slight grin appeared on her still pale face.

"How the hell?" Sean's head whipped around and he stared at her. "I mean how would you know about that?"

The look of astonishment on his face made Whisper softly laugh.

"Oh, it's an old story, and every time I'm with Luke and Jay they brag about that night."

"Yeah, well if I could have gotten my hands on the little bast. . .I mean the two of them..." He started to laugh, and she knew he got as big a kick out of the story as Luke and Jay did.

Whisper reached over and took Sean's hand, "Before we go any further – you pretending that you just happen to be on the same plane as I am," she watched to see his reaction, but Sean had been a cop too long to let on what was going through his head.

"I still think Luke persuaded you to watch out for me, since he's got a crazy notion that I need taking care of, and the way you reacted just now leads me to believe you weren't surprised that I have nightmares, as a matter of fact, I believe you expected it."

"I'll be damned" Sean muttered "and I thought I was the detective."

His smile was soft as he looked at her. He could almost see what was going on in her head, and he was sure in her place he'd want the same answers.

"You're right and you're wrong. Okay Luke did suggest that I keep an eye on you, but my being on this plane and in the seat next to you was my choice, - not his, if I didn't want to do it..." he watched as temper flared in her eyes.

Sitting up a little straighter in the seat she glared at him. She wasn't intimidated, but she decided keeping her cool was probably the best way to deal with him.

Fastening her eyes on the top button of his shirt so she wouldn't be distracted by his beautiful eyes, she said "Look, this isn't fair to you. I'm not sure how far you and Luke," then her voice became accusatory – "Was Jay in on this too?"

When she received no response, the infuriating man just sitting there with a grin on his face her voice became sharp,

"No matter whose involved, Luke had no business asking you to give up more important work to follow me around –and I'm going to be all right, so you can just get on the next plane back to Boston." and her voice became icy, "I'll even pay your return fare."

At first Sean had been amused at her attempt to argue with the button on his shirt, but then he realized that she was dismissing him.

His amusement fled. She had no idea that the thought of leaving her alone in England had never been an option, and now that he had kissed her, the thought of her being in danger made him crazy.

His voice was quiet and all the more frightening because of it, as he leaned toward her and lowered his voice. "Let's you and me get one thing straight, if I wanted to go back to Boston, which I don't, I would pay my own way, and if you think Luke wanted someone with you, you're right, however lady," his soft breath warmed her lips he was so near, "my being here was my own choice, so you might as well sit back, and enjoy the ride."

He saw her face flush with anger and her eyes flash, and he prepared for battle. Rattled by his change in tone and the fierce way he was looking at her Whisper temper had just reached the boiling point and as she opened her mouth to tell him exactly what she thought of his high-handed manner, he surprised her by attacking the one place she was vulnerable. "Why don't you tell me about that dream?"

"No." she stiffened. "I told you it's none of your business..."

"Well" he said, sitting back, "You can tell me or I'll just call Luke and ask him."

His lazy smile belied the way his eyes fastened on hers. "Either way I aim to find out what it's all about."

"You" she retorted, "Are an insufferable overbearing ass!"

Tickled, that no matter how he tried he couldn't bully her, his whole demeanor changed, and as he looked down at her his tone softened. "You're probably right, but that doesn't change anything; now tell me about your dream."

His look told her that nothing she could say would dissuade him. Why he felt it was so important she had no idea, and she had lived with it so long that once it had come and gone, she got over it until the next time.

"All right this is what happens, I'm in a place where it's damp, it seems to be filled with cobwebs and I'm frightened."

What she didn't mention was there was another person in her dreams, a shadowy figure who hovered in the background, or that there were times when her mother also appeared in her dreams. The nightmare would begin and suddenly her mother would be there soothing her. It was almost as if she wanted to tell her something. She was sure that if she told this to the man sitting next to her, he would think she was crazy.

"End of story, besides I'm getting better at handling it."

After seeing how she had just reacted to that dream he didn't think so, but he'd tackle that later.

"Have you had that dream often?"

The minute the words were out of his mouth he silently cursed. She didn't react well to being pushed, and the last thing he wanted to do was to completely alienate her. He had to stop acting like a detective and start acting like a normal person, although in his line of work sometimes he didn't remember what normal really was.

"Listen," her voice might be soft but her tone was frosty.

"I really appreciated your waking me, and the kiss was rather pleasant," a becoming blush stained her cheeks, "but I'm dealing with this myself so," she smiled at him but there was steel in it, "Back off."

Instead of being annoyed, Sean laughed...

The lady had guts. He'd seen her frightened eyes and watched her struggle to conquer her fear and he knew whatever caused that nightmare was very real to her.

Striving for a lighter note that might alleviate some of the sudden tension between them, he asked, "Ever been to Ireland?"

Prepared for battle, the question caught her completely off guard. "What?"

"Have you ever been to Ireland?"

Whisper shook her head.

"Well, if you had, you would know that we Irish believe in all sorts of wonderful things, leprechauns, fairies, angels," he paused, "and of course, pixies."

He picked her hand up off her lap and slowly caressed it causing Whisper's breath to catch in her throat.

"Now pixies are capricious little creatures and sometimes when they are bored, they steal into people's dreams. So next time before you fall asleep tuck this under your pillow." And reaching into his pocket he pulled out a tiny plastic bag and slipped it into her hand.

Whisper closed her fingers around it and looked at him inquiringly.

"Pixie dust," he said.

"Pixie dust?"

"The genuine article, guaranteed to drive away bad dreams." Bending over he whispered, "I got it from a very reliable Irishman, so it's guaranteed to work."

His eyes began to twinkle and he looked like a mischievous little boy. A warmth spread through Whisper and she couldn't help but laugh.

Deliberately Whisper opened her purse and placed the little bag into a separate compartment zipping it closed. "There" she said, "Pixie dust for a good night's sleep."

His winked at her," Guaranteed." he said.

This man obviously was possessed with a good bit of Irish blarney, and yet somehow it made her feel good to hold onto this so-called good luck charm.

Sean settled back in his seat, blessing his grandfather, who insisted that he carry this little bit of Ireland with him for luck.

Closing his eyes, he pretended to fall asleep, while remaining intensely aware of everything going on around him. Whisper's soft conversation with the stewardess, the drone of the engines, and even the conversations around him didn't escape his notice.

He had no idea why someone would want this beautiful woman dead, but somebody did. He was determined to find out who, and why. . .and stop him at all costs.

CHAPTER EIGHT

The plane set down in London, the last hour of the flight having sped by.

Throughout the trip, the tales Sean told about his family had kept Whisper laughing. She discovered he had a warm sense of humor, and a knack for poking fun at himself and his brothers. Yet, his tales about his sister held a different tone. As he told her antidotes about some of the funny situations Colleen got herself into when she first joined the force, Whisper could sense that beneath it all he was deeply worried about her. Something must have happened to his sister that triggered such a strong emotion, but she was hesitant to ask.

One thing was fairly obvious though, Colleen was not the type who would sit back and let the men in her life make decisions for her, no matter how much she loved them.

The closer they got to their destination, the more apprehensive she became. This last week had worn her out.

In addition to being worried about her father she was apprehensive about leaving her business. She knew her staff was capable but her company was not only her livelihood but her baby. She'd watched it grow from the day she opened its doors to the thriving business it was today.

Still it was fairly new, and a lot of her business stemmed from word of mouth and recommendations of clients. There was no way she could compete with the big advertising budgets of her competition, and she was worried that without the owner being available to talk individually with clients that she might lose out.

But she would have to take that chance.

And she had to deal with her fear.

Each night since her father's phone call she had prayed that she would be so worn out that she would be able to sleep, but that hadn't happened. Nights after night her dreams were filled with the same nightmare, and she awakened with her heart pounding and her hands curled into fists. There was little she could remember about the dreams except that she was very cold, and wherever she was, the room was damp and filled with cobwebs. She sensed she wasn't alone but what, or who was with her, she didn't know. She only knew she had to stay hidden so that whatever was there couldn't find her.

She glanced over at Sean and tried to discover why she found him so attractive. He certainly wasn't conventionally handsome, his hands were too big, and his nose a little crooked, but she decided as she looked at him, he was the sexiest man she had ever seen. What there was about him she didn't know, but the chemistry was there, and she sighed inwardly because she knew many other women felt the same way. It was no secret that none of the O'Brien men ever lacked for female companionship and just being near him told her why.

She also realized that after this trip she might never see him again.

It had been years since their paths had crossed. She had moved into her own apartment and her visits to her aunt and uncle weren't as frequent as she would have liked, and starting a new business had eaten up the rest of her time. From what she had learned from Luke, Sean also had been immersed in getting his business up and running and if the rumors were true, he was flat out with assignments.

Funny, she knew a lot about the O'Brien family, but she didn't know a lot about him. He was older, and they hadn't been in school at the same time, or traveled in the same circles. Questions were swirling in her head, and as soon as she got home, she was going to corner Luke and get some answers.

She sighed, no matter how much he denied it, she knew he was on this plane because of Luke, and once he left the plane his obligation to Luke was over. And since their paths had only crossed once before, the chances of their running into one another in Boston were slim. She could only thank Luke for giving her the opportunity to spend a little time with Sean, so she could get to know him, and hope the fates would intervene and she would see him again.

The pilot's voice instructed them to fasten their seatbelts, and she turned toward Sean only to find him staring at her with an intensity that made her uneasy. It was almost as if he was memorizing her features.

Discomfort at first, then she felt a blush creeping up her cheeks as she murmured his name. Even that didn't distract him, and he seemed lost to her. Finally, she touched his hand lightly, quickly withdrawing her hand when his eyes snapped at her.

"Sorry," he muttered, "That's one habit I have that drives my mother crazy. I can tune everything out when I'm concentrating on something." A grin creased his face, making her heart turn over as he continued, "Guess it's just a defense mechanism I acquired from growing up in a big family."

Whisper smiled back at him, "Oh, I have a few quirks myself, just ask Luke how I react when he startles me."

A picture of Luke sitting at the O'Brien dinner table one night, his eye swollen and a blue mark on his cheek flashed into Sean's mind. He had only been paying half attention to the conversation but now he remembered Luke had been taking a lot of ribbing about being hit by a girl.

Sean reached out and took her small hand in his with a strength that made her gasp. As her lips opened with a soft murmur, he bent and captured her lips with his, not caring about anything or anyone else, just intent on tasting her one more time.

For a moment Whisper sat stunned, then the warmth of his body seemed to penetrate even to that tiny place in her heart that was always frightened and cold.

She sighed into his mouth and gave herself up to him.

"I suppose I should apologize to you, but I'm not going to." he whispered as he released her, "I've been waiting for your kisses all my life."

"Oh, really?"

Mischief sparkled in her eyes, "That's not the way I heard it, the way your brothers tell it, you were pretty hot for Mary Margaret, and then there was the nurse at the hospital where your brother Mike works, or that secretary with the big—"

Startled Sean stared at her, "My god woman, how do you know so much about my life? I thought we only met once before."

"We did, but I just remembered a few discussions I overheard that had slipped my mind till now. As a matter of fact, I've even seen the chart in Jay's office with your name and Eric's on it. He and Luke add the names of your girlfriends, as they appear, and as they disappear, they cross them off. I believe they have a bet going as to which of you will get married first."

The look on Sean's face was priceless. "They have what? A freakin' chart? When I get my hands on those two idiots." He paused, suddenly beginning to laugh--

"And," she continued, her eyes narrowing as she pretended to give her next words a lot of thought, "After kissing you, I've decided to take a piece of that action myself," and her eyes twinkling she said, "And I'm putting my money on you."

Sean laughed, and cupping her chin in his hand he leaned close and gazed into her eyes, his eyes hot and possessive. "You do that honey, you do that. If I have my way it will be the easiest money you ever made." And grinning, he sat back.

Whisper's mouth opened in astonishment, but before she could think of an answer, the plane rolled to a stop.

Sean after unhooking his seatbelt moved out into the aisle. Reaching up he retrieved his small carry on and her purse from the overhead compartment.

He didn't step aside quite enough to let her body move comfortably past him into the aisle, and she gasped as he made a small movement that brought them closer together and she could feel the steel hardness of his thighs.

She immediately stopped and looked up at him.

Trying to look sheepish, but not quite succeeding, he stepped aside and waited silently for her to lead, and then proceeded to follow her down the aisle.

Getting through customs didn't take long since all her papers were in order and as she stood in line, she realized that Sean was right behind her. She headed for the baggage terminal, and was startled when she glanced back and saw him following.

He stood silently as they waited for the baggage to come around and as she moved forward to grab her bag off the carousel, he stepped in front of her and had it in his hand before she could react. Deftly picking up his bag and hers, he started walking down the concourse.

"Sean, where are you going?" He didn't answer just kept moving, and being much shorter she had to run to keep up.

"Sean!" Angrily she tried to grab the back of his shirt and yell at him to stop, but she didn't want to make a scene. The jerk, where was he going with her luggage?

A few minutes ago, she was practically swooning at his feet, but right now if she had a bat, she would gladly hit him with it. She knew he wasn't stealing her luggage, and he certainly wasn't some pervert who got a kick out of stealing women's clothing, so what the heck was he doing?

She caught up to him just as he stopped, causing her to run headlong into his back.

Swiftly turning, he dropped the bags and reaching out prevented her from tumbling to the pavement his big hands grasping her waist.

For just a moment he cuddled her close to him and bending down he murmured; "Don't you know I would never hurt you?"

He stepped back, and with a mock scowl asked "and if I was going to steal a woman's clothes don't you think I would look for someone more my size?"

A picture of him in a dress flashed through her mind, and she couldn't help the giggle that escaped her. With his massive shoulders, big hands and feet and that little crook in his nose, he would be one homely woman.

'You have got to be kidding," she said, the whole idea was so ridiculous that she couldn't contain the laughter that escaped her. Without thinking she reached out and gave him a quick hug.

Before she could step back, he pulled her closer and kissed her, but this time it was no gentle kiss, this one was filled with passion and unbridled desire. Her breath caught in her throat as she drank in the heady scent of male. He bent over her, then suddenly she was lifted into the air, his big arms wrapped around her. His mouth angled and he drank from her lips his tongue running gently around the rim. His arms tightened and gently pressed her body against his.

Please don't stop she wanted to say, hold me close and don't let me go. She knew people had stopped and were staring, but for the first time in her life she realized she didn't care.

Heat curled through her body and she lifted her arms and ran his fingers through his hair. She felt his body react and so did hers. She felt an ache she had never experienced before and she wanted this kiss to go on and on. . .and on.

Frightened that this would be the last time she saw him, she tightened her arms around his neck, and tilted her head to take more of his mouth. She would have to trust fate that he felt the same way as she did, and if he didn't, well she would always have the memories of these kisses.

Groaning he set her down "Not now." he growled, "But you can be damn sure that we're going to finish this." his eyes caught hers and held them – "Only I'll choose the time and the place, and it won't be on a damn sidewalk in an airport!"

Hooking his arm around her waist, and as if he had heard the questions swirling in her mind, in a low voice he murmured, "This my love, is only the beginning; I'm going to be in your life for a long time," and his eyes held a promise that answered her questions.

Releasing her, his eyes quickly scanned the street around them. "Look, I've got an appointment, but can I give you a lift somewhere? I've rented a car and it should be here any minute."

"No, thank you," she said her eyes scanning the street, "My father is sending his car, and I imagine its close by." She frowned, "The only problem is he has a new driver and I'm not sure he knows what I look like…"

"Well, he sure won't be looking for you at a taxi stand so let's move on." He bent and picking up her suitcase, waited for her reaction. All he got this time was a soft smile and he began to move down the sidewalk.

They hadn't taken more than a few steps, when a long black limousine pulled up beside them.

The driver that jumped out of the car was a full head shorter than Sean, and much older, with shiny white hair and a ruddy complexion that attested to a life spent out of doors.

He moved swiftly up to Whisper and peered at her.

"Alison? I knew it was you, your father gave me your picture --" Not waiting for a reply, he reached out and took her luggage from Sean's hand.

"Although I didn't need the bloody picture," he grumbled, "Your father must have described you to me a hundred times, and he showed me every picture he has since you were born. Worried I'd miss you? To miss you I'd have to be blind!"

He lifted the boot of the car and picked up her suitcase, and as Sean reached to help him the older man glared and mumbled something that caused Sean to grin.

Slamming the trunk shut, he turned and bowed to Whisper as if she was some visiting royalty, his voice one decibel lower than a roar.

"Name's Archibald McGinty, Esquire, but my friends call me Archie, as do a few of my more impertinent relatives". He glanced over at Sean who simply stood there grinning.

Without stopping to take a breath he continued, "I added the Esquire because it sounds more dignified, don't you think?"

Without waiting for an answer he took her arm as he rambled on, "If you're driving a limousine for a living, and hobnobbing with your betters, . . . not that I think they're any better than me," he sniffed, "they just have more money, which reminds me, I should ask for a raise, him making me drive in this crazy London traffic."

He looked at Whisper expectantly but she was so stunned by this crazy conversation that she couldn't even think of a reply.

Opening the limousine door, he waved his hand at her "Get in, get in girl, your father's been driving us all batty, could use a little rest while he was waiting I told him, but he got a wee bit snippy with me, telling me to mind my own,...well, you know how he is."

He looked to see her reaction, and seeing the stunned look on her face, his face split into a grin as he continued, "He's a tiny bit overbearing at times, but you know that don't you? Good thing he's got that nurse with him or he'd really be something. She keeps him in hand."

Only then did he take a breath as he looked over at a wide-eyed Whisper who didn't know whether to laugh or not. He told her father to take a nap? Her father a bit overbearing?

Suddenly her eyes filled with tears. She could remember her mother laughingly accusing her father of the same thing, and how he would pick her up in his arms and swing her around and the two of them would end up kissing.

The glimpse of sadness that passed over Whisper's face cut Sean to the heart and he sensed she was remembering the past.

Cursing his Irish intuition that seemed to enable him to feel her pain, he had to stop himself from reaching out and holding her in his arms until the hurt passed. Leaning down, he lightly touched her face for comfort and he realized she wasn't only remembering the past, but there was also fear in her eyes. Her skin was cold to his touch and the light had gone out of her eyes.

Carefully he hid his thoughts and his smile was reassuring as he bent to her, "Trust me you're going to be ok." He wanted to take her in his arms and tell her not to be afraid, but instead he reached into his pocket and pulled out a card and scribbling his cell phone number on the back handed it to her.

"I'm only as far away as this phone, call me anytime day or night, and I'll be there." He glanced over, his eyes meeting the limo driver's for a second, and an imperceptible nod told him that everything was going just as planned.

Archie carefully guided Whisper into the limo and after seeing her comfortably settled slid into the driver's seat. Glancing back, he saw that Sean was still standing beside the car.

"Hey Yank," he yelled, startling several of the people standing on the sidewalk near them. "Move that oversized body of yours so me and the wee girl can get moving."

At Whisper's gasp, Sean threw back his head and laughed.

Stepping back, he watched the car pull away from the curb and as it did a black Jaguar pulled into its place. The driver stepped out and handed Sean the keys.

"All set." he said and turning disappeared into the crowd.

Sean stood for a moment looking over the people who were standing or walking nearby. No one on this trip had seemed to pay any attention to them, either on the plane or in the terminal. Whoever was after Whisper hadn't shown up yet, he knew it.

CHAPTER NINE

Whisper sat quietly as the English countryside sped by, the land beautiful with a feeling of timelessness, but no matter how she tried to convince herself that she was returning home, it just didn't feel right.

She tried not to feel guilty about her lack of affection for this country, this was her father's homeland and he loved it. But returning here had not created the feeling of homecoming her father hoped for. She sighed, all she really wanted to do was turn around, catch the next plane back to the states, walk up the stairs to her apartment, and climb into her own bed.

It was quiet in the car and in her mind, she could still see Sean and the way he had bent to kiss her in the airport. She closed her eyes and relived his kiss while her imagination carried the scenario a little farther.

Her bedroom, the moon shining in, she could feel his presence in the room before he came to her. The scent of woods and spice invading her senses as he lay beside her, then reaching out he wrapped her in a warmth she had never known before. Slowly he pulled her nightgown over her head, and she could feel the stubble of his whiskers as his lips rubbed against her breasts, and then the awareness of the changes to his body, as he lay next to her, then above her.

Her eyes snapped open – she was losing her mind. She'd spent a few hours with Sean and she was already putting him into her bed. She definitely needed help. Perhaps there was a newsstand in town where she could purchase a Cosmopolitan, or at least the British version of one – there might even be a test that would tell her if she was sexually frustrated, or better yet – she should have just borrowed Sean's.

Laughing softly, she remembered the look on his face when he reached into the plastic bag with the reading material his sister had supplied for his flight. The Cosmopolitan with it cover advertising a graphic article on how a male should turn his partner on in bed, had been bad enough, but when he pulled out the second magazine and saw the title "Floral Arrangements for the Liberated Man" she had thought he was going to choke –and then the blush that crept up over his face – priceless.

It didn't matter anyway she couldn't take any test on sex because she had never had a lover. She'd been out with a few guys that tried to grope her, but till now she'd never felt the need or desire to jump into bed with anyone. She was a twenty-seven-year-old virgin dreaming about sex with a man she'd just met, she needed her head examined.

Reaching up she ran her fingers lightly over her lips. She didn't know what she expected, but she hoped it might invoke a reminder of Sean's kiss. Not that she really needed a reminder; any woman who had been kissed by Sean would remember him.

Yet as she settled back in her seat there were unanswered questions that she wished she knew the answers to.

Over the years she'd learned a lot about his brothers, but not him. She'd already picked up he had a terrific sense of humor, and when he spoke about his family, she sensed deep affection; but she would be foolish if she wasn't aware of a ruthlessness that also lay quietly beneath the surface. There was an unmistakable core of power in him, not only physical but a deeper one that said, this is who am- I make no apologies. She doubted that he would be forgiving if anyone deliberately hurt someone he loved.

The rumbling voice of the driver interrupted her thoughts,

and her eyes swept up to the rear-view mirror where she could see his face reflected. Why was that voice so familiar but the question fled as she realized that he was grinning at her and she felt like the wily old man could read her mind. Guiltily she dropped her hand back in her lap which only caused his grin to broaden.

"Well, my girl, how does it feel to be almost home? Your father told me you've been away a long time, and he's mighty excited about your returning."

The limo driver's eyes met hers in the mirror and she realized that he had the same deep dark brown eyes that Sean did.

But this man certainly was no Sean. The first thing she had noticed about him when he hopped from the limo was his pure white hair, so shiny it glistened in the sun, and he wasn't very tall, the top of his head barely coming to Sean's chin. Yet he certainly was strong, he had tossed her suitcases into the trunk of the car as if they weighed nothing, and when Sean bent down to try to help, the man had given him a look. She was sure she had heard him mumble something about impertinent kids, but Sean must not have heard it because he had just stood there grinning down at the man.

"I'm sorry," Whisper said, "I didn't quite hear your question."

"Well," he repeated "Are you glad to be back home?"

"I guess, yes and no. It really doesn't feel like home to me, I grew up in the states, and the only real family I know is there."

Suddenly she stopped, realizing that this fellow was pretty nosy for a limo driver. She looked up into the mirror and saw that his eyes were twinkling at her.

"I win," he chortled, "Your father said I wouldn't get two words out of you, you'd be too nervous to talk and here we are, you and me having a whole conversation."

Whisper couldn't contain her chuckle "Well, I wouldn't call it a whole conversation."

"Of course it is, I asked you a question, you answered it, and I made a comment...you made a comment..."

Whisper's chuckle was rewarded with a big grin. "Alright you win, it was a conversation."

"Then you better tell that to your father. And tell him to give me those five dollars in American money, not pounds. I'm going to America as soon as this job is over to join my grandson in his business."

It seemed odd that he was talking about the job being over, but maybe he was only hired to drive while her father was ill. "You're going into business with your grandson? And what business is that?"

"Well, you might say he does a little bit of this and a little bit of that, kind of minds other people's business if you know what I mean."

"Well I don't exactly," but she never got to finish her question because smoothly he cut her off.

"Did I tell you my name is Archie, --Archibald, as a matter of fact, I swear my dear departed mother must have been drinking when she named me. Can you imagine sticking that on a sweet innocent babe? Think she did it to get back at me father he was in a pub you know when I was born, – celebrating, the old man told me – of course I often wondered how he could be celebrating my birth when he didn't even know I was arriving. But then he never did call me by my name only "boy".

He swept his eyes up to the mirror grinning, "Used to burn the old girl up." He never stopped for a breath and Whisper began to laugh. "But as I said my friends call me Archie," and he continued, "I would be honored if you would call me Archie too."

"I would love too," she had to smile; she was surrounded by Irishmen today, each one more charming than the last. And although he didn't look anything like Sean, there was something about him-but just as she began to ponder this thought, Archie pulled to the side of the road.

"Want to drive?"

"What?"

His grin was all the encouragement she needed and she didn't hesitate. "Of course."

Climbing out, Archie moved to the passenger side and watched as Whisper slid behind the wheel of the big car.

"Now remember we drive on the left- so forget that stuff you learned in the states – they mess everything up you know and when we come to a round-about pay attention – I don't want to be explaining to your father how we ended up in jail!"

Before they had gone two miles Archie was clutching the door and wishing he had brought a pair of rosary beads, sure that one pair would not be enough to save them.

"Glory be girl" he said, "this isn't Boston, you can slow down and maybe we'll make it in back in one piece."

Whisper threw back her head and laughed, "I can't help it – it feels so good to be behind a wheel, do you know how long it has been since I was behind a wheel? I feel like I can finally relax."

"Maybe you can," Archie muttered, "but you certainly aren't doing much for my nerves."

As she drove down the road the scenery suddenly became familiar and she could almost hear her mother's laughter in the wind. Her mother had a reckless streak when she got behind the wheel of her convertible, and the two of them would zip around these roads with the sun on their faces and the wind whipping their hair. She could remember her own small voice crying "Faster Mommy faster," while her mother just laughed.

It was a wonderful time, at least it was until the day a red-faced policeman arrived at the door. He hadn't been able to catch her mother to give her a ticket, and instead had found her father at home.

That was one of the few times Whisper had heard her father raise his voice to his wife, and after that her mother had driven much more sedately, at least when Whisper was in the car.

Pulling over she got out, "You better drive now, it might

look odd you sitting there she pointed to the passenger side...and me over here."

As she climbed into the backseat, Archie grinned at her, "Wouldn't that raise a few eyebrows, especially with your Aunt Charlotte."

"Oh, my god, is she going to be there?" The words slipped out before she could stop them.

"Not today, she's gone down to London,"

"And Edward?"

Archie sense anxiety in the question.

"I don't know where he is, your cousin has been scarce for the last few weeks, haven't seen hide nor hair of him since he found out you were coming home. An odd duck he is." he glanced over at her. "A bit older than you, isn't he?"

"Yes, he was in his teens when my mother died, "her voice caught, "and I haven't seen him in years."

"Just as well", Archie mumbled, "he's a sullen one."

"I'm sorry what did you say?"

Archie smiled at her in the mirror, "Nothing of importance, just an old man rambling."

Suddenly she felt chilled as if a cold wind had crept into the car; and shivering she rubbed her arms to bring warmth back into them.

Archie had been keeping a close eye on her and he saw her face become pale.

His voice strangely soft as he spoke, "You'll be all right now, take a deep breath darlin', nothing is going to hurt you here. Your dad warned me you might be apprehensive about coming back."

"It's not me I'm worried about."

My god where had that come from? Suddenly she realized she wasn't afraid for herself; she was afraid for her father – and it had nothing to do with his illness. Was that why she would never return home to him?

She knew she hurt her father with her refusal to even consider coming home but she could never rid herself of the fear something bad would happen if she did. Her heart began to pound and she clenched her hands in her lap, the color draining from her face. Had she buried something deep inside her when her mother died? But how could she? She was only a child when the accident happened, what could she know, and why was she so frightened?

Archie pulled up in front of the massive doors of the mansion and before she could move, he was out of the car, and opening her door surprising her by reaching in to take her cold hands in his.

"You're home," his voice was soft and caring and tears sprang into her eyes.

"Pull yourself together girl, and remember I'll be right here if you need me." His eyes fastened on hers and suddenly for some reason she felt safer.

"Thank you, I don't know why, but you've made me feel better" she hesitated for a moment, "So I guess I'm ready."

"Good," he held on to her arm as she stepped out of the car and turned toward the massive stairs leading up to the entrance. She had only taken a few steps when one of the massive doors was thrown open and a tiny plump woman with gray hair flew down the stairs toward her.

The woman never slowed simply barreled into Whisper, throwing her arms around her and hugging her. The force of the greeting threw Whisper off balance and if it hadn't been for Archie reaching out to steady them, they both would have toppled over.

"Anna, Anna," Whisper's voice broke as she hugged the woman in return. "Oh, my god, I'm so glad to see you, I was so afraid that you wouldn't be here."

"And where would I be? You know I would never leave your father," there was just a hint of censure in her tone as she looked up at Whisper.

"I know, I know," Whisper's eyes were filled with tears as she looked down at the little woman. Anna had been with her mother before she was born and had stayed on to attend her after her birth. Over the years Anna had written to her, first to the child and then to the teenager and finally to the adult and each letter had brought her comfort. They had been full of tales of her father, but also her mother, and Whisper had cherished each one. She spoke little of her Aunt Charlotte and hardly at all about her cousin Edward but Whisper never questioned it, knowing that her aunt had a prickly personality and Edward was sullen in his best mood.

"How is my father?"

"Driving us all crazy that's how he is, he must have had me call the airport a hundred times to make sure your plane was on time. It got so that I was even trying to disguise my voice so they wouldn't know it was me again."

Archie had been carefully watching the greeting between the two women and satisfied that Whisper seemed to be handling things well, began to grumble. "Do you suppose you could let the girl go in and see her father, after all that's why she came all this way..."

Anna turned on him her eyes flashing, "Who asked you, you cantankerous old man?"

"Cantankerous, am I? Why I'll tell you--."

"Enough already." Whisper felt like laughing as she refereed the argument that seemed to be brewing.

"Come on then dearie," and placing an arm around Whisper's waist she started up the stairs, "Let the old man get the suitcases."

"Old man, old man!" Archie sputtered as his bellow followed them, and Whisper began to laugh as she felt Anna's plump body shake with mirth.

"Have to get in the last shot, or there'd be no living with him, his ego, you know, thinks he's something,"

"Anna," Whisper leaned down so only she could hear, "Why do I think you think he's something too?"

"It shows does it? I'll have to work on that," she mumbled, "He's going to have to change his ways if he wants to get me."

"Why you're crazy about him" Whisper's eyes opened wide, "You've never once mentioned him in one of your letters."

Anna shrugged Whisper's comment off. "Well, he hasn't been here very long but come along now and we'll talk about that old man later. Your father's resting so I'll take you upstairs and get you settled. He wanted to be up when you came, but Sam wouldn't let him. Said he didn't sleep at all last night and that if he expected to spend some time with you and be awake at the same time, he needed to rest now."

"Sam?"

"His nurse, you're going to like her, "she chuckled, "Keeps your father on his toes."

Whisper paused as she stepped inside the door tears gathering in her eyes; nothing had changed and it was like stepping back in time to when she was a child. The soft rugs in the massive foyer spoke of wealth, and the bust of some romantic ancestor stood in front of the stately staircase that dominated the hall.

Her breath caught in her throat as her eyes fell upon a large bouquet of wildflowers that sat on a round antique table near the door. She remembered her mother and father arguing over those bouquets, her mother insisting that wildflowers should greet their guests, since she considered herself a wildflower in a field of English lilies. It didn't matter to her how much her father and Aunt Charlotte argued that roses would be more appropriate for the grandness of the room, the wildflowers remained.

Her breath caught in her throat and she struggled not to cry out.

It wasn't fair, the wildflowers were still here but her mother was gone. Her beautiful, kind, loving mother, her playmate and friend was gone.

"I can't do this," she thought, "I have to get out of here." She turned to flee when she suddenly caught the sweet fragrance of gardenias. Slowly turning, she stared at the massive staircase looming before her. The sweet scent of the exotic blossoms was originating from there she was sure of it.

She remembered lying in her bed at night when her mother came to tuck her in, and how the scent of the flower clung to her. "Mama, why do you always wear that pretty perfume?" Her mother laughed and hugged her holding her tightly. "So I never forget my beloved south, and where I come from."

"Do I come from the south Momma?"

"No, honey you're an English rose, and the best of both Daddy's world and mine."

"You smell nice, not like Aunt Charlotte, she always smells funny."

Her mother had turned a way for a moment and when she looked down at her daughter her eyes were laughing. "Aunt Charlotte wears a perfume called musk . . . and she lowered her voice again, "it is a bit overpowering."

"When I grow up, I'm going to wear something nice like you do, and not like Aunt Charlotte. Suddenly she had an idea, "Mommy why don't you buy Aunt Charlotte a nice perfume and maybe she won't be grumpy all the time."

Softly Alise placed a fingers over her daughter's lips, "Hush, Alison you mustn't talk like that, Aunt Charlotte wasn't always grumpy," her voice dropped to a whisper, " or at least I don't think she was" she reached under the covers and began to tickle her, "Now, see what you've got me doing, you're supposed to respect your aunt and,"

Alison's voice dropped to a whisper too, "I do respect her, I just don't like her."

Their laughter mingling together, she remembered her father pausing in the doorway before he entered the room. Coming up behind her mother he caught her close to him and pushing aside her hair he had begun to kiss her neck. Her mother had collapsed against him laughing, and Whisper remembered pushing the covers aside so she could attack his legs. In a few moments they were all rolling on the bed while her father pretended to surrender. It was the same ritual night after night, and now the tears that Whisper had been holding back cascaded down her cheeks.

Two days later her mother was dead.

"Honey, are you alright?" Anna's soft voice brought her back to the present.

Whisper turned to the tiny woman, some of her unshed tears still shining in her eyes, "I can't do this, I have to go home."

"Alison listen to me," Anna voice became stern, "This is your home too, and it's time you faced your demons. No matter what you are afraid of here, it can't be any worse than the fear you carry in your heart. Now come upstairs with me and we'll get you settled in."

"I'm sorry I know I'm acting like a baby."

"You'll always be my baby," she reached out and gave the younger woman a hug, "So wipe those tears from your cheeks and come along. After you freshen up a bit you come find me and I might just have some tea ready and those cookies that you loved when you were a little girl."

Whisper began to follow and then hesitated at the bottom of the staircase.

Looking up a scene began to play out in her head. Her mother standing at the top of the staircase talking to someone, her arm outstretched. Was she trying to ward off a blow? Yet Whisper didn't sense fear, or anger in the scene, and she could see her own small hands tugging at her mother's skirt. There was a sense of urgency about her as if she desperately needed to get her mother's attention, but why? What was she trying to tell her? On god why couldn't she remember?

Alarmed at the look on her face, and the color draining from her cheeks, Anna grasped Whisper's arm, "Come back from wherever you are and look at me."

Slowly Whisper became aware that the tiny woman next to her was tugging on her arm, trying frantically to get her attention.

Yet she couldn't take her eyes off the top of the stairway as the scene slowly faded from her sight.

"She's trying to tell me something."

"Who darling? Who's trying to tell you something?

"My mother, someone was here that day Anna, the day that she fell."

"Who darlin', who?"

"I don't know."

Anna reached out and wrapped Whisper's slender body against her plump one. "Try not to think about it sweetness, it just brings back sad memories and I'm sure your mother wouldn't want that."

"Leave her be." Archie had come up behind them, and now his voice rumbled out of his chest. "Maybe the girl needs to remember. Maybe there is something she needs to know and if her mother is trying to get her to remember who are we to interfere."

"I don't believe in ghosts." Anna snapped.

"The hell you don't. . . didn't you come running out of the pantry just last week screaming there was a ghost in there rattling the pans?"

"That was different."

"It was different because your ghost had a little pink nose and a long tail and you made me carry the damn thing out into the field. Probably back in here already."

"Well if there is a ghost, . . ."

But Whisper wasn't listening, slowly she started up the stairs straining to remember exactly what had transpired that day, but her mind had closed off all other memories.

Within a few minutes Archie had deposited her bags in the room and left, while Anna insisted Whisper rest before dinner. As she slipped out of her clothes and into a light nightgown, she realized nothing had changed. Her room was exactly the same as she left it, an old teddy bear with one ear missing sat on a shelf, her books lay in tumbled heap on the floor, and the same curtains with ballerinas on them graced the windows. It was a child's room and her father had never changed it. Tears gathered in her eyes as she climbed into her bed. Somehow everything felt right, the soft covers that surrounded her eliminating the apprehension she had felt earlier, and she drifted off to sleep secure in the knowledge that for the moment she was safe.

Once Anna got back into the kitchen, she put her apron up to her eyes and silently began to cry.

"What's this? Somebody step on your foot?"

Anna turned around to glare at Archie who was leaning against the frame to the kitchen door, "Of course nobody stepped on my foot...you old fool."

He stepped into the room and put his arm around her shoulders. "Forget whatever is worrying you – she's going to be all right. She's a good smart girl and she'll deal with whatever is frightening her."

Releasing her he reached over swiping a cookie from a plate on the kitchen table, he looked over at Anna trying to hide his grin, "Now wipe away those tears, you have nothing to cry about," he moved out of her arms reach, "Unless it was the crust on that berry pie you served last night." He took a bite of the cookie savoring it before he continued, "I hate to tell you this darlin', you being sensitive and all, but last night's crust was so tough it's being used to shoe one of the horses in the stable."

"What?" Anna screeched "That crust was perfect and you know it, I pride myself on my pies"

"Ah ha," he said, "You know that old saying about pride going before a fall, well they were probably thinking about your piecrust."

"Listen you ungrateful man, you can be sure that I will never sneak you an extra piece of pie out to the garage again. You've seen the last of it," she sniffed. Although Archie wasn't very tall Anna was so tiny, she had to look up at him."

"Come now darlin', you know that the way to a man's heart is through his stomach and by golly you're half way there."

"Half way there?" Anna reared up to her full height of four feet seven inches, her eyes flashing, "What makes you think I want your heart? You old. . ."

Without missing a beat Archie leaned down and placed a soft kiss on her lips. "Try a little harder with the crust will you love?" And placing his cap on his head he began to whistle as he headed out the door.

"Oh I'll . . ." Anna's hand crept up to her lips, it had been years since she'd been kissed and although she and Archie were no longer young, it didn't seem to matter. A kiss was a kiss, no matter what your age.

Sighing Anna moved to the cupboard, she knew her piecrusts were always tender, but the pie she'd make for dinner tonight would have just a little more shortening in the crust, and who knows, maybe there was more than one kiss left in the old goat —and if there was maybe this pie just might do the trick.

CHAPTER TEN

Sean sat staring out at the circular driveway in front of the small cottage situated in the woods behind the mansion. A former caretaker's cottage, Stephen had quietly made it ready for Archie to move into.

Where the hell was he? He'd promised that it wouldn't take more than an hour to finish what he had to do, and then he would come right here. That was three hours ago.

He pushed the mug of cold tea away from him and stood up, banging his head on the beam that crossed over the ceiling and down the wall next to him. The place was small, yet cozy and clean, and it sat just far enough from the road so that his car could not be easily seen. He walked over to the small fieldstone fireplace and considered lighting a fire to drive out the late afternoon chill, but instead he wandered back to look out of the window at the driveway again, as if by sheer will he could make a car appear.

Ever since he had left Whisper at the airport, his stomach had been in a knot. He had two people watching her, and although her father was in no condition to do anything physically to guard her, the times he and Stephen had talked had reassured him that this man was sharp and nothing would escape his notice.

This feeling of deep personal involvement in a case was totally out of character for him, and he didn't like it one damn bit.

He'd always prided himself on his self-discipline, yet the first time he'd seen her picture he had known she would be special.

Damn this Irish intuition, he knew that was what had his stomach turning cartwheels; it was as if she already belonged to him.

There was one bright spot though, smiling, he congratulated himself, that bag of 'pixie dust' had been just the right touch. God bless his grandfather who had sent it to him at the office, promising that a little bit of Ireland would guarantee prosperity. He had shoved it into his pocket, intending to leave it in his apartment, and then in his haste to make the plane had forgotten about it... wasn't it lucky that he did. Maybe it wouldn't deliver prosperity, but with a little luck it might deliver something even better.

The sound of a car engine interrupted his thoughts and he watched as a sleek limousine pulled up in front of the cottage. The small man that emerged from the driver's side was whistling as he leaned into the backseat and pulled out a huge picnic basket. It always amazed Sean that this man could be his grandfather. Probably five feet ten at the most, he had the bearing of a much larger man. His face was ruddy, and his eyebrows and hair pure white, and he had the dark eyes of all the O'Brien's, but his seemed to dance when they looked at you.

Those eyes were an illusion. His family all knew that he was the bearer of a notorious Irish temper, one that to their mother's despair, most of his grandchildren had inherited.

Sean remembered as a child his grandfather coming to the states to visit the family, and when he barked an order, all of the O'Brien's would scramble to obey except his mother and his sister. Both of them could wrap him around their little fingers. His father swore that the old man was there to check up on him, and if he didn't like what he saw, he'd threatened to sweep his daughter up and take her back to Ireland. Not bloody likely Sean thought, his father would have died before he let anyone, even her father, take his wife away.

"Well Yank are you settled in?"

"What the hell is all this Yank stuff?" Stifling a laugh since he knew that his grandfather was just trying to get under his skin, Sean decided to give as good as he got.

There was nothing more his grandfather liked than an opportunity to match wits with one of his grandchildren, and Sean was always happy to oblige.

Grinning, he shot back, "Where the hell have you been, old man?" The affection in Sean's voice belied his words and brought a smile to his grandfather's face.

"Old man? Listen here Yank, I can still take you and all your brothers, and your father too and still come out without a scratch while you Yankee boy, -" he couldn't continue, laughter bubbling out of him.

Without warning, Sean reached out, wrapped his grandfather in his huge arms and gave him a hug.

Archie pretended to struggle for a moment, then he threw his arms around his grandson in a grip that was surprisingly strong for a man of his age and stature.

"You forget I raised your mother, and I can hold my own with the best of you, now that girl"

Realizing that he was showing a softer side than he wanted his grandson to see, he gave Sean a slight push- but Sean wasn't deterred by his actions, he just grinned down at him.

Finally stepping back Sean baited him, "You -- old man, couldn't hold a candle to my mother and you know it," he waited as Archie sputtered, then continued, "But you haven't answered my question, what took you so long?"

"Took a while to get your girl settled in, and then I spent some time with Anna," he shrugged, "and I guess time just got away from me."

"What do you mean my girl?" Sean could feel his ears turning red, a sure sign that there was more truth to this question then he wanted his grandfather to know.

"And Anna, who the hell is Anna?"

Archie frowned at Sean "Keep a civil tongue in your head boy, Anna is a dear friend of mine, and she can be invaluable in keeping an eye on your girl. She knows that family, and she'll watch out for her because that girl has a special place in her heart."

Archie began to remove some of the dishes from the basket he'd carried in, and placed them on the small table that sat next to the wall. "It's an interesting story, Anna had no folks of her own, and she married young. The lad was from one of the prominent families in Dublin, and because Anna was an orphan, they thought Donald, that was his name, married beneath him. They were married quite a few years when Donald took sick and died, Anna's in-laws had never gotten over the fact that he had married her, and because there were no children, they felt they had no obligation to her. She and Donald had been living in a home on their property and when he passed, they threw her out."

Sean shook his head in disgust, "I didn't think those things happened anymore."

"Well it does, a friend of Anna's who worked for your girl's mother told her what had happened, and as Anna tells it, Alise swooped into the boarding house where she was working and took her home with her that very day. She was with the missus from then on. She went to the hospital with her when Alise went into labor, and she stayed with her and held her hand until Stephen got there. From what she says, Alise had a terrible long labor and for a while they thought they might lose her. Then when Alise came home with the baby she was so weak that Anna took care of her till she was back on her feet. She loved that little girl as if she were her own. It broke her heart when the child was shipped to the states, but she could understand why."

Sean frowned, "That's an odd thing to say, she could understand why. What does she know that we should?"

Archie turned and looked at him, "All she would say was after her mother's death that the child seemed deathly frightened.

More than that I don't know, when I asked Anna to explain, she clammed right up. There is more than one mystery in that house, I can feel it in my bones, but no one will open up at least not yet." And he grinned.

"Does Anna know about me?" even with Archie's reassurances Sean couldn't conceal his worry.

"Of course not, nobody knows. But you needn't worry about Anna, I trust that old girl, I wish you could have seen them together, it was like they were never parted, all that hugging and kissing and crying, I tell you it touched this old man's heart."

"Yeah, but when you're not there, suppose . . .?"

"Relax boy, I didn't get to this age without having a few smarts. And you seem to forget that there are other people in that house that will be watching out for her."

Sean grinned at his grandfather, with the cockiness of Archie's answer his apprehension began to fade, and the tightness in his gut ease.

"Maybe you're right,"

Embarrassed when his stomach made a rumbling noise, Sean realized that he hadn't had anything to eat since he'd left the airport and he was starving, "How about it old man, isn't there anything to eat in this place?" The sound of his stomach was loud enough for even Archie to hear.

Laughing Archie reached for some plates, and two mugs, and set them on the table. "Certainly, I had Anna make us up a steak and kidney pie."

At the look on Sean's face Archie grinned, "Or maybe it was a chicken pie, yes I think that's it, a chicken pie, though you don't know what you're missing till you've tasted Anna's steak and kidney."

Motioning to Sean to take a seat Archie began to rummage around the small kitchen that was part of the main room. Soon he found the utensils he was looking for, and as he dished out the steaming dish, he kept up a steady stream of questions about the family. Sometimes Sean's answers got a smile, and when he got to the part about Colleen being promoted to detective, he was rewarded with a grunt.

"That girl needs a husband not a gun, what was your father thinking allowing her to join the force?"

Sean laughed "Tell me, were you ever able to stop my mother from doing what she wanted?"

"Good point" Archie grumbled, "Those women of ours are all alike" and he looked over at Sean, "and I think, you're contemplating adding another one to the mix."

Sean spit out the iced tea he had just sipped; he was just getting used to his feelings about Whisper and his grandfather had already picked up on it. Narrowing his eyes, he glared at him, "I just met the woman...there is no need to rush into---."

"Forget it," Archie said. "The first time I saw your grandmother we were in church. There, with my best friend Mickey I was," he tried to look contrite but couldn't quite manage it, "We were planning to do penance for the rowdy time we had had the night before, and we figured the good Lord would forgive us if we showed up at his door the next morning."

"Of course, the liquor hadn't quite gotten out of our system and as we stumbled into that church, I guess we made a little noise, because the most beautiful girl I had ever seen turned and frowned at us. Mickey leaned over and whispered to me that he intended to marry her. I looked him right in the eye, right inside those hallowed walls, and I threatened him."

He got up and carried the serving dish to the sink, "It's a wonder a lightning bolt didn't come down from the sky and strike me down right there...but," he sighed, "I wouldn't have cared, I've have crawled out of that wreckage and gone after her anyway. I told him to back off or suffer the consequences. He did, and even introduced us after church, I married her six months later."

He paused, "Would have married her before that, but her

father was a crotchety old man, had all I could do to get her out of that house."

Sean grinned, remembering the tales his father used to tell about how hard it was to get his mother Nellie away from this old man. His father had met her when he had been sent to Ireland to teach the newest police techniques in an exchange program. She worked in the office and he said he took one look at her and decided this was the one. Archie had fought tooth and nail to keep Nellie from going back to the states with Dennis, but it hadn't worked, and every year either she returned or she sent one of her children to spend a month with their grandparents.

Colleen was named for her grandmother and the family had been devastated when the elder Colleen had been diagnosed with cancer and died. She had been gone for years now, but Archie had never remarried or shown any interest in another woman till now.

Conversation ceased as the two men devoured the steaming chicken pie and the fruit Archie had placed on the table. It was a peaceful meal, the only thing causing a minor moment of discord, was when Sean asked for a cup of coffee instead of the tea his grandfather had put in front of him. Mumbling about a heathen drink, Archie moved to the stove and in a few minutes replaced the tea with a cup of something that looked like it had been made from boiled potato skins. The look on Archie's face dared Sean to say a word, and discretion being the better part of valor he didn't.

Sitting back, Archie looked carefully at his grandson. All of his grandchildren were special to him. He and Colleen had the one daughter Nellie, and although he and his wife had dreamed of having more, when he almost lost his wife with that one, he had been careful to insure there were no more. But his daughter Nellie had made up for that lack, a parcel of good healthy children she had, and he loved every one, even the one they'd adopted.

This one was special though; Archie knew they both had the same streak of independence. He wasn't surprised when he had learned that Sean had gone into business for himself. He always knew Sean would follow in his footsteps. In his day he had been quite a detective himself, hired by the government to ferret out secrets some people didn't want to give up. A bullet had taken him out of action for a while and he had ended up with a desk job.

As he studied Sean, he realized that this grandson had the look of a hunter. He was big, but not bulky, his eyes never rested, they were aware of everything going on around him. He wasn't handsome, but he knew women would be drawn to him although he seemed unaware of his magnetism. His nose was a little crooked, and that was good, a few fights were good for a man's soul, and he also had a sense of humor. "Yes," Archie thought, "he would be a good match for that little lady from Boston."

He grinned as he thought about the ride they had taken to the estate, how she had eagerly taken the wheel of that car, and what a hair-raising ride that had been! She might look fragile, but he was sure she would be able to hold her own with this grandson, and any chance he got well he might just help that courtship along.

Sean interrupted his musing, "So when you were in the house, beside your little talk with Anna did you discover anything useful? Was anyone suspicious about Stephen hiring a new driver?"

"Not a bit, though Charlotte, that old biddy of a sister of Stephen's asked me for a references, boy did you hear that? I was about to tell her what she could do with her references when Stephen stepped in, took the wind out of her sails I tell you told her that he had checked me out and that I came highly recommended. Mentioned some name I didn't recognize, but she sure did--shut her right up."

"And this Anna, you're so called friend, did she buy it?"

"Listen boy, when I sell something it gets sold, she thinks the old driver got upset at something Charlotte said and quit. Anyone would understand that. That sister of Stephen's looks like she's sucking on a lemon all the time and she snaps at everybody.

Stephen may be reserved but he's kind to everybody, except the nurse," he grinned, "there are sparks that fly between those two."

"And who else is in the house?"

"Well, he doesn't live there, but Charlotte's son Edward is in and out constantly. Seems he was adopted by Charlotte as a baby and she dotes on him.

He paused, "Now there's a funny relationship, she adores him, and he barely tolerates her. I can't explain it, it's like he resents her or something. They both live together in a large house on the estate, have for years. Anna says at one time they all lived in the mansion, but when Stephen got married, Charlotte and Edward moved out. Only not too far away. She still comes in and tries to boss him around, but he isn't having any of it, and since Sam arrived she doesn't get away with much. You know," he said, with a gleam in his eyes, "That Sam is quite a looker."

Raising one eyebrow, Sean studied the man in front of him. "Sam's too young for you."

Laughing Archie looked up at Sean, "Don't I know it, but an old man can dream can't he?"

"Sure, just as long as you don't dream in too much detail. Sam took this job as a favor to me, and I don't want her to have to worry about you."

"Me?" laying his hand on his heart, Archie looked at Sean, his eyes twinkling. "Why would she worry about me...? Just because she's a six-foot gorgeous red-head with a knockout figure, is no reason to be. . ."

"Because you're a scoundrel and Aunt Em reminded me that if you get me into trouble, she refuses to bail me out."

"Ah, Em, when you're talking to the office tell her I was asking for her. She's a cute little dish too."

Shaking his head, Sean asked, "Is there any woman who is safe from you?"

Seeming to ponder the question for a moment, finally Archie said, "Yep, Charlotte I'd rather bed a snake."

"You seem to feel very strongly about her."

"You bet I do, it's a gut feeling I have, she's hiding something and whatever it is it has made her very bitter." Archie shivered.

"Could she be behind the attacks on Whisper?"

Archie pondered the question for a moment than shook his head, "No, I don't think so, that's not her style, she'd be more inclined to tear your throat out by herself. I'd bet my reputation that she's not behind whatever is going on."

"What about Edward, you mentioned the nephew, and Stephen was rather noncommittal about him. He didn't seem to want to talk about him, what's going on there?"

"I don't know, they seem to have a love hate relationship. Sometimes I get the feeling that Stephen simply tolerates him for Charlotte's sake and other times I think he is genuinely fond of the boy."

"Damn, I wish I could get inside that house, I hate it when I have to rely on others."

"And especially when you're personally involved."

"I am not personally involved," Sean growled.

"Sure, and I'm the queen's bedfellow."

"There is one thing though," Archie paused, "When we were taking Alison up to her room, I had the distinct feeling we were being watched. It was a funny feeling, but since I had my hands full of suitcases, I thought it might look funny if I suddenly dropped them and ran around peering into some of the rooms. Whoever it was, disappeared by the time I was free and had a chance to look around. Couldn't find anyone in the house that shouldn't have been there either."

"What the hell do you make of that?"

"I wish I knew, but I alerted Sam anyway, and she is going to keep an eye on things, although with Stephen confined to a wheelchair until his operation, she doesn't have much opportunity to snoop around."

"Do you think he suspects that she's working for me?"

"Not a clue, hiring a former nurse turned detective was brilliant, I always said you took after me."

Suddenly he yawned and standing up, he pointed to the back of the cottage. "Your room is to the right in the back there, you'll find clean towels and stuff on the small table beside the sink."

"Wait a minute, when I asked you to get me someplace to stay, I didn't think it was here, and what about that sizeable check I sent you for a deposit on a hotel room?"

"Well I figured you'd be more at home with kin and all, and since I had this room in the back, I decided to rent it to you. Besides it is closer to where you want to be."

"And the check?"

"Just about covers the inconvenience of having someone here, and the food and all that stuff that goes with having a border."

He grinned at his grandson, "I do like my privacy you know,"

Starting up the small staircase, Archie turned back for a moment, "Listen lad, after you've cleaned up the kitchen, don't forget to turn out all the lights, money doesn't grow on trees!" And with a smart salute to Sean, Archie continued his climb. He had only taken a few steps when Sean called out to him. "I've been thinking".

Sean's quiet tone of voice and the serious expression on his face told Archie whatever he was about to say was no joke.

"My mother misses you and when this job is done, I would like you to consider moving to the states."

Archie thought for a moment. "You know I might be tempted; your grandmother has been gone a long time, and it's lonely sometimes, but what would I do?"

"You could come to work for me." Before the words were out of his mouth Sean realized that he would enjoy having this man work for him. For one thing his grandfather had the uncanny knack of fitting in anywhere, people always trusted and opened up to him. His mother always bragged about her father had served in the Irish intelligence and how many accolades and medals he'd won. One thing for sure, it would never be dull.

Archie cocked one eyebrow, and stared at Sean. "Is this you or your mother talking? Did she put you up to this?"

"My mother knows nothing about this...this is strictly a business deal...and well..." he paused, and while his eyes twinkled his voice was strictly business, "but being my grandfather doesn't mean I'll cut you any slack. If you can't cut the mustard, I'll just have to fire you."

Archie hooted..." Get out, why you cocky young pup, the day some kid like you thinks he can outsmart me." Archie stopped and turned around and came back down the stairs.

Laughing Sean looked at his grandfather. "You are something you know that?"

"Yes, I am Yank, and don't you ever forget it, and by the way I accept your job offer. We'll quibble about money another time, since you don't seem to be as sharp tonight as you usually are... must be jet lag or something."

With that Archie headed back toward the stairs.

Flabbergasted Sean sat there, staring at where his grandfather had been standing.

I'll be damned, the old fox got me. Not only did he have a check for a thousand from me, but I'm doing the dishes and cleaning up the place He didn't have to worry about his grandfather holding his own in Boston, Boston had better worry about holding its own with him.

Throwing back his head Sean roared with laughter right now he hoped he had more than just a little of his grandfather's blood running through his veins.

CHAPTER ELEVEN

E dward stood at the bedroom window, a glass of wine clutched in his hands staring out at the formal gardens that guarded the entrance to this ancient dwelling. Beds of flowers and shrubs were in full bloom in a riot of colors, each carefully nurtured and confined to their specified place. No wayward weed dared to raise its ugly head or one of the gardeners would dispatch it with no remorse. Yet behind the mansion the fields were alive with wild flowers and no one dared to touch them.

He loved this land and it should be his, not hers.

He'd called the airline and knew her plane had arrived on time, but he didn't need them to verify it, she was home, he could feel it. The air had changed.

Where a few hours ago there had been a calm almost serene feeling, now the air around him was charged and seemed to be humming.

Impatiently he pushed a lock of dark unruly hair off of his forehead.

He was aware of his good looks, and the fact that women seemed drawn to him; yet he was uninterested.

He had loved only once, and no one would ever be able to overcome the passion he felt for that one woman.

He poured himself another glass of wine. He'd always prided himself on his excellent control, his ability to handle any situation, at least until today, but today was different. She was home.

He smiled, long ago he had discovered the room where his uncle kept the good wine as he explored all of the hidden passages in this old converted castle.

He had made it his business to research the family history and he could name every one of the ancestors who had lived here. He recognized every portrait hanging in the family museum. He knew intimate details of their lives, their marriages, their children, their triumphs and losses, and even their mistresses.

He had studied them and learned from them. He would never make their mistakes.

"It's time." he thought, as he took out a pristine handkerchief from his pocket and carefully wiped the crystal glass, then placed it on the wine cart. He had known all along that this moment would arrive and he was ready for it.

He stepped back to the window as the limousine pulled up and he watched as the driver hurried around to open the passenger door.

His breath caught in his throat as she emerged.

How like her to sit in the front with the driver, he frowned, he didn't like the man, and he'd argued with his uncle Stephen when he hired him, but Stephen had been adamant. Not even when he'd asked his mother to intervene had Stephen been swayed.

He moved the drape aside cautiously it wouldn't do to have the family question what he was doing in this room.

He watched as Anna raced down the front steps and drew the woman into her arms. Anna's head barely reached her chin but he knew how it felt to be drawn against that ample bosom and comforted.

Stepping back, he watched as they mounted the stairs and entered the building.

A slight sound alerted him, and he slipped behind the door just in time to see Anna, Archie, and his cousin climbing the stairs.

Silently he waited, sure that they would never enter Alise's bedroom. No one entered her room. It was left exactly as it was the day she died. No one knew that he was the only one who came here. To Stephen, the room held painful memories of a lost love, and he allowed no one to change it. But to him this room didn't bring sorrow, it brought comfort.

His breath caught in his throat as he stared at his cousin through the crack. She was beautiful, not quite as beautiful as her mother, but that was to be expected, no one could be that beautiful.

He listened as Anna rattled on about how Stephen insisted on keeping all of her old dolls and teddy bears on the shelves in her room, and he had a brief moment of panic when Archie stopped and glanced in his direction.

He tried to calm himself, he'd always felt his self-control was ironclad, but today his palms were sweating and his heart was beating heavily in his chest. He thought he was prepared for anything, but the fact that she looked so much like her mother had startled him. He had expected to see more of her father in her, but instead she was a miniature of Alise.

A few times in the past, he had slipped into the states to check on her, telling his mother he had business to conduct in Boston. She had never suspected that he was lying. But he had been careful, and Alison had never known he was there. His desperate need to keep track of her had become an obsession with him.

Stephen didn't realize that he had unwittingly helped by telling them everything he knew about what was going on in her life.

Once when she was in school, he had shown up at an open house being careful not to be spotted by her aunt. Two or three times he had even been brave enough to attend her high school football games, and as she took the field with the other cheerleaders and rooted for her team, he had only watched her. But for the last few years it had been too dangerous, and he could not risk being caught. No one must ask why he was so interested in her that he would travel to the states to spy on her.

Yet those visits had proved fruitful. Sitting in a Boston bar one night he had struck up a conversation with a man who had turned out to be quite an interesting fellow. Not his usual kind of chap, but one with a vocation that he wasn't afraid to brag about. He claimed he was an arranger, and that he collected money just to be sure his boss got paid when a contract was fulfilled. When Edward asked his name he'd laughed, and said people called him Max but he wasn't sure what his real name was since he'd been abandoned as a baby.

As the evening wore on and the drinks got stronger, they moved to a booth where Max told him wild stories of how he and his boss had worldwide connections and how his boss wasn't adverse to "helping people out" – and laughing had assured him that sometimes even "helping people out of this world."

At first Edward had laughed in disbelief, but as the stories grew more detailed, and newspaper articles he'd read flashed into his head, he knew this man was telling the truth. At the end of the night Edward was apprehensive, did he know too much, was he going to wind up dead?

His companion saw the fear in his eyes and laughed, and clapped him on the back assuring him he was safe. He even handed him a card, a rather odd card with a picture of some kind of a lizard on it, and bragged that if Edward ever needed him or his boss to just give him a call. But there was no information other than the picture on it.

He never did see him again, but the next morning the bellhop stopped at his room and handed him an envelope. In it was another card. It simply had a phone number and the words, "The Arranger" on it, and that too had a picture of a small lizard on it. For some unknown reason it was the second card that made him apprehensive.

How Max ever found out where he was staying he didn't

know, because he was sure he hadn't told him. He had been tempted to throw the cards away but for some reason he had tucked them in his wallet.

A few months ago, he had called Max and left a message. The next day Max called back. When he explained what he wanted, Max just laughed and told Edward to stay near the phone he would talk to his boss and see what he could do.

Edward shivered as he recalled his next phone call, he had never heard the voice before but what made it all the more frightening was that the voice wasn't cold as you would imagine a killer's voice to be, but warm and friendly and he spoke of killing someone as if it were just another day at the office. That's when he learned that what he thought was a lizard on the card really was a chameleon. The Chameleon even patiently explained that he wasn't in the habit of killing women, had only done it once before, but because he was a friend of Max's he would make an exception for him.

That night at precisely midnight instructions were left on his answering machine that he was to get a fifty-thousand-dollar bank check as a retainer, and an address to mail it to. An additional twenty-five thousand was due when the contract was fulfilled.

He did as instructed and he never heard from anyone again, except one call a few days ago from Max saying the assignment was taking a little longer than expected.

Yet there was no doubt in his mind that what he was paying for would be accomplished. The only problem was now it would probably happen here, and not in the states as he'd instructed and that made him uneasy.

CHAPTER TWELVE

Waiting until he could hear Anna's chatter and Archie's gruff voice in Alison's room, he slipped out and down the stairway to the library. Entering, he carefully chose one of the wing backed chairs facing the windows, knowing that he would be hidden from anyone entering the room.

Being alone gave him time to calm himself. This was the family library, the room where all major decisions were made, where wills were read, and occasionally when family rules were ignored, discipline was meted out. Oh, yes, if he waited long enough, everyone he wanted to see would come to him.

The sunlight from the tall windows reflected onto the floor and he tensed remembering when it had all begun.

He was about seven, totally secure in a world that most kids only dream of.

It had been a gloomy day and the light was better in this room, so he had gathered up his sketches and water colors and come here to lie in front of the massive windows. His dreams revolved around building grand structures that the world would marvel at. As long as he could remember he'd had the desire to build, not just build, but also create pictures of his buildings with such minute details that everyone who saw them marveled that they had been created by a seven-year-old. He didn't know why he had this burning desire to create these structures but he did. It just seemed to be part of him.

He should be happy, he had everything he could want, or money could buy and yet something was missing.

Charlotte his adopted mother, doted on him, and although he had been told his own mother died at birth, and his father shortly after, there were no pictures of them so he could at least know what they looked like. Eventually he decided it didn't matter anymore, he had his mother and his Uncle Stephen.

His uncle had always been there for him. He had taught him to ride, even buying him his first pony, they had gone fishing, and hunting, and he had accompanied Stephen as he rode around the estate inspecting the buildings, and talking to the people who kept everything running smoothly. He was as much of a father as he would ever need.

His hand clutched the arm of the chair as he remembered that day.

His mother and uncle had already been quarreling when they entered the room, a vicious quarrel, their voices raised, and although he was curious, he really wasn't paying too much attention.

He was tempted to cover his ears because as usual when she was upset his mother's voice became shrill. He grinned, and shimmed closer to the windows and farther away from them. He had discovered that he was able to block out his mother's voice simply by thinking of something else, and he hoped his uncle was able to do the same.

Suddenly he stopped drawing as he heard his name.

The words were still engraved in his mind, "Charlotte, be fair, the boy has a right to know who his father is, and that he's still alive."

"He has no father, he has me, and when I adopted him, he became mine and mine alone."

"For god sakes woman, you're being completely unreasonable, you're letting your own bitterness ruin your life, the boy has a right to know who his parents are, and if I'm right about his parentage, I am sure his father will acknowledge him, and the boy stands to inherit. . ."

"You have no idea who his father is."

"I know what the gossips say, and since I am intimately involved . . ."

"You know nothing!"

"Charlotte, you're my sister and I love you, but by not telling him the truth you're making a big mistake."

"Stop it," her voice had risen to a hysterical pitch, "I won't listen to you...nobody can have him, he's mine, you can't have him, nobody can."

"I don't want to take him away from you, all I want is for you to talk to the boy and tell him, who--"

"No! I'm not going to tell him anything and neither are you, I'll never forgive you Stephen, if you say one word to him, I promise you, I'll take him and leave here and you'll never see either of us again."

Edward lay there stunned. The room had suddenly become cold, and the picture he had been drawing was no longer the magnificent structure he had been envisioning, but a make-believe picture. Just like his life.

His world was shattered, he had a father somewhere and she wouldn't tell him who it was --he wracked his young brain – who could it be? He wanted to jump to his feet and confront them – but he was afraid. Suppose his father didn't want him – and after he questioned them – they decided they didn't want him either.

He lay very still hoping that neither of them would walk toward the windows. He knew he was hidden by the large sofa in front of him, and if he didn't move, they probably wouldn't notice him.

The quarrel had gone on for a while, but nothing more was said about his father and Edward had lain awake that night trying to remember all that he had heard.

Why had his Uncle Stephen been so angry, and why had he been so insistent that he be told he had a father that was still alive.

Suddenly a thought entered his young head. Maybe the reason that his Uncle Stephen had fought with his mother was because he was Stephen's son.

Maybe he was a bastard. Yes, that was it, he'd heard the cook discussing that once, and he even knew what it meant. He had been playing in the hall outside the kitchen when he heard raised voices. Being naturally curious he had crept to the door and listened.

The gardener was telling the cook her daughter was a disgrace being pregnant and not married. The cook's voice was furious as she defended her daughter, insisting that these were modern times and no one held illegitimacy against anyone anymore. But the gardener kept saying a bastard was a bastard, no matter how modern the times were.

It had ended when the cook threw a pot at the gardener's head and he had stomped out of the kitchen. A few months later the cook quit and he heard his mother and Uncle Stephen talking about how the daughter had a little boy. Shortly after that the cook and her daughter moved away.

That was it, his young mind reasoned, his mother had adopted him because Uncle Stephen was his father, and the heir, and he could not acknowledge a bastard. Secure that he had worked out the puzzle Edward had fallen asleep, positive that one day soon Stephen would admit he was his son.

But it never happened, and when his uncle had met Alise and married her, his hopes of ever being acknowledged as Stephen's son had begun to fade. When Alison was born, he began to hope again, Stephen had his daughter, and surely now was the time to acknowledge his son.

After all Stephen's title could only go the males in the line, not the females, and that was the way it had been for centuries.

He had tried to reason with Alise the day she died, but it had been no use.

He remembered that day as if it were yesterday. He had slipped into the house through the empty kitchen, stopping only long enough to help himself to a glass of milk, and some of the cookies that were cooling on a plate on the table. There seemed to be no one around, and he had quickly climbed the stairs to Alison's room. He knew that was where he would find them both, mother and daughter.

Each afternoon after Alison's nap, Alise would go to her room and for a few hours become her playmate.

Edward knew that Alison was a lonely little girl, the nearest family with children was miles away and it was only on rare occasions that they visited. Alise went out of her way to make up for this by making sure that each afternoon Alison had someone to play with, even if it was only her mother.

Sometimes he even joined them, and had been the butler for their tea parties, and on occasion a pirate or a robber. No one knew about it, after all at sixteen Edward wasn't about to admit that he played with a five-year-old and her mother.

Yet this day was different, he had lain awake all night debating whether or not to tell her what he suspected. Would it change her feelings toward him or Stephen? He didn't think so, Alise had a warm loving heart and he was sure that she would forgive Stephen any indiscretion, after all it happened long before he married her.

He paused in the doorway to Alison's room, puzzled by the air of excitement there. Alise sparkled like a jewel and she was dressing Alison in a tiny gown that matched hers.

There was no tea set on the little table and no pirate costumes laid out. Everything had been put away. There was something going on that he didn't know about, and it worried him. He should be part this celebration, and for the first time since Alise had married Stephen, he felt like an outsider.

Up until now there had been a special bond between the two of them, which made up for the bitterness that his mother seemed to feel. Only two people escaped her sharp tongue, he and Stephen, and sometimes Stephen didn't escape it at all.

He walked over and stood behind Alise and reaching out

he touched her shoulder and she jumped with a tiny squeal, and then laughed and hugged him. Alison who had been standing on the bed gave a leap and landed in his arms and he held her close reveling in the fact that even though she didn't know it, she was his sister.

Alise had drawn Alison's hair up in a miniature duplication of hers and they laughed and pretended to curtsy to him as if he were royalty. He had felt a swelling of pride as he looked at this cute little girl with a mother so beautiful, she took his breath away. For just a moment he imagined how it would be if Stephen acknowledged him. He would take his sister everywhere. People would think they were a wonderful family, and then nobody would ever say a thing about his illegitimacy.

Of course, it would probably hurt his mother that he wanted to be Stephen's son and not hers, but when she thought about it she would understand. He would inherit the title and Alison could inherit the money. His adopted mother had already made out her will, and everything she had would go to him. He would have everything he ever wanted.

He followed the two of them out into the hall words tumbling out of his mouth. He wasn't even sure if they made sense to her but he couldn't shake this sense of urgency. She had to know what he'd heard that day in the library, she had to understand. Suddenly the words he was saying seemed to penetrate, and Alise stopped at the top of the staircase and stared at him.

For the first time he saw pity in her eyes and it alarmed him. Was this going to change the way she felt about him? Maybe he shouldn't have said anything.

His words tumbled one over the other, but Alise reached up and put a soft finger across his lips, trying to still his voice. He would never forget that day, the light from the chandelier overhead made the diamonds on her ears sparkle, and she seemed to have a glow about her that he had never seen before. He remembered thinking that if he was her husband, he would have had her painted just as she looked at that moment.

Gently he removed her fingers from his lips. He had to make her listen. He had spent the night envisioning this moment but nothing was going as planned. It was the first time since she had come into their lives that she seemed to be ignoring what he was trying to tell her. It frightened him. Up till now she had always been there to listen to him.

But not that day, and that was the day he realized that he was in love with her, with all the passion of a young man's heart.

A dull ache began behind his eyes and his fist tightened on the arm of the chair as he remembered what happened next.

She reached out to him, and stroked his cheek while at the same time, her words had stabbed him.

"Edward, where did you ever get such an idea? Stephen isn't your father, I know it. When he comes home tonight, we'll sit and talk to him, if he knows anything at all he'll tell us. If not" she hesitated, "I'll help you find out. You have my word on it."

He remembered Alison had been tugging on her mother's skirt trying to get her attention, but Alise was concentrating on what he was saying and had ignored her. But he had been beyond reason and reached out to grab her arm, determined to make her understand. She shook him off and turned toward Alison taking a step forward to pick her up—and then she fell.

All he could remember were her screams as she tumbled down the massive staircase her body coming to rest at the bottom of the staircase, her neck at an unnatural angle.

He looked at his outstretched arm and a cold chill ran up his spine. Had he pushed her? He didn't know.

He knew she was dead. Then Alison began to scream trying to get past him to go to her mother. He grabbed her up in his arms and ran down the stairs past Alise's body.

He had taken her down...

CHAPTER THIRTEEN

His thoughts were interrupted by the sound of the Library doors opening and Stephen's querulous voice snapping at Sam.

It was obvious to anyone who met Sam that her nickname did not fit. She was slender, with a glorious head of red hair and a temper to match. When Stephen's doctor sent her to care for him until the operation was over, there had been a terrible row. She had stood and listened to him rave and rant, then had taken off her coat, gotten him a glass of water and insisted he take his medicine. She had been here ever since.

His uncle's voice was soft, but with the unmistakable tone of someone used to giving orders and expecting them to be carried out. He could barely catch the words, but they made Edward smile. Stephen would never change. That aristocratic bearing and tone of voice was guaranteed to intimidate the most worthy opponent.

"I really don't care that you didn't want to take the medicine."

"Well, you better care, you're fired."

"You can't fire me, I don't work for you, I work for your doctor remember?"

"Well, I'll fire him too."

"Oh, really? And just where are you going to get another one that can do the type of surgery you need?'

"I'll go to the states and find one."

"You'll never survive the trip."

"You," he said in a tone that dripped of sarcasm, "Are a cold bitch."

"And you my friend are an arrogant, opinionated s.o.b., and I am tempted to dump you out of this wheelchair right here in the hallway."

"You wouldn't dare."

"Try me."

"Where did my surgeon find you, some prison in the states? Did you escape after murdering ten or twenty men? You wouldn't have needed a knife; you could use your tongue to cut their hearts out."

"Good one. Now grow up, your daughter's home, and we don't need her to see what a spoiled brat you've become since you've been ill!"

"Why all of a sudden my doctor insists that I have to have the nurse from hell is beyond me."

"You're just lucky I guess."

"I've thought it all over," Stephen mused, "Now that my daughter's home, I don't care what that damn doctor says, I'm going to have that operation when I'm good and ready and not before."

"Forget it buster, you'll have that operation when he says you will."

"He's a damn quack!"

"He's your best friend."

"I don't care what he is, I'm not ready. Alison's home I need to spend some time with her, there are things I have to attend to..." the wistfulness of Stephen's tone tugged at Sam's heart, but she knew that delaying his surgery diminished his chances of survival.

"You've already attended to everything. All she has to do is sign some papers and it's all settled."

"Suppose she won't accept anything?"

"Then you'll either reason with her or you'll make other plans."

"You damn Yankees have no idea what it takes to run an estate this size. You'd either give it all away or run it into the ground."

"And you my pompous friend need to talk to your daughter and tell her exactly how you feel. If she's inherited your stubborn streak – you're in big trouble."

"You're just trying to aggravate me so I'll have another attack and die."

Sam laughed at the dramatic tone of Stephen's voice. "You know, back in the states we have an old saying, "Only the good die young, and you my cantankerous friend will probably live forever."

Sensing that there was an element of fear behind his bluster Sam reached out and rested her hand on his shoulder, and just as quickly his large hand came up and covered hers.

His voice wistful he spoke, "Sam, for the first time in my life I'm scared. I've made so many mistakes. I wish I knew what there is about this house that frightens my daughter. Years ago, I should have given it to my sister and taken Alison away from here. She would have grown up in my home, in my life, and now she's a grown woman and I'm an old man."

"For heaven's sake, stop feeling sorry for yourself, you're in your prime and once you're past this operation you'll feel differently. Secondly, too many people depend on you for their livelihood, and there was no way you could just walk away from your responsibilities. Besides from all I've heard your daughter is an amazing young woman. You have plenty of time to build on that relationship, and maybe she'll even encourage you to start again, you might even meet a nice woman and start a new family."

A slight cough startled them as they suddenly realized they were not alone.

Edward rose from the chair and turned to face them. From

the words and the tone of their voices he had expected to see two people ready to tear each other's throats out, instead both of them were wearing grins and Stephen looked on the verge of laughing.

"So, Sam thinks you should marry again?"

His glance toward her was condescending and dismissive. "Obviously she never knew your first wife, or she would realize that no one could replace her, or maybe she is applying for the job herself. After all a nurse in the family wouldn't be a bad idea now that you and mother are getting older."

"Edward, what the hell are you doing here?"

Defiantly Edward looked at his uncle. "Waiting to see my cousin of course. Don't you think that the family should all be together to welcome her?"

"And is eavesdropping a new habit of yours?"

"No, as a matter of fact it's an old habit, and you'd be surprised what you can learn if you're quiet and unnoticed."

With one hand Stephen stopped the forward momentum of the wheelchair and stared at his nephew. The look in his eyes made Stephen uneasy, as if there was a message there that he should understand and didn't, and he began to rack his brain as to what Edward could be referring to.

"I thought I made it clear to your mother that I would appreciate a few days alone with my daughter."

"Oh, I'm sure she didn't realize that included," his pause was barely perceptible "family, I understood from mother that edict was strictly for friends and acquaintances not us, but if that's what you want," he turned to leave "of course I will acquiesce to your wishes."

"Wait," wearily Stephen raised his hand as if he realized the battle was already lost, "I guess Alison and I can spend some time alone together tomorrow, stay, and since you are here already call your mother and invite her over too."

The two men stared at each other animosity crackling between them.

"Sam, would you tell Anna there will be two more for dinner."

"It will be just family won't it Uncle?" Edward looked pointedly as Sam.

"It will be whoever I wish Edward," Stephen's voice had become icy, his tone challenging.

"Whatever you wish, although in our home mother and I are not in the habit of entertaining the servants."

Turning his back before Stephen could respond, Edward moved toward the desk and picked up the phone.

Stephen muttered to Sam, "I can tell this is my sister's fine work. There was no way she was going to miss being here today. She's been waiting for this moment ever since I told her Alison was coming home."

"Maybe she missed her."

"No, she didn't, she's always been jealous that I was able to have a child and she wasn't, and she used to make Alison's life miserable. The only thing that stood between her, and Charlotte's razor-sharp tongue was my wife."

He grinned, "I wish you could have met her, you would have liked her, everyone did, she was from the South, sweetest woman in the world— but don't mess with her," —he paused—"and I'd put my money on her in any battle, even against me," he laughed, "or my sister."

"She sounds like a remarkable woman, and you must have loved her very much."

"I did," his eyes were sad and her heart ached for him, "it was a once in a lifetime kind of love, but I can't live in the past any longer," his voice softened. "Lately I've realized that she would have wanted me to get on with my life, she was that kind of woman."

He looked into Sam's eyes and she saw a glimmer of his resolve. "There is someone else for me to love, and if I can just survive this operation I intend to get out of this chair and prove it."

Sam's hands tightened on the handles of the chair, and she wanted nothing more than to brush her lips over the top of his head and reassure him.

Edward dropped the phone back into its cradle and turned, "Mother is pleased that you have changed your mind."

He looked at Sam and Stephen, and he didn't like what he saw, there was something going on between them, he could sense it. Maybe they didn't recognize it, but he did, and now he had something new to worry about.

Stephen must never marry again and have another heir, which would ruin all his plans. Carefully hiding his thoughts, he continued, "and I'm going to run over and pick her up. . ."

But he never got to finish his sentence because the door to the study opened and Alison stood there.

Everyone else in the room was forgotten as Stephen opened his arms to his daughter and she ran to drop to her knees in front of his wheelchair.

"Dad," tears streamed down her face as she laid her head on his knee. "I didn't realize that you were this ill, you never let on," her voice broke, "I would have come sooner."

"Don't be silly," Stephen reached up and gently pushed a strand of hair away from her face, "That stupid surgeon insists that I need rest, and he found me this nurse," he glanced up at the woman standing behind him, "Alison meet Samantha O'Meara the nurse from hell."

Shocked, this was so unlike her father that she choked out the words, "Dad," her soft voice held a bit of censure, and she glanced up at the woman standing behind her father's wheelchair... "I'm sorry, I'm sure he didn't mean it."

"Of course he did." Sam grinned at Stephen's daughter.

The woman standing behind her father was beautiful. She wore a white pants suit and the soft top molded itself around a slender torso. But it was her hair that fascinated Whisper. It was a fiery red with chestnut highlights, and Whisper felt as if she reached out and touched it she would be able to feel its warmth. Deep green eyes were laughing at the expression on Whisper's face.

As Sam extended her hand, Whisper had just a moment to study her before she clasped it and even though she had never met this woman before, Alison's had a feeling there was more to this woman than she was letting on.

As she held Alison's hand, Sam's gaze kept sweeping back to Stephen, and with a woman's intuition Whisper realized that Sam was in love with her father.

"She's perfect for him." and as she rose to her feet the sweet fragrance of gardenias gently surrounded her. Mama approves too, she thought.

Carefully watching the women and trying to gauge their reaction to each other, Edward was not reassured by their quick acceptance of each other. Sam was a thorn in his side and he certainly didn't want any alliance forming between these two.

"Well, you've greeted everyone else; don't you have a kiss hello for me?"

Edward took a step toward her and Alison felt a cold chill passed through her at his words. Only sheer will kept her from bolting from the room as Edward placed a cool kiss on her cheek.

Fighting to be sure that her voice betrayed none of her apprehension, she smiled "Of course, how are you Edward?"

Ignoring her question Edward's voice was cold, "Tell me cousin are you back because you care about what happens to your father, or simply here to see what you'll inherit?"

Malice dripped from his words and as soon as he said them, he realized that he had made a huge mistake.

"Edward," the name was spoken in unison from father and daughter, and even Sam looked shocked.

"Sorry," he mumbled, "I don't know where that came from."

He hesitated as he looked into Stephen's face and saw raw anger reflected there.

"I'm just worried about you and I guess I resent the fact that she hasn't been here . . .while mother and I...", then recognizing that with each word he was alienating Stephen further – he stopped.

"I think I should run and get mother she'll be anxious to get here."

Pushing by Whisper he muttered, "You and I must get together soon -and talk."

Sam's eyes followed him as he left, then she glanced down at Stephen and could see red splotches appearing on his neck and face. "Stephen," she said, touching his shoulder, "Let it go."

"That miserable little son of a bitch," Stephen exploded. "What the hell has happened to him he was a decent little kid, then one day he turned into this obnoxious little bastard. If he is resentful because he was adopted by my sister, it is time he got over it I told his mother that she should," suddenly he stopped, and glancing at the two women he hesitated, "Well that's water over the bridge."

"But that's what Momma and Edward were fighting about – the day that she fell."

"WHAT? Edward was here that day?" Stephen's eyes narrowed as he stared at his daughter.

Slowly Whisper sank into a chair- "I think so – but I don't know – did I dream it? I just can't tell, everything gets so mixed up, sometimes I think I remember, and then I don't."

"You think they were discussing Edward's adoption?"

"I can't be sure but I think they were arguing about his family, and who his father is. Dad do you know?"

Stephen shook his head, "I've said too much already", he paused, "it's out of my hands, I tried to fix it long ago."

"You son of a bitch, you never tried to fix anything."

Three head swung toward the doorway and stared. Edward stood there, fists curled with anger and hate radiating from him,

"All these years you knew who my father was, and yet you never would acknowledge it."

"What the hell are you talking about?"

Edward strode into the room and stood towering over Stephen, "If you weren't in that chair you and I would deal with your deceit."

At Sam's gasp, Stephen began to rise from the chair only to feel her hand pressing him back. His face was pale, sweat beading on his brow. "Don't let that stop you!"

Sam's her voice as sharp as one of the ancestral swords that hung in the hall as she snarled at Edward.

"You obnoxious little bastard, with your nasty attitude you don't even belong here, now get out before you upset your uncle anymore."

Edward took a step forward his fists clenched, "You, a servant, are ordering me out of my family's home?"

"No, but I am!"

Shaking off Sam's hand Stephen stood, his face white with the effort and his hand shaking as he pointed to the door. "I don't know what the hell has gotten into you - now as Sam said, get out."

Grabbing the keys that he had forgotten off the desk, Edward stalked from the room, but not before he reached out and pushed Sam out of his way.

Moving to the desk Sam grabbed a pitcher of water that was there and forced two pills into Stephen's hand. "Take these. Where the hell did you get him from? He and his mother must be a throwback to some barbaric ancestor."

"You probably hit a nerve when you called him a bastard – because he is."

"What?"

But it was Whisper that answered her. "My aunt adopted him, but it is a well-known fact that his mother died giving birth and that his father is someone in the village. I remember the servants talking to mother about it.

Stephen frowned "I've heard those rumors for years, and I think Charlotte knows who he is, but she won't tell me. She'll only tell me that he was a prominent married man, and that Edward's mother was her friend, with no family and no money, and that she adopted Edward to help her out."

"And you believe her?" Sam shook her head.

"Of course I believe her, why wouldn't I?"

Her voice softened, and she looked at Stephen with disbelief. "Oh for god's sake Stephen, open your eyes."

"What do you mean?"

"Nothing. I've said enough." She shrugged. "Come on, you and your daughter can talk later," her eyes met Whispers.

"This whole thing has been too much of a strain on you and you're going to lie down before dinner."

"Suppose I don't want to?"

"Well that would be just too bad."

"Have I told you lately that you're fired?"

"Yes, three times this morning and twice last night."

"O.K., then I don't have to tell you again." Suddenly, he put his hand on the wheel of the wheelchair effectively stopping it and looked up at her with a challenge in his eyes. "Maybe Edward is right, maybe I should marry you."

"Yeah and maybe pigs can fly."

She swung the wheelchair around and headed for the double doors. "Though maybe you're right, I should marry you; that way I could concentrate on making sure that your head doesn't swell up so much that it can't fit through these doors."

She smiled at Whisper, "Want to come? I'm going to put this cantankerous old man to bed. Maybe between us we can tuck him in so tight he won't be able to move for a couple of hours – then you and I can talk."

Stephen laughed as she pushed him out into the corridor, none of them aware of the sweet scent of gardenias drifting through the room.

CHAPTER FOURTEEN

Edward slammed the door of his MG and glanced at his watch. Leaning over he placed his head against the cool roof of the little car.

He needed to calm himself before he confronted his mother.

Many times in the past this little car had been his salvation, when things went wrong in his life, he brought this vintage auto out from where it was stored, and when he slipped behind its wheel he felt as if he became another person.

But not tonight; tonight it had been all he could do not to drive it straight into a tree. How could he have been so stupid?

He'd lost it, and all the hate, the rage that had been bubbling in him for so long had just surged to the surface, and then, -- and then the bastard had sat there in his wheelchair and pretended he didn't know what he was talking about.

He pushed himself away from the car.

He couldn't believe he'd been ordered out of Stephen's home by that bitch, and then having Stephen defend her.

He paused, his eyes narrowing, there was something about her – he had a friend, a very discreet friend who would do some checking. She didn't act like any of the nurses he knew, always flipping that red hair of hers and talking to Stephen as if she were his equal . . . and to have Stephen snap at him and take her side; he felt sick.

This whole thing was spiraling out of his control.

He rubbed his temple, how was he going to explain his outburst to his mother? She would be furious. There were times when he admired her icy control but there were times when he damned it. Thank God it was Stephen's blood running through his veins and not hers. He could never live up to her expectations.

Rubbing his head, he realized he needed a reason for his outburst, something plausible that she would buy. She was no fool, and somehow she had always had an uncanny instinct where he was concerned.

Suddenly it occurred to him, he could blame his outburst on the stress of worrying about Stephen's health. She knew he loved Stephen, and worry made people do stupid things, yet why he had called Stephen deceitful was going to be a little harder.

A throbbing headache suddenly materialized and he reached into his pocket and popped one of the tiny pills he now carried. One thing he was sure of, he couldn't let this setback change his plans. He needed to see Alison alone. He wanted to watch her eyes when he talked to her. Until then, not knowing if she remembered what happened the day Alise died would drive him crazy.

He'd spent many sleepless nights wondering if she could remember anything about that day.

In his own mind there were times when everything was crystal clear and other times everything was hazy.

He shivered, he could still hear Alise's screams as she fell, and then the screams of the child. He had stood there with his hand out...had he pushed her? He knew they had been quarreling. But he just couldn't remember. In some ways he hoped Alison remembered and in others he dreaded it, what would he do if she told him he was a murderer?

Taking deep breaths, he tried to calm himself. He was becoming hysterical for nothing, after all she had been only five, what could she know?

Yet there was the possibility that Alison did remember, maybe in her child's eye she could see things he couldn't. He couldn't risk it; everything he dreamed about was at stake here. All he wanted was his heritage, to live in that grand house, to be referred to as Lord Alexander, not Edward Alexander, Charlotte's adopted bastard son.

He didn't need or want Stephen's money, and if there was some way that he could force Stephen to acknowledge him as his heir, Alison could have it all.

His dream was to have Stephen admit he was his son and heir, and then all the mocking and slights he had suffered over the years would be atoned for. Many of his friends would be shocked when they discovered that his title and ancestry was much more prestigious than theirs, and he would be gracious about it, pretending their past slurs never mattered.

He frowned, but Stephen would never acknowledge him while Alison was alive. So that must be remedied. Besides now that he had seen her, and realized how beautiful she was, there was the added danger that she would marry and produce a son.

Then Stephen would never acknowledge him.

Striding up the walk he barely hesitated as the door opened before him and he stormed through it, barely nodding at the servant who had rushed to unlock it. He began to shout his mother's name and Charlotte opened the door to the library, the book she had been reading still clutched in her hand.

"For heaven's sake Edward stop shouting you'll wake the dead."

Edward hesitated, and then he smiled, how appropriate, maybe waking the dead wasn't such a bad idea than maybe he'd be able to sleep at night.

Seeing the questioning look on his mother's face he realized that he'd better enlist her help if he wanted to get back into Stephen's good graces. They might have their differences, but Stephen and Charlotte loved each other and she could still twist him around her finger.

"Mother, I need to talk to you there has been an incident."

"An accident?"

"No, an incident!"

Glancing at the servant who was still standing in the entryway, she motioned with her head for Edward to accompany her into the library and firmly shut the door behind her.

"Calm down, whatever this incident is, it is can be taken care of." She reached up and gently touched his face.

"I'm sure that whatever is bothering you can be fixed." She smoothed the hair away from his forehead as if he were a child again and for some reason, he felt comforted. It wasn't often that she touched him, she had never been a demonstrative mother, and he had often wondered if it was because of her own parents. He could never remember his grandmother or grandfather ever touching Stephen or Charlotte and he often wondered if the reason Stephen had been so crazy about Alise was because of her warmth and affection.

His mother was a tough person to love. Her attractive exterior hid a very unhappy woman, and when Charlotte was unhappy those around her were too. Servants quit because of her sharp tongue and although he didn't consider himself a skilled diplomat it had become his job to keep peace in the household.

When they had left the main house after Stephen married Alise, he had quickly realized that the smooth-running household that he left didn't just happen. Alise treated her servants as friends and could be found sitting in the kitchen laughing and gossiping with them. His mother didn't feel the same, and over the years it had fallen to him to keep peace. He quickly realized that a little more money would smooth even the most ruffled feathers and his servants were paid handsomely for putting up with his mother's moods.

His mother's words interrupted his musings, "Would you like a drink?"

Moving toward a wine cart she selected a glass and poured

him a glass of wine and handed it to him. "Now tell me what's going on."

Throwing himself into a chair, Edward stared into the ruby red brew, then began. "Stephen's nurse threw me out of the house."

"She what?" Edward could actually see his mother stiffen and then slipping into a chair across from her son, her eyes narrowed as she waited for him to continue.

"What do you mean she threw you out? Tell me what happened . . . and what did Stephen have to say about this?"

"Nothing," Edward stared into his glass, "because he sided with her."

Sitting across from her son, Charlotte studied him. When he was upset, she could see his father in him, they both reacted the same way when angered, instead of shouting their voices became quieter, and more deadly. Edward's father had only lost his temper with her once, and that was the day she'd demanded he divorce his wife and marry her. Maybe if he knew how frightened she was he would have reacted differently. But when he refused, she had lashed out at him and told him she would never acknowledge him as her child's father.

He had stormed across the room and grabbed her by the shoulders and shook her. Only later did she realize that he was trying to make her understand that he couldn't leave Elizabeth while she was dying.

But she had been young and afraid.

She didn't have the kind of parents that you could go to and say I'm pregnant. They would have insisted that she give up her baby, and she would have found herself in some unwed mothers' home in Switzerland. She couldn't risk having her baby whisked away from her as soon as he was born and adopted by some wealthy family, and there was no doubt in her mind that her father would have arranged it. No, they could never know, and thank god for her Aunt Frances. She had understood and helped her.

But the threat to Edward's father had not been an idle one. Carefully she had covered her tracks after Edward's birth, and the original birth certificate in France named her as Edward's mother, and her lover as his father. It was hidden in a safe deposit box and only upon her death would Edward discover who his father was.

Her will stipulated that after her death, he was to be told where he could find the deposit box that housed the original birth certificate.

She had paid a lot of money for the fictitious one, the mother listed under a false name and the father simply listed as unknown. Not even Stephen knew the whole story. Although sometimes she had the eerie feeling that he surmised more than he let on.

She had spent the year with her aunt, her mother's sister, and since the two sisters had had a falling out years ago over Frances' life style, Frances had been only too happy to help her out.

Her parents had died not knowing that Edward was their true grandchild, and although there were times she regretted not telling them; at the time it had seemed to be the best and only way. Her Aunt Frances was the only one who knew the truth about the birth of her baby, but even she didn't know the name of the father. Now she had lived with this lie so long she didn't believe that that she would ever have the nerve to confess it to her son.

"Edward," she sighed, "You're leaving out something, now tell me the whole story."

"I overheard some bits of conversation and in the heat of the moment," he stood and began to pace, "I called Stephen deceitful."

Incredulous Charlotte surged to her feet. "You did what? You called Stephen deceitful? My god Edward whatever possessed you to do a thing like that? Your uncle has always been so good to you." There was dismay in her voice.

"I overheard him talking about my father and I lost my

temper." Throwing the wine glass into the fireplace, he went and stood looking out into the dark.

Carefully fighting a sense of panic Charlotte went to her son.

"Your father? What did Stephen say about your father?" Grasping his arm, she turned him toward her, and Edward was shocked to see there was no color in his mother's face.

This was a most unusual reaction from his cool and contained mother, so Edward probed, "Stephen said he didn't know who my father is, but I think he's lying. Who is he mother? And what is the name of this mythical friend of yours that was my mother? Names, mother, tonight I want names."

Up until now he'd never had the nerve to really press the issue, since every time he brought it up his mother had frozen, yet maybe tonight his confrontation with Stephen would force his mother to finally shed some light on the past and the lie that had affected his life so deeply. Now she would tell him the truth and together they would confront Stephen.

Charlotte hesitated; and although she knew she was guilty of the sin of omission, she had never lied to him. "I can't tell you."

Rage surged through him, and Edward grabbed his mother's arms and he shook her as his eyes flashed "You will tell me, I have the right to know."

But for once Charlotte did not acquiescence to her son's demands. "When I die, you'll know and not before that."

His eyes glittering with fury Edward's hands tightened, "Well, Mother maybe that can be arranged."

With a gasp, Charlotte tore herself from her son's grasp and with a surge of strength fueled by anger, slapped him with a force that sent him stumbling backward.

"Don't ever threaten me again; ever do you hear me?" Fury flushed her face. "I have told you all I intend to, now get out of my way and let me call Stephen." Her voice was icy, and she hissed the words at her son.

"We will have dinner with my brother tonight and you will

accompany me, and you will be contrite and humble, and beg his forgiveness – do I make myself clear?"

Edward stared at her; this person was someone he didn't recognize. The woman that he could so easily manipulate was gone, replaced by one that actually frightened him.

"Now go put some ice on that cheek, and get ready to leave while I make peace with my brother."

Edward hesitated, but his mother snapped, "Do it!" as she picked up the phone.

Stephen had rested all he intended to; it had been useless anyway. The words that Edward had thrown at him kept circling around in his head. What the hell did he mean by deceitful? Obviously, he had done something in the past that had affected his nephew, but he didn't have the foggiest idea what the hell it was.

The more he lay thinking about it the more anxious he became, he needed to straighten out any misunderstanding with the boy before he went in for his surgery. If something happened to him, he didn't want to go to his grave with this rift in the family.

Realizing that sleep was impossible he called Sam to help him dress, and within a few minutes they entered the library to find Whisper sitting in a chair staring out of one of the many windows that lined the wall.

"I had forgotten how beautiful it is here."

The flickering light from the logs that burned cheerily in the fireplace gave the room a radiance that seemed to surround his daughter. Motioning Sam into a chair, Stephen wheeled himself over behind the desk and leaning on his elbows stared at Alison. All he really wanted to do was to drink in the sight of her. It was like looking into the face of his wife again. They weren't identical, but still they were so much alike that it brought him comfort to look at her.

"Tell me about your trip." He already knew most of it since

Sean had contacted him as soon as she and Archie had driven away. But he wanted to hear her voice and he didn't want to discuss what had happened in this room a few hours earlier.

He watched her animation as she told him about the man she'd met on the plane, and her face had taken on a glow he had never seen before. Could he be losing his daughter already, when he had just gotten her back? He found himself glancing over and over again at Sam as if to discover what she was thinking.

Time flew by, as they covered many subjects and the anecdotes that she told about her cousins had he and Sam laughing. But he noted warily that she never mentioned any of her so-called accidents, or her gunshot wound. It was obvious that she wanted him to believe everything was wonderful in her life.

"Thank God," he thought that Sean and Luke had kept him apprised of everything going on, because this child of his seemed determined to keep him in the dark.

Watching her he noted that she favored one shoulder and her arm where he was sure the bullet had entered. But if she wanted to play the game, he intended to let her go on thinking she was fooling him.

He and Sean had agreed on their last phone conversation that if she didn't volunteer anything about what had happened, it was because she didn't want to worry him, and he was to go on as if he didn't know about the attempts on her life.

Now it was getting harder and harder not to confront her but he couldn't risk it. She would want to know what he knew, and how.

Luke had told him she had sworn him to secrecy so he had to be careful and not let on how much he knew.

She was pretty smart this daughter of his, and it wouldn't be long before she put two and two together and lord only knew how she would react to Sean's part in the whole thing.

The door opened and Anna poked her head in. "Dinner is

served" she sniffed "And she's here so you better hurry, you know how she gets when dinner is cold."

Shocked, both women stared at Stephen.

His glance shifting from one to the other, he spoke, "I know you're probably not happy about this, but Charlotte called a little while ago, and Edward is ashamed of the way he acted, and he wants to make amends so the two of them will be joining us tonight."

At the look of disbelief on their faces he continued. "And I think that all of us having dinner together is a very good idea."

He wheeled himself away from the desk and speared the women with a no-nonsense look. "We're all going to go on as if nothing unusual happened. Charlotte was really upset when she called and I could hear the tears in her voice. My sister doesn't cry easily so to be that upset is unusual for her. Dinner will be pleasant – don't you agree?"

Stephen's eyes narrowed as he caught the look that passed between the two women, and he didn't move the chair until the two of them nodded in agreement.

Dinner itself was uneventful, and even though Charlotte frowned when she saw that Sam was seated on one side of Stephen and Whisper on the other, she never uttered a word.

As Anna served coffee Stephen smiled at her, and in a quiet voice said, "That will be all Anna, please close the doors on your way out. We won't need anything else this evening."

Nodding Anna left the room and pulled the doors firmly shut behind her.

Waiting till this had been accomplished Stephen leaned backward in his chair and stared at Edward.

"I think it is in the best interest of this family if you and I clear the air. I have a few questions to ask you, and then it will be your turn and you can tell me why you believe I am 'deceitful."

He paused, his eyes piercing, "Now why don't you tell me where you were the day my wife had her accident."

"What?" only it wasn't Edward voice that responded it was Charlotte's. "What do you mean where was he? Where was he supposed to be?"

Stephen turned to his sister; his voice cool. "I'm asking Edward. Alison believes he may have been in this house that day, and I'm simply asking if he was."

"No, you're not," Charlotte's voice rose another notch, and she stared at her brother, "You're implying he knows something about Alise's death. Do you think I'm stupid?"

"Calm down Charlotte, I'm not implying anything; if he was here, he might be able to shed some light on what happened, that's all."

"Well," venom dripped from her voice as she glared at Whisper, "I find it rather interesting that after all these years your daughter suddenly remembers that Edward might have been with them the day your wife died."

She glared at her brother as she continued, "Really Stephen I'm amazed at you. Rather convenient don't you think? You're facing major surgery and all of a sudden she thinks Edward was there. What a despicable trick!"

She surged to her feet, the chair she was sitting in tumbling backward from the force of her movement as she pushed herself away from the table.

Her gaze icy she turned toward Whisper. "Of course, even as a child you did have a tendency to be rather dramatic and I suppose you thought that your father was paying too much attention to my son."

Her voice dripped with sarcasm as she continued, "Tell me dear are you worried that he'll leave some of his money to Edward? You needn't be concerned; Edward will be quite well off if something should happen to me."

She stared at Whisper, "Of course, I might remind you that my son has been here for his uncle all along, while you have been hiding out in the states."

She turned to face Stephen, "As for where Edward was on that day – he was with me – we had done some shopping and we were just returning when we got the news."

She turned to her son, "Isn't that right Edward?"

He stood, his eyes not meeting Whispers, "Of course it is Mother, but you should remember she was just a little girl and sometimes children get things mixed up."

Stephen's voice was cold as he glared at his sister, "There is no reason to attack Alison, I'm the one who asked the question, and I'm sorry if you're offended," his gaze sought Charlotte's.

"But rest assured if Edward was here that day, and he can shed some light on my wife's death, I will leave no stone unturned until I discover the truth. I believe my daughter, and if she remembers anything else, I will be in touch."

Wheeling on Whisper, Charlotte's voice was malevolent, "Home one day and you've already managed to alienate my brother from his family. If that was your intention you have succeeded beyond your wildest dreams. I should have known you'd be just like your mother and prepared myself for this."

As his mother stormed from the room Edward gave an apologetic glance to the people at the table and then quickly followed her out.

The soft sound of someone clapping had Stephen and Whisper turning to stare at Sam.

"Your sister missed her calling; she should be on the stage." Sam picked up her wine glass and took a sip before she continued, and her voice had a smile in it.

"You never did get your answer, did you?"

"What are you talking about?" Stephen growled.

"Why the way she neatly turned the tables on you, I never heard Edwards answer, did you?"

Stephen thought for a moment. "No, no I didn't."

"No, and you never will, Mama is going to keep her little boy away from here till this whole thing blows over. She knows darn well that your operation is scheduled for next week, and you're both going to have other things on your mind, yup a mighty smart lady."

She lifted her wine glass and saluted the doorway that Charlotte had just stormed through. "To our resident mama bear, who will protect her cub, no matter what."

The sound of Stephen's voice interrupted her before she could say anymore, and he had assumed an autocratic tone that both women found amusing. "Edward will tell me; I will order him to tell me."

"And if not off with his head," Whisper looked over at Sam and the two women burst out laughing.

For a moment Stephen looked stunned and then he began to chuckle too. "I guess I did sound a little pompous."

"Dad," Whisper said, and she jumped up and leaned over his shoulder hugging him, "That's what makes you – you, a little pompous, a little arrogant, and completely loveable."

"Oh, I don't know about that," Sam interrupted, "Pompous yes, arrogant yes, – but loveable – I'm just not sure about that."

Looking up into his daughter's eyes Stephen recognized the fatigue that shadowed her eyes and knowing that she would not leave the table till he did, he signaled to Sam.

Sam rose and moving impulsively to Whisper gave her a quick hug, then stepping behind Stephen's chair told him, "It's time, your highness, you've got pills to take and you're going to need all of your strength in just a few days and rest is important."

Reaching out he took Whisper's hand. "Come sweetheart, walk with me, I want to reassure myself that you are really here before I go to bed."

Whisper turned to Sam, "Would you like me to push the wheelchair?"

"Oh, we don't have to push it, he maneuvers quite well, he just makes me push when he's angry, or he's decided to act like a brat." She grinned at Whisper, "But go ahead I know he'll let you."

Glaring at Sam, Stephen's voice was crisp, "Will you two stop talking as if I have suddenly become deaf? I am perfectly capable of wheeling this damn thing myself and the first thing I am going to do when I am out of this chair..." "Well," he said, looking directly at Sam, "you'll just have to wait and see...."

"Ooh I'm scared" Sam laughed, causing Stephen's frown to change to a grin and Whisper to giggle.

"The only thing I'll hear for the next hour is how abused he is." But she winked at Whisper as she said it.

"I heard that" Stephen said, "You're fired"

"Again? Wow you just broke the record, that's five times today, let's try for six, shall we?"

Whisper shook her head; this was the most animated she had seen her father in years. This sassy nurse was good for him, and that made her happy. Tomorrow she'd have to tell him that she didn't want to inherit this estate, but not tonight, he needed his rest and so did she.

She knew her decision was probably going to hurt him, but she needed to make him understand that her heart and home were in the States. She just didn't belong here, and although she loved her father she wanted to return to her business, her cousins and maybe even a new man in her life.

Besides Charlotte was right, Edward had been here for her father all these years, and he was the one who deserved to inherit the estate, and somehow she knew he would do a good job of caring for it.

After kissing her father good night, she left him to the ministration of Sam who was chiding him about taking his pills.

As she started toward her room the fragrance of gardenias softly surrounded her. "I love you Mom," she whispered. "Thank you for letting me know you're here, and please take care of Dad, he's going to need you."

A soft breeze touched her brow and she smiled, and entering her bedroom she could almost taste the sweet fragrance of southern gardenias on her lips.

Edward helped his mother into the passenger seat of the car and then slid behind the wheel – and waited for the storm that he knew was about to erupt. He glanced over at her, but Charlotte seemed unaware of him and sat quietly staring ahead.

"Mother."

"Be quiet Edward and let me think."

In a few moments she sighed and turned to him. "You have created quite a mess. Now Stephen knows you were in the house the day Alise died."

"But you told him that I was with you."

"Do you think he believes me? Don't be foolish, he believes his daughter. If that girl told him the earth was flat, he'd believe her."

Edward's grip on the wheel tightened.

"I am going to have to make some changes in my plans because of your stupidity." She turned to him. "I want this estate to belong to you – I have always wanted this for you – but now that you've totally alienated my brother you've made it harder for me to reason with him."

Edward's voice was soft but even in the subtle light cast from one of the lights that shone into the car Charlotte could see his eyes glittering.

"The story you've told me is you adopted me to help out a friend, so you obviously know who my mother was, but what about my father? Years ago, I overheard you and Stephen talking and he was alive then – is he alive now?"

"I told you before your father doesn't matter at all, so stop badgering me. We have other things to worry about."

"I think I have a right to know, is Stephen my father?"

At Charlotte's gasp, Edward heart began to pound, maybe now he would get the answer he craved. Instead Charlotte's voice became cold. "Don't be absurd! Now start this car and let's go home."

"Mother, I need to know."

"Did you hear me? – I'm tired and I want to go home I need to think." She reached up rubbing her forehead, the diamonds she wore at her wrist glittering in the moonlight. Edward was startled to see that even in that pale light his mother was still a beautiful woman. He'd never thought of her that way, but she was. Time after time he had watched her brush men off and now he was beginning to wonder why.

Starting the car, Edward said, "You win tonight, but this conversation isn't over. Sooner or later I'm going to find out the whole story and then any decisions I make will be up to me."

"What decision? There is no decision. Think about what Alison can do to your life if she persists with this story that you were with them when Alise died. How do you think Stephen will feel if you tell him that that you spent every waking moment that you could with his wife? How do you think he will react when he finds out that his slut of a wife encouraged a teenage boy to leave his own home and spend day after day with her?"

"It wasn't like that!" Edward voice held barely contained fury. "She was warm and loving she was kind to me – never criticizing. She cared about me while all you cared about was nursing your own bitterness. Think about it mother, did you ever encourage me? When I told you I wanted to be an architect did you say it was a wonderful idea and when I got my degree were you there? No. Uncle Stephen was there even my future employer showed up - but not my own mother. Do you know how that hurt?"

"There were reasons."

"A reason good enough so that you didn't attend your own son's graduation?"

"I did attend. You just didn't see me; I even saw you laugh when you stumbled climbing the stairs to receive your degree."

"What?"

"Edward, take me home. I'm tired and this little car may be your pride and joy – but it is the most uncomfortable thing I've ever sat in. Besides I'm done talking."

"You still haven't answered my questions."

"And I don't intend to tonight, so we'll leave this discussion for another day –tomorrow is a big day for this family and I want to enjoy it."

Suddenly realizing how pale his mother had become Edward put the car in gear and its powerful engine shot forward.

"We're not done with this yet mother."

"I know." Everything Charlotte had ever hoped for was unraveling. She closed her eyes and leaned back against the seat praying that she would get home before the tears that were threatening to fall did.

CHAPTER FIFTEEN

S am stood on the balcony outside her room. Stephen had been restless tonight and two or three times she had gone quietly to check on him. She smiled as she recalled how he looked in bed. Sitting in that wheelchair gave him the illusion of being frail, but he wasn't. He was tall, slender, his hair dark, and as far as she was concerned with just the right amount of gray around his temples. His arms were strong and as she worked with him, she couldn't help but notice that the muscles on them were tight and firm. He was handsome but not in the conventional sense. His nose was a little too long and he had frown lines between his eyes, but who wouldn't Sam thought, with the dragon-lady and her son for relatives.

How Sean persuaded Stephen's doctor to go along with ordering a nurse and a wheelchair for Stephen she would never know nor did she want to.

For a brief time, she had been married to an O'Brien, a distant cousin of Sean's, but Jim was always out looking for adventure. He'd met her when he had jumped from a moving car and broken his arm. Only later did she discover that he had been trying to get away from some jewel smugglers that he had turned into police. She had been working the late shift in the emergency room, and was in fact getting ready to go home when they rushed him in. He began his pursuit of her that very night. After a whirlwind courtship, two months later they were married.

It didn't take him long to leave again. Within a month after a particularly passionate night of lovemaking, she awoke to find a note on the pillow beside her. He had been hired by the leader in some remote area in Africa for a special assignment, and he would contact her when he got there.

That call never came. Instead of finding the poachers he had been hired to apprehend, he'd stepped on a snake that hadn't taken to it too kindly, and he had died before they could get him to the village for help.

Although they were not immediate relatives, when they heard about Jim's death, Nellie and Dennis sent Sean over to help her. Boy had she needed it.

His affairs were a mess, and surprise, surprise, there was another wife and two children he'd forgotten to mention. She was sure that if that snake hadn't gotten him first, she would have. She'd taken back her maiden name to eliminate any confusion, and then turned over the small house they'd bought to his wife, and also his insurance policy. That way there wouldn't be the confusion of two Mrs. O'Brien's. It wasn't much but it would keep a roof over their heads till Sarah, the children's mother, could get on her feet. Life is funny she thought, at the memorial service she and Sarah had sat for a long time and talked about Jim. They had both fallen for a fast talking, good looking Irishman with a sense of humor, and although he was a scoundrel, they both agreed they would miss him.

"O. K. Jim," she thought, "I'm sure you had the last laugh, I just hope there isn't another wife tucked away somewhere that I haven't found out about yet."

As she started back through the large sliding glass doors that led to her bedroom she hesitated. I'll check one more time she thought, Stephen had felt a little feverish to her earlier in the evening, but she had chalked it up to the excitement of his daughter coming home, and the confrontation with his sister and nephew.

She could just imagine how Stephen would react when he discovered that putting him into a wheelchair was just a ploy worked out between Sean and his doctor. He'd be roaring, still the virus he'd caught that damaged his heart valve was nothing to fool around with, and now he was facing major surgery to correct it. Maybe being confined to a wheelchair and having a nurse on hand made sense, especially since it got her into the house.

From the corner of her eye she caught a movement in the wooded area outside the house. Quietly sliding behind one of the pillars she watched as a figure furtively crossed the lawn and started toward the library doors.

"Ah," she thought, "someone who knows that door lock is broken." She stepped into the hall and waited. Her room was at the end, so anyone coming up the stairs would come into her view before they could see her.

She was astounded when she spied Edward slinking into view. He paused when he got to the stop of the stairs but she had stepped back into the doorway, out of sight. He carried nothing in his hands that she could see, but he made her nervous anyway. He reached out and quietly pushed open the door to Alison's room.

Slipping off her slippers she followed him, hanging back till he was in the room. Then sliding behind the door so she could see, she watched and waited.

He did nothing. He simply stood by the bed and watched her. The soft light from the hallway bathed her face, and her shallow breathing revealed that she had fallen into a deep sleep. Once he reached out with his hand as if to touch her, but then pulled it back, and simply stood staring at her until he turned and silently began to leave the room.

Sam waited till he had a few steps into the hall and then pretending to close the door to Stephen's room. "Edward" she said, and he started, then turned slowly to face her.

"Yes?"

"What are you doing here at this hour of the night?" Glancing down at her watch, "3:30 is a pretty early hour to go visiting."

Edwards eyes narrowed and his tone as he replied was dismissive "I'm not in the habit of explaining what I am doing to the hired help so if you will excuse me."

"Fine with me" Sam said, turning away, "You can explain it to Stephen in the morning."

"Wait."

Slowly Sam turned around, she didn't like the look on Edward's face as if he smelled something unpleasant, but she never let on she noticed.

"If you must know, I was worried about Alison and I came to reassure myself that she was all right. That little scene earlier was upsetting to all of us, so I decided to check on her."

"At 3:30 in the morning? Couldn't you have waited till daylight?"

"No. I couldn't sleep, and obviously you couldn't either," he suddenly realized that Sam was a very attractive woman. Her red hair was hanging loose around her shoulders, not pulled back in the severe bun she wore during the day, and even without makeup her skin was flawless. She was no youngster, but that only added to her allure. The only other woman he had loved had been older, and since then no young woman had appealed to him.

He only hoped that he didn't have to hurt her too. "Now does that satisfy your curiosity?"

"Yes," she smiled, "It does. So, we'll forget we ever saw each other tonight, all right?"

"Thank you...there is no need to have the whole household in an uproar because of my concern for my sis err... cousin."

"No need at all, so I'll just say goodnight," and turning Sam headed down the hall, her arm at her side and her elbow jutting backward. She didn't trust him, not one bit and if he made a move, she'd be ready!

Getting to the doorway of her room she glanced back, but

he was already gone and hastily she moved through her bedroom slipping onto the balcony and watching till he left the house and slid back into the trees. She stood for a few more minutes till she was sure he was gone, than pulled the cell phone out of her pocket and hit one number. Within seconds, Sean was on the phone.

"What's going on?"

"Good morning to you too boss."

"This had better not be a social call, what the hell time is it anyway?"

"Its 3:30 here and 10:30 in the states."

"Jesus, did you call to give me a G. D. international time check or do you have something intelligent to say. What the hell is going on?"

Laughing, Sam held the phone away from her ear, he might not have the polish of some of the men she knew, but he was the best boss she'd ever had. After the mess with Jim was straightened out, he had hired her, trained her, and she now headed up his British operation. He had singled her out for this assignment and she knew it must be important to him.

'What do you know about Edward?"

"Not much, only that he's her cousin why?"

"We need to find out more, I swear that tonight he was going to call Alison his sister, instead of his cousin."

"When tonight?"

"Oh," Sam said, "About five minutes ago when I caught him in Alison's room."

"What?" his roar threatened to shatter her ear drum and again Sam pulled the phone away from her head.

"He was in her room, but it was weird", she said thoughtfully, "he didn't do anything, didn't say anything, never touched her, just stood there looking at her. I tell you it was spooky. It was like he was seeing someone else."

"That's it? Just looking? Were you there the whole time? Is there anything else I should know?" One question rumbled on top of another and Sam hoped he would run out of breath soon so she could get a word in. Finally, he slowed and she sighed as she answered.

"Yes, I was there the whole time, and no that's it but can you have someone start on that right away, if she really is his sister, we should know it."

"Don't worry, by tomorrow night we'll know everything there is to know about Cousin Edward." Sean's tone was vehement.

"Thanks, and Sean, thank you for being so gracious about my waking you up, it really was appreciated," and with a laugh she hung up leaving him sputtering on the other end.

She was still laughing as she slipped into bed she really loved that man, not in a romantic way of course, he was like a member of her family and she would do anything for him, but it sure was great fun to set that Irish temper off.

What Sam didn't know, was that Sean was sitting on the bed in his room at the cottage a huge grin on his face. He loved sparring with Sam, sometimes he won, but mostly he lost, she had a quick wit, and an easy laugh, and she would zing him and then hang up, how the heck you were ever going to get the last word in, when there was nobody to hear it.

Dialing the phone, he hit conference and immediately two phones rang.

The background noise when Connor answered caused Sean to growl and Eric to shout. Connor couldn't hear the words, but he knew both of his brothers were yelling, so he disengaged himself from the woman who was sitting on his lap and stepped out of the bar and onto the sidewalk.

"Where the hell are you?"

"I am at a retirement party for a friend at the High Hat Club. My work day ended at 6:00 tonight so therefore I'm on my own time and I don't…"

"For the amount of money I pay you, you should be available whenever I need you."

"Enough," Eric roared. "I'm taking a double shift tonight and I don't need to be listening to you two bickering, I have to get some sleep. I've got a bunch of rookies on the street, and god knows what they'll get into."

"Sorry," both brothers spoke in unison

"O. K. that's better." Eric's voice softened, "Now would you mind telling us what's going on?"

"There are a couple of things I need done, Connor -I need you to call our branch office in the morning, find out everything you can about Charlotte and Edward. I want to know when he was adopted, where, and how Charlotte a single mother got him. Who his natural parents are where they live...I want anything and everything. Then call Luke, see if you can find out something from his side of the family, how well they know Charlotte, do Stephen and Charlotte have any relatives in the States? What does she feel about Whisper? Did Luke's side of the family know about the adoption, did Stephen's wife know anything she might have shared with her sister? I don't like what I feel in my gut, and if we're going to find out who wants Whisper killed, we're going to start right at home."

"Well, now that you mention it," Eric spoke softly, "R. W. and I were going to call you in the morning anyway....it seems that the money paying for a contract on Whisper didn't originate from the U.S. So far neither of us can find out where it originated from, but we've got a couple of snitches working on it."

"Jesus," Sean said, "We might have flown her right into the killer's hands."

"Yes, and no," Eric paused "All I know is the word on the street is that the hit man is still here in the states, why nobody knows, so whoever up-fronted the money may have to try to kill her himself."

"You think it's a man, not a woman that's after her?"

"Yes," both men spoke at once.

155

Eric answered. "How many women can tamper with an elevator or a car?"

Connor continued, "I agree. But what has me puzzled, if my sources are correct, this killer doesn't work cheap, but in this instance it's almost like he's doing a friend a favor. There was no bickering about money."

He paused, "At first that threw me, I thought it might be a woman because if a woman wants you dead, she wants you dead and the money be damned, but I can't see a woman getting palsy with a murderer, so palsy in fact he gives her a price break."

"Christ" Eric said "You talk about hiring a killer as if it were like buying a new car. A god damn price break from a killer?"

"From what I've learned this guy demands six figures to even consider a job, and he's doing this for a couple of thousand. What does that sound like to you?"

"Good point. Sounds like our killer is helping a friend out – now if we can just find the friend."

"Why don't we start by letting me get some sleep?" They could hear Eric's yawn. "When I go in I'll take one of the rookies out with me in plain clothes and hit the street and some of the bars and see what we can find, although whoever this guy is, nobody has ever seen him. He seems to delight in keeping everyone guessing."

"Call me as soon as you learn anything," Sean growled, than his voice softened, "and Connor, I'm sorry I made that crack about your pay I didn't mean it, I'm just going nuts here, and not being able to do anything and just sitting around is driving me crazy!"

"Well," Connor drawled, as long as you brought the subject up, I've been meaning to talk to you about a raise."

There was no answer, and the only sound both men heard was a dial tone.

"I'll be damned," Connor muttered, while half way across the world, with a grin on his face Sean reached to turn out the light.

"Thank you, Sam," he thought as he settled under the covers, "Just hanging up is a great technique and no one can say I'm not a quick learner."

CHAPTER SIXTEEN

The next morning Luke strolled into the office where Jay was hunched over at his desk studying a file.

Jay barely glanced up until Luke spoke.

"What are you studying so intently?"

"The Eppsone case, you know we're due in court this afternoon." He sat back and grinned, "Looks like this could be a winner for us, the guy not only stole from his company, and he also stole from his wife and her family. Know who they are?"

"Yes," said Luke.

"Well, I didn't. If I hadn't mentioned the name to my brother Eric, I would still be thinking he was just a small-time schmuck who didn't know better. But this guy must be nuts, he was messing with the big boys."

Jay grimaced, "I wouldn't want to be in his shoes when he gets to prison. Daddy is really upset that his little girl got hurt, and the bimbo the son-in-law was spending all the company money on has apparently skipped town!"

"Some people are just stupid, I guess. Well good luck with it."

Luke walked into his office and gathered up some of the papers from his desk as Jay jumped to his feet and followed him.

"Whoa, what the hell do you mean good luck with it? You're supposed to be doing the closing arguments."

By the grin on Luke's face Jay knew he was in trouble.

"Well it's going to be a little hard to present the closing arguments when I'll be on my way to Paris."

"Paris? Why the hell will you be in Paris?"

"Visiting a relative, well not my relative exactly, but Whisper's great Aunt Frances. It seems that Aunt Frances knows where all the family skeletons lie, and I am being sent to ferret them out."

"Though," he said, "I understand that she was quite a gal in her time so I'm kind of looking forward to it."

He opened his briefcase and stuffed a file into it, then looked over at Jay. "Last night about midnight I got a frantic call from my mother demanding that I get back home as soon as possible. Seems my parents had a late-night visit from your brother Eric, who had been sent to get some questions answered."

He frowned, "It sure seemed a little unusual to all of us since the questions Eric asked were all related to the Alexander side of the family, not our side, and they centered on Charlotte and Edward. So Eric showed up to interrogate us."

"Interrogate you?" Jay couldn't believe what he was hearing.

"Well there is no other word for it – When I arrived at the house Eric had already been there for an hour and neither of us left till three this morning."

He yawned, "Anyway I learned a lot from that visit, my parents knew a lot more than I thought. It seems years ago Aunt Frances had a falling out with her family, and she and her sister Judith never spoke again."

He laughed softly, "I believe her family even referred to Frances as a courtesan."

But she's about seventy now, and they tell me she's still a beauty, so I'm heading to Paris to do whatever is necessary to learn every secret that dear old Aunt Frances has squirreled away in her brain."

"And as far as Eric interrogating us," he grinned at Jay, "If he ever gets a law degree, we're hiring him, I never got such a grilling in my life, and god he went back to when Whisper and I were kids. He had my mother practically pulling out her hair he asked her so many questions, but she thinks that if anyone knows anything about Whisper's family history it will be Frances. So," he paused, "Before I knew it, I had agreed to visit dear old Aunt Frances in Paris, and see if she can shed any light on Edward's adoption."

"Edward's adoption? What the hell does her cousin's adoption have to do with anything?"

"I don't know, except it seems Edward and his mother showed up last night for dinner, there was a confrontation between Charlotte and Stephen, and later Edward paid a late-night visit to cousin, Whisper, while she was sleeping.

"He what?"

"That's the weird part, when confronted by Sam, he claimed he was just making sure she was all right. But Sam said when she challenged him, he slipped, and almost called Whisper his sister. Of course he caught himself, but whatever he said set the wheels in motion."

"So, I'm doing this case alone today?"

"You are, so don't blow it, we need the money."

"You're flying to Paris on a moment's notice to wine and dine some old lady, and you tell me we need the money?"

"That's right, I've got some plans for the future and . . ."

Jay quirked an eyebrow at him... "Does your plan for the future include my sister Colleen?"

Luke didn't answer just stood there grinning at him.

Realizing he wasn't going to get an answer, Jay continued, "You're crazy you know? If I had the money you inherited, I would be sitting on the Rivera drinking champagne with a beautiful blonde."

Luke raised an eyebrow, "Would you?"

"Naw," Jay said disgustedly, "I'd still be sitting here, studying this case and hoping I don't mess it up this afternoon, especially now that I know who Daddy is."

"Relax, he doesn't know you that well, he'll only have one kneecap broken."

"Hey, we're representing the company this guy ripped off remember? Not Daddy, why should he care if I mess up?"

"Maybe you didn't do your homework as well as you think you did. Who do you think owns the company?"

"Shit, I'm representing the mafia."

"No, you're representing all the little stockholders who have money invested in the company, and that's all. Daddy bought the company to make sure his little girl was well provided for. Only son-in-law decided he could have his cake and eat it too!"

Jay looked at Luke for a moment and seeing the twinkle in his eyes threw his head back and laughed.

"Thanks for the words of encouragement."

"Listen," Luke said, leaning over the desk, he placed his hand on Jay's shoulder. "You'll do just fine I e-mailed you the notes for the summation this morning ...very early this morning."

He gave him a little shove, "I'll call you tonight." and picking up his things he walked out.

The trip to Paris was uneventful and Luke used the time to study some of the notes he had taken last night while his mother was talking to Eric.

Stephen and Charlotte's mother Judith, and Frances were the only children of a very prominent English family, a family that had not only carried a title that went back for centuries but was extremely wealthy. Yet their offspring couldn't have been more different from one another. While Judith, the eldest daughter did all the things expected of her, including marrying the man her family chose, and settling down near her parents, Frances was involved in one scandal after another. When she was thirteen, she stole a horse from a neighbor because she believed he was abusing it and hid it so well her father had to buy the horse from his irate friend.

At eighteen she ran away with the married son of one of her parent's friends.

The fact that the husband and Frances had been in love since they were children didn't seem to matter, nor did the fact that he had been forced to marry a much older woman to save the family estate. The two of them slipped away to Paris and lived there for several years until he was killed in a boating accident. These circumstances were of no consequence to her parents, and shocked with all the scandals, they cut Frances out of their lives.

Following suit, Judith never visited or encouraged her children to associate with their aunt. But each of the children when they were old enough, sought her out and found her to be a warm and loving human being – a far cry from the stiff and unbending Judith.

After her lover died, Frances, an exceptionally beautiful woman, had modeled for a few months until an older man had fallen in love with her and taken her for his mistress. When he died several years later, he left the bulk of his estate to her and there had been a nasty court battle. His heirs had tried all sorts of schemes to discredit her, but the old gentleman had been shrewd and his will was ironclad, and the fact that he had left his children well off had worked in Frances' favor. Her picture had been all over the newspaper and before the ink was dry on the lawsuit another rich man had stepped forward and swept her off her feet.

From then on according to Luke's mother, she had a bevy of men who were only too happy to keep her in the lavish style to which she had become accustomed. There had been even one or two gay protectors, drawn by her vivaciousness, and her friendship, and had been more than willing to have the outside world believe that they kept her as a mistress, while in actuality her home was the perfect place for them to meet their lovers.

Over the years there had been some lovers that really cherished her, and she had lived with her last lover for fifteen years until he had a stroke and died. But Frances had been prudent, and when she had gotten too old to attract a protector, she simply began living off the wise investments she had made.

Listening to his mother last night, Luke realized that Frances was probably lonely. Going from being the toast of Paris, to sitting on the sidelines had to be tough and since he needed whatever information she had, and she needed a little fun in her life, it would be the perfect trade off.

When the plane landed, he was whisked through customs, found his hotel and prepared to set his plan in motion.

Calling the number his mother had given him, he prayed Frances had never changed it, and when a male voice answered he was relieved. Frances made a habit of never engaging a female to work for her, she had never liked competition and from what he understood didn't to this day.

"May I speak to Frances? Tell her it's Luke Noonan from the states."

He waited a few moments and then a soft voice came on the phone. "Luke? Darling, whatever are you doing in Paris?"

"Hi Frances, how are you?"

He waited patiently as she answered. Over the years she had kept in touch with his family sending holiday greetings and gifts and making an occasional phone call. The gifts Frances sent to Whisper for her birthday had always been unique, and some had caused his mother heart palpitations. She finally got used to the Great Dane puppy Whisper received for her seventh birthday, but she drew the line at the llama, for her tenth.

Just thinking about it made Luke grin, and his voice conveyed warmth which Frances immediately picked up on.

"I'm here on business and my mother wanted me to call and tell you she said hello."

"I always loved you mother, Annette and Alise were always so warm and kind to me," she sniffed, "Not like some of my other family members. Did you know the two of them used to visit me whenever they were in Paris?"

"My mother and Alise?" Luke sounded surprised.

"Yes, the three of us had such fun together."

"And," her voice dropped as if as if sharing a secret, "Just before her accident Alise called me and told me that she thought she was expecting, and that was before she even knew for sure. She was so excited and she swore me to secrecy."

She sighed, "What a shame that she had to die as she did, and so young, it broke my heart, but here I am rattling on. I've forgotten, why did you say you were calling me?"

"I'm calling for two reasons, one because my mother asked me to look you up," he paused hoping that was the right beginning, "and second because I would love to take you to dinner."

"Take me to dinner?" delight warmed her voice, then she paused "Perhaps you might like to dine here instead?" Her tone was gracious but Luke detected a little disappointment."

"What?" He let his voice convey just a little bit of horror... "I don't think so, it isn't every day that I get to take someone as beautiful and well-known as you to dinner. Why the stories my mother used to tell me..."

Luke waited, hoping he hadn't laid it on too thick and was relieved when he could practically hear her purr as she answered, "And they're all true. . ."

"How about I pick you up . . . around nine?" Glancing at his watch he had quickly calculated a time that he was sure would suit her. He hoped having a much younger man paying attention to her would make her mellow enough to tell him anything he wanted to know.

There was a pause, and then she laughed. "Yes, that will be fine, I'm looking forward to it," and he heard the click of the phone as she hung up.

He sat in his hotel room and chuckled, she never even asked if he needed directions, she just assumed that he would know where to find her.

He was willing to bet money that dear old Aunt Frances was

planning what she was going to wear, even as she was allowing him to persuade her to accompany him.

Well, he intended to knock her off her feet, and lifting the phone he ordered a huge bouquet of flowers to be delivered to her home, and then another call assured him of a limousine to take them to dine wherever her little heart desired.

Promptly at nine, the limousine pulled up in front of her lavish estate, and Luke bounded up the stairs, but before he could knock, a butler opened the door and escorted him in. Ushering him into the study, Luke wandered around for a few minutes and was surprised to see the book shelves filled with books he knew were antique and priceless. He was more surprised to see that the classics obviously were well read with pieces of paper marking special pages and passages. As he browsed, he realized that Frances was a very unusual woman intelligent, well read, and he was sure with an innate theatrical presence that knew how to build suspense. He bet she'd been doing that for years. But he was in no hurry, this was how the game was played, and he intended to win it.

Exactly fifteen minutes later, Frances threw open the doors to the study and glided in. He couldn't be sure she even took a step, she seemed to slide along the floor toward him. Luke was startled, she wasn't at all what he expected.

Her hair was a soft champagne color and her makeup understated. She had soft blue eye shadow on, but it was very subtle and obviously used to draw attention to her vivid violet eyes. Her dress was the same shade as her eyes, the material flowing around her, and he suddenly realized that her figure was very trim with a tiny waist. Boy, he thought admiringly, she must have really been something in her day.

Laying down the book he had in his hand, Luke moved forward and bending raised her hand and kissed it.

Frances stepped back and looked up at Luke her eyes twinkling. "Well" she said "Are you surprised or disappointed?"

At the look on Luke's face, she laughed, "I'm sure that you've heard that I am, how do you American's say it —a fallen woman, and I have to admit that I considered having a little fun with you." At the look on his face she threw back her head and laughed.

"Not that kind of fun, dear boy . . . your mother would skin me alive and it took me years to get back in her good graces after that llama fiasco."

"Well you have to admit having a llama in your front hall is a little disconcerting especially when it ..."

"I know, I know, perhaps it wasn't the best idea but I read about this petting zoo in the states and the idea of Alison having her own llama to pet appealed to me!"

She reached out and took his hand, "When I talked about having fun with you, I considered wearing an old Gloria Swanson outfit l had for a costume party. What a story that would have given you to tell back in the states, and then I said oh to hell with it – I'll just be me --- so here I am," she said.

Luke threw back his head and laughed, she was absolutely right, his mind had dredged up every stereotype of a fallen woman he had ever seen and not one of them looked anything like the charming woman standing in front of him.

On impulse he leaned down and gave the tiny woman a hug which she returned with a laugh, stepping back she fluttered her eyelids at him, and in an exaggerated purring voice, said, "Oh If I was only 20 years younger."

Which, Luke thought, would still make you about fifty, but he just smiled at her and said "Twenty years ago you could not have been any more beautiful than you are today," and suddenly he realized he meant it.

"Oh, you dear boy," but he caught her glancing at her watch, and he knew she was anxious to be off.

As he guided her into the limousine Luke realized that Frances hadn't even bothered with the pretense of asking him where he would like to go, she gave the driver an address, and twenty minutes later they were stopping in front of an older but obviously very elegant restaurant. Luke leaned forward and instructed the driver to return when he called. He had no intention of rushing this dinner, and he would stay all night if he had to.

As they entered the lavish dining area, he could feel many eyes on them, so he carefully placed his hand solicitously on France's back as they followed the maître'd to their table.

A hovering waiter reinforced Luke's opinion that this was no ordinary lady, and glancing around he realized that much of the conversation in the room had stopped. One pair of eyes in particular caught his attention, and he found himself staring into the cold eyes of an elderly gentleman sitting by himself at a corner table.

"I'm not going to be challenged to a duel am I Frances?" he whispered, indicating the man with a slight tilt of his head. "I left my pistols at home and I'm pretty rusty right now."

"Don't be silly," but she leaned over and ran her finger up the back of his hand as if she was telling him something intimate that she didn't want anyone else to hear.

"These Frenchmen are so jealous, and Francois and I had a fight...um...I mean a slight disagreement two weeks ago and now he is punishing me by not calling."

"But," she sat back and smiled intimately at Luke," I intend for him to sit there and watch, while I flirt and carry on with you."

Luke laughed, and shook his head. "Frances, you really are something!"

"I know, but I won't be here forever and I intend to enjoy every minute I have left, so," and she gave him a big smile, "as you Americans say, let's eat, drink, and be merry."

Luke signaled to the waiter and in just few minutes they had placed their orders and a bottle of chilled wine and some fruit and cheese had been set in front of them.

Frances waited until the waiter had finished filling their wine glasses and then with piercing blue eyes addressed Luke, "Now, dear boy, why don't you tell me what it is you really want, I may be old, but I'm not stupid. You didn't just drop out of the blue, for some reason you made this trip to Paris to talk to me . . . though I must admit those flowers were a nice touch," she leaned toward him pretending to look totally enamored while her voice hissed, "So let's have it."

Then leaning back, she threw a slight smile in the direction of her elderly admirer, while Luke tried not to spit his wine all over the table.

"Why do you think that?"

Well for starters, how old are you?"

"Thirty-one."

"Well dear, as the younger generation would say, that just doesn't compute. Although I am flattered that you wanted to spend the evening with me, I simply don't believe that you wanted to take me out because your mother suggested it."

Delicately she waved her hand around encompassing the room, "This is Paris after all a city filled with beautiful women, and to most men a phone call would have sufficed. No dear, there is more to this than you are telling me. Besides" and she smiled, "at my age I need a man who takes his glasses off when he gets into bed with me at night, definitely not one with keen eyesight."

Luke threw back his head and laughed, as Frances continued, dropping her voice intimately, "Do you see my friend over there, when he takes his glasses off, he's blind as a bat. And in his mind, I am still twenty years old and that," she grinned at him as she leaned back, "Is my kind of fellow."

Luke started laughing again, and he picked her hand up off the table and kissed it. "You dear lady" he said, "Are obviously too young for me."

As the waiter approached with their meals, Luke lowered his voice, "But you're right, I do need something from you, but now that you and I've met, we will do this again – and without any hidden agendas."

"Don't be silly dear boy, although I would love to see you again, and I hope I shall, that's what life is all about you use me to get whatever information you need, and I will use you to force that dreadful old man to the altar. After all I am too old to be traveling around with a Miss in front of my name. And he has enough money for us to go around the world at least twice, she grinned, "and maybe more."

"Is that what you want?"

"Absolutely."

Luke leaned across the table and gently kissed her. Her lips were soft and her breath sweet.

Sitting back, he grinned, and then laughed out loud when Frances whispered,

"Very nice dear but somehow lacking, after we are married, I will have Francois give you some hints on how to kiss, maturity does have its benefits you know."

Dinner passed pleasantly as they discussed far flung members of her family. Frances was really interested in how Stephen was doing, and she seemed to know more about what was going on in the family than Luke would have believed.

Finally, Luke found her looking at him speculatively and he knew it was time.

Lowering his voice, he worried that she would take offense at his questions and he was somewhat reluctant to end the evening on a sour note. But Whisper's life was at stake and if Sean thought these questions were important then damn it, he'd have to risk her anger. Quickly he brought her up to date on all the things that had happened to Whisper, eliciting a gasp from Frances when he told her about the shooting. Finally, he got around to the questions he needed answer to.

"What can you tell me about Edward's adoption?"

Frances frowned, "That's what this is all about? Edward's adoption? Lord, I would have thought that Charlotte would have straightened this whole mess out by now."

She eyed Luke speculatively, "There is no hidden motive behind these questions is there? My niece may be a little hard to take, but I don't want her hurt."

"No," he assured her and told her about Edward's visit to Whisper's room and his slip of the tongue.

There was no smile on her face as she listened and her eyes were narrowed. "I don't think Charlotte would be behind any attempts on Alison's life, she would have no reason to. She has inherited enough money from her my sister and her husband to last her through this lifetime and another, Lord knows her mother and father were tight enough."

She grinned, "You probably already guessed that my sister and I were never close. She never approved of my life style and lord knows I would have killed myself if I had to spend one week with her husband." She shivered.

Putting her coffee cup down she leaned forward," But Edward wasn't adopted, my dear, he is Charlotte's natural child."

The shock on Luke's face caused her to laugh. "You never expected that did you? I'll tell you what little I know, his father was a married man, from what Charlotte told me, a very prominent married man. His wife was very ill, they had married very young, one of those arranged marriages." Frances paused, "Stupid thing to arrange your child's marriage, they rarely work out you know, if you knew how many of my lovers," she hesitated, and then laughed, "well, never mind."

"Anyway, due to the wife's health, after the first year it became a marriage in name only. He and Charlotte had known each other forever it seems, and they were thrown together at parties, at races, and in clubs. Charlotte is an excellent horsewoman and he had an exemplary stable, so they traveled in the same circles. Before long they were seeking each other out and of course they fell in love. And, when you're young along with love comes lust. She sighed, "Thank god for me those days are over."

She grimaced, "and of course, foolish girl that she was, she got pregnant. He was all set to ask his wife for a divorce, when the doctor told him his wife was dying. Of course, with the English honor and all that, he wouldn't leave her, plus his wife's family begged him not to tell anyone how ill she was. So Charlotte never knew – all she knew she was pregnant and her lover refused to marry her.

He begged Charlotte not to do anything about the baby, Charlotte came to me crying, she was young, in love, and pregnant; and also very angry and bitter. She had no one else to turn to, Stephen was away in the military, she knew her parents would never understand or forgive her. Family name and all that. She took a chance coming here, because my sister Judith, never did approve of my life style. She told them that she was coming to France to study with a famous dress designer. How they ever bought that I'll never know," Frances shuddered, "Have you ever seen how that poor girl dresses?"

Luke tried not to laugh, the disdain in Frances voice cracking him up.

"Instead she stayed with me until the baby was born, and then she left. I hired a wet nurse and the baby seemed to thrive, then one day she returned. By then Edward was six months old. She told her family that one of her dear friends from Paris had passed on, and that she had to come and take that poor baby back with her. The fools bought it of course, if they took a real close look at Edward, they would have known he resembled her, but she was their daughter and I suppose they had no reason to be suspicious."

"And the father?"

"She never told me who he was, and to be honest I didn't care. It was a terrible lesson to learn, and I know she was extremely hurt by the whole thing. I did counsel her to tell Edward the truth when he was old enough, but I don't think she ever did. As a matter of fact, I am sure of it, because I haven't heard from her in years and I believe it is because I know her secret."

"Yet, you told me."

"Yes, I did, because I know you're really worried about Alison and now that I know the whole story so am I. When you called, I could sense something was going on, no one hops on a jet and flies to see some old lady unless there is a very good reason for it. I can't believe Charlotte or Edward is involved but," she hesitated, "I don't know Edward very well, just what I've heard through the so-called grapevine."

"We can't leave any stone unturned, as I told you after the attempts on Alison's life, we are checking everybody and everything out." Luke couldn't succeed in keeping the anxiety out of his voice.

"Well, if you find the father of Edward, he might know more about this whole thing than either of us. I told you he was a very prominent man and as I recall Charlotte told me later that his wife passed away around the same time Edward was born. But having a little more of Judith in her than I like, she never forgave him. Follow that trail and maybe you'll find some of the answers you're looking for." Frowning a little she seemed perplexed. "Though what Edward's birth has to do with any of this I don't know."

"Neither do I, but maybe what I have learned will help fill in some of the blanks."

He smiled and stood up motioning to the waiter to refill Frances' wine glass. "Will you excuse me for a minute?"

"Certainly."

And walking away he headed in the direction of his elderly rival.

"Follow me," he murmured as he passed the man's table. Stepping around a corner he waited and in a moment the man stood before him, anger radiating from him.

"Make your move," he told the old man, "or I'm taking her back to the states with me."

"Listen you gigolo, Frances is going nowhere with you."

"Well, old man, you make your move or I do. Take your choice."

"Why she's old enough to be your mother."

More like grandmother, Luke thought, but he wasn't going to back down now. "All right, you had your chance. See ya," and he started toward the men's room door.

"Wait, how do you know she will forgive me? We had a terrible row."

Reaching out Luke grasped the man's shoulder. "I thought you Frenchmen prided yourself on being great lovers, now if you don't think you can take her away from a nobody from the states," he shrugged. "Well, we'll see."

"Yes, we will," and with a strength that belied his appearance, the old man straightened up, turned and headed back to the dining room.

Luke stood in the hallway and waited ten minutes, grinning when he saw that he was returning to an empty table. Both Frances and her admirer were gone. The waiter hustled over, handed him his dinner bill and a note. The note said only two words, "Thank you!" But he laughed when he noted that the bill included not only their meals but that of his rival's, and two bottles of chilled champagne to go.

Luke counted out the cash and handed it to the waiter. But before he could leave, the waiter turned back to him a perplexed look on his face, "Oh, and she said to tell you," and he frowned as if it didn't make any sense. "You will get an invitation to the wedding."

Luke was still laughing as he started toward the door. He would see her again, he couldn't believe how much he had enjoyed this evening, and if the old girl did get her admirer to the altar, well damn it, he would be there. Tomorrow he decided he would arrange to send her another gigantic bouquet of flowers, maybe he'd send her one a day for the rest of the week, after all a faithful admirer just didn't give up that easily.

CHAPTER SEVENTEEN

Snapping his cell phone shut, Sean sat at the tiny table in his grandfather's cottage a cup of tea steaming in front of him. He lifted the cup to his lips grimacing as he took a sip. Today he was going to a get a cup of real coffee, god knows he needed it, not this warmed-over dishwater.

The phone call from Luke had certainly been interesting and enlightening. In addition to describing Frances in detail, and even admitting to being half in love with the old girl, Luke had told him that it was true. Frances had confirmed it, Charlotte was Edward's natural mother

He sat back staring out the window at the fields that surrounded the tiny cottage.

His own family was really close, loving each other, fighting for, and with each other and even intervening when they felt it was necessary. When his brother R.W's wife left him, he'd hit bottom, but the family had rallied together, gone to his apartment and dragged him home. They'd all known Leslie was the wrong woman for him, but he thought he was in love while the family recognized it as being in lust.

She used sex as a weapon against him and god knew she was sex personified, tall, and willowy, with pouting lips and a body to die for. Only they all recognized it as the shell it was, that is everyone but R.W. It was only after she was gone, he finally admitted she'd been addicted to drugs. It had taken some time, but now R.W. acknowledged that she'd never wanted to get clean, and her leaving was the best thing that ever happened to him.

Sean sat back and rubbed his forehead, somehow he just couldn't understand a family that kept secrets from each other, especially one that involved a baby. If Charlotte was Edward's mother, as Frances claimed, why hadn't she ever told her son the truth? After all Edward was no kid, and her parents were long gone, and after all these years what did she have to hide?

And who was Edward's father? Why hadn't he surfaced somewhere along the way- and damn it - did any of it matter?

Absently stirring the tea in front of him, he tried to make sense out of everything he knew. If any of this had a bearing on Whisper's so-called accidents, he was missing it. It sounded more like a plot from a soap opera than a reason to want to kill someone.

Sighing Sean glanced out the window. All of this inactivity was driving him crazy. He was dwelling on things that might have no bearing at all on the case. But then again, suppose they did? He couldn't shake the feeling that if he missed something, overlooked some slight clue, it might have devastating consequences.

A chill ran up his spine. At a time like this he really missed his brothers. He knew Eric and Jay were trying to find out something about the trigger-man but he wished they were here. A few good arguments, maybe even a couple of fists thrown and he'd feel better. A slight laugh escaped him that was what was wrong---it was just too damn quiet.

He smiled as a thought occurred to him, maybe he should fly his mother over here and set her loose in the village. In two days, she'd have all the answers. When Nellie started asking questions people just gave up information whether they wanted to or not, lord knows he and his brothers did.

Sean pulled out his cell, he'd warn Sam to be extra careful, and not to feel safe just because she was behind the walls in that house. He didn't like puzzles and this sure was turning into a giant one. If anyone in that family was behind the attempts on Whisper's life, they would be dangerous. Cornered rats were unpredictable.

But before he could call, Archie came bounding down the stairs whistling some tune that Sean didn't recognize, and he was quite sure that the composer wouldn't either.

Archie grinned as he spotted Sean, "I see you're having breakfast without me, I'm glad you decided to take advantage of my hospitality."

"Hospitality hell, I'll bet you used this tea bag for your own cup before you threw it into the pot for me."

Archie's eyes twinkled, as he denied Sean's accusation, yet it was obvious that he was enjoying himself.

"Where are you off to today, Yank?"

"I haven't got any plans. I'm waiting for a call from either Eric or Jay. When I talked to Jay yesterday, he told me that he has set up a meeting with the women on Whisper's staff hoping they might know something, and Eric's chasing down leads on the streets."

Deciding not to share Luke's phone conversation about Charlotte and Edward with Archie just yet, since it might not have any bearing on anything, and left alone Archie's snooping might uncover some nugget of information that would tie everything together, or better yet, even lead them in another direction.

"Now," Archie said lifting his head, and checking the mirror to see that his tie was neatly centered on his shirt. "If I were you, I'd wander down to the fairgrounds today, they're showing some mighty fine horses and I'm sure there will be a filly there you might be interested in."

Sean snorted, "I don't have time for that, I'm waiting for Eric or Jay to call, and watching horses jump over little hedges and fences would drive me crazy. When R. W. and I race at the reservation, it's always bareback on a stallion, not on some little pansy of a horse with its mane braided in ribbons."

"For shame, lad, you're turning into a Yankee snob, I know

your father takes you and your brother back to R.W.'s people every year, but there could be one little filly at this show you won't want to miss."

"Why what's so special about this one?"

"Well, it's a family tradition that at the Queen's cup, the opening ceremony is always led by an Alexander and if I don't miss my bet, Stephen will be there. His father and his grandfather, and lord knows how many more of those stubborn men opened this event, and I don't see him being the first to break with family tradition, no matter how sick he is. As a matter of fact, two horses from the estate will be pulling the carriage that he will be riding in. And I'm pretty sure that pretty daughter of his won't be letting her father out of her sight.

Heading for the door, Archie turned around and looked at Sean, "Are you cooking dinner tonight, or are you taking me out?"

Sean had taken a sip of his tea which he promptly choked on. "I thought meals went with this deal. You know bed, breakfast, meals. Lord knows I paid you enough."

"Tsk, tsk, all you Yankees think about is money. Is that my tea I see in front of you boy? Then that's breakfast. Anything else is up to you, but since I don't want you to be eating alone, being as you're my grandson and all, I thought you might like me to go to dinner with you, as your guest of course."

He glanced back as he pulled the cottage door open, "You better hurry it's not polite to be late to these things, the English take pride in being prompt you know."

He glanced down at his watch, "Glory be, I should be on my way to pick the family up right now," he frowned at Sean, "in the future I would appreciate you're cutting down on the chatter while I'm getting ready for work, I get paid by the hour you know." Then he grinned and closed the door.

A few seconds later the door opened again and Archie poked his head back in, "And don't leave the dirty cups in the sink boy, I like to keep the place tidy. . . and you've only got about a half hour to get there if you don't want to miss the opening ceremony."

A grin on his face, Archie closed the door, and the curses that left Sean's mouth were colorful and appropriate.

Emptying his cup, he looked down at the sink. Archie obviously had more than a cup of tea for breakfast, yet he expected him to clean up the mess. Laughing Sean realized that he was having more fun trying to keep one step ahead of his grandfather than he'd had in a long time.

Maybe later today he could find some willing woman in the village to come and clean this place, otherwise the old man would probably be expecting him to mop floors and wash windows.

He hurried back to the tiny room his grandfather called the guest room and fumbled in the closet for something to wear. He knew these things could be fairly formal for some people, but he'd be damned if he'd wear a suit. Reaching into the suitcase, he pulled out the only pair of dungarees he'd brought, luckily, he had thrown them into the suitcase at the last minute, and pulled out the flannel shirt that hung in the closet.

So, he'd look like a Yankee, well that's what he was, and if someone didn't like it, too bad!

CHAPTER EIGHTEEN

A s he pulled into the parking lot, he realized that his grandfather wasn't kidding, this was obviously a big deal.

The fairgrounds were littered with horse trailers the owner's colors proudly flying above them, grooms currying horses, others being paraded, and in the midst of the bedlam, people shouting good wishes to one another. It was obvious to Sean, as the horses strutted by, that these animals were well cared for and loved.

He stood wondering how to get to the main grandstand since people seemed to be leading their animals in every direction; then decided that it might be good to wander around for a few moments till he got his bearings.

He didn't realize, as he carefully looked over the crowd, that he was inviting a few stares himself.

It had nothing to do with the casual clothes he was wearing, which did earn him a few frowns, but more with his aura of total masculinity. His shirt was tailored to fit and hugged the muscles in his upper arms, and his legs were encased in fitted dungarees. With his dark hair and eyes, and the small scar on his upper lip he looked the epitome of a modern-day pirate. Many of the single women and a few of the married ones let their imaginations run wild and envisioned him in a scenario that gave rein to the type of lover they thought he would be.

None of them would have been disappointed.

He heard a trumpet blow and followed the sound, stepping up to a fence to admire the pomp of the opening ceremonies. He leaned against the rail as the judges arrived in open carriages and began to circle the field. The horses drawing the carriages were obviously the pride of every stable, and the horses seem to know it their heads held high, and an arrogance to their gait. The beauty of these animals drew admiring murmurs from the crowd and as each trotted onto the field the crowd cheered.

Leading the procession was Stephen, and Sean was pretty sure the woman handling the reins was his sister Charlotte. Sean was surprised to see how attractive she was. From listening to Luke and Archie he'd thought they were talking about a wizened old crone, instead there was something about this woman that many men would find attractive.

A few blond curls had escaped from the bun she had pulled tightly to the back of her head, and they softened the contour of her face. She had a slight build and as they circled nearby, he could see that her complexion was creamy. It was obvious from the way she looked at her brother that she loved him, and that feeling was reinforced when Sean saw her laugh at something he said and reach over to pat his hand.

"She's a street angel and a house devil", said a soft voice behind him.

Startled, Sean swung around, looking down in the laughing eyes of Whisper. She was wearing a riding habit that complimented her tiny waist, and the soft hues of gray and blue seemed to accent the blue of her eyes and the pink of her cheeks.

His chest tightened and he had to curb the impulse to pick her up and carry her away from the crowd to somewhere warm and dark.

She moved up closer to the fence looking out onto the field, where the carriages were circling. "I guess that wasn't very kind of me, was it? "She hesitated glancing over at Sean as she continued,

"But I remember when I was small that I always had the feeling she didn't like me."

"Why?" Sean probed.

"I don't know. Even now I have the feeling that she resents me," she shrugged, "I still don't know why, I haven't been around in years."

Sensing a hidden sadness in her, Sean leaned over, and with an exaggerated leer looked closely into her eyes. "But I like you enough for both of us," and he gave her his best impression of Groucho Marx, wiggling his eyebrows at her.

Whisper burst out laughing, causing several people to turn and stare at them. Lightly punching him on the arm, she said, "Follow me, I know the best place to watch the competition."

Walking behind her as they threaded their way through the crowd, Sean held his breath. If he kept looking at the trim little bottom walking ahead of him, he knew he might embarrass himself. This was no time for his body to assure him that it approved of his interest in this woman.

Trying to think about something else, and also being acutely aware of the danger she was in, he began to carefully study the people around them as they moved through the crowd. But there was no instinctive warning of eminent danger and when she reached back to take his hand and she inadvertently rubbed against the front of his dungarees Sean groaned.

Finally, she pulled open a gate leading up to a small building he hadn't noticed before. She pulled a key from her pocket and unlocked a side door and then led him up a narrow staircase. When they reached the top, he found himself in a small room encased in glass, with windows floor to ceiling on three sides. There were red velvet cushions on the seats, and a bar tucked into a corner.

"Wow" he said, "Somebody knows how to live."

"My father had this built so my mother wouldn't have to sit in the sun while she watched him compete."

She laughed, "You know, she was from the South, but for some reason she couldn't tolerate the sun, and my father couldn't tolerate her being uncomfortable, so he built this for her. She ran her hand over one of the velvet seats in the back row.

"She always sat here, she had a tendency to jump up when she was excited, and she didn't want to block anyone's view. She was that kind of a person."

"And right here was where I would sit," and she pointed to a seat next to her mother's where the cushion had been built up, so a child could see over the adults in front of her.

Sean could tell that she was very close to tears, and knew these memories although sweet, had to be painful to her.

Reaching down he picked her up into his arms, and sitting down in her mother's chair, he held her close as the tears finally came.

"Did she hold you like this?"

Whisper nodded, her bright hair tickling his chin. "Well," he said, "I bet she knows that someone is sitting in her chair, holding you right now, and she's happy about it."

"Why, you big old bear," Whisper's voice was like velvet caressing his skin. "You're a softie and I thought all of the O'Brien men were so tough."

Gently wiping away a tear that was slowly rolling down her cheek, Sean smiled as he answered her. "We are tough, except where our women are concerned. My mother," he grinned, "can turn my father inside out when she wants to, he lasts about one day when she gives him the silent treatment."

Absently he ran his finger across her cheek stopping just short of her mouth. "I remember one time, she kept asking him to put up shelves in the basement for things she needed to keep on hand, with a family our size she was always running out of stuff, but somehow he just never got around to it."

"So being the kind of woman she is," he grinned at her, "Irish women can be very tricky you know. She took things into her own hands. I'll never forget that day, when my father came home from work, she had already fed all of us kids, but there was nothing warming in the kitchen for him." He laughed, "When he asked her about dinner, she told him she had run out of the ingredients that she needed, and she had no intention of running to the store at that late hour. She suggested that he have some cereal since there was plenty of that."

Whisper laughed, "And then what?"

"Then she took my sister and went to visit a friend. I remember the exact time she returned, because all evening long my father kept asking us what time it was. Finally, about ten o'clock, she walked in, passed right by him, and went up to bed. The silence in our house was deafening. All of us boys crept around afraid to set him off; we knew his temper was simmering just below the surface."

"Why, would he hit you?"

Sean laughed, "Hit us, never! He would just holler, and believe me you haven't lived until you've heard Dennis O'Brien holler."

"Did she get her shelves?"

Sean grinned, "You know it! Lucky for us it was a Friday night and there was no school the next day, because at two o'clock in the morning all of us boys were routed out of bed to help my father build shelves."

"No way!"

"And the next morning," and he began to laugh, "my mother was up bright and early and when we came down for breakfast, there was pancakes, waffles, bacon and sausage, and my father wore a big grin on his face for the next week. To this day he takes visitors down to the cellar to see the great shelves he and his boys built."

"Does he tell them the whole story?"

"No, I don't even think he even remembers it, the last time I heard him talking about those damn shelves, they were his idea.

He claims he did it to save my mother running to the grocery store for staples."

Whisper looked up at him laughing. The tears in her eyes were still sparkling, and he thought he had never seen anyone as beautiful. Her nose was a little pink and there were track marks of tears on her cheeks, but she seemed to glow, and like a moth of the flame he bent to kiss her. Softly he touched his lips to hers, giving her time to back away if she wanted to.

He had been surprised when she had let him hold her, knowing that Luke had told him that even as a child she seemed to be leery of a man's touch, or maybe it was because she was cuddled across him like a child, whatever it was, he was determined not to frighten her, and all the moves were going to be hers.

But Whisper staggered him; she reached up cupping his head with her small hands and pulled him down, so that his kiss had to become more demanding. He held back, letting her take the lead. Sighing a little, she pulled him closer still, while she angled her mouth across his.

Oh my God, Sean thought, she's killing me! And he turned her until he could feel her breasts pressing against him.

He pushed his hands up into her hair, and then he pulled away long enough to run his tongue lightly over her soft lips. Rather than fight, or push him away, she opened her mouth ever so slightly and retaliated by running the tip of her tongue over his.

Luke, he thought, is going to kill me and I don't care this woman belongs to me and no one is going to hurt her in any way.

The sound of muted voices startled them both and Whisper moved as if to stand.

But Sean's arms tightened around her as he whispered, "Darlin' if I were you, I would stay right where you are for a minute, otherwise when you stand up and leave me; you are going to embarrass us both."

Suddenly Whisper became aware of the rigid flesh that was pressing against her bottom.

Unexpectedly she giggled. "Did I do that to you?"

Sean pretended to look around, "Well," he drawled "since I don't see anybody else here," he grinned at her, "I guess that leaves you as the culprit."

"All right then, let's really give them something to talk about," and she pulled his head down for one last kiss.

Charlotte and Edward stopped in the doorway of the room, and Charlotte's voice was icy as she spoke. "Really Alison, is this what you learned in the states? To make a public spectacle of yourself?"

Sean raised his head and stiffened; Charlotte might look like an English rose but she obviously was a cold bitch. Preparing to give her a taste of his Irish tongue, he suddenly felt Whisper's finger across his lips. Raising an eyebrow, she looked at him and after a second he nodded.

Pushing herself out of his lap, she turned to face her aunt and cousin. "Unless I'm mistaken, Aunt Charlotte, the way my father had this building constructed, we can see out, but no one can see in. Has that changed?"

Surprised by an attack from someone she had always considered an unworthy opponent, Charlotte began to sputter. Although Whisper voice was soft, the tone was unmistakably sarcastic.

With a cool smile, Edward admonished his mother, "Careful Mother, the little cat has claws."

Surging to his feet, Sean glared down at Edward. "Just who are you calling a little cat?"

Startled Edward stepped back, although his eyes glittered with animosity.

At the vehemence of Sean's words, Charlotte slid closer to Edward. There was something about this man that was intimidating, and she was sure she and Edward both recognized it.

Whisper placed a light hand on Sean's arm, and although the smile she bestowed on him was warm, there was an unmistakable message in it, back off.

Grinning down at her, he realized that this little woman had just given him an order —without saying a single word.

Deciding to make peace before things got out of hand, Whisper looked at her aunt. "I'm afraid things got a little out of hand here," she nodded toward Sean, "Charlotte, Edward, this is Sean O'Brien, my friend from the states."

At Sean's derisive snort she turned and looked at him, daring him to say a word, "A dear friend from the states."

"That's better." Sean murmured, and Whisper gave him a look that promised retribution.

But Charlotte, still smarting from watching Edward being intimidated by Sean, was in no mood to let it go.

"If," she said, pure malice in her tone, "He's such a good friend of yours, why hasn't your father ever mentioned him?"

"Maybe," Sean answered before Whisper could reply "It was because he didn't know about us, we only met a short while ago, and because of his illness we were waiting for the right moment before we told him that we are about to announce our engagement."

Whisper stepped back, the heel of her riding boot causing a sharp pain to run through Sean's foot and up into his leg, but Sean never grimaced.

Glancing up at him, eyes narrowed, Whisper was astonished to see him grinning down at her, unspoken words hanging in the air between them, in her mind she could swear she heard him say, do your damndest I can take it.

Startled Charlotte looked from one to another. "Well if that's the case, I'm sure congratulations are in order, but perhaps I'll wait for the big announcement." She stared at Whisper, her voice challenging, "You never know what might happen."

"And you, "she turned toward Sean, "if you are to become a member of the family, please don't embarrass us by calling her by that ridiculous nickname her cousins gave her. You will remember to refer to her as Alison."

Turning, she spoke to her son in a voice that permitted no argument, "Come Edward, I prefer to watch the competition somewhere else."

Edward looked at Sean, and then at Whisper, his eyes narrowed speculatively, but he didn't say a word, just turned and followed his mother down the stairs.

Spinning around Whisper gave Sean a shove and being caught off guard he stumbled backward into the seat behind him. Even sitting he could just about look her in the eye and he tried hard to hide his amusement as he gazed at the spitfire standing in front of him. Her hands were on her hips and her stance one of defiance as she glared at him.

"Enough is enough, first you just happen to be on the plane next to me, then you just happen to kiss me, then you just happen to be at this horse show and now you just happen to announce our engagement. Are you out of your mind?"

Sean laughed, there was one good thing about being in love with a woman who couldn't shout, even when she was angry as Whisper obviously was, her voice still sounded like velvet.

"Do you know what my mother always told me? A good defense is a fast and thorough offense." And grabbing her by the waist he pulled her into his lap and began to kiss her.

For the first few seconds Whisper pushed at his chest, not ready to make nice, then she gave up, and began kissing him back. Finally, he raised his head, "You know" he ran his tongue across her upper lip effectively stopping anything she was about to say. "Much as I'd like to spend the rest of the afternoon with you, I think I'll skip the rest of this competition, I have to go out and get you a ring, and after all we just became engaged."

Still in his arms, Whisper looked up at him, "You are a crazy person. Why did you tell them we were engaged, do you know what will happen now? She'll be on the phone telling everyone she knows what just happened, it will be all over in an hour that

I'm engaged and I didn't tell my father yet. Just how far do you intend to carry this and a better question is why?"

Seeing the intent look on her face Sean realized now was the time to level with her. "Look, I admit things are probably moving a little fast for you, but for starters, I'm crazy about you, have been from the moment I first saw your picture."

"My picture?"

"Yeah, Luke brought it to my office, some of the things that have been happening to you lately had Luke worried, and as I told you on the plane, I was coming to my branch office in London anyway and when he asked me to keep an eye on you... I agreed."

Not exactly the complete truth, but close enough. "Neither of us wanted you to be alarmed so we arranged for me to be on your plane, but my kissing you was strictly my idea!"

Tenderly he brushed a curl off her forehead, "He brought the pictures to my office to remind me what you looked like," as if I could ever forget he thought, "and then I met you. It only took the few hours we spent together on that plane and I knew you were the one I've been waiting for."

He pulled her closer to him, 'Look I'm no kid, and maybe I moved a little fast for you, but if you're the least bit interested in pursuing this relationship, I think we can make it work."

As Whisper started to respond, he bent and kissed her again. "Wait. Before you say a word let me finish. I'm sorry if I've just placed you in a tough position; and if you don't feel the same about me then I have trapped you in a bogus engagement. But" he hesitated, "if you do, I meant what I said about getting that ring."

Whisper smiled at him, they might both be crazy but knowing from her own past how quickly love and happiness could be snatched away, she decided to take a chance and drawing his head down she whispered in his ear, "Go get that ring."

Sean's whoop of joy almost shattered her ear drums, and she laughed as he bounded up out of his seat and lifted her in his arms swirling her around.

"I love you."

Neither knew who said it first nor did they care. An old song kept repeating itself in Sean's head. Ah, he thought, it's true, what a difference a day makes.

Carefully setting her down, he suddenly became serious. "I want you to promise me that when I'm not with you you'll be careful."

"Do you really think I'm in danger?"

"Yes..."

"But why? I don't think I have any enemies."

"Lots of people get hurt when they don't think they have any enemies. But someone takes a crazy thought into his head, and innocent people do get hurt."

"Sean, "she paused, her voice questioning. "What am I going to tell my father? I mean you just appear out of the blue and suddenly I'm engaged to you?"

"Tell him the truth, we met, we fell in love and today I asked you to marry me. Lots of people meet and fall in love, and get married within weeks, and as a matter of fact I know a few." He thought about his grandfather and grandmother who met after church one day and were married just months later, and his mother and father who married after two months. "Your father will be happy to know that you have someone to watch over you, and it might even make his surgery a little easier."

"Somehow I missed your asking me to marry you – I got the engagement part – but did I miss something?"

"Honey you're not about to miss anything. If you didn't hear the words it was probably because I was saying them in my heart – but if you need to hear them, Will you marry me?"

Bending, he kissed her again, but it wasn't a kiss of lust, it was a kiss of love, and this kiss carried a promise with it.

"Yes, yes, I will."

"Now darling, after I get that ring, you invite me to dinner, so I can talk to you father and we can show the world what a happy couple we are."

Whisper frowned, "I forgot, tonight we have a big party at our home right after the competition ends, many of the people who are here today will be there, as well as the few relatives we have left."

A look of horror crossed over her face, "Oh, my heavens, you just told Charlotte and Edward we're engaged and they'll tell my father before I can see him."

"No they won't, I'm sure your father didn't stay for the competition and we'll tell him right now."

Pulling his cell out of his pocket, Sean turned slightly away so that she wouldn't see that Stephen's number was already programmed in. As the phone rang back at the house, Sean pretended to dial the numbers she was telling him.

Sam's cool hello went unanswered and she listened carefully as she heard Sean's voice instantly realizing that Sean wanted her to hear his end of a conversation. She raised one eyebrow when she heard him ask Whisper, "Do you want to tell him about our engagement or should I?"

"Let me," she said and she took the phone from Sean's hand.

"Hi, Dad," she paused and delight colored her voice, "Oh Sam is that you? May I speak to my father?"

"Well he's resting, Alison, but if you wait just a minute, I'll take him the phone."

Mouthing the words so that Sam couldn't hear, Whisper said "I really like Sam; she's so good for my father."

Nodding, Sean waited anxiously till Stephen took the phone. What the hell had he been thinking? He should have called Stephen first, told him that this wasn't a job to him anymore, this was personal. Sure, he had returned Stephen's retainer before he had even met her but... Sean began to sweat. Suppose when she found out that he had been hired to protect her, she didn't believe that he had fallen in love with her, how was he ever going to get her to understand? Would Stephen blow it? Would her father tell her that he had tried to hire O'Brien Detective Agency, and think this was just a job?

He held his breath.

"Daddy," Whisper began, "I know this sounds crazy, but I've met the man I'm going to marry. You remember I told you about him, His name is Sean O'Brien and he comes from the states. I've known his family ever so long, but I haven't seen him till just recently."

She paused listening, and she turned slightly away from Sean, which made his heart begin to beat faster. What was she going to say when she got off the phone? How could he prove to her that everything had changed the minute he had seen her picture? He wasn't sure that he would even believe his story if he was in her place. He'd just have to work like hell to make sure she trusted him.

"Yes, daddy I do think he's wonderful, o.k. I'll tell him." Snapping the phone shut she handed it back to him, a perplexed look on her face. "He said he was delighted for me, and I couldn't have made a better choice. Now why would he say that, he doesn't even know you?"

Thinking fast, Sean pulled her into his arms, "No, he doesn't but Luke does, and maybe your cousin has mentioned my name a time or two."

"I bet that's it, Luke's always talking about your family, and I am sure he mentioned you to my father. My father always said, he felt like he knew all the O'Brien's."

A look of horror crossed her face, "Oh no, Luke! . . . I need to tell Luke; suppose he hears it from someone else? And my Aunt Annette and Uncle Craig how are we going to explain what happened?"

"Honey, you and I will cross that bridge when and if we ever come to it," he softly murmured. Grabbing her hand, he started leading her toward the stairs, "Come on now, I've got things to do, and so do you. How did you get here?"

"With Edward."

"Well I'm taking you home, and do me a favor will you honey? Don't ride with him anymore I don't like him. What time should I be back?"

"You don't even know where I live."

"Since I'm taking you home, that won't be a problem…"

"But I came with Edward."

"Too bad, let him take the dragon lady home instead," he grinned at her, "It'll serve him right."

Trying to catch her breath as she followed Sean, she tugged on his hand, "Slow down, the party starts at eight and they won't start serving dinner until nine."

He stopped short causing her to run into the back of him, and giving him the opportunity to swing around and catch her up into his arms. Nose to nose, he looked into her eyes, "What are these people barbarians? Dinner at nine? Don't they know people like me need to nourish our bodies earlier than that?"

"People like you," and she looked him up and down slowly with a twinkle in her eye. "Probably eat more than the staff will put on the buffet table," and she laughed.

"Well, honey, if you don't want to be embarrassed, I suggest you warn them that I'm coming and that I like to eat."

"Oh, I will, I will," and she poked him in the ribs when he set her down, and took his hand as they headed for the parking lot.

CHAPTER NINETEEN

S ean stood in the doorway of the cottage glancing at his watch for what seemed to him the hundredth time. Where was Archie? He said he'd be home early and here it was almost seven o'clock. He had promised Whisper that he would be there by eight.

He glanced into the mirror that hung over the rather faded couch that hugged one wall. His grandmother had loved that couch. He remembered the year she bought it. It was one of the summers when both Eric and he had come over for a visit. Grandma had saved the money herself out of profits from the sewing she did for the town seamstress, and she was really excited.

Sean grinned when he thought back on it, Grandma had wandered around the store for what seemed like hours, a disgruntled husband and two teenage boys trailing after her; all the while Archie loudly grumbling that their old couch was good enough. Finally, after returning to this couch three times she had proudly pointed at it and told the salesman she'd take it. That's when the fun began.

Archie made the mistake of loudly proclaiming that he wasn't paying for some local fellow to deliver it when he had two strapping grandsons right there. It was the first time he had ever seen Grandma lose her temper and such a sight it was! Needless to say, the couch was delivered and Archie never said another word about it. And even now, long after Grandma was gone, whenever

Archie moved, whether for a long term or short assignment, that old couch went with him. And he was sure if his mother ever persuaded his grandfather to move to Boston, somehow that couch would be going along.

The headlights of the limousine caressed the trees as Archie pulled up in front of the cottage and bounded out. He pushed open the door barely glancing at his grandson.

"Can't eat with you tonight, forgot all about having to work. Got to park cars for this big shindig their having...though why grown men can't park their own damn cars is beyond me."

Still muttering he headed for the stairs and then stopped, turned, and stared at Sean.

"You," he said, "Are one fine looking grandson. I never realized how great you look when you're dressed up." He circled back and strolled around Sean looking him all over.

"Yeah you'll do. Of course, you're not as handsome as your brother Jay, but in a pinch, you can hold your own."

"Grandpa" Sean said, "I need to talk to you."

"Grandpa? Suddenly I'm grandpa? What happened to you calling me Archie or crazy old man?" The old man's eyes twinkled as he looked up at Sean.

"Everybody calls you crazy old man, especially after you went out on that fishing boat with nothing but the clothes on your back for six months."

"That wasn't crazy; it was just a little misunderstanding that me, and the captain had while drinking a few pints of ale. I thought he said six hours. But never mind that did you get arrested while I was gone? I noticed you and Alison disappeared during the show – you didn't do something you shouldn't did you?"

"No, I didn't do something I shouldn't, I got engaged."

"YOU WHAT?"

"Look, I know it's a little unorthodox, but Whisper and I are engaged."

"You're not engaged, you're crazy I'm calling your mother,"

and mumbling to himself he headed for the phone that sat on a small table next to the couch.

"Archie, Grandpa, listen to me." Sean moved quickly to prevent his grandfather from dialing the phone. "She's not going to change my mind. I'm in love with the girl."

He watched as his grandfather dropped the receiver back into its cradle.

"The only problem is" he continued, "I don't want her ever to think that my wanting to marry her has anything to do with my being hired by Stephen and Luke. That's why I need to talk to you."

Dropping down onto the couch Archie ran his hands up and down its arms as if receiving comfort from it. "You grandmother loved this couch you know, and when I came here, I just couldn't leave it behind." He sighed, "So what do you want from me?"

"I want Grandma's ring."

"You really are that serious, are you?" Archie's voice was husky.

"Dead serious."

"I know that your grandmother told you before she passed on that she wanted you to have her rings, you being the oldest and all," his eyes were piercing as he gazed at Sean. "But, I need to ask you one more time, are you sure this is the one? I can't have you handing her ring out to every Jane, Susan and Sally."

Sean went over and sat down beside his grandfather taking his hand in his. "Were you sure when you saw first saw Grandma?"

Archie's eyes glittered with unshed tears. "I'm as sure today as the day I met her." Pulling his hand from Sean's he stood, "Alright then, the ring is yours but so help me," —and then he stopped.

"I'll go get it"

Within minutes he returned with an antique white jeweler's box clutched in his hand. Handing the box to Sean he smiled up at him. "If this girl brings you as much happiness as you Grandmother did me – you'll be one lucky fellow."

Sean bent down and kissed his grandfather's brow and immediately Archie started sputtering.

"Cut that out, I'm not into all that mush." but even as he spoke, he put his arms around Sean waist and gave him a quick hug – than pushed him away.

"I suppose that means you're going to the party too, well hurry up now, you don't want to be late, besides, this way I won't have to park your car – it will already be there."

Sean laughed and grabbing his keys off the table opened the door. "Maybe I'll come home a little early so I can send you out to get my car – I might even slip you a tip."

He ducked as a magazine came flying at his head.

Parking his car to the side of the mansion where the valet had directed him, Sean walked into a room that took his breath away. His whole apartment could probably fit between these four walls with room to spare.

Before his eyes swept the room and the people gathered there but his Irish intuition told him there was no threat among these guests –at least not yet.

He moved to the side of the massive room, a plate of untouched food in his hand. There must be a hundred and fifty people here, and obviously Whisper had been kidding when she told them there might not be enough food to feed him. Buffet tables laden with every kind of dish imaginable were scattered around the room and waiters were constantly refreshing drinks. In the midst of all this Whisper floated from guest to guest, smiling shaking hands and greeting people. Her father proudly accompanying her maneuvering his wheelchair as if it were a chariot.

Whisper had only been able to spend a few minutes with Sean since he arrived before being commandeered by her father and she hadn't been able to leave his side since.

But that was all right, it gave him a chance to continue to look over the guests, but so far nothing had seemed the least suspicious.

Sam caught Sean's eye and nodded toward the hallway. Waiting a few seconds after her signal, he slipped from the ballroom and down the hall and into the first room he came to.

Luckily it was the library, and he perched on the corner of a desk as he waited for Sam to appear. She looked stunning tonight, her flaming red hair set off by the soft white gown she wore. He noticed that her jewelry was understated she only wore a gold watch and earrings. Somehow though she managed to look more regal than many of the guests who he was sure wore every pricey piece of jewelry they owned.

Sam slid into room soundlessly and pulled the door shut behind her. She moved swiftly to him and kissed him on the cheek. Long ago they had considered a closer relationship, but soon realized that there just wasn't enough chemistry between them to make it work. So they settled for being friends along with a truly beneficial business partnership.

"You first," Sean smiled at her, "and may I add that you certainly look beautiful tonight."

"Thank you." Sam's smile was warm. "You not so bad yourself – of course your brother Jay," then she laughed at the look on his face. "Only kidding,' she perched on the arm of a nearby chair and grinned at him, "Well you certainly set everybody on their ear with all this engagement stuff."

"You think so?"

"I know so, Stephen can't wait to get you alone to find out what is going on, Charlotte came storming into the house and began screaming at Stephen about his daughter. And Edward," she frowned, "stood behind her –looking sick. I don't know if it was because Mama was upset – or if he was disturbed by this turn of events."

"What was Charlotte screaming about?"

"Seems she feels that her son should be Stephen's heir because Alison hasn't been around in years, and Edward should be entitled to everything. And if Stephen named Edward as his heir, he would automatically inherit this property and the title that goes with it."

"And how did Stephen react to that?"

"Like any father, he told her to get out, but not before he told her that everything would go to Alison and then to any children she might have, and not to Edward. That's when she made a fatal mistake, she told him that Alison's mother was an American floozy and that Alison wasn't entitled to anything."

"Oh boy." Sean grimaced thinking of how his father would react is someone disparaged his wife and or any of his children.

"Oh boy is right, I had to restrain Stephen, and I swear if he got up out of that chair, he would have strangled her."

"Wait, this doesn't make sense," Sean shook his head, "According to my sources, Edward has plenty of money of his own — so all of this really circles back to that damn title and this estate. You'd think in this day and age. . ."

"Listen, over here this is big stuff, and just because you and I don't get it, don't think that wars haven't been fought over this stuff."

She moved toward the door, "I need to get back before Stephen misses me." She swung around and looked at him, "Did you have anything to tell me?"

"Only that Edward isn't adopted, Charlotte's his real mother."

Sam didn't look surprised, which puzzled Sean.

Sam pondered this for a moment. "No wonder she went crazy. Now everything is starting to add up. Edward is really the first male heir in the family, and she thinks he's entitled to inherit this estate and the title even though he's not Stephen's son."

She frowned, "If you and Alison get married . . . and there's a son. . ." she didn't finish, but changed direction on Sean, "Has anyone found out who Edward's real father is?"

Completely confused by the workings of a woman's mind, Sean shook his head. "It's a long story, but it will have to wait. We have to get back or they'll be looking for us." He started toward the door and then turned back, "Snoop around a little, and see if you can find out anything, I don't know if this whole thing has any bearing on what's been happening to Whisper, but we've got to eliminate all possibilities., Eric told me his friends on the street say the money that paid for the hit man, came from someone here in London. He's still chasing it, but so far no luck. It's like chasing smoke, but I'm beginning to think it's not money that put Whisper's life in danger, but something else."

She grinned at him, "Keep in touch peasant."

Sean laughed "You're fired..."

"Sure, just like you fired me the last three times. She laughed, "Between you firing me, and Stephen firing me at least three times a day, I just might get a complex."

"I doubt it."

"Yeah me too." And opening the door she slipped into the hall.

Sean waited a few moments before he left and once he got back into the ballroom he moved to stand beside the massive fireplace that dominated the room. Conversation ebbed and swirled around him, none of it of any interest to him until he heard a cold voice next to him.

"When is the big announcement?

Sean turned and looked into a pair of eyes that didn't even try to mask their hostility.

"Well," he answered, his voice cool, "I imagine whenever the little lady and her father feel the time is right. Personally, it can't come soon enough to suit me. Too many of these fellows are just itching to get near her."

Both men's eyes followed as Whisper turned to greet a late comer. Sean's chest tightened as he watched her, she was especially beautiful tonight. The gown she had chosen was the color of an antique pearl and swirled around her as moonlight would an angel. Then the man she was talking to reached out and pulled her into his arms. Instinctively Sean started forward toward them a red haze beginning to form before is eyes.

He was surprised when Edward's hand shot out and stopped him.

"Don't make a scene," he hissed, It's a distant cousin she hasn't seen in years, happily married and if you will look a little to his left you will see a tiny blonde that's due to deliver his baby any day now."

Glancing at Edward, Sean was surprised to see a look of pride on his face as he gazed at Whisper. This was totally unexpected. What the hell was going on here?

"Alison is beautiful but Alise, her mother was exquisite," he stopped and his voice became wistful "She was beyond compare, other women faded beside her, and she was soft and warm. She cared about everyone; she was a breath of fresh air in a world where protocol and rank mean everything. Everyone loved her and it's no wonder I, I mean no wonder Stephen loved her so."

My god, Sean thought, he would have been just a kid, but it was obvious he had been in love with Whisper's mother. How old could he have been fourteen, fifteen? He remembered how he had felt about his first girlfriend, and when she moved away, he had been devastated, but to lose your first love to death. He couldn't imagine how that would feel.

Subtly the expression on Edward's face changed, and a look of anger swept across his face only to disappear behind the bored façade that Sean was used to seeing.

Following Edward's gaze, he watched as Sam wheeled Stephen from the room.

"Devil take her," he muttered, "She won't let any of us near him. He doesn't need a nurse; this family is perfectly capable of taking care of our own."

He turned to Sean, "If you will excuse me," but as he turned to leave a slender man, obviously in his fifties stepped in front of him.

"Edward," he nodded to both men, "Perhaps you'd like to introduce me to your friend here, I've heard so much about him, and he and I have something in common although he doesn't know it."

At the perplexed look on Sean's face he smiled, "I'm Andrew St. James. And I know my name means nothing to you – but your brother Senator Dan O'Brien and I have met several times in Washington. As a matter of fact, the President just appointed your brother and me to serve on an international commission working to share art and artifacts between our two countries."

"Art and artifacts?" Sean burst out laughing. Dan was the only one of all the O'Brien's that couldn't draw a straight line with a ruler.

"Yes, I was sitting next to him when the President appointed him to the Commission; and I might add," and he grinned, "He has a very colorful vocabulary when he's not happy. Taught me a few words some that perhaps I'd rather not know."

He extended his hand, glancing over at Edward, "And since Edward seems to have forgotten his manners, and he also seems to have forgotten to mention it, I am also this scamp's boss."

"I apologize, Baron St. James.," Edward mumbled.

Sean racked his brain, of course, his file on Edward said he worked for one of the most prestigious architectural firms in London, and as he recalled, this man was the owner.

"Sorry," Edward voice was strained, "but the two of you seemed to hit it off so quickly- I forgot you didn't know each other."

"No harm done," the Baron laid his hand on Edward's arm. "Edward, I believe your mother is glaring in this direction, haven't you paid sufficient attention to her tonight?"

"That woman," Edward muttered, "Is going to drive me crazy, every week she wants me to meet one of her friend's daughters. If she doesn't run out of friends soon," and he looked at the two men for sympathy. "And the ones she picks usually give me nightmares for weeks."

This was a humorous side of Edward Sean hadn't seen before, and he found himself studying him. He was handsome with his dark good looks and that brooding demeanor and the way he held himself reminded Sean– Sean eyes narrowed as he glanced at the Baron.

"Listen," Sean leaned down as if to whisper, "I'll match any one your mother's offerings against some of the trolls my mother's brought home for me." He straightened up and grinned at the look on the men's faces.

"Oh, oh, she's coming our way." Nodding his head, it was the Baron who spoke as Charlotte walked toward them.

"If she insults you this time, ---"

Sean was surprised to see that it was the Baron Edward was addressing.

"Don't let it bother you my boy, your mother and I go back a long way and she just likes to remind me she knows things about me I'd rather not have anyone know. So we're just going to let her jibes go shall we?"

"All right, but I don't know why you haven't fired me because of the way she treats you."

"Fire you? That will never happen. Now run along, meet the girl and make your mother happy." But the Baron had to stifle a laugh when he saw the homely little blond that Charlotte had in tow.

They watched as Edward met his mother in the center of the room, graciously smiling as he took the arm of the young woman she escorted.

"One of these days, that boy is going to murder his mother, and I'm going to hire the best attorney in London and do my damndest to get him off."

He laughed and extending his hand to Sean continued, "I

hope that you and I will meet again soon. I can't wait to tell your brother I met you."

And with a soft smile on his face he turned to watch a small brunette who was heading their way. Taking his hand, she led him off into the crowd.

"Well, well," Sean thought, "The plot thickens."

He watched as St. James and Edward mingled with the crowd, and he cursed his Irish heritage that gave him a strong sense of intuition, and right now he had the eerie feeling he had just met Edward's father.

A cold hand slipped into his and he looked down into Whisper's face. Her beauty still took his breath away, but he could see the slight tinge of blue beneath her eyes.

"Can we slip away for a moment; my father wants to talk to us."

"In a minute," and as the orchestra started to play a romantic love song, he swept her into his arms and led her out onto the dance floor. As her held her close, he was aware that many of the guests turned to watch them, and that the women in the room were sighing over the beautiful young woman being held so tenderly in his arms.

"I'm worried."

"Shush, there's nothing to worry about."

"But how do I explain our engagement, we just met and I'm sure Dad will think we've lost our minds."

"No, he won't." Sean remembered Luke's words about Stephen pursuing Alise across the world after only meeting her just once.

"I think he'll understand." he said softly.

Taking her hand, he led her off the dance floor and out onto the balcony.

It was a balmy night but she still shivered as he pulled her into the shadows and away from the windows. Slipping out of his jacket he draped it over her shoulders and then looked down and laughed.

The sleeves brushed the stones of the balcony and it hung as an adult overcoat would on a child. Taking the sleeves, he wrapped them around her and then pulled her forward into his arms.

"Now" he said, "Let's put to rest any worries you have about your father."

And reaching into his pocket he pulled out his grandmother's antique engagement ring.

"This was my grandmother's and when she was dying, she insisted that as her oldest grandson I should have it for the woman I married."

"But" Whisper stuttered, "Are you sure you want me to have it? You've only known me a little while, maybe you'll meet someone else later. . ."

"Do you honestly think so?" Sean pulled her even closer his mouth just inches from hers. "Tell me you don't feel the same way I do. Tell me you didn't feel something from the moment we met."

"I can't but this is crazy. We barely know each other."

"No, we've known each other forever; it's just that this is the first time we met in this lifetime."

"You really believe that?"

"Of course I do, I've waited all my life for you, and now that you're here you think I'm going to let you go?"

Whisper sweet breath touched Sean's lips and with a soft groan he lowered his head and kissed her. What started out as a kiss of commitment quickly burst into flame as the two lovers strained to get closer. The coat unwound from around her slim body and fell to the floor unheeded as the heat from their embrace enveloped them.

It was Sean who broke away, lifting her hand to kiss the palm before he slid his grandmother's ring onto her finger. The diamond was small but surrounded by emeralds, and the setting exquisite. It caught the light of the moon and glittered and danced upon her hand.

"It is so beautiful." Tears glistened in her eyes as she looked up at Sean.

"I could buy you a bigger one, but I won't. This ring brings with it a promise of love and happiness, my grandmother guaranteed it." He looked into her eyes. "If you accept it, this is the real thing. No play acting, or pretending, as of this minute we are engaged and I'm hoping before too long we'll have taken this one step farther. Just pick the day," he grinned down at her, "and I'll be there."

Whisper lifted her hand and stroked his cheek feeling the soft stubble underneath. Just like his beard she knew that this man could be prickly. Was she worried about it? No. And then she laughed.

Sean's eyebrows drew together and he looked down at her with a perplexed expression on his face. Not sure what that laugh was about.

Whisper stood on tiptoe and lightly kissed his cheek. "Stop frowning Sean O'Brien, I will be happy to marry you – I was just thinking you and I are in for a heck of a ride."

Letting out a whoop, Sean picked her up in his arms and twirled her around never setting her down as he began to kiss her thoroughly. Finally, it dawned on him that Stephen was waiting and he reluctantly let her slide down the length of his body.

Whisper was delighted to feel his hardened response to their kiss and the fact that her own heart was beating erratically thrilled her. This was it. This was why no other man had ever set her senses on fire. Sean was right, they had been waiting for each other, and no one else in this lifetime would do. Somehow, she wasn't afraid when she was in his arms. She knew she had a reputation for being an ice maiden, and not liking men to touch her, but this was different. In his arms she felt safe and as if she had finally found her home.

Grabbing his coat off the floor and then taking her hand, he led her along the balcony and into the ballroom. The fact that his tie was crooked and that her lipstick had disappeared seemed not to matter to either of them. They looked like a couple in love and people smiled as they passed by.

Only one person didn't smile.

He had watched and listened from his place of concealment and now he knew he had to do something. He would see to it that Whisper never married this man – and she would never bear him a son.

CHAPTER TWENTY

The only things that were new in the room Whisper and Sean entered, were the computer and the modern desk where Stephen sat, papers piled neatly in front of him.

Sean winced as he noted the quiet elegance of the furniture, and although no connoisseur of art, even he recognized the worth of the paintings on the walls.

This was no Boston office decorated by an ex-cop, this was true aristocracy.

"You," he whispered, "Are going to have to do something with my office."

In mock horror she whispered back, "Now I know why you want to marry me to get your office redecorated for free."

"Oh no…. I've been found out." He grinned at her, but the softness of his gaze told a whole different story.

"Sit down, sit down." Impatiently Stephen addressed them.

Sean frowned. This wasn't the controlled man that he had spoken to on the phone so many times, or the one who obviously adored his daughter.

He watched Stephen's hand tremble as he reached for a glass of water, and there were blue rings of fatigue under his eyes. He should be upstairs in bed not sitting here looking like the angel of death was hovering at the door.

"Sam" Stephen snarled, "Help me here."

Silently Sam uncurled herself from a large overstuffed corner chair where she had been quietly sitting and moved to the desk. Leaning over Stephen, although she spoke softly, her voice still carried. "Keep acting like a spoiled brat and so help me, I will find the dullest needle I have when I give you your shot tonight-get my drift?"

Sean swore that he saw a glimmer of a smile on Stephen's face as he told her, "You're fired."

"Yeah right, I'll leave right after you get your shots. Now what do you want me to do?"

"There are three piles of documents here, give one to Alison and one to Sean." He pulled the third pile toward him, and then waited as Sam handed the papers to the two of them and returned to her seat.

"This" he told Whisper, "Details exactly what will be yours if I don't survive this damn operation, and in any event, it will be yours when I die. Take a minute to go over it and then we will discuss it in detail."

He sat back not even glancing at the papers in front of him.

Sean ran through the first page startled at how much money and property Whisper stood to inherit. His mind raced as he realized the importance of this document. She was to inherit a great deal of money, in addition to this huge estate. There was only one stipulation that had Sean's eyes opening wide. Unless Stephen married again and had an heir, his title would go to Whisper's first-born son. This proviso went back to a time when the ruling king bestowed the title on a distant ancestor. Yet Whisper could lay claim to the title of Lady Alison Alexander.

"Oh my god," he thought "If we have a son, he'll be an English Lord," and then a devilish thought crossed his mind, maybe he'd have Archie and his brothers call his son by his title. They would have a fit. His thoughts were interrupted when a soft but determined voice spoke.

"No."

"What? What did you say? Did you say no? You're telling me no?"

It was obvious from his tone of voice and its volume, that this was not a word Stephen heard very often.

Standing up, Whisper moved swiftly across the room and dropped to her knees beside her father's wheelchair.

She placed her hand on his knee and looked up at him, her eyes pleading for understanding.

"I can't accept any of this, I just don't belong here anymore, and my life is back in Boston. I have a business, friends, and a family."

"I am your family." Stephen's voice was icy.

"Yes, you are, and I love you dearly, but Dad, please don't ask me to do this, I have a new life, a new business, a new love," she glanced at Sean, "This isn't home anymore, I need to go back to Boston and pick up where I left off."

"Is it because of him?" he nodded in Sean's direction, "because you've decided to marry him?"

"No," she glanced at Sean, "I had made up my mind to talk to you before I met Sean; as a matter of fact, it was the same day that I received your last phone call asking me to come home that I decided. I did some soul searching that night and I realized that I needed to stay where I was. Please try to understand."

Although her voice was pleading Sean could see Stephen stiffen, and he knew her pleas were falling on deaf ears.

Ignoring the glacial look on her father's face she continued. "Please can't you leave it all to Edward? He wants it. Declare him your heir, he and Charlotte will both be thrilled."

"Never," for a man in his condition his voice was amazingly strong, and Whisper leaned away from him startled by its intensity.

"He will never be my heir. If it wasn't for him, I would have my wife and," his voice cracked "you would have a mother."

"Dad," Whisper put her arms around his shoulders and leaned

her forehead against his. "You don't know what happened that day any more than I do."

"Don't you? In my heart I think I have always known there were three of you in the house that day. You even said you think you remember him being here. Did you see Charlotte's reaction, when I brought it up? That wasn't anger . . . it was fear. She's afraid her son had something to do with your mother's death – and so do I. The question is why was he here that day? If he was innocent why did he run away? Why didn't he stay and try to help? And why were you alone in the wine cellar and who brought you down there?"

"Dad, be reasonable he was a teenager, if I am not mistaken and he was here, he must have been frightened."

"Or guilty."

"Guilty? Guilty of what? It was an accident."

Stephen's eyes glittered. "Murder... that's what."

"Murder?" Whisper stumbled to her feet, her hand covering her mouth. "Why would you even think such a thing? He loved her, he really loved her. He would come here all the time. He played with me; he talked to Mom for hours. I was young, but I remember that. Why would he hurt her?"

"You tell me. Did they argue that day? Did he touch her?" Stephen's eyes glittered, "What happened? You're the only one who knows, and you've never told a soul what you saw. What did you see Alison, why did you scream so much you damaged your voice? And why were you hiding in the wine cellar? Why? Why?"

With each questions Stephen's face got whiter, and Sean jumped up and scrambled to Whisper's side, pulling her back into his arms, and forcing her to lean into him.

"That's enough!"

Sam surged to her feet and pushed past Sean and Whisper, whipping the wheelchair away from the desk. Her tone was angry but also anxious.

"I told you it was a stupid idea to do this tonight. But did you listen? No? Do it your way. Well now you managed to get both you and your daughter so upset neither of you will get any sleep tonight." Furiously she shot at him, "I'm going to stick your needle into a block of wood first so it will be nice and dull before I give it to you. It will match your head."

In unison both of them spoke. "You're fired!"

Only Sam continued on, "Yeah right, so I'll leave right after I get you to bed."

As she wheeled Stephen toward the door she stopped and turned to Whisper. "You want to kiss this blockhead good night?"

"Of course," Whisper pulled free of Sean embrace and ran to her father.

As she bent down his arms slipped up around her and he held her close.

"I'm so sorry" his voice became barely audible. "But I'm afraid I'll die never knowing what really happened that day. I know you were just a child, but I think the reason you never came back home was because you were afraid."

"Oh Dad, if I could tell you I would, but I can't remember myself." Her voice broke, "Don't you think I've tried and tried?"

She laid her cheek against his, and she kissed him murmuring soft words that only he could hear.

Over their heads Sam and Sean's eye locked, and he was startled when she gave him a big wink. What he figured was a bitter confrontation between Stephen and Sam obviously wasn't. As Stephen raised his head and looked at Sam there was exhaustion in his eyes, but there was also admiration for the redhead who had so quickly taken control of the situation.

"Alright, you shrew, let's go. I'm ready for bed now."

"You were ready hours ago but you're just too stubborn to admit it."

"It's too bad that we aren't allowed to throw unruly servants in the "tower" anymore. You'd be carried there in an instant."

"Yeah and it's too bad you didn't spend more time in the states and you'd have learned that I come from a democracy buster and don't you forget it."

"A democracy modeled after ours."

"Yours was just the pilot program – we perfected it!"

Their voices faded and although they couldn't hear the words, Sean and Whisper could still hear them arguing.

"Jesus," Sean shook his head, "I feel like I've been in a war zone."

He walked over and pulled her into his arms, "Are you all right?"

"Nonsense, that was mild, you should see him when he is really on a tear."

She grinned, "She's terrific with him."

"I thought you'd be coming to his defense and agree she should be fired."

"What, and have him give up?"

The look she gave him was pitying. "You may be a great detective Sean, but like most men it's obvious you simply don't know a thing about women and how we handle the men in our lives. Right now he needs a good fight, sort of like a warrior preparing for the battle of his life. Sam knows this. So she gives him a worthy opponent. If she babied him, he might give up, but every time he fights with her it just reinforces the fact that she thinks he's going to get well. After all who would fight with a dying man?"

"Thank god I'm not a woman I don't think I'd ever get the hang of this stuff. To me a fight is a fight and ..."

Whisper stepped closer and laid a finger across his lips. "Thank god you aren't a woman. Where would that leave me?"

Suddenly her eyes widened and she put her hand to her head as she shivered and slumped forward, her arms clutching him as she fell.

Sean reached out and caught her to him, alarmed to see that the color had drained from her cheeks. Sweeping her up into his arms, he dropped into the nearest chair, and pulling his jacket open laid her body close to his, folding his jacket back around her so that his body heat was against her. He rubbed her arms and kept murmuring to her until his warmth began to flow into her.

Reaching down he took her hands. They were ice cold. He began to rub them trying to bring some warmth back into her body. Her breath was erratic and she seemed to be staring into space and he became frightened. Her eye lids fluttered and a soft sigh blew against his cheek. He could feel his heart pounding in his chest and he realized that he had never been as frightened in his life.

"Whisper, honey, where are you? Whisper," he bent down to kiss her only to discover her lips held no warmth.

Slowly her eyes opened and she stared up at Sean a bewildered look on her face.

"Good god woman, are you trying to kill me? What the hell happened to you?"

"I was there . . . I remember some of it. "We were at the top of the stairs, Mama and Edward were talking, he said something to her and she said. . ." She paused, obviously struggling to remember more of the conversation, "No Edward," then she was tumbling down the stairs and then-"

"And then?"

"And then I don't know, that's all I can remember. But she looked so beautiful that day just like a princess." Her voice was wistful, "There were just the two of us and we spent the whole morning in the kitchen cooking southern dishes. She had sent to the states for some collard greens, and sweet potatoes, all kinds of things she loved, and she said Daddy was going to have a fit, but then she hugged me and told me that she had a surprise for Daddy and me."

Tears glistened in her eyes. "It was years later when I was a teenager that my aunt told me that my mother had found out she was pregnant, and that was the surprise she was planning to tell Daddy and me."

As he listened Sean realized that somehow Whisper's memory had taken her back to that fateful day, and she was seeing events through the eyes of a five-year-old. She shuddered, and he sat perfectly still not saying a word, just holding her in his arms until her eyes closed and her breathing became soft and even.

He wanted to clutch her to him and smooth away all her worries and fears, yet he was afraid for her. Her mind would take her just so far and then no further. Why?

Had she witnessed a murder? Was that why her life was in danger? Maybe it wasn't the title, maybe the reason her life was in danger was much more sinister.

He bent his head and laid his lips upon her forehead. This was obviously linked to the dream she had on the plane.

What ever happened the day her mother died must be coming back to her in bits and pieces and obviously it scared her,

He settled back in the chair. He wished he could call Archie and tell him not to wait up. If he had to sit here all night he would. Her even breathing told him that she was sleeping peacefully and he remembered that on the plane she had told him she hadn't been sleeping well.

The door opened a crack as Archie poked his head in. Seeing Whisper sleeping in Sean's arms, he tiptoed in, being careful not to disturb her.

"Did you call me?" he mouthed.

Sean just stared at him stunned.

"No, but I was thinking about you, I was afraid you'd worry if I didn't get home tonight." Sean's voice cracked a little as he whispered his answer.

"Oh, o.k. then, I'm done for the evening and I'll just toodle along home. See you in the morning."

"Wait, how did you know I wanted you?"

"I heard you call my name."

"But I didn't."

"Don't get your shirt in a tangle boy, in this country lots of strange things happen." And with a grin he gave a jaunty wave before pulling the door shut behind him.

CHAPTER TWENTY-ONE

S am slipped out of her robe and shivered. What she wouldn't do for some heat. She grinned, preferably body heat. She hadn't been married all that long but one of the things she really loved was having a warm body to cuddle up to on nights like this. The locals said all this dampness was good for a woman's complexion but it sure wasn't good for someone who slept alone.

She slipped between the sheets and sighed, maybe there was no warmth here but these silk sheets sure felt good. When this assignment was over, she would splurge and buy herself a set, if you couldn't have a man to sleep with, at least you could sleep with silk. Smiling softly, she acknowledged that it wasn't that she hadn't gotten offers but somehow there was always something missing and she just wasn't the type to hop in and out of a man's bed.

She hoped Stephen would rest easier now that his daughter was home, although she didn't like the scene she had witnessed earlier. That daughter of his had a mind of her own, and all the money and titles in the world didn't seem to impress her. Maybe she had more of her mother in her than Stephen realized.

Sam had heard snippets of gossip here and there, about Stephen's wife, and although she had looked like a sweet southern belle, she was no one to push around.

She wished she could have seen the confrontations between her and Charlotte. It was a well-known fact that Charlotte was jealous of all the time Edward spent here, and the servants said when she went after Alise, she ended up on the proverbial short end of the stick. She thought she would probably have liked Alise, everyone seemed to, the only problem was, and they would probably both end up in love with the same man.

Reaching out she shut off the small lamp on the antique table beside her. Sighing, she hoped that tonight she would get a full night sleep. But she doubted it. Since she had taken this assignment, every night she felt the need to get up and check on Stephen, and she knew tonight would be "no exception". He probably didn't require her constant vigilance, but somehow it made her feel better to know he was all right. And putting him in that wheelchair had been a stroke of genius. There would have been no way to contain him, especially knowing that his daughter had been the target of an assassin.

She closed her eyes but her mind wouldn't stop racing.

Sure, she had an exciting new career as the head of Sean's London's branch, and he had even sent his brother Connor over to train her, but she had never quite gotten over the need to take care of other people.

Her heart and soul were in nursing and maybe when she got back to London she would volunteer in a children's ward at the hospital. The one regret she had from her short marriage to Jim was she had never gotten pregnant. She couldn't understand her husband's reluctance to having children until after his death, when she found out he already had two.

She had to remember to send birthday presents to them. She and Jim's first wife had gotten to be good friends, and she was reluctant to find out if he had ever divorced her.

She hated to think she'd fallen for a guy who would have deserted his kids and their mother. But since neither of them knew for sure, they had decided to let sleeping dogs lie, or in this case a sleeping rat.

She pulled the pillow up into a bunch under her head, and then sat up slightly and punched it.

Damn Stephen, the scene she witnessed downstairs kept playing over and over in her head. Didn't he understand that some women don't want everything handed to them and obviously Alison was one of them?

During that scene tonight, she would gladly have hit him in the head with one of those ancient swords he had hanging on his walls.

Autocratic, sarcastic, then the next minute utterly charming and loveable, she was in love with a fool, and she damn well better get over it. When this job was done so was the relationship.

Lying back down, she mused there were some things that she had learned about him that surprised her. The façade he put on for other people hid a soft and a worried heart. He loved his daughter and she had watched him each time he had talked to Alison on the phone. When he hung up there had been such a look of sadness on his face that it had broken her heart. Whatever he was afraid of had to do with this house. No man who loves his child as he obviously did, sent her away unless he was afraid for her. That's what puzzled her. Afraid of what?

A soft groan interrupted her thoughts, and she pushed the covers aside and pulled on a soft white silk robe. She loved the color white. Maybe it was vanity but her red hair seemed to glow brighter when she wore white. Other people hated their red hair, but she loved hers and always had since she was a little girl. Being called red or carrot top never bothered her, and as a matter of fact she always dressed to complement its vivid color. That was her only source of pride, at least she hoped it was.

Silently moving into the room next to hers, she crossed to the bed her soft hand gently touching Stephen's brow. He was cool to the touch so he had no fever. She lifted his hand and took his pulse, steady as a rock, and so no problem with his heart, what the heck was wrong then? She leaned forward to listen to his breathing when it happened.

Swift as a snake Stephen's arms wrapped around her and tumbled her onto the bed next to him. She opened her mouth to protest and then it was too late.

His body was hard, even the weeks he had spent in the wheelchair hadn't softened it. He ran his tongue around her lips while his hand traveled up and began to caress her breast.

"What the hell do you think you are doing?" she whispered.

"What the hell do you think?" he whispered back.

"What I think is that you are crazy, now let go of me."

"I can't."

"What do you mean you can't?"

"If I let go of you, you're going to leave and then I won't be able to make love to you."

"You're not going to make love to me so forget it!"

"Oh yes, I am, and you are going to help because," and he groaned dramatically, "I am in such pain."

"You are not in pain." But as she tried to sit up, she discovered that during their whispered conversation he had thrown one leg over hers and she was quite securely tucked under him.

"Have you ever heard of sexual harassment?" she hissed, "I could sue!"

"Sexual harassment? Isn't that where someone has to cooperate in order to get ahead?"

"Yeah, well something like that."

"Well, you are already making a lot of money, you're your own boss, I can't promote you – so I don't think that applies. But if I am going to be sued than I think I should at least reap the benefits of this harassment stuff."

And he ran his tongue around her lips driving the breath from her body.

Trying to scoot away from his body she pushed ineffectively

at his chest. "Look, this isn't going to work, I'm not into one-night stands."

"Neither am I, and don't think that I haven't thought about making love to you long and hard." In the muted light from the hall way she saw his grin, "If you'll pardon the pun."

"What the hell does that mean?"

"It means, I've asked myself a dozen times if I really want to have a shrew like you in my life," he waited for his words to sink in then softly he continued "and the answer is yes!"

"A shrew like me?" Sam's voice began to rise "What do you mean a sh" ...her irate tirade was cut off abruptly as his lips cut across hers and he gathered her securely up to his body.

He lifted his mouth from hers just long enough to look into her eyes. "If you tell me to stop I will, but you'll be giving up the greatest lovemaking you'll ever have in your life."

"What makes you think you're so great?"

"I'll show you!" And with surprising strength he grabbed the front of her nightgown and tore it open.

Sam was shocked, he wasn't supposed to be this strong; the doctors all thought he would be losing his strength, and instead he seemed to be getting stronger. And the fact that he felt well enough to make love scared her to death, could they have made a mistake in the diagnosis, or was the medication working better than they had hoped.

But all thoughts fled from her mind when he bent his head and took her nipple in his mouth. His hand began a downward path spreading her legs and caressing her. Her breath became shallow, and she closed her eyes tightly all feeling centering on his hand and the things that he was doing to her.

It was obvious that he was not a passive player in this love game, she could feel the steel of his body lying next to her and he reached down and took her hand wrapping it around the source of his desire. Between the feel of his lips on her breast and his caressing hand Sam thought she would die. Her legs opened voluntarily to his caress and she turned into him.

He slipped into her, draping one of her legs over his so that they faced each other. "Are you alright?" he whispered.

She opened her eyes startled, Jimmy had been a good lover, but not one who took the time to make sure that she was getting as much out of his lovemaking as he was.

"Do you want me to stop?"

She groaned, "No don't stop."

"Good, I lied, I don't think I could."

He began to move in her slowly, very slowly, taking his time. Constantly watching her, listening to her breathing. When her breathing became rapid, he slowed down, barely moving, and then increasing slightly every time he felt she might be coming down. He kept her at a peak for what seemed like hours, until she couldn't stand it another minute. She tried to force him to increase his pace by moving her body against him, but he just slid away from her.

"You bastard" she whispered," Just do it!"

"Shame on you, a lovely young woman like you with such a nasty mouth." He plunged into her, "Take it back."

"I'm going to kill you when I get up."

"Shame, shame, and you a nurse."

He lifted himself up on one elbow and she realized that the fog had lifted and the moon was shining down on them. His eyes glittered in the moonlight and his voice was deadly serious. "Sam, are you protected? I haven't taken any precautions; there could be consequences to this. Shall I stop?"

"NO!" then her voice softened, "No, to both questions."

"I was counting on that." And he covered her lips with his and began to move within her with a rhythm that sent her soaring.

His lovemaking was all he promised. He never took, but that he gave, if she seemed to be slowing down, so did he, and they finished together, and she knew that he had planned it that way.

They lay still entwined until she realized that his breathing had slowed and that he was falling asleep. She started to sit up to pull her nightgown together praying she could get back to her room before anyone saw her, when he reached out and pulled her back down beside him.

"You're not going anywhere."

"I need to get back to my room before anyone sees us."

"You're not going anywhere." and he pulled her close and wrapped his arms around her.

"Autocratic"

"Shh. . ." he laid a long thin finger across her lips," I'm tired and you're probably pregnant so you'll need your rest."

"What?"

"You said you weren't protected. No pills… no anything right?"

"No," she squeaked.

"Then you're probably pregnant. I haven't made love in a long time, and I imagine I'm pretty potent, and with your peasant background," he waited until that last remark sunk in before he laughed, "you probably got pregnant the minute I touched you."

"Why you insufferable jackass"

"Sam," there was no longer teasing in his voice, "I'm in love with you, and if I make it through this operation, we are going to get married, pregnant or not, so shut up and go to sleep."

He pulled her closer to him. "We'll talk about it in the morning. Or rather we'll probably fight about it – but whatever –right now I am exhausted."

All the things that she was about to say drifted out of her mind. Now was not the time to argue with him. She could do that tomorrow.

She grinned, he expected that anyway. She placed her head under his chin and cuddled into him, she was in love with him too, and what ever happened in the future, this promised never to be a dull relationship.

She listened to his heart, and the beat was sure and steady. She had been afraid for a few minutes when they made love, but his breathing had not become labored.

At least not the kind of labored that foretold a heart problem. Maybe this was good for him, just maybe making love was what he needed to reassure himself that he was going to be okay. And who was she to question the why, or the fact that he turned to her tonight, and told her he loved her. And if for some reason he didn't make it through this operation, --- but she wouldn't let her thoughts go there, -- at least she would have the memory of this night–and if there was a baby–then this night would be even more special!

CHAPTER TWENTY-TWO

S ean stepped out onto the front stoop, the air was crisp not damp, and he considered taking a walk. Maybe some exercise would clear his mind. Archie had his cell phone number, and he wasn't meeting Whisper until dinner. She'd begged off saying she needed some time this morning to straighten out a few things, and although he hated to leave her alone, the last thing he wanted to do was make her nervous by crowding her.

He had only taken only a few steps down the driveway when a car careened up the drive and slammed to a stop in front of him.

"Get in, get in, she's in trouble."

Archie sounded agitated and Sean ran toward the car. "What the hell do you mean she's in trouble?'"

"I've been calling and calling; I called your blasted phone and I couldn't get through and then I called the cottage phone and you didn't answer."

Vaguely Sean remembered hearing something in the background, but Archie had so damn many clocks around, he had dismissed the sound.

"She's gone."

"What the hell do you mean she's gone?"

"She left in her father's car a few minutes ago, I overheard her talking to Anna, and she's going to the village to run some errands. Her father told me to bring the car around for her, but when I got there with the BMW she was gone. Earlier I tried to tell her I'd drive her but she was having none of it. Said the drive would do her good, help her to clear her head."

"So?"

"So?" Archie jumped out of the car; his voice having taken on a screeching quality. "Smell this." and he shoved a rag covered with dark spots under Sean's nose.

One whiff and Sean face grew pale. "Where was it?"

"Right where Stephen's sports car was parked."

"And that isn't all." Archie's voice boomed, "The car she's driving is her father's M. G. and it's always locked in a garage. When I came in this morning, I spotted it, thought it was in the driveway for someone from the village garage to pick up for a tune up, the old man always keeps it in tip top shape. And how the hell she got it I don't know; it's always locked up."

"Which way are we going?"

"North, but you won't catch her — that girl has a lead foot — when you get married you need to have a talk" ... the rest of his comments were cut off as Sean started off at a run toward his Jag.

"I'll catch her...are you coming old man-?"

Archie debated internally as he looked at Sean, "Aw to hell with it, I might as well go out in a blaze of glory with my grandson, as die in bed in an old man's home."

"Of course, I'm coming with you — how about I drive, me knowing the way and all."

The look Sean gave Archie should have sent him up in flames, and Sean heard Archie mutter, "Well it was worth a try."

He scrambled into Sean's Jag and they took off tires screaming, with Archie hanging on for dear life.

The sleek car never hesitated and responded to Sean's every move as it slid around curves and ate up the miles.

"Slow down, slow down, I think she's just ahead of us."

Sean had already spotted the tiny red sports car and his heart began to race. That thing would crumple like a piece of tin if she hit anything.

Archie leaned forward, his eyes staring intently at the little car just ahead of them.

"She must know by now that she doesn't have any brakes, but what she doesn't know, is that around that next bend in the road is a hill...with a curve at the bottom." Archie's breath quickened as he glanced over at Sean.

"What am I going to meet on this road?"

"With any kind of Irish luck," he blessed himself. "You may not meet too much traffic coming the other way. Of course there's a chance you'll run into a farm truck, or a straggler, but this is a farm road and it's not usually busy at this hour of the morning."

He paused, then groaned, "Tempting fate I am. Run into a farm truck, I must be out of my mind."

A smile flitted across Sean's face before he spoke, his tone grim, "Check your seat belt, we're in for a rough ride. As soon as we catch her, I'm going to pull up beside her."

"You're what?" Archie could feel the hair on his head starting to stand on end.

"I'm going to pull up beside her, you signal for her to put the engine in neutral and I am going to push her into the first open field we see."

"You're a crazy person," but Archie reached up and gave his seat belt a tug to make sure it was securely hooked.

Sean hit the gas, and pulling up beside the small sports car, laid on the horn. But Whisper never looked over at him. It was as if she was oblivious to everything except the car she was fighting to keep on the road.

With no brakes the small car was gathering speed and Whisper's heart was hammering and she suddenly felt sick. She wasn't an experienced driver and the intricacies of this little car baffled her.

On the last curve she had stepped on the brake and it had dropped all the way to the floor. The hand brake hadn't worked either and she was terrified.

Frantically she fought to control the car, her only thought to stay on the road. It took a few moments for her to realize that there was a car next to her and that its horn was blowing. She glanced over and her white face alarmed Sean.

"Damn, she's too scared to respond to us."

Archie kept his eyes on the road as he scanned the road ahead. "Fear will do that sometimes."

"I've got to stop her before she gets to the bottom of the hill and that curve with all the trees..."

He glanced over at Archie. "I'm going to have to bump her, then I'll pull in front of her."

Archie's voice was strained, "You haven't got much time, if you're going to do it-- do it." He narrowed his eyes frantically trying to recall everything he remembered about this road.

Suddenly he sat up, "Listen there's an open field up ahead, but she's going to have to go through a hedgerow to get out into it."

Sean spoke his voice controlled, "Good, maybe the bushes will slow her down and her instinct will be to throw her arms up in front of her head when she sees them coming."

"Are you ready?" Sean glanced at his grandfather desperately wishing he had stayed safe at home.

"I'm ready, though I wasn't planning on meeting your grandmother just yet and there's a fifty-fifty chance I will."

"Naw," more like seventy-five."

Archie's voice held disbelief. "More like seventy-five we'll make it?"

"No, more like seventy-five we won't, now if I lose control and we crash- I'll put in a good word for you upstairs."

"Saints preserve us you're the devil himself making jokes at a time like this."

"Worked didn't it?" He glanced over at Archie.

"O. K. the hedge is coming up, now hang on. When she sees me turning my car into her she'll try to avoid me. With luck where she enters the field it will be fairly level."

A feeling of pride tightened Archie's chest; his grandson had nerves of steel. His voice never betrayed the emotion he must be feeling, and his decisions seemed cool and calculated.

Sean accelerated the Jag till he was beside Whisper again, then he turned the Jag into the smaller car and gently bumped her. Catching the car just in front of the tire, the impact forced the small car to turn, wrestling the steering wheel out of Whisper's hands.

She felt the slight jar as her car was gently bumped again, and heard the sound of scraping metal and glancing over she saw the car had moved up beside her again.

Oh my God it was Sean driving. What was he doing here? Her brain couldn't seem to compute anything that was happening.

Again the car touched her, only this time with more force. The larger car again making contact with her front fender.

Sean swore. "This isn't working. I can't hit her any harder!" He glanced over at Archie. "Hang on, I'm pulling in front of her."

Suddenly he accelerated, swung in front of her, and hit the brakes in an effort to slow both cars down.

Instinctively Whisper seeing the brake lights, turned the steering wheel as she tried to regain control and avoid hitting the larger car, but it was too late.

The car swung off the pavement and Whisper screamed as a large wall of bushes loomed up in front of her. As soon as the car hit the bushes it began to slow, but the soft dirt of the field and the ruts from years of plowing tossed the small car around as if it was a toy.

Even though she was buckled in, the spinning of the car had her head hitting the side window.

Abruptly Whisper's wild ride came to an end, as the car spun completely around and mounted a small stone wall at the far end of the field.

Seeing the sports car come to a stop with the front end up on the wall, Sean threw his car into park and jumped out. Racing across the field he wrenched open her door and reaching in shut off the engine.

Whisper was unable to speak, fear robbing her of her voice. Sean ran his hands over her body, checking for any sign of injury. Finding nothing broken and the only significant injury he could see was the bump that was rapidly developing on her forehead, he unbuckled her seatbelt and hauling her up into his arms he carried her away from the small car.

Her body was shaking violently and tears were running down her cheeks. With her clutched in his arms he ran across the field to his car. Archie was out and had opened up the back door. Sean climbed into the back seat; Whisper still cradled in his arms.

"Get us to the nearest hospital." he barked.

Archie didn't hesitate, he scrambled behind the driver's wheel and in just a moment the Jag was back on the road.

Sean held Whisper tightly. Now that it was over fear tightened his stomach. His lips caressed her brow and his mouth come away with the taste of blood.

"Oh, my god, she's bleeding. "Carefully he moved her hair aside and inside her hairline was a jagged gash.

Archie glanced in the rear-view mirror and the look on Sean's face persuaded him he'd better step on it.

"It doesn't look deep but it's a nasty gash, and she may need stitches."

"Probably hit something like the mirror or the window."

Moaning slightly Whisper opened her eyes. She looked into Sean's concerned eyes, but it was apparent she was still dazed. "What happened?"

Sean didn't trust his voice so he was happy when Archie answered from the front seat.

"Bit of an accident Princess, but Prince Charming here came to your rescue. Of course, maybe he still looks like a bit of a toad to you…"

"Shut up," Sean growled…but the fact that she was alive and safe in his arms made his voice crack.

"The brakes failed."

"I know honey" Sean rubbed her arms reassuring her that she was safe. "Do you remember what happened to the brakes?"

"I don't know, I stepped on the pedal and it dropped to the floor and then the hand brake wouldn't work." Her voice drifted off as the anxiety and tension of the episode took its toll. Her eyes closed and only then did Sean allow his feelings to be reflected in his face.

"Step on it she's going into shock!"

Archie glanced into the mirror and shivered. Sean's face reflected anger, a deadly anger that frightened Archie with its intensity.

Sean's voice was soft but with a piercing quality to it. "I'll kill the son of a bitch."

"Now Sean, don't go jumping to conclusions.

"Conclusions hell, those brakes lines were cut. And when I find out who did it."

He never bothered to finish, simply bent down and after gently pushing a stray strand of hair away from the gash softly kissed Whisper's brow; all the while thanking God for keeping her safe for him.

CHAPTER TWENTY-THREE

The ride to the hospital seemed to take hours, but in reality, was just a few minutes. Before Archie had time to completely stop the car Sean jumped out Whisper still cradled in his arms.

Bursting through the doors his bellow startled the nurse who sat at the console in the middle of the hall reviewing charts.

"Get me a doctor."

The nurse looked over at the giant of a man whose face reflected anxiety and anger, and made a quick decision to do exactly what he asked.

Within a few seconds a tiny birdlike man, his gray hair standing on end came bustling down the corridor.

It only took him an instant to take in the scene, and in a voice that belied his size demanded to know why the patient had not been placed on a stretcher.

The nurse's answer was precise and to the point, "She hasn't been put on a stretcher, Doctor, because---" and she glared at Sean, "I can't get this gentleman to put her down."

"Well, I certainly can. You," he said pointing at Sean, "Follow me!" And he strode into a nearby cubicle.

Sean followed and tried to lay Whisper on a small hospital bed, but his arms seem to have acquired a will of their own. Each time he bent to lay her down she was still cradled in his arms when he straightened up.

"Put her down!"

The diminutive doctor had a roar that would do justice to a much larger man, and glaring at Sean his words were razor-sharp, "I hope you haven't done her any harm by carrying her."

Sean's reply was just as sharp, "I did a body check before I lifted her, and I couldn't count on an ambulance getting here as quickly as I could."

Finally realizing that standing beside the bed with Whisper in his arms really didn't make any sense, he carefully placed her on the bed, but he couldn't make himself let go of Whisper's hand until her eyelids began to flutter.

The doctor pushed past Sean, then glaring at him, the tone of his voice reflecting his sarcasm, he asked, "Are you a doctor?"

Sean's glare would have intimidated most men, but not this one. "No, but I spent plenty of years on the Boston streets as a cop, and I can probably check out an accident victim as well as anybody you have here."

The doctor took a second to turn and stare into Sean's eyes, and seeming satisfied with what he saw, he turned back to Whisper. With hands that were surprising gentle for such a brusque manner, the doctor brushed the hair away from Whisper's brow.

"Now, honey, "he said, "You didn't fall off your pony again, did you?"

"Not this time, this time I wrecked Dad's car." her voice was soft as she answered.

"So, he can afford a new one, do him good to part with a few pounds anyway."

Sean watched as a weak smile lit Whisper's face as the tiny doctor tenderly wiped the blood away.

Somehow he knew there was a close connection between the two of them, and even though she had grown up in Boston – this man must have been a part of her life before she moved there. Someone she obviously remembered fondly.

Waving the nurse off who was hovering nearby, the doctor

turned and getting what he needed from the tray beside the bed, gently cleaned the gash on Whisper's head.

"Nasty cut you've got here, but don't worry I'll take care of it, and maybe order a few tests just to be on the safe side."

"Now," his eyebrows lowered, the doctor's gaze swept over the two young men, obviously interns, who had silently entered the room.

From the pained look on their faces Sean realized that these two men were terrified of this tiny dynamo, and he had to suppress a grin.

With just a nod toward Sean, the doctor ordered one of them, "Please show this gentleman where he can wait, and then come right back."

Without hesitating, the intern turned to Sean "Please," he said, "Follow me."

When Sean didn't comply as quickly as he wished, he gave him a gentle nudge, his glance pleading with him to comply.

Sean paused for a moment, reluctant to leave Whisper, yet realizing that he should go, and allow the doctor to check her over.

Sean turned at the sound of Whisper's soft voice, "Sean, I'm okay," she murmured, "Please do as they ask."

Stepping close to the bed he bent and softly kissed her, ignoring the men in the room.

He tried not to grin as the young intern moved in beside him and taking his arm murmured a quiet request for Sean to follow him. It was obvious the young doctor would rather face Sean's wrath, then to displease the diminutive man leaning over Whisper.

With one last look at her, Sean stepped out into the hall.

Archie was leaning against the wall, and falling in step, they followed their escort toward a small room at the end of the corridor. Pointing them toward it, the intern turned and sprinted back.

With a grin at his retreating back, Archie led him into the small room as he filled him in, "I called Stephen and told him what was happening. The man went crazy. It was all I could do to persuade him not to come here. I told him she was doing fine… she is, isn't she?"

Sean looked at his grandfather and suddenly realized that his face was ashen. Alarmed he took his arm which Archie immediately shook off.

"Are you o.k.?"

"Of course I'm o.k. – girl scared the living daylights out of me that's all, and I won't rest easy until I'm sure she's all right. Besides, that crazy ride with you didn't do much for me heart."

"Heart? Is something wrong with your heart?" Alarm tinged Sean's voice.

"Don't be an ass boy, it's just an expression. My heart's just fine, besides it's probably better than yours at this point. After all, my fiancé isn't lying in a hospital bed with all those good-looking young doctors staring at her while her toad of a fiancé waits outside."

Sean grinned at his grandfather. "You can't rile me, she loves me."

"Well there's no accounting for some women's taste."

"You're sure Stephen's not coming here?"

"I'm sure. Sam won't let him. Besides, while he was on one phone with me, he was ordering Sam to get on another line and call the garage where the car's last tune up was done. I'm sure by now they're already on their way to get it. He shook his head, "For a man who's supposed to be so sick, he has a powerful voice when he's angry."

"They're going to find the brake lines were cut."

Archie didn't hesitate, "I know. The whole thing was a set-up. The car parked out in front," he stared at the drab wall in front of them, his voice perplexed as he continued. "Whoever did this somehow knew she was going to the village. And also, how to get the car out of the garage without being seen."

He shook his head, "All the doors to that garage are locked and have been since I came to work here. One of the first things I did was check all the entryways and exits and the outbuildings. Damn place is creepy though, little holes in the outside walls that are really entrances . . . passageways and tunnels that date back lord knows how long, ..." he paused, "don't think I've found them all yet. But as far as the garages are concerned, Anna told me that some local kids broke into them awhile back to have a smoke, thinking they'd never get caught, big mistake, one of them was stupid enough to drop his wallet- and once that was discovered---well they've been locked tight as a drum ever since."

"How many bays in that garage?"

"Five."

"How often do you check the doors?"

"Every morning when I arrive, and again before I leave."

"Nothing amiss this morning?"

"Nothing."

A puzzled look crossed Archie's face. "Since I didn't bring the car around and since she didn't have a key to the locked garage, who the hell put that car out in front?"

"Somebody with keys to that car and the garage. Who else has a set?"

"Nobody but me and Stephen."

"Somebody has them."

"Well if they do none of us knows it, that car is Stephen's prize possession and he won't allow anyone to drive it, not even that nephew of his."

"Edward wants to drive it?"

"Pestered the hell out of his uncle to get his hands on it, but the old man was adamant. No one drives it."

Sean had to contain his grin at the description of Stephen as an old man. It was obvious, with the exception of the surgery he was facing, the man was in his prime.

Their conversation halted as the doctor bustled toward them, a frown on his face.

Stopping in front of Sean his voice was annoyed, "Stubborn girl, she wants to go home, doesn't want to worry her father. I'd like her to stay overnight, but oh no, she says the stress on her father would be too much. Father and daughter, two peas in a pod, stubborn... going to take a strong man to handle that one."

His eyes narrowed and he stared at Sean, "I'd like to know a little more about the bullet wound, and also the old wound on her forehead, but she won't tell me a thing, says it's all water over the damn and she doesn't like to keep talking about it. But, I did get the name of the hospital in Boston where she was taken, and I have a friend who is head of the E R there, so I'll be finding out the information for myself."

Sean groaned, while Archie grinned, "A friend that's head of the E R in Boston? Michael O'Brien?"

"Yes, do you know him?"

"He's my brother."

"And you are?"

"Sean O'Brien and this is my grandfather Archie."

The doctor's laugh echoed through the hallway. Then his demeanor changed and although he smiled Sean could sense a bit of worry in his words. "Told me she's going to marry you, think you're man enough for her?"

His eyes grew wistful. "She's just like her mother, drips milk and honey till you cross her. Then she'd scare the devil himself."

He laughed at the look on Sean's face. "You're in for a ride, boy, Alise always managed to keep Stephen in line, even though I don't think he ever knew it. Why I watched her" - he shook his head softly as he remembered incidents he'd witnessed.

"Well never mind...I have to admit I was a little bit in love with her myself. She always made me laugh." He paused, his voice softened, "I would have slain dragons for that woman."

Then he looked at Sean and grinned, "And you're going to have your hands full with her daughter, she's a combination of both of them, Alise and Stephen."

He couldn't contain his chuckle, "I remember when she was about four years old I made the mistake of telling her that one of her dolls wasn't very pretty, and she informed me in that autocratic tone of her father's, that I might be a doctor for people, but I didn't know anything about dolls, then she walked away, her little nose in the air. Tell you I laughed for a week over that one."

His voice broke as he continued, "I was there when she was born, and I was with her right after she lost her mother."

He shook his head, "Damn shame, damn shame, almost killed Stephen."

Then suddenly realizing that he was rambling, he seemed to mentally shake himself.

His eyes pierced Sean, "I will have one of the nurses give you something to take home with her for the pain. She has some bad bruises and I had to add a few stitches in her head. I want to see her in two days and bring her here so I can see her myself, and be sure to watch for any sign of concussion. Wanted to do more tests – but she was having none of it –."

He began to turn away and then swung back his demeanor somber. "Tell her father there is going to be no more postponements; he is to be here on next Friday. And tell him I'll be doing the surgery myself."

Sean stared at this tiny man, who issued orders without seeming to take a breath. So much for the English reputation of being stoic.

"Oh and see that my god child has plenty of fluids and wake her up every couple hours or so, and I expect an invitation to the wedding, and be sure to tell Mike to get some invitations while I'm in Boston, and set up a schedule for us, so I can visit some of your Boston hospitals. Can always learn something from your chaps," - his eyes twinkled, "or maybe they can learn something from me." He issued all these orders without taking a breath, and suddenly what he said registered, and Sean's hand whipped out and stopped his retreat-, "Wait – did you say she's your godchild?"

"Of course, broke my heart when Stephen sent her to Alise's sister." He shrugged, "But she's back now and I expect to see a lot more of her in the future. And," he emphasized his words with lowered eyebrows, "You had better take better care of her or. . ." he glared at Sean, "You will answer to me"

"That's a promise I can easily make," Sean grinned down at him from his much greater height only to realize that this man was not the least bit intimidated by his size. "But you never told me your name."

"Don't intend to," his hand covered the badge on his chest. "Want you to see Stephen and your brother Mike's reaction when you describe me to them. They'll know who I am."

He grinned, "And tell Stephen I said he still can't play cards worth a damn."

Archie started to laugh and then choked it back when the doctor swung around and looked at him. "Last time I talked to Stephen he said you're a pretty good card player too."

He looked Archie up and down carefully. "But I'm not averse to taking your money either. Call me after Stephen gets back on his feet."

With that parting remark he turned and strode back down the corridor.

"A damn card shark, that's what he is," Archie muttered, "I've a good mind-."

But Sean was standing there a stunned look on his face. "What the hell kind of a detective am I...I never even looked at his name tag or asked his name when he came into the room!"

Archie's voice was soft as he answered, "I guess you're the

kind of a detective who only has eyes for the woman he loves. Especially one who's hurting."

But Sean wasn't listening he was already striding back down the hall toward Whisper.

It took a while before the wheelchair arrived, and Sean knew it was the doctor's way of keeping Whisper where he could check on her if he needed to. Since she kept drifting off to sleep, he and Archie were content just to sit and watch her, till finally she was awake, and after she was carefully placed in a wheelchair, they were escorted by a nurse toward the exit.

Archie, her medication clutched in his hand, ran ahead.

Somehow while they were tied up in the hospital Stephen had arranged for the Jag to be towed away, and a black sedan was sitting in front of the exit.

A tall older man was waiting by the car, and seeming to know exactly who he was looking for, walked over and handed a set of keys to Archie, then climbed into a car that was waiting for him.

Whisper pushed herself up from the wheelchair, but stumbled a little as Archie opened the car door.

With an oath that brought a blush to the nurse's cheek, Sean swept Whisper up into his arms and climbed into the back seat. His legs were cramped and his head touched the roof but he didn't seem to care, all that mattered to him was that she was safe in his arms.

Later he would confront the many questions buzzing through his head but now all he cared about was getting her home and into bed. Then he and Archie would talk.

CHAPTER TWENTY-FOUR

Sean sat in the darkened room, shifting in a chair that was too small for his lanky body. He reached out and touched Whisper's hand reassuring himself that she was still all right. Every time her breathing changed his heart stopped. Jesus what kind of a detective was he anyway? A million times since her accident he had berated himself. Was the fact that he was in love with her getting in the way of his common sense? No one got hurt on his watch, and here was the woman he loved lying in front of him with stitches in her head and a possible concussion.

He shifted again, trying to stretch his legs and considered closing his eyes for a few minutes. He knew sitting here all night was stupid, and tomorrow he would pay for it, but tonight there was no way he was leaving her alone in this house.

Stephen's reaction to his daughter's accident had been exactly as Sean had anticipated. Gone was the calm, cool father that Sean had gotten to know, instead he was simply a man whose only daughter could have been killed, or murdered was the more likely scenario.

The fact that it was his car that almost took Whisper to her death seemed to prey on Stephen's mind, and he was so irate Sam had to give him a sedative and insist that he go to bed. That was smart since the more Stephen became upset, the more Whisper responded to his fears. By the time Sam had Stephen calmed down, Whisper had been clinging to Sean, and he had been the one who carried her up to her bedroom.

Swiftly Sam had taken charge, and now Whisper was tucked in her bed every quiet breath reassuring him that she was sleeping peacefully.

He wanted to let go of her hand, but somehow, he couldn't.

Having her soft hand in his was the link to the future, their future, and the thought of having someone almost tear that future away from him was unbearable.

He knew that to many people this was a crazy match.

He was older than she was, and harder.

He had seen the seamier side of life, and she saw the good in people.

He knew things that were going on in the intelligence community that would scare most people to death, and she thank god was blissfully innocent of all them. But none of it seemed to matter.

His head said slow down and think about what you're doing, but his heart said forget that, grab her, hold on tight, and never let her go.

Grinning in the dark he decided this was the one time his heart got the last word; and if his head didn't like it, that was just too damn bad.

The door to the room was slowly pushed open and the willowy silhouette of Sam appeared. He couldn't see her face, but quietly she gestured to Sean to follow her. For a moment he hesitated, then realized that Sam would not call him from Whisper's side without a damn good reason.

Gently he uncurled Whisper's hand from his, and laying it back on the bed followed Sam from the room.

She didn't speak and only gestured to him, leading him toward what he thought might be her room so they could talk without being overheard.

Only she surprised him, she led him down the hall, then

stepped into a small corner room that was cluttered with children's books and toys. Scattered around were doll houses and tiny plates, cups and saucers, and the curtains at the windows looked like they had teddy bears on them. He smiled as he spotted small trucks tucked in a corner. If this was Whisper's playroom, she obviously wasn't afraid to play with anything she liked.

"Come here," Sam led him directly to a bookcase filled with all manner of books, some, from the looks of them dating back to a much earlier period in some other little girl's life.

"Steven and Charlotte's playroom too?"

Sam nodded, and then swiftly ran her hand over the books on the middle shelf obviously searching for something.

"I was in a hurry when I discovered this so I just shoved it back on the shelf, and it's going to take me a moment...ah- here it is."

She pulled a slender volume from the shelf that had obviously been well read. The binder was torn and it looked like some kind of jelly had been smeared on its cover and dried into a purplish smear.

"Black Beauty." Sean raised his eyebrow quizzically. "So?"

"So this." She unfolded the paper cover that protected the book and pulled a small envelope from between its folds. "It dropped out today when I was in here looking around. I picked the book up because I had read it as a child, and when I spotted it, I couldn't resist."

She opened the envelope and handed the contents to him. There were three pictures in there, and a newspaper clipping.

The first one was a young woman laughing up into the face of a man who; from the looks of him had just tumbled from a horse. His riding outfit was stained and he had a chagrined look on his face as he gazed down at her.

Sean studied the woman, she looked familiar but somehow, he couldn't place her. She obviously loved this guy whoever he was, because the look on her face was soft and she had her hand on his arm. You could almost feel the emotion.

"Charlotte." Sam said.

"What?"

"Charlotte, much younger, softer and prettier. Probably in her late teens, early twenties."

Looking closer Sean could see that Sam was right, the hair fell around Charlotte's face in soft curls, and the riding outfit she wore clung to her curves. Although he couldn't see the full face, just her profile, he realized that the pretty young woman he was looking at was Charlotte.

"I'll be damned." This girl was totally different than the shrew he had seen and dealt with lately.

"That's not all, take a close look at the guy she's smiling at."

"Shit," as recognition dawned, "I met him at the reception the other night." Stunned, he looked at Sam. "He's Edward's boss."

"Bingo.

"He's owns the firm Edward works for."

Suddenly some of their conversation from the other night played back in his head. The words that he'd never fire Edward, and even though he seemed to be joking, his comment that if Edward ever lost it and killed his mother, he would hire the best attorney in London to defend him.

He slid that picture to the back and stopped and stared at the next one. There staring up at him in the next picture was a very pregnant Charlotte. She was obviously unhappy about having her picture taken because her arm was extended and her palm was up trying to block the photographer. He tried to make out what the sign behind her said and then he realized it was in French.

The third picture showed the same woman but in a much different mode. This picture of Charlotte showed a woman in a hospital holding a tiny baby in her arms. The look of love on her face as she gazed at the infant was the portrait of an adoring mother and her child.

But it was the newspaper clipping that really caught his attention.

The paper was tattered, but Sean could still make out that the man in this clipping was the same one that Charlotte had been laughing with in the first picture.

But this one had a picture of another woman standing with him and the caption underneath said this was the last picture the paper had of Baron and Lady St. James before her illness.

"Crap." Sean said. "St. James is Edward's father!"

"That's what Archie and I thought. Only the guy was married."

Her eyes narrowed as she glared at Sean, "So when were you going to tell us that Charlotte was Edward's birth mother?"

Sean's head whipped up. "I purposely didn't mention that Charlotte was Edward's mother till I could verify the information that Luke told me."

"You mean from Frances?"

"Jesus, how much do you know about this whole thing?"

"Probably everything. Archie and I figured out Charlotte was Edward's real mother about two days after I arrived. Watch him when they're together, when he frowns, he gets the very same line in between his eyes as she does. And if you had bothered to look closely you would have spotted the fact that one of Charlotte's ears is slightly larger than the other, just like her son's. We just didn't know who his father was.

"And you didn't tell me?"

"And you didn't tell us what you knew?"

"I'm the boss."

Sam snorted. "You could learn something from your grandfather, he had it figured out in no time."

"And the brakes?"

"Archie's working on that —they were slit, just as you thought, then he spent the balance of today contacting everyone in the village he knows that makes keys, he'll find out who had a duplicate made."

Sean ran his fingers through his hair, "I think I need to have a talk with St. James. I'm sure he knows he has a son – and if my suspicions are correct its Edward that's behind Whisper's accidents and her shooting."

"Okay for the sake of argument let's say you're right – but why? He has a lot of money in his own right, left by his grandmother and grandfather. He will inherit all of his mother's money, what else could he want?"

"A title, Stephen's title and this place. I think he's obsessed with owning everything that belongs to Stephen."

"Give me a break who would kill a cousin over a title and a damn piece of land?"

"Maybe somebody who is obsessed with this stuff." Sean shuffled through the pictures once again. "We damn sure better find out if he's behind this, before Whisper has any more accidents."

"Give me those." She reached out and took the envelope out of Sean's hand carefully replaced the photos and clipping in it.

"Charlotte obviously doesn't want them in her home in case Edward should stumble across them, and she rarely comes here now that I'm here. So I think the safest place for them is right back where they were." She replaced the envelope and walking over pushed the book back into its place.

"Now," she said, "Go back to Whisper and try to get some sleep in that chair, while I climb into my bed between silk sheets and dream of John Wayne. Ah, John Wayne," she sighed, "My hero."

"How about dreaming about a live hero instead of one that's passed on."

"Look you dream your fantasies and I'll dream mine – or

maybe tonight I'll prefer someone like Tom Selleck – move on from the rugged type to a more sophisticated..."

"Witch." He muttered, with a grin.

"Peasant" she murmured as she walked out of the room, her laugh softly following in her wake.

CHAPTER TWENTY-FIVE

Sean slammed the car door and resisted the urge to turn around and give it a good kick. Archie had begun laughing hysterically when it was delivered.

Sure it was a BMW, but it was large, black and dignified, and nothing like his Jag, which although a sedan, had been sleek, and a bright blue.

Why the hell his London office even kept this monster around was beyond him. Then a picture slipped into his mind of the desk jockeys' Sam had hired to do the computer investigations and he grinned. He was willing to bet one of them had ordered this for the office staff to use. They'd love it.

Considering the jolt, the Jag took in the accident, it wasn't in too bad shape.

The guy from the garage, after walking around and shaking his head – had told him that they should have it fixed in a day or two.

Too bad Stephen's little sports car was totaled but that was the breaks.

He and Stephen had agreed that they would total ten of them if it kept one hair on Whisper's head safe.

He stopped, and looked up at the massive building in front of him.

The Andrew St. James Building were scrolled across the top, but there was something wrong. The lettering was off center.

There was a large gap between the name St. James and the word Building. A major error for an architectural firm, and he couldn't imagine the man he'd met the other night allowing it to stay that way.

Unless, and the more he studied it the more it made sense, unless he intended to fill in the blank with the words 'and son'.

Shaking his head, he walked into the foyer and was immediately impressed with the subdued, and very staid atmosphere that greeted him.

Grinning, as his Irish sense of humor kicked in, he had the most absurd urge to put his head back and bellow "anybody home?" just to see what kind of a reaction he'd get.

He was willing to bet four or five security guards that were hidden somewhere would have a heart attack.

Glancing at the piece of paper he had in his hand, he spotted the bank of elevators to his right, and walking over he stepped into a state-of-the-art elevator and hit the 10th floor button.

When it reached the 10th floor, Sean stepped out, facing a set of large forbidding oak doors with the words St. James painted in gold lettering on them.

Very impressive, Sean thought and probably very expensive. Somehow, he could picture Edward and St. James fitting right in here. Too bad the little bastard didn't stick to architecture and not attempted murder.

After yesterday, there was no doubt in his mind that Edward was behind this whole thing. Nothing else made sense. Since Stephen's illness they hadn't done a lot of entertaining, so strangers weren't wandering around the house.

The key to the sports car was kept in a locked drawer in Stephens's desk, so who ever had it duplicated knew exactly where it was.

Archie would scour the village till he found who'd had a duplicate key made, but he'd put his money on Edward, even before they got the answer.

Clumsy little bastard. The mechanic said the brake linings were slit, but they leaked slowly, which is why Whisper hadn't lost control of the car before they got to her. So far all of his attempts to kill Whisper had been foiled, and Sean believed that there was someone somewhere watching over her.

All those near misses. . . suddenly a picture of Whisper's mother flashed into his head, and not questioning why, he glanced up, whispering a silent thank you.

Opening the door and stepping inside, Sean noted that the interior of the St. James office was everything he expected. Formal, with what appeared to be a plastic looking secretary sitting in front of the double doors that he guessed led into St. James' private office.

Everything on the woman was precise. She was so perfect that he was afraid if she smiled, she would crack and shatter into a million pieces.

There were no pictures of her family to mar the clean look, no flowers, no knickknacks. Just a computer and a few file folders.

In comparison, Aunt Em's desk always looked like a bomb had gone off on it, but she knew where everything was, and if anything was moved, she knew that too.

The woman looked up at him, and he'd heard the phrase 'curled her nose' but he had never seen it done before. He realized that he must look pretty bad, not having shaved in two days and wearing the same shirt he had on the night before. There were blood spots on his shirt, and he was sure that his jacket looked like he'd slept in it …which he had.

He'd thought about taking the time to change, but he felt an urgent need to get here and talk to St. James before something else spiraled out his control.

If he upset the plastic princess's sensibilities, that was just too bad.

"I would like to see Baron St. James."

For just a moment he thought he caught a glimmer of approval at the use of the title, before the shutters slid down over her eyes again.

"Do you have an appointment?"

She damn well knew he didn't, and for a second, he considered simply pushing by her and entering the office on his own, though he was afraid she would probably have a stroke if she had to deal with someone entering her boss's office without her permission.

Rapidly losing patience, particularly since the look on her face continued to be dismissive. Sean's voice took on an authoritative tone that had opened many doors in the past for him.

"Ma'am… either tell him Sean O'Brien wants to see him, or I'll tell him myself, and somehow you just don't look strong enough to stop me."

"O'Brien? Another Irish barbarian," she muttered, and putting her nose into the air, she pulled open one of the double doors, glancing back at him with a message that plainly said …don't you dare move.

If he was his brother Patrick, who was the mischief maker of the family, before she had been gone a minute, he would have shifted all of the papers in those folders in such a way it would have taken her two days to straighten them out.

It cheered him up just to think about it, and reminded him to call home to see how everyone was doing.

So far, at least the last time he had talked to his brother Eric, there had been no more attempts on his family's lives. But he still felt uneasy, and he ached to get this mess cleaned up so he could get back home and find out who the hell this guy was that wanted to kill his family.

The massive door to the inner office opened and the secretary walked out, her stiff demeanor reflecting her unhappiness about admitting him.

"The Baron will see you now," she sniffed, as St James himself followed her through the doorway, issuing instructions, "and cancel all my appointments till I tell you I'm available again."

Horror crossed her face as she spun around and looked at her boss.

"But the Prime Minist-"

"Can wait — you call his staff tell them you will call back when I am free."

His tone brooked no argument, and the secretary looked sick, obviously canceling an appointment with the Prime Minister for an Irish barbarian didn't make her happy.

Grinning, Sean walked into his office as St. James carefully closed the door.

"Sit down, sit down," he gestured Sean into one of the leather chairs that flanked his desk. When he was sure that Sean was seated, he slipped into a leather chair behind his desk.

"Would you like coffee, tea, a drink?"

"Coffee? Real coffee?"

"Real coffee."

Sean could feel himself salivating. "Coffee thanks — no cream or sugar."

When St. James spoke into the intercom ordering coffee, Sean could hear the secretary's voice muttering.

With a grin on his face St. James leaned back and studied Sean, "Are you here to ask me, or to tell me?"

"A little of both."

St. James sighed, "I was afraid of that."

Sean sat back in his chair and crossed one knee over the other, preparing himself in case this turned into a long session.

St. James didn't speak until after a steaming cup of coffee had been delivered to Sean, and a hot cup of tea to him. Sean didn't miss the fact that the beverage had been delivered on a sterling silver tray, and that the secretary had tried to hide a sneer as she served him.

St. James waited until Sean had taken a few sips of the delicious brew, and then after carefully studying Sean began.

"Why don't you start out telling me what you know, and then if I'm so inclined, I'll fill in any blanks"

His gaze pierced Sean, "Only I should make myself clear before we start, I will determine what I'll tell you and what I won't. I've had you checked out, Sean O'Brien, and you may be tops in your field, but I'm tops in mine, and I know where to draw the lines.'

Sean grinned, "Pretty good. . . architect. . . draws the lines huh? How long have you been planning to use that little line on me?"

St James looked at him for a moment, and then he burst out laughing. "I thought it was pretty good myself, but it just came to me a moment ago."

He stood and walked to a sideboard and carried a silver pot over and replenished Sean's coffee.

"I can't believe I'm drinking a cup of real coffee. The stuff my grandfather has tastes like boiled potato peels."

"I understood you're quite fond of it, so every morning since I met you, I've had my secretary order a pot. Unfortunately, we had to throw yesterday's out, but at least today's isn't going to waste."

"Yesterday's?"

"Yes. I fully expected that after our introduction the other night that you would show up here."

When Sean didn't answer, he continued. "Now that we've dispensed with the amenities, would you mind telling me why you're here? It's about Alison isn't it?"

Sean was puzzled, "Yes, and no, but why did you think I'm here about Alison? I wanted to talk to you about what happened yesterday and to see of you could shed any light on it."

A frown crossed St. James's face. "About yesterday? I don't know what you're talking about. I thought you were here to discuss the investment that Stephen made in Alison's' name in the firm."

He seemed puzzled as he looked at Sean, "When I first went

into business, I had two silent partners, one was my father who is since deceased, and I inherited his share of the business, and Alison. She was just a baby at the time, but Stephen had such confidence in my abilities that he made an investment in the firm in his daughter's name. He was, and is a dear friend. Since the announcement of your engagement I thought you might come around to find out the status of it. It is quite sizeable you know. Through Stephen, I offered to buy her out many times, but I don't think she even knew, because he always turned me down. Told me when Alison was old enough, she could decide. Then things drifted along and I never approached her."

Sean interrupted —a frown on his face. "No! I'm not interested in any information about her investments, nor am I interested in what she's worth," he growled. "I am more than able to support my wife, and any family we might have. But now you've put a new wrinkle into my thinking. Just how bad do you want that investment, bad enough to have her killed?"

St. James surged to his feet, his face red with anger. "Are you out of your mind? I love that girl, she was my excuse to get into that house. She was bright and lively and she filled a hole in my heart that only a child could fill."

At Sean's puzzled look, he slumped back into his chair, "Well, if it isn't about money than what the hell are you here for?"

"How about to find out what you might know."

"About what?"

"About the attempts on Whisper's... I mean Alison's life."

The color drained from St. James's face and his hand shook as he lifted the teacup to his lips. "What the hell are you talking about? Of course I heard about her accident; it was all over the papers this morning...but you said attempts on her life."

"Three, before yesterday that we know about, and there could be more, we came across those when we were investigating her shooting."

"Shooting?" the cup St. James held clattered as he replaced it on the saucer.

"Yes, a shooting, and we think the shooter was hired by someone over here. We've traced the money to an English branch of an American bank, – and that branch is here in London, and since she hasn't been here since she was a little girl, the likelihood of her having made an enemy over here is pretty remote."

"You don't really think I had anything to do with it do you?"

"No," Sean hesitated for just a moment before his eyes narrowed, and he stared at St. James. "No, but I think your son did."

"Edward? My god why?" Suddenly he caught himself, and he looked at Sean appalled at his blunder.

Sean gazed at him compassion in his eyes. He felt sorry for the man. What must it be like to have a son that you couldn't acknowledge? It must hurt like hell.

"Look, we already know Edward is your son, so you're not letting the cat out of the bag."

"Letting the cat out of the bag?" He looked perplexed.

"Old Yankee saying, but forget that, if Edward is behind these attempts, we need you to help us find out why."

The look on St. James' face changed and his voice became cool, "Why should I help you? You already know he is my son, but what you don't know is I will do everything in my power to protect him."

Restlessly he stood and walked to the table where the coffee carafe sat, and walking back he poured fresh coffee in Sean's cup.

"But I can tell you this, it doesn't make sense. The boy has all the money he needs, he is paid handsomely here, his mother has money, I don't know what else he could want."

"How about a title, and that grand piece of property he grew up on?"

"Titles? A dime a dozen over here, and he stands to inherit the

St. James holdings which are larger than Steven's and Charlotte's combined."

"But he doesn't know that does he? He thinks he was adopted...he doesn't know Charlotte is his mother."

St. James looked sick. "I know. But let me tell you the whole story and then maybe together we can figure out what to do."

He walked to the sideboard and although it was early morning poured himself a glass of whiskey.

Holding the glass up, he signaled to Sean.

"Thanks, but it's a little early for that stuff, I'll stick to the coffee."

"As a rule, I'll have a glass of wine with dinner, and believe it or not – it's an American wine- grapes grown in California... but I have a feeling I'll need more than that today to get through this story."

He slumped back into his chair, and Sean waited, as he stared into the glass clutched in his hand.

"My late wife and I were childhood friends, our parents inseparable, and it was more or less decided from the time we were born that we would marry. I liked Elizabeth, she was fun, kind, warm and loving, and if I didn't feel a great passion for her, nor I might add, she for me, that was all right.

Up until the time I fell in love with Charlotte, I had never felt any great passion for any woman.

When we were first married, Elizabeth and I went everywhere together, and then a few years later she stopped going.

She never let on how ill she was, and she swore her doctors to secrecy. She insisted that I continue to show my horses, race, and to go to parties, and that she was content just to stay home and read, and do the things she liked.

Our garden was the most beautiful in the neighborhood. Little did I know that she had employed a gardener to do the work because she was too weak.

I was young, stupid, and selfish," he twisted the glass in his hand, "I never suspected a thing. I knew she was thinner, and pale but I thought it was because she stayed in the house too much."

He took a sip of his drink, and then stared off into space. His voice was soft as he began to speak again, as if it had to strain to tell the rest of the story.

"Anyway, I was assigned to mentor Stephen, older chaps who had graduated from Academy always took the younger ones under their wing. So, because I spent so much time with her brother, Charlotte and I were thrown together constantly. We both loved horses, and the races, so we also had that in common. Then Stephen left to fulfill his military duty, and by that time what little love life I had with Elizabeth had ceased altogether."

He stared into the glass he held tightly in his hand, and although he hadn't taken a sip it seemed to be giving him comfort. "Even though I was married, I had fallen in love with Charlotte, I wasn't just in love with her, I was consumed with her."

He looked at Sean, his face reflecting his pain, "And I still love her."

He paused and the stillness in the room seemed to be laden with sorrow,

"When I realized that I was on the brink of committing adultery I stopped seeing her. Contrary to the popular opinion of her now, and yes," he looked at Sean, "I know she has the reputation of being a shrew, but at that point she was understanding, and she knew what I was going through. Every time I ran into her, and she was out with another man my heart bled. For six months we avoided each other, until one evening there was a particularly fierce thunderstorm.

The Queen's Day race was to be held the next day and our horses were stabled in the same barn at the Fairgrounds. We both went to check on our mounts. It was late and there was no one else around. The lights went out, she screamed, I went to her . . . and it was the most glorious night of my life. We just came together. . . I was her first."

He looked at Sean for understanding. "Guilt ate me up, after that night I stayed away from Charlotte, but it was tearing me apart. I can only imagine the hell she went through, and what she was thinking. What I didn't know was, that was the night Edward was conceived."

"Six weeks later, Charlotte came to me in a panic, she told me she was pregnant and she demanded I get a divorce and marry her. I had just hung up the phone from a call from Elizabeth's doctor telling me she had only months to live. She was suffering from a rare blood disease. Needless to say, I reacted badly, I told Charlotte I couldn't get a divorce, that Elizabeth was dying, and that we would have to make other arrangements."

"Unfortunately, she took that to mean I wanted her to have an abortion, when that was the last thing on my mind. To this day I don't know what made me say that. Panic, stupidity, god knows. She slammed out of my office and within a week left England. I traced her to France and her Aunt Frances. I called, I went there, I did everything I could to make it up to her – but she wouldn't see me. Finally, I hired a private investigator to watch over her. He was an old school chum, and I trusted him explicitly." He looked over at Sean, "and he never let me down."

He stood up and began to pace, pain etched on his face. "I was in the hospital with Elizabeth when he called. My wife was dying. and the woman I loved was giving birth. Have you ever heard the old saying hell on earth? Well that's what I went through. I held Elizabeth's hand as she took her last breath, and I wasn't with my son when he took his first. I was scared to death when Charlotte returned to England without our son, I was afraid she had put him up for adoption. I should have known better. She had concocted this elaborate scheme where she adopted her own child. Do you know that the birth certificate has a fictitious name for the mother and says father is unknown? --Unknown." He took a sip of his drink.

"Yeah, I do."

"So, Edward could never even find out I was his father even if he went digging."

"After the baby was born didn't you try to claim him?"

"He was born the same day my wife died. As soon as the funeral was over, I went to Charlotte and asked her to marry me. I told her to hell with propriety, people would understand and if they didn't that was too bad. I wanted to give my son my name. She turned me down, said I hadn't wanted the baby when he was born, and now he was hers, and hers alone. I tried to explain, but she got up and walked out of the room. Six months later she brought my son home. She handed her parents and Stephen that story about some friend dying and her adopting her baby boy… and they bought it."

"I had my attorney send her a letter demanding parental rights, and her attorney replied that Charlotte was prepared to go to court and say that she was with a lot of other men. He was very specific, if I wanted Edward to be labeled a bastard with that kind of background, then pursue it. I dropped the whole thing."

"After all that you're still in love with her?"

"Of course, could you turn your love off for Alison just because she did something stupid?"

"No."

"I rest my case, and in this instance I'm as much at fault as Charlotte is. I should never have given up; I should have kept after her. I missed so much of his growing up. Thank god for Stephen, I used to take him to lunch once a week just to find out how my son was. He never caught on, I was careful to ask about everyone, but every little nugget I found out about Edward I tucked into my heart." He reached into his desk. "Here is his first tooth, I bribed a servant to bring it to me, and his first drawing," he laid a child's drawing of a building in front of Sean.

"I was thrilled when he went to school to become an architect, I made sure he won one of the St. James scholarships. Slipped that one by Charlotte till it was too late for her to do anything about it.

Came storming into my office prepared to draw my blood, almost caused my secretary to have a stroke. That was the last time I had the opportunity to kiss her" – he grinned at Sean – "it was the only way I could shut her up. Then I turned the tables on her told her if he didn't accept the scholarship because of her interference, I would go to him and tell him I was his father. She slammed out of here, but never said a word to him about it. You can imagine how I felt handing him that piece of paper at his graduation."

"And then you offered him a job...and left a spot at the top of the building to say 'and son'."

"Caught that did you? A lot of my friends thought it was just a blunder and I am happy to let them think that."

Placing the empty liquor glass on his desk, he stared at Sean, "Now that you know my whole story, let's get back to why you think Edward is behind these attempts on Alison's life."

"Yesterday the brakes failed on Stephen's sports car. Alison was driving."

"Brakes do fail from time to time."

"Especially if they've been cut."

"Cut?"

"Right, and the car was in a locked garage. Nobody had a key. Only Archie and Stephen."

"Well if nobody had a key that rules out Edward doesn't it.?"

"Not necessarily, I have Archie checking to see if a duplicate was made in the village."

Suddenly St. James became pale, and he reached to steady himself on the desk. "Oh my god, if I'm right, he won't find it - the duplicate key may have been made by one of my employees who was going up to Hanover Square. It was a few weeks ago. We were in a meeting and when he got up to leave, Edward tossed him a key and asked him to have a duplicate made. Told him to be careful, there was only one of them. I thought it was odd because he is very friendly with the locksmith in a nearby village, went to school with his son. And he is always trying to steer company business his way." St. James looked sick.

Sean's voice was soft, knowing the pain that St. James was feeling. "Look, keep an eye on Edward will you. There is a reason behind this whole mess and it's going to take all of us to figure it out."

St. James frowned. "Should I tell Charlotte?"

"Absolutely not, she'll tell Edward and then we might not be able to prevent a tragedy here. I'll keep in touch. Take Edward to lunch, see if you can find out anything, but for god's sake don't show your hand, or your son may panic if he knows we're suspicious, and end up in more trouble than he is already in."

"Don't worry. I'll keep him so close to my side he'll think we're welded together. I have a big project that needs a lot of work – and as soon as you leave this office, I'll assign it to him. He and I will work closely on it, and I'll try to find out what is going on in his head."

"Thanks, and I'll keep in touch." Sean threw a card down on the desk. This is my private cell if you're worried about anything – or suspect anything call me. It's on twenty-four seven.

"Twenty-four seven?"

"Yeah shorthand for twenty-four hours a day –"

"Oh, and seven days a week." He grinned, "I love to learn these quaint sayings that you Americans use."

Reaching into his desk drawer he pulled out a card, and handed it to Sean. "Nobody has this number, not even my secretary, so if it rings, I will know it is you. The number is blocked so I only call out on it, and nobody calls in. But I will unblock your number."

Sean couldn't help feeling compassion for the older man. What would he do if he had a son he couldn't acknowledge?

Standing Sean smiled, "Come on over to the states, and I'll take you to a few pubs in Boston, where you'll learn more than you probably want to know about quaint American sayings. Especially if there's a football game on the T.V."

"I look forward to that, and as a matter of fact I have a convention coming up in your city in the fall."

Sean reached over and grasped St. Andrew's hand, but there was more to the touch than just the normal handshake of two men. There was a warmth to it as he held on a moment longer than usual.

"If I were you, I'd clean up this mess with Charlotte. It may take you awhile, but nothing ventured –"

"Nothing gained, "St. James laughed "I know that one."

He followed Sean to the door and with a wink turned and spoke to his secretary, "You can call the Prime Minister back now, say two o'clock will be fine."

He leaned toward Sean, "The staff has already warned me, he wants money – as a matter of fact a lot of money for a favorite charity, and he'll be glad he got in to see me at all."

"Are you going to give it to him?"

"Of course, being the Prime Minister and all." and with a smile he shook Sean's hand one last time and retreated back into his office.

Sean glanced over at the secretary, who was still glaring at him, and he bent forward over the desk forcing her to lean back, "Thanks for everything sweetheart." He blew her a kiss and then winked at her.

Her gasp caused him to laugh, and kept him smiling all the way out of the building. He guessed he had more of his brother Patrick in him than he even knew.

CHAPTER TWENTY-SIX

Sean stood staring out of the kitchen window at the fields behind the estate. Soft flowers dotted the landscape and he suddenly realized that while the front and sides of this stately building had formal gardens, the fields behind were filled with wildflowers.

He remembered Whisper telling him that her mother believed that God showed the world his love by displaying his palette of colorful wildflowers to them; and he knew Stephen let these fields grow naturally for a reason.

He took a sip of the steaming tea Anna had made for him, and decided that he was actually beginning to acquire a taste for the stuff. Maybe he'd keep a few teabags in his office just in case, no better yet, he'd have Em get one of those little balls that you put tea leaves in, and a thing to heat water. Oh my god what was happening to him?

Here he was thinking about making tea – next he'd be ordering curtains. He'd better get this mess straightened out and back to the real world before he totally lost it.

This morning he'd taken Whisper for a short ride, but she had been so tense that after a half hour he brought her back and carried up to her bedroom. Although there was no sign of a concussion, she still had a headache, and he was worried that she would continue to have one until they caught whoever caused her accident.

He couldn't tell her what he suspected because he had no proof. Even the fact that Edward might have had a key made in London would prove nothing until they could tie it to Stephen's sport car. He had his whole staff in London on the case, even his computer geeks, but of course he knew they would probably do all their checking from their desks.

Whisper was smart there was no denying that, this morning out of the blue, she'd told him she knew the brake lines hadn't just failed but been deliberately cut. Yet when he asked her who might have done it, she became totally silent.

Either she had her suspicions, or she was trying to shield a member of her family. Any other time he might have pushed her for an answer, but one look at the stitches in her head and her ashen face, and he decided this wasn't the time.

What really worried him was the faith that she'd had, that she was safe in her father's home was now shattered.

The nightmares had returned with a vengeance, and even during the short nap this afternoon she woke trembling and crying. Sam gave her a dose of the medication the doctor prescribed and it had soothed her. When he checked a few minutes ago she was still sleeping. On top of that, Sam had to give Stephen something to relax him and make him sleep, because he kept insisting he be wheeled into her bedroom to check on his daughter. What a mess.

Stephen had gone ballistic when he was told that his operation had been scheduled. He'd called the hospital and shouted and cursed at the doctor.

A smile creased Sean's face, that little doctor didn't seem to care how big or how powerful he was, he let Stephen rant and rave and when he was all done, simply said, "Be here Friday morning," and hung up.

Defeated, Stephen knew he had no choice, he was going to enter the hospital on Friday and undergo surgery on Saturday.

Just as he glanced at his watch for the tenth time, Sam walked in and heading straight to the steaming teapot, helped herself to a cup.

"Jesus, what a mess."

She slumped rather than sat in the chair at the table.

She was scared to death, but it had nothing to do with what was going on in this household. This morning when she got out of bed, the room had swayed crazily, and she had barely made it to the bathroom before she threw up.

A cold sweat broke out on her brow. It must be the flu, it had to be the flu, and symptoms of being pregnant couldn't show up this soon...could they? Damn Stephen with all that talk about how potent he was.

"Funny that's exactly what I was thinking. Waiting for some missing pieces to fall into place, – and not knowing what, is driving me crazy."

He sat down beside her, staring into his cup as if the answers would magically appear.

"We know the money came from here, but we can't trace it back to Edward." He rubbed his brow. "Until we know for sure that St. James's employee made a duplicate key to Stephen's car, we're at a dead end. Usually I know who or what I'm after but, in this case..." -- he looked over at Sam and frowned, she looked awfully pale to him.

"Are you all right? You don't look too good."

"Thanks a lot, what do you expect, this family is a bunch of lunatics, and I never know when one of them is going to show up with an axe, and murder us all in our beds."

Sean laughed, which caused Sam to grin, and then laugh too.

"I'm just tired and I'm worried about those two upstairs. Maybe I should check on them." She started to rise, but Sean's hand stopped her.

"Sit down." and he reached into his pocket, "I hid one of these up in Whisper's room and one in Stephens's when I was here the other night."

"A bug, you left a bug?"

Her face became bright red and she punched him on the arm. "How long has it been there? I mean what night? The night of the accident?"

"No, the night we announced our engagement."

"Are you out of your mind? You didn't tell me and you left—" her face flushed "You son —of-- a . . ."

Reaching over he placed two fingers over her lips effectively stopping her tirade, "Don't worry – I'm a detective – but I am also a very private detective —and I know exactly when to shut a bug off." He grinned at her.

"Oh," Sam groaned, "How am I ever going to look Stephen in the face when I know you heard everything!"

"No, I heard nothing. So don't worry."

He tried to hide his grin because the look on her face was a cross between utter terror and pure fury. Realizing that he'd better defuse her temper before the situation got out of hand, he glanced toward the doorway. "Do you have any idea why we're sitting here – I've got a few other things that I- "

Sam shrugged, "Don't ask me, ask your grandfather, he's the one insisted on this meeting. Loves everything to be dramatic..."

No sooner were the words out of her mouth than Archie appeared in the doorway.

He smiled at both of them as he crossed the room and poured himself a cup of the still steaming brew. Putting a finger to his lips, he tiptoed toward the large stove that dominated the kitchen and pulled open the oven door.

Reaching deep into the cold oven he withdrew a plate filled with scones and he carefully placed the delicious pastry on the table.

Dropping his voice as if the walls had ears, he murmured,

"Anna thought I'd never find them, but it takes more than a short, pretty cook to keep anything I want away from me."

Sean looked at Sam and raised an eyebrow, and was rewarded with a grin.

Archie bustled around the kitchen quite at home, and a few seconds later, had settled himself at the table and placed a bowl of sweet whipped cream between them.

"Well?" He addressed Sean, "What have you learned?"

Sean grinned, these two worked for him, but you would never know it. Sam said anything she liked, and was completely comfortable mocking him, while Archie obviously thought he was the boss.

"Everything we already knew, St. James verified. Edward is his son and Charlotte's his mother. It's kind of a sad story, Charlotte came to him to tell him she was pregnant the same day he found out his wife was terminally ill and only had a few months to live. Needless to say, he didn't react too well. She left the country and had the baby in France. He had his attorney check the birth certificate, but Charlotte was very clever, it says mother deceased and father unknown, baby to be adopted by Charlotte. So there is no way that Edward can find out his real parents through any birth records. And neither of them is about to tell him."

He stared down into his cup, as if seeking some answers, "You know St. James still loves her. It obviously wasn't a one-night stand. And I came away from that meeting knowing that St. James will move heaven and earth to protect Edward, and although he didn't say it, Charlotte too. So we're at square one, but I did get him to agree to keep an eye on Edward."

Archie turned to Sam, "and what did you get?"

"Nothing, either Stephen is too stupid to see it, or he doesn't want to acknowledge that Charlotte is Edward's mother."

"Stupid? I thought you were a little sweet on him and you call him stupid?" Sean grinned at her.

"Shut up, men can be stupid and still loveable – just ask any woman."

"Well, if you children will stop bickering, I'll tell you what I learned." Archie took a sip of his tea and a bite of his scone."

"Old man," Sean said "If you know something we don't, I am personally going to wring your neck if you don't spit it out."

"And I am going to hold you down while he does it," Sam glared at him.

"Tsk, tsk, you children are so impatient." Wiping his chin with a napkin, Archie sat back.

"This afternoon when Anna and I were sitting here, at this very table as a matter of fact, she had just put those scones in the oven and the aroma was making my mouth water. Then I asked her…"

"Old man," Sean practically shouted the words, and Sam pushed her chair away from the table preparing to throttle him.

Laughing at their reaction Archie continued, "O.K. hold your horses, I casually led the conversation around to Edward, in the event she knew something that didn't seem like a big deal to her – but might be a big deal to us – and low and behold," he took another sip of tea, and a bite of scone which he chewed very slowly, a move which left Sean wondering how his own mother would react when she learned her son had murdered her father. She'd probably understand it.

A devilish gleam in his eye, Archie continued. "Once I got her started she was a wealth of information. In the beginning she sputtered a lot and wasn't too complimentary about him or his mother, but then she began to reminisce. Seems he was a pretty good kid when he was younger."

He took a bite of scone and again chewed very slowly, watching the hackles beginning to rise on Sean and Sam. After what he considered just the right amount of time he continued,

"One afternoon when Alise and Alison were out shopping he stopped by. Naturally Anna sat him at the table to give him cookies and milk while she peeled potatoes. That woman can make a mean pot of potatoes, melt in your mouth they do, rich with…"

He started to laugh when his grandson began to push himself away from the table. But before Sean could finish his move, he continued.

"He was pretty upset that day and that was why he was there to see Alise. He often came to her with his problems, seems she had a way about her that would make a big deal for a teenager seem small in the scheme of things. But since she wasn't here, he laid it all on Anna." He studied the two sitting across from him wondering if they would even understand.

"There had been a class election that day at the Academy, and the chap he was running against for Class President was a mean little son of a bitch. Right before they were to vote, he passed around a paper saying that it would be a scandal to have a no name little bastard as president of their prestigious class. Although he had some friends who stuck by Edward, he lost the election."

Archie shook his head, "Anna says he was a sensitive little bloke and even though he blustered and tried to hide it, the meanness of the whole thing broke her heart it did, and even after all this time as she began to tell me the story, " Archie hesitated, "Anna began to cry. She said she put her arms around him and held him for a long time-- and then the bombshell."

He glanced at Sean, "He confided to her that when he was about six or seven, he overheard Stephen and Charlotte talking about him being adopted. Pulled the rug right out of his world."

"Pulled the rug right out from under him."

Archie glared at his grandson. "Do you want to hear this story or not, or would you rather just get your knickers in a twist correcting an old man? I've got a good mind …" and he moved as if to stand up.

"If you make one more move, I will personally take you down."

But it wasn't Sean that spoke it was Sam. "Now spill it."

"All right, don't get into a snit. Seems he knew he was adopted but…here's the kicker it seems he also overheard them say that his father was alive. And …well… he thinks its Stephen."

"What?" In unison Sean and Sam spoke, as Sam surged to her feet knocking over the chair she sat in.

"That's ridiculous, Stephen would never have a child and not acknowledge it."

"Well you know it and I know it – but in a child's mind, Stephen as his father might make sense. From what I've learned Stephen was very good to him, took him everywhere with him. Treated him like a son and he knew he was adopted – so as he got older, he reasoned that big sister was covering for baby brother and had adopted his illegitimate baby."

"Oh my god," Sam said, "No wonder he's so messed up, he thinks his uncle is his father."

"He kept insisting to Anna that one day Stephen would acknowledge him. She tried and tried to tell him that Stephen was not his father. Even then she had her suspicions about Charlotte, but she never could talk him out of it. He swore her to secrecy and she never told that story to anyone till now."

"Oh my god there's the piece we've been looking for." Sam's voice shook… "That bitch, look what's she's done to her own son with her lies."

Sean stared at Archie his voice slow as if he was contemplating each word before he said it. "So he thinks he's entitled to the inheritance, and Stephen's title because he's Stephen's natural son. Which would also account for his standing in Whisper's room just staring at her, he thinks she's his sister."

"Yeah a sister he's willing to kill." Archie's voice became cold.

"We've got to get Charlotte and St. James to tell him the truth. As long as he thinks Stephen won't acknowledge him, he's dangerous. He already tried to kill her yesterday, and now I'm pretty sure he hired the guy in the states. With her out of the picture, I'll bet in his mind he figures Stephen will acknowledge him, and he will have the recognition he obviously craves."

"What's ironic here, "Archie mused, "Now that we know that St. James is willing to acknowledge him as his son, he stands to inherit a larger estate and a more prestigious title than the one his uncle has. Then he can thumb his nose at all those little bastards that made his life miserable as a kid."

"Yeah, but we've got to get one of them to tell him." He looked at his two companions, "Which one?"

"St. James," Archie and Sam spoke as one.

"Forget Charlotte, she's harbored this secret too long and I don't think she's about to divulge it now." Sam shook her head in disgust.

"Sam's right – go for the father, if he realizes how bad things could get for his son, he might have the leverage to talk some sense into Charlotte."

Flipping open his cell phone, Sean hit speed dial. A second later St. James was on the phone with him.

Hastily Sean filled him in about what they had learned and the oaths that St. James uttered carried to the other two.

Sean began to frown and he rubbed his forehead as he listened intently to what was being said on the other end.

Finally flipping the cell closed, he looked at them. "For the first time since he began to work for his father Edward didn't show up at the office today. He knows they are working on a big project but there was no call, no message, nothing...and Charlotte doesn't know where he is either."

Sean face reflected his worry. "So, as of this moment nobody knows where he is, or what he's up to. Both of you stay alert. Sam you're going to have to tell Stephen what's going on, and I'll tell Whisper. We were waiting for things to break open, and I think we're about to get our wish."

He grasped Sam's shoulder, "You be careful hear me? God knows where the little bastard is, and he has the element of surprise on his side, and he knows this place a hell of a lot better than we do."

Sam nodded as she pushed herself away from the table. Up to now she had never been afraid, but just in case there was a little person nestling inside her she wasn't going to take any chances.

CHAPTER TWENTY-SEVEN

Archie opened the library door and motioned for Andrew St. James to enter.

He hesitated for a moment when he saw Charlotte, but then crossed the room and sat down on the coach beside her. He reached for her hand and when she tried to pull it away he stared at her their eye contact electric. "Don't" he said, "It's time." A quick sob escaped her and then she grasped his hand tightly.

"All right, what the hell is going on?"

Stephen's voice was hoarse with exhaustion as he glared at Sean. "Do you know what time it is?"

"Last I looked it was about five in the morning."

"Are you out of your mind? What is so damn important that we had to get together at this hour?"

"Hush, you'll know soon enough." Sam voice was soothing rather than impatient and he looked at her questioningly.

Sean gazed around the room. All the players he had contacted had arrived. St. James was the last player except for one, and he nodded to Archie. "Ask Anna to come in here."

Archie went to the library door, pulled it open, and bellowed Anna's name.

"Jesus," Sean muttered "I could have done that."

Anna's small body burst into the room and she barreled into Archie unmindful of the other people gathered there. Without a pause, she poked her finger into his chest, her eyes glaring at him. "Don't you ever, do you hear me? Don't you ever call me like that again!"

Archie stepped back, startled by the fury on her face. "I'm sorry darlin' – I just thought…"

"That's the trouble with you – you never think." Then suddenly realizing that she had an audience her face became scarlet, and she put her hand over her mouth and turned to leave.

Archie reached out and took her arm. "Come in sweetheart, you're an invited guest to this meeting and you sit right next to me." He pulled two chairs close together and patted one, motioning for her to sit.

Sniffing and putting her nose in the air Anna sat – but as far away from Archie as she could.

"That's it then." Sean walked over and closed the library doors. Turning, his face grim, he looked at Charlotte, "Did you hire someone to kill Whisper?"

"What?" Charlotte and St. James both surged to their feet, St. James taking a threatening step forward.

"Don't be preposterous, she may have her faults but she would never hire someone to kill her own niece."

"Then did you do it?"

His eyes swung to St. James, but like a jungle cat springing to the defense of her mate Charlotte snarled at Sean.

"This is crazy!" Charlotte's voice cracked. "He'd never do such a thing, and what would he have to gain? He has everything."

"Everything but you …and my son." St. James turned toward her and although the words were meant for her alone, the others in the room heard the pain in his voice as he reached for her.

Shocked, Charlotte looked up at him… "But I thought—"

"Sit down both of you!" Stephen's eyes were bleak as he stared at the two of them, St. James's words echoing in his head.

Although Stephen's voice shook, it was curt, a sign of a man trying to control his anger. "You can hammer out your personal lives later. What I want to know is why Sean even thinks that one of you might have hired someone to kill my daughter."

"Well, to be honest, I don't," there was pity in his eyes as he glanced at Charlotte and St. James, "I just wanted to prepare them . . . because," Sean looked over at Stephen, "I think their son did."

"You're crazy; Edward would do no such thing . . .tell them—" Charlotte voice shook as she looked pleadingly at St. James.

"Then how do you explain the fifty-thousand dollars that was deducted from your personal savings account here in London and transferred to a bank in Boston? My staff was able to trace it that far – and then somehow it disappeared. No record of it ever having been withdrawn – yet somehow it's gone."

"That's a lie, I never sent any money to Boston – why would I – I'd have no reason," she looked pleading at St. James.

As Sean raised one eyebrow and waited, her voice became a whisper, "Only Edward and I have access to my funds and he would never do such a thing."

"Wouldn't he? What does he want, Charlotte, that he doesn't have now?" Sean's voice was harsh.

"Nothing, he has a job that he loves," she glanced at St. James, "he has money he inherited from my parents, and he'll inherit mine, what else could he want?"

"How about the truth, how about knowing who his real parents are, not the fictitious ones you made up for him." Sean cool demeanor belied the anger that will building inside of him.

As he spoke, Sean moved behind Whisper's chair reaching down and gently rubbing her shoulders, knowing that the words she was hearing were tearing her apart.

"He thinks you're his father," Anna looked directly at Stephen, "and that you won't acknowledge him." Her voice trembled as she uttered the words.

"What?" Charlotte and St. James spoke as one – and Charlotte's face became ashen as Anna's soft voice reached her.

Charlotte surged to her feet but St. James reached out and pulled her down holding her close to him as her voice broke,

"That's a lie, where would he get such an idea? I was so careful. . ."

But now that she had spoken up, Anna mustered the courage to continue, and her voice became firm as her eyes locked with Charlotte's.

"From you and Stephen, he overheard the two of you arguing when he was very young, he was in the library when Stephen was questioning you about his parents — and from what was said he decided that you adopted him to keep him from being sent away as a baby. He thinks that Stephen got some village girl pregnant and that you as his older sister came to his rescue." She waited for her words to sink in.

"Oh my god, no," there was pain in St. James' voice.

"Charlotte," Stephen's voice was shattered as he looked at his sister, "Why in god's name didn't you confide in me, why in all these years didn't you tell me you were really his mother? And you," Stephen turned to St. James, his eyes narrowed in anger.

"You were my best friend, I turned to you for advice, and even comfort when my wife died. If my sister wouldn't tell me, why wouldn't you?"

St. James stood and moved away from Charlotte, walking to the windows that dominated one wall of the room, he stood staring out and then slowly turned and faced the man who was his friend.

"Do you know how many times I wanted to, Stephen? Why do you think I was always so interested in what was going on with your family?" his eyes sought Charlotte's. "Because it was my family too!"

His voice broke and it was obvious he was trying to control his emotions. "Didn't you think it unusual that I showed up at the hospital when Edward had that car accident as a teen, and that I bought him his first bike, and puppy?"

Stephen's face was grim. "Jesus, was I that blind?"

"No," he answered "You just never questioned my motives, you had no reason to, I was your friend; and now you ask me why I didn't tell you...if you want the truth, it was because I was a coward."

St James glanced over at Charlotte whose head was bowed, tears running down her face.

"I was afraid if you confronted Charlotte, I would lose them both. You have to realize that Charlotte was very angry and bitter at what she viewed as my betrayal, and I was frightened that she would take my son and leave and I would never see either of them again."

He paused, "Not that I blame her, I've regretted for years that I wasn't honest with my wife so I could acknowledge Edward when he was born. It would have been rough on all of us, there would have been scandal and pain, but we would have weathered it. No worse than the pain I have borne all of these years not being able to acknowledge my own son."

He looked pleading at Charlotte, "The sad truth is that I think Elizabeth would have understood and been happy for me. She was a good and true friend."

Charlotte stood and took a halting step toward the door when Stephen's soft voice stopped her. "Sit down, we can't do anything about the past, but we sure as hell can do something about the future." He turned to Sean. "What do we do now?"

"I'd like to answer that." Everyone's head swiveled toward Sam. "The first thing we do is recognize that we are dealing with a man who thinks that he has been lied to for years – which he has," she looked accusingly at Charlotte- "Only the lie he thinks he knows ...isn't the real lie."

Sean lifted an eyebrow at her as she continued.

"Let's look at the facts, at this point Edward thinks that Stephen is the father that never acknowledged him. He feels hurt, betrayed and very, very angry. He is torn, because I believe he really loves his cousin, but he is afraid that she stands in the way of the one thing he craves and that is acknowledgement by his father."

At Charlotte's soft cry of dismay Sam turned to her, "I never really liked you because I didn't understand you – maybe in your place I would have done exactly what you did, who knows? But as his mother, and his father," she looked at St. James, "but let's be clear here, if he comes to you, hiding or protecting him will cause him more harm than good."

Charlotte's face blanched, "I suppose as a nurse, you've seen this kind of thing before."

"No," Sam said, "I've seen the consequences of this kind of thing more in my other line of work...working as a detective for Sean."

"Working for Sean?" the voices weren't all in sync but the startled tone of their voices was.

"Yeah," Sean said "and Archie too."

"I knew about Archie, but you," Stephen glared at Sam, "How much did you do in the line of duty?"

"Oh, lots," she grinned down at him, "But not what you're thinking."

Anna's eyes snapped as she rounded on Archie, "and all the time you sat in my kitchen, eating my pie, you were really spying on me."

"No, sweetheart, eating your pie was my idea; it had nothing to do with my job." He picked up her hand and kissed the back of it, "I was trying to get close to you so you might not think of me as an old man – but someone who . . ." He grinned at her. "But we'll talk about that later."

"So," St. James said, "Three of you in this room are detectives and..."

"And like you, we want to stop your son from doing something he will regret the rest of his life...." Sean's voice was cold and his eyes glacial as they stared at St. James and Charlotte.

"But let me make myself perfectly clear," his hand tightened on Whisper's shoulder causing her to wince,

"If it comes down to a choice between Edward or Whisper's life …. As far as I am concerned there will be no choice, do you understand what I am saying?"

St. James moved to Charlotte's side and took her hand. "There will be no choice, we will do everything we can to keep our son and Alison safe."

"All right then," Sean turned to Charlotte, "When did you see Edward last?"

"Saturday, he said he was running up to London. But he'd be back for work on Monday."

"But he never showed up."

"No," St. James shook his head, "No, he's been gone three days, and he didn't call either, very unusual for him."

"So, he's been gone since Saturday, didn't show up for work on Monday and no one has heard from him or seen him." Sean paused, "It's my guess he's getting ready to make his move. Friday Stephen enters the hospital for his surgery, if anything happens to Whisper, and Stephen doesn't survive his operation - correct me if I'm wrong – it all goes to you…right?" And he looked at Charlotte.

"Yes, but I…"

"I'm not accusing you of anything – let's just say Whisper meets with an accident and Stephen doesn't make it…what happens to Stephen's estate and …his title?"

"It all reverts to me, and my heirs."

"Now let's say for the sake of argument it isn't the money Edward wants but to be declared Stephen's heir. What happens then?"

"Well under normal circumstances I would petition the Queen to give everything to Edward."

"Right, so Edward becomes Stephen's heir and inherits what he believes is rightfully his."

"Oh my god, Charlotte, what the hell have we done?"
St. James' voice trembled.

For a moment Charlotte was beyond speaking, her face drained of color. When she spoke, her voice shook with fear. "Do you believe he will try to kill Stephen too?"

"I wish I could answer that, but no one knows what is going on in his head. My gut tells me he'll make his move before Friday but we can't even be sure of that."

Sean glanced at Stephen, his tone rueful, "He might even be counting on the fact that if you lost your daughter you might not want to live."

"What can we do?" Charlotte voice was desperate and she clutched St. James' arm.

"Well since he doesn't know St. James is his father, he won't expect him to be involved. I want him to stay with you tonight, you can't be alone, but he is to stay out of sight. If Edward comes home, neither of you is to confront him, just contact me immediately. If he thinks he's cornered we don't know how he'll react, understand?"

He turned to the others, "That's why I had you all here so early in the morning, we don't know where he is. He may even have returned and be hiding out somewhere. If we make him suspicious, we'll never be able to smoke him out. From now on, everything in this house goes on as usual. Only nobody leaves it except Archie. If Edward is watching we can't raise his suspicions."

Sean surprised them all by turning to Anna. "He may come to you first. He's confided in you in the past and you never betrayed his trust. He may want you to know his side of the story before he strikes. You can't let on that you know anything. Can you do it?"

For a little woman her voice was surprisingly strong, "I don't want anything to happen to either of those children, Alison or Edward, of course I can do it. He'll never suspect I know anything."

"Okay then, its six-a.m. starting now everything goes back

to normal. He nodded to St. James, "You go to work, in case Edward shows up."

"But you don't think he will do you?"

"No, I don't."

"Then," Sean continued, "Find a way to get back to Charlotte's estate without using your car, I don't think he'll be watching her place, but we can't take a chance." His voice was firm, "If we want to catch him unaware and prevent a tragedy, we can't raise his suspicions."

Charlotte's voice was soft, "I was going into London today, I can pick him up in the hotel parking lot near his office, and when we get closer to home, he can lay down in the back seat. I always park my car in the garage so there's no chance Edward will see him...unless he's in the house."

"Not bad, -- o.k. with you?" he looked at St. James who looked astonished by her words.

Recovering, he grinned at her, and then Sean. "Do you know what a terrible driver she is? I'll be lucky if I make it to her place alive."

"Can't be any worse than her niece." Archie murmured trying to keep his voice low, but Whisper turned to him, and for the first time since the meeting began, she smiled, "I heard that."

"Meant you to." He smiled back at her.

"What about me?" Stephen's voice was impatient, "Am I to just sit in this wheelchair and wait for something to happen?"

Before Sean could answer Sam did. "Yes, you are to remain your cantankerous self, in that wheelchair and in this house. If by any chance Edward gets to us, everything has to seem normal, and there couldn't be anything more normal than you snarling at me."

"And me?" Whisper looked at Sean.

"I will be picking you up at 9:00 we will go into the village and shop," he grimaced, "we will have lunch and then I will bring you back. Your routine will stay the same. I don't believe he will strike during the day, too many people in and out. He's coming after you tonight or tomorrow night, and we'll all be ready."

"You're so sure?" Charlotte stood and took a step forward. "Please don't hurt him, this is all my fault."

"It's our fault.' St. James moved to her side.

"I'll do what I can, but..." he looked at the two of them, compassion on his face as he knew he was talking about their only child.

"But understand I won't let him hurt her."

"We can't ask for more than that." St. James took Charlotte's arm, "What time will you pick me up?"

"What time do you want me to?"

"You and I have a lot to talk about, so I'll leave early, is two o'clock all right?"

"Two o'clock is fine." As Charlotte moved toward the door St. James followed her, their voices mingling.

"Do they have a chance?" His eyes worried, Stephen looked at Sean.

"I would guess that all depends on what happens with Edward, but I'm hopeful."

Realizing the frustration Stephen must be feeling knowing he couldn't get out of his wheelchair and do more to protect his daughter Sean eyes narrowed.

He turned toward Stephen, "One thing bothers me Edward seems to be able to move in and out of this place without being seen. Can you draw us a map and mark every entrance and exit, even the ones that aren't normally used?"

Stephen nodded, a look of determination on his face, "I know every little spot where you can enter and exit this place, and I have plans in the study that detail every architectural change that has been made over time. Come on detective. . . I mean Sam", his sarcastic tone told Sam she was in for a rough ride when they were out of earshot of the others.

Sam rose from her chair, and moving behind Stephen's

wheelchair raised an eyebrow at Sean, but he simply smiled at her. She knew that they had already gotten a complete set of those changes from the office in London.

Then she grinned, this was Sean's way of giving Stephen something to do, and she was also sure he was going to drive her crazy checking every little detail, plus raising hell over her role in this whole thing.

Anna stood and without even glancing in Archie's direction headed for the door.

Realizing that he had a lot of explaining to do, Archie jumped to his feet and followed, "Now darlin' about that kiss- when I kissed you in the kitchen. . . that was definitely not in the line of duty – that was my own idea." his voice trailed off and faded as he followed Anna down the hall.

Suddenly alone in the room, Sean turned around and reaching down picked Whisper up in his arms. Sitting down on the couch he began to nuzzle her neck as he murmured reassurances to her.

"Does he really want to kill me?"

"Honey, this is a man who believes that he has been lied to for years. He craves recognition by the one man he believes is his father. Only unfortunately because of all the lies, he has chosen the wrong man for that role. Compound that with the fear that as long as you're alive, Stephen will never acknowledge him, and you have a man on the edge.

He ran a finger across her lips and followed it with a soothing kiss. "Now that we're getting married, he knows any son we have will be in line to inherit your father's title. He believes our son would be stealing his birthright and he can't let that happen. You're the one thing that stands in the way."

Instead of anger, tears ran down Whisper's face. Reaching up she cupped his cheeks in her hands. "I feel so sorry for him, please try not to hurt him."

"I promise to do all I can," his voice hardened, "But you better understand, I will do whatever it takes to keep you safe."

He ran his tongue around her lips and then followed it with his mouth. She sighed and his tongue swept into her mouth in the most intimate of kisses until he she began to move in his lap causing changes in his body that had him groaning.

Abruptly standing her up, but still holding her in his arms he settled her a little farther away. "There is no way I am going to make love to you in your father's library, so no matter how you beg," he grinned down at her, "I'm going to have to turn you down."

Whisper gasped at his words, and then she laughed. And reaching up she softly kissed his cheek. With a twinkle in her eye she dropped her voice, "Listen if we make love in here, I'll still respect you in the morning."

"It is morning," he kissed the top of her head, "But once this mess is straightened out, you'd better pick a date and it better be soon, or I'll be dead from frustration before I can make it."

Suddenly serious, she looked at him. "How about in six months?"

"How about in six weeks?"

"Six weeks?" For all its softness Whisper's voice took on a screeching quality. "I could never plan a wedding in six weeks."

"Alright then," a devilish delight lit up Sean eyes, "I'll plan it."

"Are you out of your mind?" She levered herself away from him, "No man, no matter how much I love him is going to plan my wedding." Sean could see the wheels turning in her head and he knew that he'd lost her.

"I'll have to call the girls in the office and tell them we've set a date, this doesn't give them much time and my aunt Annette will need to fly over...so we can start,"

Sean bent down and gave her a quick kiss. "Do you know what time it is? Call your aunt and the girls later you and I need some sleep."

She glanced at her watch, "Do you have any idea what time it will be in the States?

"Give it a little while, then call them and if you wake them so be it – and call my sister too will you? Let her have the privilege of telling the rest of the family."

Yawning, Sean ushered Whisper out the door then he smiled. Instead of being worried about Edward he had just given his bride-to-be something else to think about. Let her plan the wedding – and to keep himself sane – he'd concentrate on planning the wedding night.

CHAPTER TWENTY-EIGHT

E dward slipped into an alley and pulled the grey wig from his head. He stuffed it into a trash barrel, and pushed the black gloves in behind it. He didn't know about the wig, but he was sure those gloves would be on somebody's hands before he had been gone ten minutes.

He patted the gun that was nestled in the pocket of his jacket. There were only a few places to buy an illegal gun in London and he had known right where to go. In school he had only one close friend and Philip's father had served on an international task force that was trying to stamp out crime in the UK. Philip used to tell him stories about how his father and his colleagues would raid the shops down here searching for narcotics and guns. He never thought he would need that information...till now.

He smiled to himself, even if they questioned all the shopkeepers down here none of them would remember him.

The black livery outfit he had concocted had been assembled in pieces, a jacket here, the pants purchased someplace else, and the boots, now that was a streak of genius.

He had purchased the boots, cheap ones, and then set about destroying them. But the final stroke had been when he had placed steel rods that showed, on either side of one of the boots. The extra weight made him drag his foot, and he stooped as if in pain. The only thing he had worried about was his hands, they were a young man hands, but the gloves had solved that problem nicely.

No one would connect that sad old limousine driver, with him. He had furtively glanced around the shop as if he had been sent to do something that he didn't want to do. And even mumbled about his employer being a devil.

The shop keeper had fallen for it, and when it was time to leave, even hastened to open the door for him. He laughed; imagine selling illegal guns but still rushing to open the door for a crippled old man. People amazed him.

Now, where to get rid of the rest of his clothes. He slipped into the employee entrance of a nearby hotel he had checked out earlier in the day. Being careful not to be seen, he took a service elevator to the rear of the second floor. He exited and stepped around the corner, ah, luggage, ready to be loaded into the limo and then into a plane and just where he knew it would be. Bending, he silently began to check the suitcases, until he found one piece where the lock had not been secured. These American's were too trusting.

He grinned when he saw it was filled with a woman's clothing. Pulling a few pieces out he slipped out of the jacket and stuffed it into the empty space. He'd spotted a room where the door was ajar and he tossed the clothing in there. He knew the woman's clothes would be found, and when the woman called the hotel looking for them, they would send the missing pieces to her. No one could accuse him of being inconsiderate.

He had registered here under a false name, Jim O'Brien. Sam's dead husband. Only this Jim O'Brien would be a little different. He reached down and pulled the metal rods out of the boot and undid the top button of his shirt then pulled the oversize shirt part way out of his pants. Reaching into his front pocket he pulled out the cotton balls stored there and stuffed a few into his cheeks. From his back pocket he extracted and unfolded a baseball cap with a blond ponytail sewed into the back and pulled it onto his head.

He took the stairway down to the lobby waiting until he was sure that there were other people milling around the reception desk, then he stumbled to it. He kept his head down as he asked if there were any messages for him, and when the receptionist said no, he asked her to check again, and when she shook her head, he sighed and mumbled about the fickleness of women.

He hesitated for a moment as if he couldn't make up his mind, and then asked for his bill and paid it in small bills. A look of pity crossed the woman's face as she took the money and she quickly averted looking at him. He wanted to laugh, a poor slob of a fat guy, stood up by some woman. Anything she remembered about him would be tainted by her feelings of sympathy.

Quickly, he returned to his room, and taking off the remainder of his clothes he stuffed them into the one lone suitcase that he'd bought. Reaching into the closet he pulled out the outfit he'd brought from home. His mother would remember and recognize this jacket, she had bought it for him.

After he killed Alison, they might try to tie him to Alison's death, since he would be the one to gain the most, but he was pretty sure he'd covered his trail pretty well. They'd never be able to trace the gun, and the storekeeper would remember selling it to a chauffeur with a decided limp.

Stephen would be devastated when his only daughter was murdered during a burglary; but he and his mother would rush to console him.

It had to happen before Friday. Stephen went into the hospital then, and if he didn't survive the operation – well that would be even better. His mother would see that everything would go to him. She could petition the court to grant him Stephen's estate and title and as the last heir, even an adopted one, they might grant the petition. Or maybe he'd get St. James to petition the Queen.

His employer seemed genuinely fond of him, and if he played his cards right maybe the old boy would help. Well, he'd cross that bridge later. Right now, he had to concentrate on getting Alison out of the way.

His hand trembled as he reached for the door knob; he had wiped everything clean, now he had to get out of here without being spotted.

Even with all of his plans in place he wasn't sure he could do it. She was his sister for god's sake. But then he remembered that he was the rightful heir, and Stephen had never acknowledged him. It wasn't his fault —it was Stephen's. If he had done what was right – well, now there was no question, it had to be done.

Before he had made these plans, he had tried one last time to get in touch with his "so called friend".

He had explained to the gruff voice that answered the phone that he needed to get a message to him. He had explained the whole story, the operation, that Alison needed to be eliminated now. He had waited in the hotel for hours, waiting for the return call. When it had finally come the news had not been good. There was no way that his friend could do the job in the time frame that Edward needed. He had another assignment.

For a moment he had hesitated, then he told the gruff voice, that he was sorry but he would have to do it himself. The man had laughed hysterically, then told him this was unique, his boss had never been fired before. The way he laughed had sent chills down Edward's spine. He had heard nothing since, and he hoped his friend had taken the news well, or he might be a dead man walking.

He stole a washcloth from the bathroom and rapped it around the handle of the suitcase. Stepping into the hall he spotted some suitcases waiting to be taken to the lobby by the valet and quickly reading the destination on one of them scribbled the same destination on the tags that he had purchased.

One thing was sure; he couldn't go home just yet. Carefully

opening doors, he finally found a service entrance and slipped out into the alley behind the hotel.

Casually, he strolled a few blocks then finally hailed a cab, and directed the driver to another hotel just blocks away.

He had the driver let him out in front and paused being sure to make a big show of handing the cabbie a good-sized tip so he would remember him. Entering the lobby, he looked neither right, nor left, being careful not to make eye contact with anyone. He slipped behind a pillar and waited till the elevator was empty, then rode it to the fifth floor. Taking a key from his pocket he let himself in and moved to the bar to pour himself a drink, he usually preferred a good wine, but not now, now he needed a stiff drink and scotch would do just fine.

The next step was making sure he was seen in this hotel. It had been brilliant taking two hotel rooms, paying cash for one and using his credit card for this one.

He rode the elevator down to the lounge, chatting with the other passengers in the car, and making sure to tip the bartender amply so he would also remember him. He had one bad moment when a lone male came and sat beside him and it reminded him of how he had met his other so-called friend.

He wanted to reach into his pocket and check for the gun, but the guy proceeded to tell him he was there on business and to show him pictures of his kids back in the states.

Edward insisted he show the pictures to the waitress, knowing she would remember that he had cared enough about a stranger's kids to involve her in the conversation.

He ate a leisurely dinner and then stopped by the reception area to leave a wakeup call for the morning. He needed to establish where he was every minute. He had checked into this hotel yesterday morning, and the other one in the afternoon. His bill would reflect his time here, and he had receipts from two of the museums in town. Obviously, he had been touring the museums when someone else had bought the gun that killed Alison. The fact that he was in London when the gun was bought was just a coincidence.

Buying the tickets had been a stroke of genius. He had stopped to talk to the woman who was selling admission to the exhibit, wandered around for a little while . . . and then managed to spill a cup of tea. He had slipped a huge tip to the maintenance person, and apologized profusely for bringing the tea into the museum. A few minutes later he had sneaked out a side door and returned to the seedy second hotel, pulled on his disguise, bought the gun, and then waited till the change in shift to check out. The whole thing was brilliant.

When they asked him why he had chosen this particular time to go to London, his explanation would be simple. The stress of having lost his temper with Stephen, and the argument with his mother, was due to the fact that he was concerned about Stephen's upcoming operation. That he was in London, and not home when Alison was killed, would devastate him, but his mental health had been in jeopardy and he'd needed to get away. Even the fact that he hadn't called work would be in his favor. That was out of character for him and his boss would testify to that if necessary.

There was only one wrinkle in all his carefully made plans and that was Sean O'Brien.

Sean. Engaged to Whisper and – a private detective.

He had called a friend in Boston and casually asked if he knew anything about the O'Brien family explaining that his cousin was engaged to an O'Brien.

What he had learned had seriously shook him. The O'Briens were all involved in some sort of law enforcement. Now he knew he had to be doubly careful not to leave any clues that would point to his involvement with Whisper's death in any way. Wouldn't it be ironic if he could somehow point the finger of suspicion at Sean, but the likelihood of that happening was next to impossible.

And Archie. Anna had let it slip that that damn limo driver was Sean's grandfather He had always been leery of him. He had tried to get Stephen to fire him to no avail, and even his mother had defended him. But somehow he made him nervous. He had a way of looking at you that made you think he could sense things about you no one else knew. Anger swirled inside him. This was all Stephens fault — if he had only been honest none of this would be happening. But now it wasn't only Whisper —but Sean and his grandfather he had to contend with.

Determined to take his mind off what he was planning, he turned on the TV just in time to catch the news. A diplomat at an important world conference had just been assassinated. No one saw the perpetrator, or could identify him. The police were scrambling and sirens were wailing in the background as the reporter spoke. He had been shot, the ironic part was that paramedics had been called to the scene prior to the shooting for a false call, but they had not been unable to save him. Edward noticed something unusual about that ambulance. All of the other people were dressed in white, but not the driver of the ambulance. He wore dark blue.

Shit, his hands began to shake, the drink he had poured for himself sloshing onto the carpet. The cameras had panned the scene and picked up the ambulance driver who looked directly into it. Edward could swear he was laughing. He couldn't see anything distinguishing about him but- those eyes, he knew those eyes, his so-called friend had told him about those eyes- one was brown and one was blue. Edward stumbled to the bathroom and threw up. He had just fired a notorious killer. Was he next?

His cell phone began to ring and he shook as he answered it. The voice was gruff, but laughing. "Got the TV on?"

"Yes," he knew his voice shook but he had no control over it.

"Well, my boss said to tell you not to worry, he got a good laugh out of being fired by a punk like you, but don't call him ever again understand? And get rid of your cell phone now, this number had better not show up anywhere." He hung up.

Edward tossed the phone across the room as if it had suddenly become a deadly snake. Then realizing what he had done, he ran to it and picked it up, He opened the back and pulled out the batteries, frantically he pulled at the wires, till he suddenly realized that there were records somewhere with all his phone calls on them. They were playing with him and he had fallen for it. He tossed what was left of the phone into the wastebasket and switched off the TV.

It was going to take more than one drink to help him sleep tonight, and he took the bottle over to the couch and proceeded to get seriously drunk

CHAPTER TWENTY-NINE

Sean was restless, today had been tedious, viewing and reviewing every scrap of information he could find about the Alexander family, their friends, their business associates, hoping that he would be able to find someone other than a member of Whisper's family that might be the culprit.

No such luck. Everybody had checked out squeaky clean.

He rubbed his forehead, damn it he needed action --not more paperwork- but all of his probing seemed to be going nowhere.

If it was Edward, so far he hadn't made a slip. There was nothing concrete to tie him back to the attempts on Whisper's life.

He lay stretched out on the bed, his hands behind his head trying to figure out how and if Edward's would strike again.

He'd removed his shoes which was his only concession to trying to get some rest. For some reason his nerves were stretched tight and there was a bad feeling in the pit of his stomach.

The fact that Whisper lay sleeping in the room across from him and that he could see her doorway from where he lay still didn't reassure him. His office staff had painstaking gone over every detail they had been able to find about the place, but Sean was worried that there were entrances that they would never know about. He'd thought he'd given Stephen a task to keep him busy, but damn it, he had marked places in this old monstrosity that had shown up nowhere else.

As he pointed them out to Sean, he admitted he hadn't check any of these entrances in years and there might even be some others he had forgotten about. This place was hundreds of years old, and although the family lived in a part of the estate that had been renovated, there were parts of it that no one bothered to visit. But someone who had explored this place as a kid, might know exactly where those entrances and exits were; and how to get in and out without being seen.

His cell phone vibrated, and he sat up dropping his feet to the floor.

"You better come home, "Archie's voice trembled," I've called the police...our place has been ransacked. I don't know what they got of yours but...everything is gone." Sean could hear tears in his grandfather's voice and his voice seemed hesitant and slurred, "and your grandmother's couch is ruined."

Sean tried to keep his voice calm but his heart was racing, and his palms damp. Archie's voice, always crisp and clear was raspy and broken and Sean stomach clenched in fear. "Never mind the couch— are you all right?"

"Fell when I came through the door. Broken chair in front of me, tripped over the damn thing. I think I hit my head."

Before Sean could ask any more questions, the phone went dead.

Jesus, what the hell was he going to do? His grandfather obviously needed him, and if he went to him, he left Whisper alone.

He hit a speed dial number on his cell and St. James's sleepy voice answered. "I hope this is not another call to one of your early morning meetings, Charlotte and I just got to bed." He paused, "Unfortunately in separate rooms."

"I think Edward's back".

"He's back, how do you know?" St. James was fully awake now.

"He might've left his calling card at my grandfather's place. St. James heard the anguish in Sean's tone,

"Archie's been hurt, I was talking to him . . . and then he was gone, I can't take a chance that he might need medical attention. Wake Charlotte and get over here. If he shows, you two may be the only ones who can handle him. If I can't be here...you have to be."

"We're on our way!"

"Oh--and be careful when you enter – let Sam know it's you – she's got a gun and she knows how to use it – I don't want any accidents."

"Jesus, Sam with a gun, I'll be lucky if she doesn't shoot Charlotte."

Although worried, Sean had to smile as he snapped the cell shut then slipped on his shoes. At least through this whole thing St. James hadn't lost his sense of humor.

But something else kept was nagging at the back of Sean's brain. Suppose it wasn't Edward. Could it be whoever was after him and his family? Had Archie just gotten in the way? Could this be part of mysterious attempt on Colleen's life? Could someone have followed him here for some kind of revenge? And could that someone still be in the cottage with Archie? Questions but no answers circled in his brain.

He quietly pulled his gun from its holster as he stepped into the hall, but there was no sound and his instincts assured him that there was nothing suspicious going on. He paused for a moment but he had no sense of danger. He counted on that; it had kept him alive in a lot of tough spots.

He was torn, should he stay until Charlotte and St. James arrived? But suppose Archie needed immediate medical attention. If something happened to his grandfather because he didn't get there on time- he'd never forgive himself. He was also counting on St. James breaking all records getting here, and god knows Sam could handle a gun as well as anybody he knew.

Silently he crossed the hall and looked down at Whisper. For a moment he wondered if he should wake her and then realized that sleeping she was in less danger than if she was awake. She looked innocent and fragile, with dark circles under her eyes and her breathing soft. He was banking on the fact that Edward had been here once before and hadn't harmed her while she slept.

If Edward got this far, he would still have to get through Sam, and any kind of noise would alert Whisper to trouble. He bent and laid a soft kiss on her brow, and as she stirred, he stepped back and waited a second till she settled down.

Swiftly he crossed the hall and entered Sam's room, and clasping a hand over her mouth, woke her. She came up out of the bed swinging and it was all he could do to keep his hand clamped over her mouth and try to contain her arms at the same time. "God damn it, will you hold still," he whispered.

When she realized it was Sean holding her she quieted, but her eyes still shot sparks and promised retribution as soon as she was free.

"Calm down, either Edward's back or I got big trouble."

Seeing the worry on Sean's face, Sam reached up and peeled his hand away from her mouth. "What do you mean?" she whispered.

"Archie's place has been trashed and he's hurt. I believe that whoever was there was after me, not Archie."

"How badly was Archie hurt? Did he call an ambulance?"

Startled, Sean realized his grandfather hadn't told him any details.

"I don't know he mumbled something about falling over a chair, and he sounded disoriented. I can't tell if it was from being hurt or the trauma of having his place wrecked."

"Then get out of here and let me get dressed."

"I've got St. James and Charlotte on their way here too."

"Terrific, I don't just have to deal with a lunatic son, but with his crazy parents as well."

"You'll need the help. I've watched St. James and I think he can hold his own, under that three piece suit the guy is in perfect shape and I think he'll give Edward a run for his money if he has to."

As Sam swung her feet to the floor and fumbled for her robe, Sean continued, "Listen keep your gun with you at all times. Stay where you can see Whisper and Stephen's rooms, but stay out of sight, and for god's sake don't leave for any reason. If it is Edward, make him come to you. No matter what you hear – you stay put understand!"

Leaning down he kissed the top of her head, "Be careful. Whisper and Stephen are still asleep so for all intent and purposes you're alone."

"Better that way, Stephen would want to do something immediately and your fiancé," she grinned, "would be telling me not to hurt the little creep."

She reached up and caressed his cheek, he was as close to family as she would ever get. "Now, get going, Archie needs you...and tell the old guy I love him." Her voice broke.

Swiftly Sean reached out and gave her a quick hug, and was gone.

CHAPTER THIRTY

S am moved silently around Stephen's room.
She thought she'd heard a noise, but she couldn't tell what the sound was, or where it was coming from. It sounded like a thump and it wasn't a sound she normally heard in this house.

Swiftly she went to Stephen's bed, glad that he had refused to take a sleeping pill tonight. Placing her hand over his lips, she softly called his name. When his eyes opened, she hissed at him, "Don't make a sound but get up, I have to go wake your daughter. Someone is here."

Trying to move silently and fighting the dizziness that swept over him, Stephen pulled himself up, and watched as Sam ran from the room.

She wasn't surprised to see Whisper already sliding her feet into her slippers while wrapping a bathrobe around her.

"Where's Sean?" she whispered.

"Archie's hurt and he went to him. It's you and me girl."

"And Dad?"

"He's awake, but we can't count on him he looks pretty woozy to me."

"If it is Edward, how are we going to get Dad out of here? He can't take this stress."

"You're going to take him down in the lift, while I scout around downstairs."

"Shouldn't I come with you?"

"And leave your father alone? I don't think so."

She pulled the gun from the pocket of her robe as she continued, "We have to buy time, Charlotte and St. James are on their way – but lord knows when they'll get here."

Horror laced Whispers voice as she stared at the gun. "You're not going to use that are you?"

"Only if I have to."

She cocked her head listening, then lowered her voice to a whisper, "Sean told me to let Edward come to me, but I can't, the thud I heard sounded like it came from Anna's room, I can't take a chance that he's hurt her."

Sam started from the room and then stopped. "Wait, instead of using the lift, which Edward will hear, is there a back stairway?"

"Better than a stairway, there's a wall in the playroom that opens out, and a passageway leading to the library."

"Lord, you people are creepy, passageways, stairways, and rooms that nobody knows about."

Whisper suddenly felt defensive about those long-ago ancestors who had built those hidden passageways. "This is a very old estate and they needed these things to protect them from their enemies."

"Yeah, and it was probably a member of your own family that was trying to do them in."

Before Whisper could respond, Sam motioned for silence. Faintly, they could hear Anna's voice, it sounded as if she was loudly scolding someone, but they couldn't quite make out the words, nor could they hear the voice of the person she was talking to.

Wave of relief swept over both women, "She's in the downstairs hall – and she must be warning us he's here." Whisper already soft voice dropped so that Sam could barely hear the words. "I have to go to her."

"You're not going anywhere. You take you father down that passage and get him the hell out of this house. Hide somewhere, you'll be able to tell when it's all clear. With St. James and Charlotte's help we'll be able to get him."

As Whisper hesitated, Sam gave her a shove. "Do it!"

She turned to leave, but Whisper grabbed her arm. "You may have the gun, but now you take an order from me — you be careful," and she bent and gave her cheek a quick kiss.

The two women separated at the door, Whisper heading for her father's room and Sam toward the stairway. Sam reached into the pocket of her robe and grabbed her cell — she needed to alert Sean that someone was here. Hitting speed dial to Sean's cell she put in 911 and then dropped the phone back into her pocket.

Gun in hand; she cautiously slipped down the stairs, staying close to the wall, pausing now and then to listen. The scent of gardenias drifted around her and for a moment she hesitated, where the hell did that come from? Shaking off the feeling that she was not alone, she proceeded cautiously.

Then she heard the sound again, was it a door opening? But where? This damn house was full of doors. Which one was he hiding behind? She shivered, now she knew why the story of the lady and the tiger was so scary. The guy in that one didn't know which door to open — and neither did she.

Reaching the bottom of the stairs she paused, straining to hear something. There was nothing.

She kept her back to the wall as she headed for Anna's room. She needed to know Anna was all right. She loved that old girl — and nothing had better happen to her. If he'd hurt her — well, she'd cross that bridge when she came to it.

She gripped the gun in her hand a little tighter. Could she really use it, shooting at a paper target was one thing — but a person? She tried to control her breathing although her heart was beating so hard that she was afraid the intruder, whoever it was, would be able to hear it.

The wall ended and she had only taken two steps when he struck.

He'd stepped out of an alcove under the stairway, and swung the butt of a gun at her. But she caught the movement from the corner of her eye, and she swung around trying to avoid his blow. Shoving his gun into his pocket he reached out and grabbed her arm fighting her for her gun. Could she shoot him? The thought only fleetingly crossed her mind and then she realized she could. She would do anything to protect Stephen and Whisper.

He held her gun hand in the air as she wrestled with him trying to bring it down to pull the trigger. He had the advantage of height, weight and athletic ability, but she had rage on her side. Her Irish temper crackled through the air, as she struggled with him trying to get her knee into position to bring it up between his legs. She flailed out with the hand that was not in his grip and raked her nails down his face. He twisted and bent her back forcing her to try to keep her balance while she resisted. Finally, he outmaneuvered her, and squeezed her gun hand till the blood and the strength drained from it; and the gun dropped harmlessly to the floor.

"Good night Sam," he said as he drew back his fist and catching her on the cheekbone knocked her to the floor. He waited a moment to be sure she was out cold, and when she didn't move, he stepped over her, and headed down the hall.

Nothing was going as planned, when Anna had surprised him in the hall all hopes of this looking like a burglary-murder had gone out the window. Now it was just revenge. But maybe revenge would even be sweeter. After he killed Whisper, the whole world would know he was Stephen's son. He could even see the headlines in his head, "Father's failure to acknowledge son, leads to sister's death."

Why maybe he'd even suggest it to a reporter when they caught him, and they would catch him because Sean and his family would never rest till whoever killed Whisper was caught.

He glanced back at Sam but she hadn't moved. Two down, two to go, and these were the two that mattered. He'd left Anna safely tied up and locked in her room. There was something ironic about her being tied to the chair with her own apron. He hoped she was able to see the humor in it. He knew she wasn't strong enough to pull free of the knot he'd tied but he'd felt a strange compulsion to comfort her before he left. He'd bent and kissed her forehead, and her eyes had reflected such sorrow for a moment he had contemplated giving the whole scheme up. He was counting on the fact that she would never give him up to the police. She loved him.

He paused for a moment; the element of surprise was gone. Stephen and Whisper would have heard his scuffle with Sam; she certainly had made enough noise, he smiled softly to himself, you could never count on commoners to go quietly.

Now he was sure Whisper would try to get Stephen out of the house. He was in no condition to fight, so she would try to get him away from here. She'd never bring him down on the lift, because that would alert him.

No, she would bring him down through the hidden passageway from the playroom. He knew she would remember it.

He had discovered it quite by accident. When he was young, he had stumbled over one of his trucks, and stretching out his hand to stop his fall, had hit the latch that held it.

A door had opened revealing a dusty tunnel and he had crept down, his little heart pounding until at last it ended. He stopped to listen to the muffled voices and realized that this tunnel led straight into the library. He could hear his mother and his grandparents discussing horse feed, but he soon became bored and had returned to the playroom. The only other person he had shown it to was Alison.

Ironic wasn't it this secret they shared would lead her right to him.

He slipped into the library. Crossing the room, he slid behind the heavy drapes and waited.

Whisper held her father up.

Sam's screams had frightened her and it was all she could do to keep her father from trying to rush to Sam's aid. His own weakness had frustrated him, and she had forcibly dragged him into the tunnel assuring him that once he was hidden, she would go back after Sam.

Motioning to her father to lean against the wall, she stepped into the library and listened, there were no sounds, and nothing seemed amiss. Then moving silently back into the passageway she steadied her father as he moved into the room.

Swiftly she guided him to the portable wheelchair that always resided behind the desk and helped him into it. Now all they had to do was get through the large glass doors leading to the portico and onto the stone path in the garden and after that there were plenty of places to hide.

A soft sound caught her attention and she swung around to face Edward as he stepped out from behind the drapes, a gun clutched in his hand.

"Father," he said, "Alison...how wonderful that we can all be together...finally."

CHAPTER THIRTY-ONE

Andrew St. James grabbed his clothes from the chair where he had placed them just a few hours earlier. Throwing the vest and jacket aside, he grabbed his shirt and pants and pulled them on.

He left his socks on the floor and scooped up his shoes as he headed for Charlotte's room.

The glow from the hallway spilled over her as he entered the room, and his breath caught in his throat. She lay on her side, her face flawless in sleep and the frown she usually wore erased. He ached to reach out and touch the tangle of brown curls that spilled across her pillow finally freed from the tight bun he detested. She looked like the young girl he had fallen in love with and he sighed wishing things had been different.

Reaching out he touched her shoulder. "Charlotte, wake up."

Startled she sat up, her silk nightgown falling open, affording him a look at two breasts that to his eyes had only grown more beautiful.

Not allowing his tone to convey any of his thoughts he reached out a hand to help her up. "Archie's hurt, his place ransacked, and Sean's on his way there now. He thinks Edward did it."

Charlotte gasped, as he continued, "We have to get over to Stephen's right now. I pray God it was someone else not Edward, but no matter, we're needed over there." He hesitated for a moment, "Sean said Sam has a gun and isn't afraid to use it."

Charlotte scrambled from the bed, her face white, as St. James sat down and pulled on his shoes. Not caring that he was in her bedroom, she pulled the nightgown over her head and threw it on the floor, and stumbled into her closet. In a few seconds she was dressed, and he grinned when he saw her.

Her choice of clothing was a testament to just how frightened she was. The khaki slacks were designed for riding, while her top was a low-cut midnight blue piece of confection obviously intended for evening wear.

She had riding boots clutched in her hands, but she didn't stop to put them on, just ran past him calling for him to hurry up.

If he wasn't so worried, he knew he would enjoy watching her come apart, and the girl he had fallen in love with emerging from the bitter woman she had become.

Racing past her down the stairs, he yanked open the massive front door, and reaching behind him, grabbed her hand, forcing her to run down the steps and across the lawn toward the garage.

"Come along darling, we haven't got much time." He glanced over at her, even though her face was pale and she had on no makeup, he still thought she was the most beautiful woman he had ever seen.

He'd never stopped loving her, and the few women who had drifted in and out of his life paled in comparison to that emotion. Once or twice he had contemplated a serious relationship with another woman, then somewhere he would run into Charlotte and he knew the other relationship would never work out.

He'd loved her so long that if Charlotte wanted him back, no matter what the circumstances, he'd go, so why risk breaking someone else's heart.

He threw open the garage door and skidded to a stop, Charlotte crying out as she viewed the destruction in front of them. The hoods on her two cars were open and parts of the motors lay strewn around the floor. The headlights were smashed, and one windshield was shattered.

"It seems our son is a little angry."

"Oh my god, Andrew what are we going to do?" Tears poured down Charlotte's face and she began to shake.

St James reached out and pulled her into his arms. "Charlotte stop crying and listen to me. Where is that classic sports car that Edward is so proud of?"

"You mean the one he takes to the car shows?"

"Yes darling, that one."

"But I don't have a key."

"Never mind that…where is it?"

She pointed to a small building that was situated alone at the far end of the lawn. "It's locked in there."

St. James rummaged around in the garage, and spotting a small hatchet that was hanging on the wall reached for it. Grabbing her hand, he pulled her across the lawn only slowing down once as Charlotte stumbled. He waited for a second to be sure she wasn't hurt, and then putting his arm around her waist he dragged her toward the small building.

Reaching the building Charlotte watched in surprise as St. James stepped up to the double doors and with one swift blow destroyed the lock.

"But I don't have a key to this car. Only Edward. . .." Panic crept into her tone.

St. James glanced at her, then grinned,

"Not to worry." Pushing open the doors he moved swiftly to the sleek little sports car and rolling up his sleeves, unlatched the hood, and began to work on the engine.

"What are you doing?"

"Hot wiring it."

"You're what?"

St. James didn't answer just continued searching for what he needed. Within seconds the engine roared to life, and he slammed the hood shut. "Get in."

"But the doors are locked."

He walked to the driver side of the car and swung the hatchet again, destroying the window, and reaching in unlocked the door.

"Brush out the glass and get in." He didn't bother with his side, simply sat down and put the car in gear.

Reaching over, he pulled her head to his and swiftly kissed her savoring every moment that it lasted. "No matter what happens tonight, I want you to know I never stopped loving you." Before she could answer he hit the gas and the sleek car shot out of the garage.

CHAPTER THIRTY-TWO

Sean sat at the table looking at the destruction that surrounded him. Curtains were torn off windows, chairs smashed; the table where he now sat had been overturned. His laptop lay in pieces on the floor. Cupboards emptied, and the thing that had brought his grandfather to his knees, his grandmother's couch was slashed. He shuffled the papers that he'd gathered up, and tried to put them in some semblance of order.

Anna had slipped about Archie being Sean's grandfather – but he knew that for sure now. Archie's favorite picture of the family, the same one he had in his office, was torn from its frame and ripped into small pieces.

Somehow in his worry about Whisper, he had forgotten that he was also a threat, and that he might be a target too. If he married Whisper, and they had children, those children would also be Stephen's heirs. To the little bastard's way of thinking it was probably better to take both of them out before anything could happen.

He'd sent Archie upstairs to clean up and change his clothes.

Archie had been covered with blood when he arrived, the wound to his head bleeding profusely. He'd wanted to take him to get stitches when he saw the extent of the wound, but he'd had to settle for cutting some tape to make a butterfly bandage to hold the skin together; since the old man insisted he wasn't going anywhere.

Of course he was, as soon as he was dressed, he was taking him back to the estate. He'd been gone long enough and he didn't like the idea of leaving them alone too long.

He reached out and took a slashed pillow from the couch twisting it around in his hands, wishing it could offer him some comfort.

Tonight was the only time he had seen his grandfather in tears since the day they buried his grandmother. Red hot anger swept through him as he recalled coming through the door to find his grandfather sitting on what was left of Grandma's couch. He had this pillow clutched to his chest, and the anguish Sean had seen in his eyes had torn him apart.

He knew Edward had done this, this destruction had been done by someone in a rage, and he vowed that when he got his hands on him, he would make him pay for breaking the old man's heart.

There was one thing to be thankful for, Archie had taken Anna out for the evening and that they had stopped on the way home for a drink. If Archie had been here, he shuddered to think about it.

This room had been destroyed by someone in a frenzy, and although Archie was wiry and tough, he would have been outmatched in this battle.

His gut told him that the secrets this family harbored had finally come home to roost. Now where the hell was Edward?

He pulled his cell from his pocket and tried St. James' number again. He had called as soon as he had taken care of Archie wound, but St. James hadn't answered. Since he couldn't get him, he was counting on the fact that he was already at the estate. Now all he wanted was to put Archie in the car and get back to Whisper.

Pride, stupid pride, what a mess it could make out of people's lives.

Tomorrow this whole charade was going to end. He had extracted a promise from St. James that as soon as they caught him, Edward would learn who his real parents were. And then after the parenting thing was straightened out...he was going to beat the crap out of him.

He was startled when his beeper went off and glancing down, he saw Sam's number, followed by 911. Knocking over his chair in his haste to get to the door, he heard Archie's feet hit the floor.

"Where are you going?" Archie scrambled down the stairs.

"Sam just beeped 911."

"Wait, I'm going with you..."

"I haven't got time for you to dress..."

"To hell with the dressing, I have as much at stake here as you do."

Sean was already at the car door, as Archie slipped into the passenger side.

Glancing over, even with the urgency of the call on his mind, Sean had to grin, Archie's white hair was standing on end, he had one slipper on, and his shirt was half in and half out of his pants. The sleeve of the jacket he had clutched in his hand was caught in the car door but Archie didn't seem to notice.

"Hold on old man, you're in for the ride of your life."

"And me without my rosary beads!" Archie made a quick sign of the cross as he looked up as if praying for divine intervention. The only thing that ruined his theatrics was the grin that was plastered on his face.

Sean simply groaned; his grandfather never changed he'd probably be making jokes as he got to the pearly gates. If he even got that far.

The ride to the estate was quick, Sean never letting up on the gas, careening around corners and blowing through roundabouts.

"I've seen this kind of ride on the telly," Archie muttered, "and from now on that's where I'd like it to stay."

Sean didn't answer, and slamming on the brakes he was out of the car, yanking open the door to the mansion with Archie close on his heels.

CHAPTER THIRTY-THREE

Sweat dotted Edward's head and his eyes were wild as he looked at father and daughter.

Stephen pushed himself up from the chair and although his movements were unsteady, his voice was strong.

"Edward, listen to me this is all a big mistake."

Stephen's words enraged Edward, and he moved to the wheelchair and using his hand, hit Stephen across the face, splitting his lip and knocking him backward.

"Now I'm a mistake, am I? You should have thought of that before you got some girl pregnant." Gesturing wildly, he pointed the gun at Stephen.

"Well, your big mistake was in never acknowledging me."

His voice began rising hysterically." Why wouldn't you? Why couldn't we have been a family? Why did you take my sister away from me? I loved you both, but I loved your wife Alise most of all. She cared for me, she loved me." He turned toward Whisper pleadingly, "Didn't she?"

At Whisper's nod, he continued, "I didn't mean to hurt her, you know that don't you? It was an accident. I couldn't have pushed her —I couldn't have . . .she fell, she fell. . ." Tears streamed down his face.

"What do you mean it was an accident?" Stephen struggled to stand.

"Why do you think you had anything to do with my wife's

death?" He stumbled to Edward and grasped his arm. "Tell me what happened that day. What did you do?"

He held on trying to force Edward to look at him. He quick glance pleading silently with Whisper to run.

Whisper reached behind her, her hand searching for the heavy paper weight that had been on her father's desk as long as she could remember. It wasn't round but was elongated and very sharp and inside it was held a tiny shield that depicted the family coat on arms.

As Edward screamed and grappled with her father, she grasped it in her hand and swung its sharp edge toward Edward's face. But Edward caught a glimpse of her movement, and thrusting Stephen aside, he raised his arm and deflected the blow so it glanced off his cheek. The edge of the paperweight opened a gash and he brushed the blood away with his hand.

Rage radiating from him, he doubled his fist and hit Whisper, but the punch that knocked her to the floor infuriated Stephen. He pushed himself from the desk where he had landed, and frantically he reached out, his only hope to divert Edward's attention and give his daughter time to escape.

He grabbed Edward's arm grappling for the gun just as the room began to darken, and he clutched his chest before he fell.

"You've killed him, you've killed him," Whisper screamed as she fought to get to her father, but Edward grabbed her arm dragging her behind him.

"This is going to end exactly where it started." He twisted her arm behind her back, and pushing her ahead of him, forced her through the hall. Pausing before an ornate panel that was part of a wall located under the stairway, he slapped a carved figure on it, and a hidden door swung open.

The hand that held her arm tightened as she stopped in horror and stared down at the stairway in front of her.

Dampness permeated the air, and the cold drifted up toward her. She could see cobwebs high on the stone walls that surrounded the room. She began to tremble; this was the room of her nightmares.

She planted her feet halting Edward's forward movement till he gave her a shove, and she lost her balance tumbling a few steps before he steadied her and stopped her fall.

"Did you hurt your ankle? Test it before we go any further."

Whisper stared at Edward, what was going on here? She knew he had every intention of killing her, but when she stumbled he stopped, because he was worried about her. None of this made any sense.

She held her ankle out in front of her, using the one hand that was free to hold onto the rail and steady herself, as she pretended to twist and turn it as if checking to see if it would hold her weight.

She moved closer to the rail; sliding her thumb under the belt of her robe to untie it. She desperately needed to buy time, she didn't know where Sam or Anna was, but she knew Charlotte and St. James were on their way.

Losing patience, Edward gave her a forceful nudge, and grabbing her arm thrust her toward the bottom of the stairs. As she reached the last few steps, she suddenly twisted her arm free and jumped, throwing him off balance. He stumbled, then stood holding the sleeve of her robe in his hand as she escaped from his grasp.

She ran down the narrow passageway darting in and out of the rows that held the hundreds of casks of wine, and frantically trying to keep the shelves filled with bottles between her and Edward. Ducking down she held her breath and listened. Damn this earthen floor it made it impossible to hear where he was. There were no creaking boards or other sounds to betray his whereabouts.

She hoped the dark shadows would be her friends as she crouched down and tried to steady her breathing. She could hear him cursing as he tried to see her in the dim light of the ancient sconces that were the only illumination in the dark dank room.

She concentrated on staying low and moving silently ahead of him. It was a deadly game of hide and seek.

She recognized that her white nightgown was a flag and she briefly considered taking it off, but stupidly, vanity seemed to be playing a role in her thought process. There was no way Sean was going to find her dead, dressed only in a bullet hole. She wished she had had time to put on makeup, so when Sean found her body, he would be impressed with how great she looked. Oh my god, she thought, I'm losing it.

She considered lying on the ground but if Edward found her, she would have to scramble to get up. No better to stay crouched down. She scooted ahead a couple of feet but she couldn't see him. Where the hell had he gone?

Her screams echoed around the vast room as Edward's hand snaked out from behind her, and grabbed her by the hair. He dragged her up, a snarl on his face, his eyes narrowed with rage.

"Nice try you stupid girl, you're just prolonging the inevitable." He stared into her face his eyes glittering, then he pushed her in front of him the gun jammed into her back.

Then they heard it.

Edward stiffened as the muffled sound of running feet and voices reached the two of them. "The son of a bitch has found us."

Grabbing her by the arm he snarled, "Move, move!"

A wave of relief surged through Whisper's body. Although she knew she was dealing with a mad man, she also knew that inside that enraged mind was a man who so far hadn't been able to kill anybody.

Taking a chance, she swung around her hands going to his face, but he was too quick for her, he grabbed her arm and twisted it behind her, forcing her to cry out in pain. She tried to bring her leg up to debilitate him, but a fierce blow to her face sent her to her knees. Grabbing her hair, he pulled her to her feet, "I'm done playing games, get up and come with me or when your boyfriend shows up ... I'll kill him."

Stumbling, she forced herself to move ahead. Sean was too large a target; he wouldn't stand a chance against this gun, and she was afraid that Edward would carry out his threat.

Gasping in horror, she stood staring at the ancient oak door looming before them. This was one entrance she and her father had forgotten about. Cobwebs covered the walls nearby and the gray hue of the stones that surrounded it blended with the ancient wood. The marks in the dirt in front of the door showed that it had recently been forced open and as she glanced up at Edward, she realized he was enjoying her fear.

Now she knew why no one saw Edward leave the day her mother died; he had used this door to escape.

He had carried her screaming down here, past her mother at the bottom of the stairs and had placed her behind one of the wooden whiskey casks. She had been inconsolable screaming and screaming for her mother.

Edward had sat in the dirt beside her, trembling with tears running down his face. She remembered as her crying slowed, he had taken the bottom of her dress and wiped away her tears.

"You must never tell anyone I was here; do you hear me?"

She remembered staring at him, "Why?"

"Never mind why...do you promise?"

"But I need to tell them that she fell- because. . ."

"You will tell them nothing- do you hear me?" He took her tiny shoulders and shook her.

"You mother is dead, and if you tell" – he leaned over her and stared into her eyes "If you tell anyone – I will come back and I'll kill your father too!"

As the memory and his words echoed in her mind, Whisper slowly turned toward Edward, "Oh my god, you're the reason I stopped talking, you told me you were going to kill my father – and I believed you, oh Edward, how could you? I was only five years old." Her throat closed up and all the other words she was about to say failed her.

CHAPTER THIRTY-FOUR

S ean pushed open the massive oak door, pausing to listen for any sound that might tell him where anyone was.

Suddenly he realized that Sam was sitting on the floor; cradling Stephen's head in her lap. Blood was running down the side of his face and dripping onto the floor, and his face looked pasty while his lips had a bluish tinge.

An ugly bruise on Sam's cheek was already purpling, and she had trouble speaking through split lips.

"The fool tried to get to her but he was too weak. He only got this far before he collapsed." Her voice broke and she realized she was babbling.

"Where is she?" Sean's voice was calm but Sam shivered as she looked into his eyes.

"I don't know, he knocked me out." Noting the rage in his eyes she warned him. "Don't let your anger take over – remember he's got a gun!"

Darting around the two of them Sean called back to her "Is Stephen going to be all right? And where the hell are Charlotte and St. James?"

"I don't know, Stephen's unconscious, but I've called for help."

"I'll kill the bastard if anything happens to any of you."

Pushing past Sean, Archie was running ahead, "I have to check on Anna, then I'll help you look!" Pushing open the kitchen door, his heart began to hammer. Pots were bubbling on the stove but no one was around. Moving with astonishing speed, he began pushing open doors that led to other parts of the house.

Finding a door that he knew led to the servants' quarters he tried to push it open. But it would only open partially. Not enough to see what was holding it closed.

"Sean, I need help here!"

His voice echoed in the vast hallway and Sean turned and sprinted toward the sound.

Pushing Archie out of the way, he gently used his considerable bulk to push the door inward.

Anna lay on the floor in front of him, the chair she had been tied to laying on its side.

Dropping to one knee he felt for her pulse, it was faint, but it was there. Edward hadn't killed her.

Seeing the blood that was pooling under her head, he gently pushed the hair back from her forehead to find an ugly gash that was bleeding profusely.

"I'll kill the bastard." Dropping to his knees Archie reached into his pocket and grabbed a knife he carried there cutting Anna free from the chair,

"Hang in there darlin'...you and me got a lot of living to do yet."

Suddenly she opened her eyes and stared at him.

"He's got her!" she whispered.

"Who's got her? Where are they?"

"Edward. He dragged her down the hall toward the wine cellar...I think that's where he took her." She scrambled trying to get up.

"Leave me, go get her before he kills her...he's mad, and it's all Charlotte's fault," she continued." If only she'd told him who his father really was. . ."

Placing his arms under her, Sean lifted her onto her feet. "Take her," he told Archie, "and bring her out into the hall with Sam, the ambulance is on its way."

"But," Archie started, but Sean cut him off. "I've got it!"

"Now where the hell is the door to the wine cellar?"

"Wait here." Archie pushed Anna down into the chair she had been tied to.

"Follow me; I know where it is."

Close on the old man's heels, Sean marveled at Archie's stamina. At the end of hall hidden behind a stairway Archie stopped, and looking over the panel for a second, reached out and hit an ornamental scroll. Immediately a door began to swing open but impatiently Sean grabbed it and yanked it the rest of the way. Archie started forward but Sean pushed him out of the way.

"Go see to Anna, make sure that's she's still all right."

Without hesitation, Archie turned and raced back down the hall with a swiftness that belied his years.

Peering down into the gloom, Sean saw the ancient stairway, the dirt floor and the cobwebs. Cold and dampness permeated the air. His breath caught in his throat as his mind flashed back to Whisper's nightmare and her panic on the plane.

What the hell kind of a place had this been to leave a five-year-old? It was like a scene from a horror movie.

With a bellow Sean leaped, landing only once before he was at the bottom. It was dark and damp, only an ancient yellow light bulb casting a faint light on the chamber. More like a cave than a room, it walls were stone, with rows of shelves filled with bottles of wine in every shape and size.

"Whisper, where are you?" Sean's shout echoed through the massive room.

A muffled shriek and then silence.

Sean's heart began to pound; he had never been so frightened in his life. Even working the streets, being stabbed, and caught up in life and death situations on the Boston streets, he had never felt this gut-wrenching fear, but when someone you love is in danger. . .

He started down the dark aisle straining to hear any other

sound that might give him a clue as to their whereabouts. There were shadows everywhere, deep dark recesses where anyone could hide.

A slight sound behind him told him Archie had followed, and as he glanced over at him, Archie smiled, that simple gesture assuring Sean that Anna was safe otherwise he knew Archie would have never left her.

Silently, Archie made the motion of a door opening.

"Another exit?" Sean mouthed.

As he nodded, Archie slipped ahead and beckoned, and Sean saw they were headed for the far end of the cellar. Because of his smaller size Sean allowed Archie to lead the way knowing he could probably get closer with less chance of detection.

They slid to an outside wall, Sean silently thanking god that the floor was dirt so there was no sound to alert Edward as to their whereabouts.

But Edward knew he was here and would have recognized his roar as that of a warrior preparing for battle.

Rather appropriate Sean thought, that the battle between the two of them would take place in this old castle.

He only hoped for Whisper's and Stephen's sake it would not be a battle to the death.

A flash of white straight ahead had the two men dropping down. Sean peered between the shelves carefully keeping his head out of view. He could hear the sound of angry voices, and as he crept forward, he could see them.

Edward was struggling to hold Whisper up, obviously trying to drag her through a door that Sean would never have known existed if Archie hadn't alerted him.

Although slender, she had managed to make herself dead weight, her arms hanging loosely at her side, and her feet dragging on the ground. Edward was cursing, trying to hold her upright while still holding the gun against her.

Creeping closer Sean could barely hear Whisper's voice, but

he realized that she was trying to calm Edward down, and that the man was crying. He was mumbling words that didn't make any sense and Sean strained to hear what he was saying.

"She wouldn't listen, no one would listen. I tried to tell Anna but she kept babbling about my mother and St. James. She didn't make any sense. I had to hit her, I had to shut her up; she was all mixed up."

Fear crept into Whisper's voice. "Did you kill her?"

Shocked, Edward paused, "Of course I didn't kill her, I only put her to sleep, just like I did Sam."

He stopped and listened, he had heard that blood curdling cry, but not a sound since. He had to get control of himself, panic was beginning to muddle his brain.

All he needed was a few more minutes to get her through the door. He knew he was tiring, his arms ached from dragging her, and although her build was slight, she had managed to make herself an unwieldy burden.

Sean peered from behind the shelves having shoved Archie behind him. He had to get Edward's attention so that the gun he held would be trained on him. He frowned as he stared at Whisper, she had obviously put up a hell of a fight, because he could see a small ribbon of blood running down her neck from the cut on her face.

Her nightgown was ripped, one sleeve completely torn off and one of her shoulders was bare. If she had any other injuries, Sean couldn't tell.

A red haze descended over his eyes and the temper that he always worked so hard to control was unleashed.

This man would never get the opportunity to hurt her again because he was going to kill him.

Sweeping his arm over the shelf in front of him, the ancient bottles of wine smashed together, falling to the floor, breaking and spilling as they went.

The sound had Whisper raising her head, as Edward halted, staring into Sean's furious eyes.

Rage emanated from Sean as he stood a few feet away, his face chiseled in stone and his voice low and deadly. "Let her go... now."

He loomed so large over the two of them and his demeanor was so terrifying that her mind superimposed the picture of a giant bear over him. Only this bear was not here to do her harm, he was here to protect his mate.

"Don't be stupid," Edward's voice trembled, "I have a gun at her back and I won't hesitate to use it."

"Kill your own sister, kill your own flesh and blood?" It was a gamble and Sean held his breath as he waited for Edward's reaction.

Edward seemed to hesitate, and for a second Whisper was astonished at Sean's words till she realized Edward didn't know the truth.

Sean raised his gun, "I'll tell you only one more time, let her go —or you're a dead man."

"You'll never shoot me. . .you'll be afraid of killing her."

"You don't know me very well," Sean's voice was cold, "What I aim at I hit, and you'll make a pretty picture for all your snobbish friends with your brains splattered all over these walls."

Edward's body began to shake as Sean's eyes narrowed.

Slumped over Edward's arm, Whisper realized the upper part of Edward's body was exposed, and she knew Sean had his target.

She couldn't let that happen. She couldn't let Sean kill Edward. Their lives would forever be tainted if he had to kill a man to save her.

She pushed herself upright startling both men. Pulling Edward's arm straight up from around her waist — she bit down hard on it. He tried to shake her loose, the gun waving wildly in the air, and Sean was on him in an instant.

Grabbing Whisper, Sean yanked her from Edwards's grasp.

Flinging her to the side, he began to punch him, his massive fists pulverizing Edward. Blood cascaded down his face and a mean looking cut opened up over his eye.

Although no match for Sean, Edward began to strike out blindly, his rage at being thwarted providing him with strength that surprised Sean. But the more Edward jabbed, the harder Sean's blows became until he realized that he was holding Edward up and that his head was lolling backward.

"Stop, stop."

Sean suddenly became aware that both Whisper and Archie were hanging onto his arms as they clung to him like burrs. He had already flung them off twice only to have them return again. They were determined to prevent him from delivering a blow that could kill Edward.

Dropping Edward to the floor, Sean stared at his handiwork, Edward's pretty face now looked like raw meat, and although he had landed no life-threatening blows, he was satisfied that Edward wouldn't be hurting anyone for a long time.

He reached down and grabbed Whisper pulling her close, the feel of her body reassuring him that she was safe. With trembling fingers, he lifted her chin to gently kiss her when he spotted the blood on her face.

Her cheek was swollen and her eye looked puffy. With a bellow, he tried to move her away from him, with every intention of going back and hitting Edward again. But Whisper took advantage of his momentary hesitation and dropped over his arm so he had no choice but to hold her up or let her fall.

"Neat trick." He whispered as he gathered her close.

Voices and the sound of running feet alerted him that they were no longer alone.

First St. James, and then Charlotte burst in. Charlotte took one look at her son, and pushing Archie out of the way, ran to him, dropping to the dirt floor and cradling her son's head in her arms.

"Look what you've done," she screamed at Sean, but St. James moved in front of her and dropping to his knees in the dirt looked at Edward's face.

"Shut up Charlotte. I don't believe there is any permanent damage, is there?" He looked over at Sean for reassurance.

"What?" Disbelief colored Charlotte's voice, "Look at his face."

"No," Sean said, "He looks worse than he is, it's mostly flesh that's discolored, but I didn't hit anything vital..." the look he sent Charlotte was far from friendly.

"Thank you," St James voice was husky.

Still kneeling in the dirt, St. James reached out and took his son's face into his hands. "Edward, listen to me."

Though he could barely move his lips, his words slurred, he lifted his face to St. James, tears making tracks on the dirt on his face.

"I couldn't kill her...I wanted to...but I couldn't... I kept seeing her mother's face in front of me, pleading for her daughter's life."

"Hush Edward," St. Andrew's voice broke, "I want you to stop talking and listen to me, really listen to me." Gently he turned Edward's face toward him, "I am your father Edward– not Stephen, you're Charlotte and my natural son."

Edward struggled to open one eye, the other already sealed shut by the swelling.

"What?" disbelief colored his voice.

"Your mother and I have made some terrible mistakes, and you've paid for them, but that ends now, do you understand me? I will try to make amends; I promise you that tomorrow's newspaper will announce that I have acknowledged you as my son."

He sat back and smiled softly, "That's what you always wanted isn't it? To belong, not to be called a bastard – but to be acknowledged as someone's son. Well now you know the truth – you are my son."

Disbelief and anger on his face, Edward's voice was slurred, "Stop lying to me. . . why should I believe you—if it was true why didn't you ever tell me? You were my friend, my employer, why would you hide the truth from me? You're lying to me. Everybody lies to me. You're just trying to protect Stephen."

"Stephen? Don't be a fool. Do you think so little of your uncle that you believe if you were his son, he wouldn't acknowledge you? Your uncle is one of the most honorable men I know and I will spend the rest of my life trying to regain his trust."

Forcing himself to focus but barely able to speak, Edward winced in pain as he stared up into his father's eyes. "I'm your son not Stephen's ...are you sure?"

"That," St. James said, as he ran his finger up alongside Edward's cheek, wiping away some of the blood, "Is a stupid question, and when you see the portrait of your great grandfather Henry there will be no questions in your mind – you look just like him."

Edward tried to turn his head to look at Charlotte, "And you're really my mother?"

"Yes, you're really mine."

Pain laced his voice as he stared up at her, "Why didn't you tell me? Why did you let me go on thinking I was Stephen's son?"

Charlotte's face was strained as she recognized that her lies had almost her cost her her son. "Because you never told me what was going on in your head. I thought that you accepted the fact that your parents were dead, and then, and then I was afraid to tell you, afraid you would stop loving me when you learned the truth."

At the sound of voices and of people running down the stairs all conversation ceased as a man and a woman rounded the corner and came to a halt in front of Edward.

"Jesus," one man said, his eyes taking in the scene, "What the hell happened to him?"

"He ran into the shelves that hold the wine bottles" he

gestured to the broken bottles that littered the floor, "and he fell and cut himself." St James' voice was crisp as he answered.

"That don't look like no...."

"I assure you that I know what I am talking about young man," St. James' eyes narrowed, an unmistakable threat in them.

"Perhaps I neglected to mention that I am Baron St. James and this is my son Edward? Tell your superiors that I will be down to make out the accident report myself. Now would you please stop talking and get my boy to the hospital, his mother and I will be following shortly."

He looked over at Charlotte who was still cradling Edward's head close to her breast. Her blouse was covered with blood and tears ran down her face as she kept kissing her son's brow and whispering, "I'm sorry, I'm so sorry."

Although he felt compassion for her pain, still there was anger in his heart for what she had put their son through, and also at himself for his own cowardice.

"Are you coming with me or do you prefer to drive yourself." His voice was cool.

"I'm coming with you." She watched as the attendants lifted Edward's head from her lap and winced when he cried out in pain. "Be careful, please be careful," tears ran unheeded down her cheeks.

"What about Stephen, you know the man in the hall upstairs?" Sean's voice was cautious, afraid what the answer might be.

"Oh, he was sitting up and cursing when they lifted him on to the gurney. That man can really swear I tell you; I learned a few choice words from him just helping them out." He grinned, "Luckily somebody ordered two ambulances, and although he put up quite a fuss, he left in the first one."

He turned to Sean, "What did he do, run into a wall too, or that little redhead that was with him?"

He laughed but when no one else even smiled, the nurse with him muttered, "Shut up you muttonhead, and go get the gurney."

Looking at the closed faces that surrounded him, the attendant took off and was back in record time. Leaning down the female attendant murmured soothing words and took Edward's hand for a moment before they began pushing the gurney over the dirt floor toward the stairs.

"We may need help getting him up the stairs," she looked at Sean, then glancing down at his bloodied knuckles hesitated, "But maybe you don't care to assist."

"Of course, I'll help. Will you be all right?" He reluctantly let go of Whisper.

"I'll be fine."

In just a few minutes Sean was back and he frowned when he realized that St. James and Charlotte hadn't followed their son to the ambulance.

Looking around with narrowed eyes, Sean's voice was cool. "Where's his gun? Sean's eyes pierced St. James.

"I'll be damned; I don't know I didn't pick it up." Startled he turned to look among the bottles that were strewn and broken across the floor.

Only one person in the room had been aware of the exact location of the gun since the fight, and it would have remained that way if a slight movement hadn't caught Archie's eye.

He'd watched as Whisper slipped forward and lifted one corner of her nightgown and using her foot slid the gun under it. Even after all she's been through, he thought, the girl's protecting her cousin.

In a way, he admired her, protect the family, he understood that. If Sean got his hands on that gun, it would go straight to the police...but if the father got his hands on that gun – it would go nowhere.

He sighed, he'd be damned, he was breaking all his own rules, but it wouldn't hurt to help the girl out, so he moved closer and bent over picking up a large piece of glass then showed it to Sean.

"Boy, get this girl's bare feet out of this mess before she gets cut, and bending down as if to retrieve more pieces, he blocked Sean's view as he brushed the hem of her nightgown aside and slid the gun back under a nearby shelf.

"Come on, come on," he said, "The girl needs to get dressed and we need to get to the hospital. That cut on her cheek should be looked at, and I'm sure she wants to check on her Dad. And," he added "I'm driving since I'd like to live long enough to see my next birthday."

He started down the aisle, stopped and turned around scowling at Sean, "And how much of a bonus are you planning to give me boy? I took my life in my hands here, and if it weren't for me..." he grinned at Sean, "Better yet, never mind the money, I saw one of those flat screen TV's on the telly," his voice trailed off as he turned and headed down the aisle, nodding and then giving a conspiratorial wink to St. James as he passed him.

St. James waited as Sean scooped Whisper up in his arms, but Sean surprised him by stopping directly in front of him,

"She," he nodded at the woman in his arms who was watching him with wide eyes, "slid the gun under her nightgown and my grandfather pushed it under that lower shelf."

His eyes narrowed as his gaze shifted between Charlotte and St. James. "But let me make myself perfectly clear, I had better never see or hear about that gun again, understood?"

"You knew," Whisper squeaked.

"Of course, I knew where that gun was every minute, I just wanted to see what you were up to, and obviously that old fox upstairs thought he would help you. Bonus nothing," he grinned, "I think I'll dock him for aiding and abetting."

"You don't have to worry." St. James was stunned by this turn of events, he knew that Sean was a by-the-book cop, and he thought for sure the gun would end up in Scotland Yard's hands. "I'll see that it disappears."

He turned to Charlotte. "Are you coming?"

She stood and walked over to Whisper and lifting a shaking

hand she gently pushed the hair away from her niece's face. "I'm sorry, I'm so sorry."

"It's going to be all right, just take care of Edward, I'm going to be fine." and bending from within the safety of Sean's arms, she placed a soft kiss on her aunt's cheek. She knew it wasn't going to be easy for the St. James and Charlotte to mend their difference but she was sure in time they would work it out.

Charlotte turned, her eyes searching St. James' face for reassurance and whatever she saw reflected there gave her the courage to slip her hand into his. "I'm ready."

"Come along then." And he turned carefully guiding her down the narrow aisle toward the stairs.

"Are you angry at me?" Whisper's voice was tentative.

"Angry at you? For what? No, I'm mad at myself for leaving you alone. I'm a detective damn it, and I should have seen this as a ruse to get me away from here. If I'd have been smart, I'd have sent Charlotte and St. James to Archie."

"No." Whisper's voice was soothing, and she reached up and ran her hand over his cheek, "You did the right thing, I had Sam and my father, and even Anna, each of them bought us time, but if anything had happened to Archie, none of us could have forgiven ourselves. But what I really want to know if you are mad about the gun."

He stopped moving and looked down at her, "Tell me why you did it."

"Because I felt sorry for him – he couldn't shoot me – I knew it. When he was dragging me down the stairs I stumbled – and he asked me if I was hurt. He even stopped for a moment to let me test it my ankle. He was threatening to kill me... but he was worried about my ankle. It didn't make sense. And even when I fought him when we got to the door, he kept mumbling about my mother, and kept saying forgive me Alise. I knew he would never do anything to hurt my mother... and killing me. ..." her words trailed off and she suddenly began struggling.

"Oh my god, put me down, put me down," Frantically she pushed herself out of Sean's arms, and dropping to the floor she totally disregarded the broken bottles and ran back the way they had come.

Beyond where the shelves housed the bottles of wine, stood rows of casks and Whisper slipped down behind one of them and dropped to her knees. Cobwebs covered the area and because it was so far from the light, there was a musty odor. "It's here, I know it's here." She thrust her hands in the opening and the crevices between the casks, until finally she sat back something small clutched in her hand. Tears poured down her face, and she held a tiny object up for Sean to see.

"What the hell is that? A safety pin? You came running back here to get a safety pin?"

"Not just a safety pin, but 'the safety pin'. The one I was holding when my mother fell down the stairs. The one she was going to use to temporarily fix the hem she'd torn."

Sobs shook her as she twisted the pin around in her fingers. "We were dressed alike, and she didn't want to change because it would upset me, so she decided to wait until later to sew it... she was going to use this, so she handed it to me and asked me to hold it so she wouldn't forget it."

Sean had to strain to hear her words because her voice faded.

"Edward was there and the two of them were arguing. I was used to that, they used to argue about everything. The girls he dated, the clothes he wore, even his haircut."

She looked up at Sean, "Now I realize he just wanted her to care about what was going on in his life."

"We were at the top of the stairs, and she turned to talk to him when I saw that her heel was caught in the hem of her gown, I tried to tell her, but she was talking to Edward and she didn't listen to me" – Whisper began to tremble "Oh my god, she didn't listen, I could have stopped her fall, I could have prevented my mother dying.

"No, you couldn't – you were five years old," Sean gathered her up in his arms and sat back on the earthen floor holding her. "And then what?"

"Then she turned, her foot tangled in the material and she started to fall and Edward tried to stop her, he grabbed for her arm, but she slipped away from him and she tumbled down the stairs. I began to scream, and I screamed and screamed... He picked me up, I remember he was shaking and crying as he held me, and brought me down here. He thought he killed her, but he didn't ---he tried to stop her fall. He kept repeating that he'd killed her, and that if I told anyone he would kill my father too. I was afraid. I stayed hidden where he left me. Later they found me, but I had decided to stop talking. I was confused; if he killed my father then I would have no one. Later they sent me to my aunt's and I knew my father was safe. I was afraid to come back, suppose I said something and Edward found out. It was better to stay where I was."

"You poor kid," Sean kissed her forehead and wiped the tears from her cheeks. He pulled her closer and wrapped his arms around her willing the warmth from his body into hers. He held her tightly as all the years of fear and hurt were washed away in her sobs.

As soon as she got control of her emotions, she took his face in her hands and softly kissed him. "Come on Sean O'Brien, we have to get to the hospital and see my father, and then talk to Edward. He needs to know that I remember. He needs to know that he tried to save my mother's life and that both of us spent years needlessly blaming ourselves for my mother's death. He needs to have a new life and I can help him get started on it."

CHAPTER THIRTY-FIVE

S ir Guy was waiting for Stephen at the emergency room door and after working frantically to stabilize him, rushed him into surgery. The strain of fighting Edward for the gun had elevated Stephen's blood pressure to a dangerous level and only the timely arrival of the ambulance saved his life.

At first the prognosis had been grim, but Sir Guy was determined not to lose the battle for Stephen's life. After a grueling eight-hour operation, he walked into the waiting room and held out his arms to Whisper. She'd fled to him sobbing with fear but even as he held her, the eyes he turned toward Sean had been cautious. The virus had done quite a bit of damage to the valves around Stephen's heart and they'd had to be replaced, but the heart muscle itself had suffered nothing permanent, but the next few days would be crucial.

For seven days Stephen drifted in and out of consciousness. During that time Whisper and Sam left his side only to eat and sleep. Sean worried about both of them, but remained silent because he knew that when he had been stabbed his family had been with him around the clock and if it was one of his own family lying there, he'd be doing the same.

On the eighth day Stephen's fever finally broke and his breathing became less labored. Standing by his bed Sir Guy grinned at Whisper. "The bloody bastard is pretty tough, isn't he? Knew he'd live, I owe him 50 pounds, and he'd never die without collecting the money."

Although his words were cheerful, it was obvious to all of them that the battle to keep Stephen alive had not been an easy one. Sir Guy's eyes were bloodshot, and the hand that reached out to touch Stephen's brow trembled. His hair was standing on end where he had run his fingers through it and his usually pristine smock was rumpled. They all knew that throughout the ordeal he'd appear on the ward at all hours of the day and night to check on Stephen and his temper was so short that when he did, nurses would run and hide.

Assuring them that Stephen had finally turned the corner, Sir Guy left after flatly stating it was his intention to go home and get roaring drunk before he went to bed, and the nurse in the room sighed with relief which earned her a scowl.

Not once since his admittance had Steven been alone, even Archie and Anna had come, taking their turn to sit by his bedside. The tiny family that once had been Whispers now had grown into mammoth proportions. Sean's brother Connor popped in during his layover in London while heading for an assignment, and Whisper talked every day to Sean's mother. Her aunt, uncle and Luke, kept in close touch as they waited for Luke's brother Chris's baby to be born. It was a critical time for their family since there had been complications and they were afraid to leave Boston until after the baby had arrived safely.

One after another the O'Brien siblings called Sean every day. At first Whisper had been overwhelmed with the outpouring of love and concern that came from his family but it didn't take her long to realize that the O'Briens' already considered her part of their lives.

Finally, Sam prevailed on Whisper to go home and rest, after assuring her that should anything change, she would call.

Sam was been resting in a chair beside the bed, her eyes closed when a weak voice spoke her name. She opened her eyes to see Stephen staring at her.

"Boy, you sure look like hell."

"What?" Sam jumped up and went to his bedside, her cool hand brushing the hair off his brow even as she answered him. She tried to hide her grin and she pasted a scowl on her face. Here was the man she loved lying in a hospital bed looking like the wrath of god, and he had the nerve to tell her how awful she looked.

"Listen you, do you know how long..." tears of relief pooled in her eyes.

"Come here and kiss me."

His hand shook but there was no mistaking his autocratic gesture and Sam laughed.

"What?"

"You heard me, kiss me."

Bending over, Sam braced herself on the bed intending to place a cool soft kiss on his cheek, but with surprising strength Stephen reached up, and putting his hand behind her head pulled her down meeting her lips forcefully with his. His lips were dry and cracked from the fever that had overwhelmed his body, yet Sam felt she had never had such a wonderful kiss in her whole life. Her very being centered on his lips and tentatively she touched her tongue to his.

"No way." Stephen groaned and gently pushed her away, while the wisp of a grin lit up his face. "We'll get into the serious stuff after I have had a chance to clean up. When I kiss you the next time," he tried his best to leer at her although the attempt was rather feeble. "It will be one you'll remember, not one where you say 'gross' at the end."

"Gross?" Sam raised one eyebrow at his use of American slang, then gently pushed the hair back from his forehead and replied with a laugh.

"You're a nut," ...she ran her hand softly from his jaw to his cheek, as if memorizing his features with her touch. "I'm glad you're back."

"Yes," he said with satisfaction in his tone, "I'm back. Gave you a bit of a scare, did I?"

"No," she lied, "It was a piece of cake, but I'm glad to know you have a heart, there have been a couple of times lately when I wondered." She bit her lip to keep from pouring out all the anguish she'd felt as she watched him fight the pain. Twice she had broken down and had to leave the room.

The look Stephen gave Sam had her heart pounding, and his voice was solemn as he spoke. "Pull your chair closer to the bed so I can hold your hand while we talk."

Frowning, Sam complied, suddenly frightened. Was this where he'd tell her he didn't need her anymore? Her stomach knotted. Stephen had become her whole life, yet she had known when she had taken this assignment that it was only temporary. Now that his daughter was safe, and he was on his way to recovery, it was probably over. He wouldn't need her when he left the hospital.

He held her hand while he stared at her, his gaze making her uncomfortable. "You know that I loved Alison's mother very much, don't you?"

It was a question that really didn't require an answer and as he spoke, Sam's eyes roamed hungrily over his face. There was a blue cast to the skin under his eyes and his gaunt cheeks emphasized how ill he had been. She longed to climb into his bed and hold him close, but stiffening her spine, instead she prepared for the worst.

She only hoped that she would be strong enough not to break down in front of him. After what he had just been through an emotional scene was out of the question. Her hand instinctively dropped to her waist protecting the tiny life that she hoped was growing there.

With no idea of the thoughts swirling in her head, Stephen continued. "After Alise died I thought I would never love again, that my love for her was a once in a lifetime love. But I was wrong," his hand tightened on hers, the strength of his grip bringing both pain and joy to her.

"I love you Sam and I want you to marry me."

Before she could answer, a grin lit up his face. "So for both our sakes, since neither of us is getting any younger," he watched as sparks began to build in her eyes and happily he stoked the fire, "And I hesitate to mention this, but just last week I happened to notice a few gray hairs among all that glorious red you're so proud of .. ." He waited with anticipation for the explosion that he knew would be coming shortly, "I think we should consider getting married very soon."

He wasn't disappointed, stunned Sam pulled her hand free and thrust it up into her hair reassuring herself that it was as full and luxurious as ever. Then realizing what his last statement had been, she gasped, "We should what?"

Jumping to her feet she leaned over him, "Are you out of your bloody mind? What makes you think I'd want to marry you? You're opinionated, autocratic, bossy..." She sputtered, then glared at him, "Are all those drugs you've been taking making you delirious?"

Stephen raised an eyebrow and smiled, "Really Sam, a few days without my stimulating presence and you've become addle brained"

"Stimulating presence . . . addled brained? Listen you pompous ass. . ."

As soon as she spoke, he laughed, gone were the soft comforting words he'd heard as he'd fought the pain, he'd never tell her, but her words and Whisper's had been the anchors he'd held onto as he fought his way back from god only knew where.

Now with her sharp tongue of hers back in true form —he couldn't be happier, and he was looking forward to spending the rest of his life striking sparks off this redhead.

He wondered for a moment if he should tell her now that

God had given him another chance, he didn't want to squander it. He was determined to be part of a real family again, a family built around Sam, his daughter and eventually his son. He was sure that together he and Sam would have a son.

No one would ever know that Alise had appeared to him while he was unconscious. "Fight" she had whispered "It's time to begin a new life, for the sake of our daughter and your son." He would carry her words with him to his grave, but he would never share them

Especially not now, this was Sam's time, and he had just proposed to her, now it was her choice, she had a career she obviously loved and one she was good at, would she throw it all away to be his wife? Of course she would, his heart answered, she loves you.

Not knowing what he was going around in his head, Sam stood staring at Stephen while she contemplated smothering him with his own pillow. He was waking up from death's door, and the first thing he requests is a kiss and then he follows that up with a marriage proposal, were the pain medications still affecting his brain?

Sean and Whisper stood in the doorway watching and listening, Sean pretending to cough to cover his laughter, while Whisper just smiled.

Spotting the two of them Stephen motioned to his daughter. "Come in sweetheart, and I'll tell you exactly how this woman abused me while you were gone."

He pointed to a chair close beside him, and as she settled in it, he winked at her. "Now," I want you to be completely truthful, do you think that there is anyone in this world who would consider me," he paused "to be a pompous ass? And more importantly do you think Sam should marry me?"

Although his smile was impish there was concern in his eyes. How would this precious daughter of his react to his wanting to marry Sam? He had just gotten her back and would his wanting to share his life with another woman impact upon his relationship with her.

Whisper looked at over at Sam and winked, and then hesitated as if she was deliberating what her reply would be. As her father waited, Whisper rubbed her chin and stared up at the ceiling, enjoying her father's discomfiture.

"Well?" he finally exploded.

"I'm thinking, I'm thinking."

Finally, laughter in her voice, she answered, "My answer is yes to both questions."

"What?" But he squeezed her hand as he turned for support to Sean. "Now my only daughter is turning on me..." he paused for a moment then grinned, "we'll forget about the first answer, but she did say yes, she thought Sam should marry me, didn't she?"

Sean had no opportunity to reply, because Whisper leaned over and answered "I did say yes, but I have one condition, that you and Sam get married before I leave England so I can be part of it."

"But that is impossible" Sam stammered .... You're leaving in two weeks."

"No," Whisper looked over with affection at this woman who would soon be her stepmother and she smiled softly. "There's been a change in plans, we're getting married here in six weeks, Sean and I talked it over, and we've decided to stay here till then so that Dad can give me away. Sean is going to work out of his London office until the wedding."

"Oh Lord you're going to be working out of the London office?" Sam looked at Sean with a laugh, "In that case, I quit!"

"Too late, I already decided to fire you. I can't have my mother-in-law working for me, especially one with a smart mouth like yours."

"Good lord man," Stephen's interjected, "Believe me, there's nothing wrong with her mouth, as a matter of fact. . ."

"Stephen!" Sam's face pinked with a becoming blush as her eyes narrowed as she glared at him.

There was love and a little regret shining out of Stephens' eyes as he tightened his grip on Whisper's hand, 'Nothing makes me happier than to know I'll be giving you away to Sean, but," Whisper caught a glimpse of the tears in Stephen's eyes before he glanced away.

"I wish before I had to give you away," his voice broke, "That I had had the guts to find out what was behind your fear. When you were a child and needed me most, I let you down," regret colored his voice, "our lives would have been so very different."

"You didn't let me down Dad, you did what you thought was right- people here depended on you, and you couldn't just get up and leave. And maybe we didn't get to spend a lot of time together but there was never any question in my mind that you loved me, and you know I loved you."

"Thank you." Her words gave Stephen comfort. He looked at this daughter of his with pride shining out of his eyes. She had inherited not only his wife's beauty but also her warm heart.

Suddenly an idea occurred to him. "You know I was just thinking, how would you feel about a double wedding?"

The fact that as he spoke his head turned, and his eyes were focused on Sean. Whisper instinctively realized that her immediate family was very small and although they had a lot of distant relatives that would attend, her father probably wanted Sam to be surrounded with the same loving warmth that she knew she would be.

Sean had already admitted to her that Sam had been an O'Brien at one time, and although there were some questions as to the legality of the marriage that didn't matter, once an O'Brien . . . always an O'Brien.

As she looked over at Sean, he nodded, and she let go of her father's hand and moved to Sean to hug him. He wrapped one arm around her while fishing in his pocket.

He kissed the top of her head as he placed a small white jeweler's box in her hand. Snapping open the lid her breath caught in her throat. Nestled inside was a wedding band to match her engagement ring. The ring she wore was designed with a single flawless diamond in the center surrounded by tiny emeralds, but the wedding band had a perfect emerald in the center, and was surrounded by tiny diamonds. She slipped the ring on her finger and moved to the window to let the ring's stones dance in the brilliance of the afternoon sun.

"Your grandmother's wedding ring." Tears ran unheeded down her cheeks. "And it fits perfectly."

Sean moved to hold her. "It was the ring of a special lady — and now you're my special lady."

"I'll cherish it till I die — then," her smile was soft - I'll pass it on to my son." Love shone out of her eyes as she looked at the man she had promised to marry.

Whooping Sean picked her up, twirling her around in his arms.

"Leave it to an Irishman to always upstage you" Stephen said with mock disgust, although the smile playing around the corner of his mouth gave his true feelings away.

"What's going on in here? I could hear the shouting in the hall." A rather stern looking gray-haired nurse poked her head in the door.

"Come in, come in you can help us celebrate. We're getting married," Stephen said.

"All of you?"

"It's kind of complicated," he grinned. "I'll explain it to you later."

Walking to the bottom of Stephen's bed, she placed her hands on her hips, "Since I'm the one who had to put up with you — and all your relatives through this whole thing —and especially that cranky old man who hung around here — I'd better get an invitation to this wedding."

"Archie, Archie was here?" Surprise colored Stephens's question. "I thought he hated hospitals?"

"Archie? The nurse's eyes narrowed, "Is that what his name was?"

"I can't think of anyone else who would fit your description of 'cranky old man' except Archie."

"Old lecher is more like it," she sniffed, "I made the mistake of bending over in front of him to straighten your pillow, and" . . . she hesitated long enough to be sure she had everyone's attention. "He patted my bum he did, with his girlfriend resting in the chair right next to him. I was going to give him a real set-to I tell you, but he hushed me so I wouldn't wake her up.

Then her eyes twinkled, "He had the nerve to throw me a kiss as I left the room." She tried her best to sound irate but it was obvious to all of them that she was really enjoying herself.

"Did you report him?" Sean's voice was strangled as he asked the question.

"Of course not," she snapped, looking at Sean as if he were out of his mind for making such a suggestion, "He was just having a little fun. . .besides. . . my bum has always had some kind of fascination for men – so I'm kind of used to it."

Gazing at the ample proportions of the nurse's bum, Sean struggled to keep his composure. "Well I'll talk to him when I see him."

"Tell him Hilda mentioned it –oh, and if he should ask, I only work four nights a week and he can call should he want to apologize." She gave Stephen a wink just before she strolled out the door.

They waited till they were sure she was out of earshot before the room exploded with laughter.

It was obvious that Stephen was tiring and as Sean and Whisper turned to leave, a pained look stole over Stephen's face and his mood became very solemn.

"Wait, I need to know what happened to Edward." He looked

to Sean for answers afraid what he might see on his daughter's face. "I've put off asking any questions about what happened that day because," he studied each of them in turn, "I was afraid to find out. But now I need to know. What happened to Edward and where is Charlotte?"

Sam, Sean and Whisper glanced at each other.

It was Sean that answered, "There was a fight in the wine cellar, I won, and after a brief stop in the hospital to be patched up, St. James took Edward to Scotland. He's being cared for there."

"That's it? You had a fight and he landed in the hospital?" Stephen began to softly laugh. "Why the hell is it if you ask an Irishman to tell a story he'll drag it out for two days, but when you want some information, he gives it to you in two sentences? I'll never understand the lot of you. There has to be more."

"And no charges have been filed." A fleeting look of sadness crossed Whisper's face as she picked up where Sean left off. "Charlotte is with them. St. James made it very clear that from now on he is in charge, and he told Charlotte that she is not to interfere in any way. He also insisted there will be no more secrets. Edward now knows the whole story, and also that his father has publicly acknowledged him as his son."

Wonder colored Whisper's voice "Dad, I don't know how Uncle Andrew pulled it off, but the morning after our incident, there was an article in the Daily Sun where he told the whole story about Edward's birth. He talked about how sick his wife had been and how he and Charlotte had fallen in love, and how noble Charlotte had been to bear his son alone and spare his wife from knowing he had been unfaithful.

He made himself the villain of the piece, but all the editorials in the paper sang his praises for his courage in finally admitting his mistakes, and acknowledging Edward. He and Charlotte were married with a special license by a vicar two days after the story broke.

"You know," Sean grinned at Stephen, "I never was too

impressed with this title stuff, but it sure buys you a lot of understanding and forgiveness in the press over here."

"Of course it does," Stephen scoffed, "We English grew up understanding that all throughout history our monarchy had their mistresses, it was just a fact of life, and we are a very forgiving people, but," he chuckled, "It couldn't hurt that Andrew has the controlling interest in the paper."

At Sam's raised eyebrows, Stephen picked up her hand and kissed her palm, "Of course even with the little indiscretions my ancestors might have engaged in,'" he looked at Sam, "I would never cheat on my wife."

"Or she might kill you," Sam muttered.

Sean looked at Stephen, "Are you up to clarifying a couple of points that have been bothering me? Where were you when Edward was born and why didn't you know Charlotte was pregnant?

Stephen paused, "I was fulfilling my military service in the RAF and I was rotated out of the country for a full year. Why?'

"Í was just thinking how different things would have been if she confided in you."

"Maybe, maybe not," Stephen's face was grim, "Ours was never a warm, close family and the family reputation was all that mattered to my parents. I don't know how they would have reacted had they known. And since I was younger than Charlotte, I'm not sure I would have been much help. But damn it, I wish she had given me the chance, maybe I would have surprised myself."

"Don't even start," Sam said, "Maybe doesn't build bridges… this family needs to start anew, and rehashing the past isn't going to help.

"You," she looked closely at Stephen "need to move on, make peace with Edward and your family, forgive him, and realize the hell he must have gone through for all these years thinking he'd killed your wife."

Perplexed Stephen looked at Sean "He really thought he

killed my wife? I knew he was there that day . . .but..." he stopped. "I guess I knew deep in my heart he could never kill Alise, he loved her."

Sean walked closer to the bed and looked down at Stephen trying to determine whether or not he was strong enough to hear about his wife's death. Reassured, he nodded to Whisper.

"Your daughter remembers everything that happened the day your wife died and if you feel up to it, she'd like to tell you the story."

Whisper moved to the top of the bed and kissed her father's forehead and then took his hand.

"Mama was so happy that day, she told me there was going to be a new baby, but I wasn't to tell anyone because she and I were going to surprise you that night. She gave the servants the day off and we spent the morning in the kitchen preparing for our celebration. I was so thrilled to be wearing a gown like hers that even when she stepped on the hem of her gown and tore it, she decided not to change. She handed me a safety pin and told me she would repair the rip later, that the pin would hold it temporarily. I know she kept that gown on to please me," tears glistened in her eyes.

She closed her eyes, "Dad, I can see it all now, we were all at the top of the stairs, Edward was insisting that he was your son, but Mama said "No, she was sure he wasn't, but that she would talk to you and make sure the question of who his father was would be cleared up."

The tears she had been holding back now slid in silent testimony to the pain Whisper was feeling as her mother's final moments played out in her head.

"Mama turned to reach for my hand.... but her foot caught in the material of her gown, and she started to fall, Edward reached out to grab her, but she slipped out of his hands. She was screaming as she tumbled down the stairs, and then she stopped.

I started running down the stairs after her …and I remember Edward stood staring down at his hand…

"Oh Dad, all these years he thought he pushed her…but he didn't… he tried to stop her fall."

Her voice broke and Sean quickly moved and gently pulled her into his arms. Brokenheartedly she continued, "Then Edward followed me down and picked me up; I remember I was hysterical and I clawed at him as we passed her. Somehow even then I knew she was dead. He carried me down to the wine cellar. I remember he was shaking as he held me, and I was screaming and screaming, and he put me in a corner of the cellar and told me if I didn't stop screaming, he would kill me too. Somehow that didn't frighten me, but then he told me if I ever told anyone what had happened, he would find out about it…and kill …you."

"Oh my god," Stephen's voice was grim "No wonder you stopped talking… somehow in your young mind, you must have thought if you got away from that house, I'd be safe."

Whisper nodded.

"And all this time he thought he was the son that I wouldn't acknowledge and he grew to hate me."

"He was torn," Now it was time for Sam to intercede, "He loved you, but he hated the part of you he saw as cowardice in not acknowledging your own son. Now is the time for you to make peace with Edward and your family, forgive him for what he's done, and understand the torment he went through thinking he killed your wife. After all, the man is your own flesh and blood nephew."

Stephen's voice was cold as he stared at Sean, "Somehow in this 'poor Edward scenario that you all have obviously concocted in your heads, you've missed the fact that he tried to have my daughter killed. How do you expect me to forgive that?"

"He didn't, did he? He was a frightened sick man…. and all you can do is forgive him, and help him cope with the major changes that are taking place in his life." Sam's voice was soft.

Stephen didn't answer. He looked at Sean, "Ironic, isn't it, after all he's put us through, he'll inherit through his father an enormous estate and a title that's older and more prestigious than mine."

There was silence in the room at his words, then addressing no one in particular. He said, "I'll try to forgive him, although I make no promises…. but you?" he looked at his daughter, "What about you --he tried to kill you. Can you forgive him?"

"I've already forgiven him…he brought me Sean."

"Have you forgotten how many times he tried to have you killed," Stephen's voice was bitter.

"No, but that's over." Pushing herself out of Sean's arms, she bent over and kissed her father's cheek.

"And now Sam and I need to make some phone calls, six weeks isn't very long to plan a wedding."

"Make sure you tell everyone that it's to be a double wedding…" and his eyes full of mischief he continued, "I've been thinking it over and it'll be cheaper that way. One chartered plane for both families, one parson, one church…" Stephen could barely contain the amusement in his voice.

"Cheaper? Cheaper?" …even though Whisper's voice was soft, it still managed to sound like a screech to the rest of them…

With a wink at Sean, Stephen moved in for the kill, "Do you think we'll get a cheaper rate on hotel rooms and . . . food.?"

Ignoring the women, Sean grinned, "I'll ask Archie to see about the church I spotted on the corner of the village green and he can check on two limousines…" he paused, "No make that one – one of us can ride in the front with Archie… and I suppose we have to have a minister and a priest, I'll tell him to get two that get along well together."

Stephen picked up "We'll have the reception in the garden that will cut down on the cost of flowers…and …."

"Wait a minute," horror colored Whisper's voice as she glared at the two men – nobody is riding in the front seat with Archie."

She glared at them, "Sam and I will be making the arrangements not you two"—then she got a stricken look on her face- and she turned to Sam, "I promised the girls in my office they could help plan the wedding. They'll kill me if I tell them now that they can't."

"They can still do it, I'm a better detective than I am a wedding planner and I admit I'm not very good at that domestic stuff."

"Good thing you're marrying me for my money. I'm sure whatever you two plan will be expensive." Stephen expression was expectant as he waited for the explosion.

"Marrying you for your money, I don't need your money you pompous ass, I'm perfectly capable of . . ."

"Really darling you're going to have to come up with some other phrases 'pompous ass' is getting a little old and you will have to marry me for my money, you could never afford to send my son to Cambridge on a detective's salary."

The color drained out of Sam's face. "What.... What do you mean?"

Throwing his good intentions and caution to the wind, Stephen went for it, "I mean darling if you're not pregnant now, at my first opportunity to bed you, you will be!"

Sean grabbed Sam as she slid toward the floor everything was moving too fast for her, first a marriage proposal and before she even had a chance to accept, this lunatic was planning on starting a family.

Stephen watched as Sean helped Sam into a chair and then with a laugh turned to his daughter, "These Irish are so dramatic aren't they honey?" He squeezed his daughter's hand. Only she was aware of the tears sparkling in her father's eyes.

Swiftly Whisper rose and crossed to Sam and dropping to her knees in front of her.

"Please tell him yes, nothing would make me happier."

Standing she extended her hand to Sam, "Let's go get a cup

of tea, six weeks doesn't give us much time, I'll have the girls close the office and fly in next week for a few days. They'll need time to order the flowers and food and dresses...and she paused "I think I'll ask Colleen to stand up for me...and..." when Whisper paused for a breath. . .

Sam interrupted "That's a great idea, and I'll ask Anna....

The two women walked out of the room; the two men forgotten.

"You were brilliant," Sean said... grinning at Stephen "A double wedding-"

"Brilliant, or else we're two of the dumbest men on the earth – lord knows what those two will plan." He became solemn, "I'm glad they're gone for the moment. What about the man that tried to kill my daughter in Boston?"

"Already taken care of, Eric, Colleen, RW, and my father have already put the word out on the street that the contract has been pulled because the money is no longer available."

"Will that work?"

"It will work, these guys kill for profit...no money ...no incentive. And with Edward unable to get his hands on any funds, there will be no payoff. But the funny part of the whole thing is, the word on the street is Edward had already fired him."

Then Sean began to laugh at the stunned look on Stephen's face, "Imagine the big balls he's got. . Your nephew fired a hit man!"

Stephen couldn't believe his ears. "Fired a hit man?"

"Yes."

"He must have been out of his mind."

Solemnly Sean looked at Stephen. "I guess that's understood."

"I still can't believe he wanted her killed."

"He was sick and if it's any consolation, he's having a hard time living with what he's done. Charlotte calls every day to check on you, and St. James called me yesterday, now that Edward knows the whole story, he's learning to deal with the deceptions in his past."

Reaching out, Stephen extended his hand, which Sean grasped. "Thank you for bringing my daughter back to me."

"No, I need to thank you for giving me a woman I promise that I will love and cherish for the rest of our lives."

A puzzled look crossed Sean face and he raised his head and sniffed the air in the room, as a poignant smile crossed Stephen's face.

"What is that? Can you smell it?" He glanced around as if to discover where the scent was originating from. "Whatever it is, it's great."

"Yes, I know," Stephen said, his smile soft, while in his eyes Sean saw a glimmer of sadness. "It's the scent of a gardenia."

EPILOGUE

S ean studied the pictures that Whisper had left on the table. It was obvious that she was trying to decide where to place them in her wedding album.

She had been a beautiful bride in her white gown, carrying a bouquet of wild flowers, with one pure white gardenia tucked in the center. Sam's gown was pink...what the heck had Whisper called it, blush pink. And she carried wildflowers too, but without the gardenia.

Everything had gone smoothly, even that little dust up with Eric. When he had arrived at the church with a bright red bow tie when all of the rest of the groomsmen wore black, R. W. and Patrick had offered to take him outside and teach him a few manners. But Whisper had stepped in laughing when Eric explained to her, he expected to be her favorite brother-in-law so he needed to stand out from the crowd.

Looking at the photos of Stephen, he frowned a little, it had taken Stephen longer to recuperate than they had hoped. The exertion the day of Edwards' breakdown had caused Stephen more trauma than the doctor had counted on. Even though still weak, he had insisted on escorting his daughter down the aisle. With Archie guiding the wheelchair, he had stayed beside his daughter, and then with tears in his eyes had taken her hand and given it to Sean.

Sam had waited for Stephen at the altar, and after bending to give him a soft kiss, the service had begun.

It had been a wonderful wedding. Even though for Sam and

Stephen it had been their second, they certainly acted like kids, hugging and kissing all through the reception.

And he, Sean thought disgustedly, had acted like a kid himself following his new bride around like a puppy. His face still turned red when he thought about how he had almost followed Whisper into the ladies' room. If Colleen hadn't grabbed his arm, he probably would have.

Why the hell they had decorated that door with flowers he'd never know...looked like every other damn door to him.

His brothers would never let him live that down.

All of the O'Briens had been there along with Whisper's aunt, uncle and cousins, even Aunt Frances with her new husband and various relatives that he knew he'd met but couldn't remember, and even a few of Sam's relatives had flown in.

Charlotte and Andrew didn't make it, preferring to remain in Switzerland where they son was in counseling. But each bride received a beautiful gift.

Their honeymoon had been cut short, he had been called back on a special assignment for the government, but other than that everything had turned out perfectly.

Six weeks later, over a fabulous candlelit dinner she claimed laughingly that she had prepared, even though he had spied a box from a nearby restaurant hidden under the sink, she told him she was pregnant.

It didn't matter about the food anyway; he was so scared he lost his appetite. All the horror stories he had ever heard about pregnancy, and things that could go wrong had frightened him to death.

Whisper never knew it, but the next day he had slipped off to see his mother. As they sat over a cup of coffee, in her cozy kitchen, he was finally able to confess his fears. Smiling softly his mother had gotten up, walked over to a drawer in the counter, and after rummaging around for a moment, pulled out a family picture. She didn't say anything, just handed it to him. He looked down at the faces of all of his brothers, and his sister, children his mother had borne, and when he looked up his mother raised an eyebrow, and then just smiled at him. He went away feeling much better.

Once a week Sam and Whisper talked, comparing notes on their pregnancies, and sometimes he thought, comparing notes on their respective husbands.

Sam had been disappointed when she discovered she wasn't pregnant when she and Stephen got married, but his father-in-law had confided in Sean that he had remedied that problem a short time later.

Sean grinned contentedly; life was good. No more attempts had been made on Whisper's life or for that matter on any of his brothers and sisters.

There was no question in his mind, he still intended to find the bastard who tried to kill her, and threatened his family, but so far there were no leads.

Colleen and Eric were still grilling the street snitches but they all scrambled for cover when pressed too hard. He'd never seen such fear of one man before.

Whisper waddled into the study where Sean was working. There was no other word for it Sean mused, she waddled.

Grinning, Sean decided that this might be a good time to tease her just a little, the baby was due any time now and she had been a little grumpy the last few days.

Looking up at her with a twinkle in his eye, "You're really cute when you waddle like that...you know kind of like a duck."

"Like a duck.... I'll give you a duck," hands on her hips she glared at him.

"You," she said, emphasizing her next words by pointing her finger at him, "are supposed to be telling me I am the most beautiful woman you have ever seen, not comparing me to a duck."

"Oh, you're that too...but ..."

The grin left his face as she winced, and he was on his feet in a minute, "What's the matter?"

"Oh nothing" she said "the pains are about five minutes apart..."

"The pains are five minutes apart! The pains are five minutes apart!" Sean's voice shook. "Why the hell didn't you tell me?"

The room in front of Sean started to shift, and he put his hand against the wall to steady himself.

"Sean," Whisper snapped... "Don't you dare faint on me!"

"Men don't faint, "Sean growled, as the room settled back down, but suddenly his stomach felt a little queasy.

"Besides your sister says that new babies take hours to arrive, and..."

"My sister!" Sean roared, "What the hell does she know about new babies, she's never had one! For god's sake call my mother, she'll know..."

"I. Am. Not. Calling. Anybody!"

"When my water breaks than maybe I'll call..." As if on cue, Whisper looked down at the puddle suddenly beginning to appear on the carpet.

"That's it." Sean pushed away from the wall, and leaning down picked his wife up holding her close, heedless of the growing stain on her maternity smock, or that the front of his pants now had a large water spot.

"The suitcase...Whisper gasped..."

"To hell with the suitcase..."

"But everything I packed ..."

"Can be picked up by my sister later...you know the one with all the good advice, maybe she can get that right at least!"

Kicking the door open, Sean carried Whisper out to the car, bundled her in, and kissed her lightly on the lips as he fastened her seat belt.

From there on everything was a blur to him...on the way to the hospital she kept wincing, and he kept asking her to hold on, pleading with her not to have the baby in the car, growling that he didn't want any of his damn brothers delivering his baby.

All Whisper did was laugh.

Exactly five hours later, little Hope Alise O'Brien was born. Mother and child were doing fine but for a time there seemed to be some question as to whether or not the father was going to make it.

Sean had stayed with her as long as allowed, but when he had gotten pale and lightheaded numerous times from nerves, he had been politely escorted out of her room.

His brothers had laughed so hard that they had been admonished by the nurses.

Finally, the doctor came out and motioned to Sean. With Eric on one side, and Jay on the other, they walked him to the double doors of the maternity ward. "How is my wife?"

Grinning, after spotting Sean's white face, the doctor said, "She's fine and obviously doing better than you are."

Picking up on the doctor's cue, Eric turned to Sean, "Can you make it from here or do you want us to carry you in to see your wife and daughter?" But before he could even finish the sentence, he burst out laughing.

"Don't be an ass." Sean growled, and shrugging off his brothers' hands, he followed the doctor.

Within a few minutes, the blinds to the nursery were pulled up and Sean stood there in a green hospital gown holding his new daughter. The O'Briens stood outside the window in awe.

Holding his baby girl in his arms, he turned her so that all of the family could see.

Already she had soft blond fuzz on her head and they could tell her features were delicate.

"Thank god she doesn't look like him, we'd never be able to marry her off," Eric started laughing as Colleen punched him on the arm.

"Hush," Nellie said, tears running down her face. "She's the most beautiful baby in the world."

"And our first grandchild." Dennis wrapped his arms around his wife "Wouldn't Archie be proud?"

"I am proud," at the words O'Brien heads swung around as one.

"What the hell are you doing here?" Dennis' look of disgust had his children grinning.

"Didn't think I'd miss this birth did you, I had a hand in this match you know. If it wasn't for me..."

"You did not!" Dennis interrupted.

"Oh, yes I did," and proudly he continued...."and I got to hold that little one before her own Dad or granddad did!"

"You did not." Dennis eyes became slits.

Archie turned to his daughter Nellie, laughter in his eyes, "Do you remember me telling you that this fellow wasn't too bright...have to repeat the same thing over and over. You could have done better you know..."

"Archie" . . . Dennis began. . . "You're kidding, aren't you?"

But Archie interrupted him, "I beg to correct you boy, but me and Anna, came directly here from the airport, I told the doctor we had just gotten off the plane from Ireland, and that the great grandma here would just die if she didn't get to hold that baby. Nicest Irish doctor in the world, took me right in there, and as soon as they cleaned her up, why me and Anna got to hold her.

"Dad, I can't believe you." Nellie started to laugh, "You claimed Anna was the great-grandma and you got in there to hold the baby-."

"Of course I did, did I tell you that the doctor's name was O'Neil and that I knew his great grandpa."

"You knew his great grandfather?" Dennis' voice was disbelieving.

"Well, I must have, I knew a pile of them, and as for Anna being a great-grandma... she is," and reaching down Archie held up Anna's hand that was sporting a bright new shiny wedding band.

"She finally wore me down, threatened me with no more cooking, so I had to marry her to insure I would get some decent meals. Besides, I kind of fell for her along the way, and everybody else was getting married so I said to myself--ah, what the hell- so here I am a married man again."

Nellie grabbed Anna and gave a whoop of joy as everyone crowded around the two of them. Sean looking out from behind the glass was perplexed until Archie dragged Anna to the window and held her up her hand, then a grin broke out on Sean's face. He gave Archie the thumbs up sign, and then turned and held up his daughter. Archie looked at his grandson and this first great grandchild of his, and grinned.

With the arrival of Luke and his parents and the two families crowded around the glass in front of the nursery, the hall became a mad house, until a nurse stepped out and reminded them they were on the maternity ward and she would appreciate some quiet.

Nellie, Dennis, and Whisper's aunt and uncle were allowed to stay, but the rest of them trooped down to the cafeteria, to wait their turn to see their new niece and the proud parents.

Standing up on a chair and holding up one hand, Archie called for silence. Immediately everyone stopped talking, waiting to see what bombshell Archie was going to drop this time.

"Children," he said, "I haven't been able to tell Whisper yet, but as you know, Sam is pregnant...I mean was pregnant... just before we got on the plane today Anna got a call, Sam had a little boy this morning. Everyone is doing well, so there's joy in our two countries today and I suggest we drink to health and happiness for both these little families.

He lifted his coffee cup high in the air, and a dozen or so cups joined his. As they all took a sip, Archie looked at Anna and shook his head muttering "Vile stuff," then looked over all his grandchildren that were gathered around him and smiled.

"And I imagine Whisper's aunt is breaking the news to her right now."

For a moment there was silence and then everyone was on their feet hugging each other.

"What do you think?" Luke asked his eyes intently staring at Colleen.

"I think I'm going to go out and buy the biggest doll I can find for my niece, and a giant teddy bear for Whisper's little brother. She smiled at him.

"Want to join me?"

"You want me to go along to carry those monstrous things you plan to buy, or because you crave my company?"

"Both, and it wouldn't hurt either if you decided to split the bill with me…. after all they're related to you too."

Luke looked at Colleen warily. "Why do I think I'm going to end up paying for everything?"

"Because you have a suspicious mind that's why." But the grin she gave him was decidedly impish.

"Alright, you got me, let's go" Standing, he offered her his hand and her brothers watched as she slipped her hand into his.

Jay sat nursing his coffee and watched them leave.

"What do you think?" Eric nudged him.

"I think she will lead him a merry chase until she catches him."

"I agree." and Eric lifted his coffee cup in a silent salute to the departing couple.

Three days later, Chameleon sat in his dining room drinking a cup of coffee and listening to his wife chatter on about a broken clasp on her diamond bracelet. Ignoring her, he began to rifle through the paper till a name in the birth announcements jumped out at him.

His hand shaking, he lifted the paper to get a closer look. A baby girl, another O'Brien. God would he ever get rid of them all?

He thought back to the wedding that he and his wife attended in London. The cathedral had been crowded so they had slipped into a seat in the back row. The fact that they hadn't been invited didn't bother him. He was not there to celebrate; he was there to see them all together.

The scar that Sean wore over his lip was a gift from his kid brother. The stupid kid. He had told him not to strike out on his own, and while he was in Rome on a job, the kid had been arrested for trying to pull off a robbery while high on drugs. He'd ended up killing one cop, and assaulting another. Sean O'Brien.

Someone in that jail didn't like him, and he was killed before he could come to trial. That killing had never been solved by the cops. But a few thousand bucks later he had found out who the killer was, and that guy had met with a fatal accident. But it was Sean he blamed. Of course the kid never could keep his mouth shut, but Sean should have realized that Eddie could only kill somebody when he was high. The kid should never have gone to that stinking jail, he needed to be rehabilitated not killed.

He had already found a place for him to go — he was going to take him out of the country — away from the bad influences here - but he never got the chance, his brother, his only relative, the kid that he had supported from the day their mother died of an overdose, was gone. It had been the two of them against the world. Now it was one.

He had a score to settle with the O'Briens and he would. It was too bad he had made one mistake killing that Police Lieutenant's daughter but that had been an accident. He had thought it was the O'Brien brat Colleen that he had shot.

He frowned, even though the contract on Sean's wife had been pulled, he had still gotten paid. Why?

Then he began to laugh, the guy that had ordered the contract was afraid of him, he bet the little weasel paid the balance himself. Good, showed what a poor businessman he was.

His wife's voice finally got through to him. He looked over at her. Empty headed piece of fluff. She was getting on his nerves, but he needed her right now. She was part of his cover.

"Shut up." he snarled, "I'll get your bracelet fixed." He knew just where to have it done. The same little jeweler in Indonesia who made all his jewelry, especially the small replicas of a chameleon that he always left.

Softly he laughed, making his wife's eyes widen in alarm. She was afraid of him, afraid to go, and afraid to stay.

He reached into his pocket and threw a small jeweler's box into her lap. Cautiously she opened it, nestled in the red satin was a diamond ring. "This should keep you happy till I get your damn bracelet fixed." His head swung around and he gazed out of the window at the sky visible from his fifteenth story condo.

He would give anything to know how the brothers reacted when they opened the small jewelry boxes that held the gold key chains that Sean had bought for his groomsmen. Instead of that gift, Eric's held a small jeweled replica of a chameleon. He grinned, he hoped it hadn't caused too much of a stir. Of course, the fact that the tiny note he placed in the box might have given them a few bad moments cheered him considerably.

"My wedding gift to the newlyweds is priceless, none of you died today." And he laughed.

CPSIA information can be obtained
at www.ICGtesting.com
Printed in the USA
LVHW091922231020
669657LV00005B/44